An Argument of Blood

An ARGUMENT OF BLOOD

BY

MATTHEW WILLIS AND J. A. IRONSIDE

www.penmorepress.com

An Argument of Blood by Matthew Willis _J. A. Ironside
Copyright © 2017 Matthew Willis _J. A. Ironside

ISBN-13: 978-1-946409-14-0(Paperback)
ISBN-13: 978-1-946409-15-7 (e-book)

BISAC Subject Headings:
FIC014000FICTION / Historical
FIC032000FICTION / War & Military
FIC031020FICTION / Thrillers / Historical

Editing: Chris Paige
Cover Art :
Cover Illustration by Christine Horner

Address all correspondence to:
Penmore Press LLC
920 N Javalina Pl
Tucson, AZ 85748

OATH AND CROWN,
BOOK 1

"I am afeard there are few die well that die in a battle; for how can they charitably dispose of any thing, when blood is their argument? Now, if these men do not die well, it will be a black matter for the king that led them to it" Henry V, Act IV, Scene 1

Dramatis Personae
The Saxons:

Royalty:

Edward the Confessor – King of England 1043-1066

Alfred Ætheling – Edward's elder brother

Æthelred ('the Unready') – Edward's father

Emma of Normandy – Mother of King Edward, aunt of Duke William

Harthacnut – King of England 1040–42

The House of Wessex:

Godwin of Wessex (originally of Sussex) – Jarl of Wessex

Gytha Thorkilsdóttir (JHEE-taa) – A Danish noblewoman, Lady of Wessex, wife of Godwin and mother to nine of Godwin's children

Sweyn Godwinson – (seVEHN) the eldest of the Wessex children, Jarl of Gloucestershire, Herefordshire, Oxfordshire, Berkshire and Somerset

Harold Godwinson (or Harold of Wessex) – Jarl of East Anglia, Hereford and later Wessex

Ealdgyth – (ALD-jheet) Eldest Daughter of Godwin and Gytha, wife of Edward and Queen of England

Tostig – (THOR-stig) third son of Gytha and Godwin, Jarl of Northumbria

Gyrth – (GERTH) fourth son of Godwin and Gytha, made Jarl of East Anglia, Oxfordshire and Cambridgeshire

Gunhild – (GAHNH-hihl) Second daughter of Wessex

Leofwine – (LEOV-wine) sixth child of Godwin and Gytha, Jarl of Kent, Middlesex, Surrey, Hertfordshire and Buckinghamshire

Ælfgifa – (ALF-ghee-faa) Third daughter of Godwin and Gytha

Wulfnoth – last child of Godwin and Gytha

Edith the Fair - (or Edith Swannesha/ 'Swan-neck') wealthy Saxon noblewoman with lands in Cambridgeshire, Suffolk and Essex. First wife of Harold Godwinson

Beddwen – (BETH – wyn) a Welsh woman who acted as nurse to Godwin and Gytha's children and later to Harold and Edith's

Suela – (SOO-ay-laa) a beautiful Ceorl and trusted servant to Queen Ealdgyth

Aofra – (AY- frah) a pretty, ambitious girl, ward of King Edward and married to his trusted Thagn, Bealdric

Camus – (KAM-mus) The royal physician

Alfwine – (ALV-wine) a monk and adviser to Harold in his Jarldom in East Anglia

Caedmon – (KAD-mun) a non-conformist, radical monk belonging to the Celtic Rite Christian Church, resident advisor of Godwin and teacher of Ælfgifa

Nessa – A Pretani born ceorl in Harold's household

Ulfric – one of Harold's vassal thagns

Dubhne – (DOVE-nee) an old blind monk at Westminster Abbey

The French:

Henri I (Capet) – King of France 1027-60

William I ('The Bastard'/'The Conqueror') – Duke of Normandy

Robert I ('The Magnificent'/ 'The Liberal') – Duke of Normandy 1027-35

Herleva of Falaise – mother of William I, and his half-brothers Odo and Robert, Count of Mortaigne

Ralph de Wacey – William's fourth and last guardian

Gallet – a loyal knight of William's

Helisande – daughter of William's master of hounds, later married to Gallet

Bourdas – William's valet and then his squire

Grimoult du Plessis – A Norman nobleman, lord of Plessis

Neel – Viscount of Cotentin, a Norman nobleman

Renulf – A Norman nobleman, the Viscount of Bessin

Hammond ('with the Teeth') – Baron of Cruelly, a Norman nobleman

Guy of Burgundy – a relative of Duke William, the grandson of William's grandfather Duke Richard I

William fitzOsbern – advisor, steward and childhood friend of Duke William, and son to William's former guardian, Osbern

Hubert de Ryes – a knight, loyal to William during the first uprising against him

Raoul de Ryes – eldest son of Hubert de Ryes, knighted by William

Henry (or Hubert) de Ryes – second son of Hubert de Ryes, also knighted by William

Lanfranc, Bishop of Bec – one of William's closest advisors, an educator and negotiator

Raoul de Taisson, a Norman lord of uncertain loyalties

Roger de Montgomerie – a relative of Duke William and one of his chief counsellors

Mabel de Bellême – wife of Roger de Montgomerie and heiress of lands in Maine

Roger de Beaumont – a distant cousin of Duke William's, and one of his closest supporters, noted for his beard (an unusual accessory for Norman nobles)

Jean Bellin, Lord of Blainville – a loyal lord who managed the Duchy while William fought the rebellion

Baldwin V, Count of Flanders – Duke William's father in law, Count of Flanders 1035-67

Matilda of Flanders – Married to Duke William c.1053

Berenger – Norman guard at Falaise

Asce – Norman guard at Falaise

Eustace ('aux Gernons' – 'The Mustaches') **of Boulogne** – a relative of Duke William, and Count of Boulogne

Geoffrey of Anjou ('Martel' – 'The Hammer') – Count of Anjou and rival to Duke William

William of Arques – Duke William's uncle, lord of Arques and Talou

Mauger – Archbishop of Rouen and Duke William's uncle, brother of William of Arques

William Talvas (de Bellême) – head of the powerful Bellême family of Maine

Saxon place names:

Wintanceastre – Winchester - the seat of Saxon power in the last unbroken kingdom of the Heptarchy, Wessex

Deorham – Durham, where Harold set his household whilst he was Jarl of East Anglia

Cnobheresburgh – a castrum in the Jarldom of East Anglia where the first Irish monastery was established in 630 AD

Caerdid – Cardiff

Grantaceastr – Cambridge

Gwynedd - one of the Cymry kingdoms in North Wales

Jórvík – York

Londinium – The Roman capital of Britain, abandoned early in 5th Century

Lundenwic – Anglo-saxon London. The 'city' was established a mile or so from the original site of Londinium in 7th Century and was used as the capital until 11th century.

Westminster – at the time a small settlement on Thorney Island surrounding the early incarnation of Westminster Abbey, where later Westminster Cathedral was built. It is likely Harold Godwinson was crowned here although much of the work was funded by Edward the Confessor during his reign.

Stamford – one of the Danelaw five burghs, a small walled town in Lincolnshire. Stamford bridge was the site of the battle between Harold Godwinson and Harald Hardrada

Douvres – Dover, part of the Jarldom of Wessex at the time.

Fulford – a small village near York, site of the battle of the same name.

Pefensey – Pevensey, a village on the coast of East Sussex where William the Conqueror landed his fleet.

Hæstingaceaster – Hastings. The town near Battle, that gave name to the battle of Hastings.

Jarldoms of England:

Northumbria

East Anglia

Wessex

Kent

Mercia

Hereford

Huntingdon

(Norman place names are all rendered much as their modern French equivalents)

CHAPTER 1

THE sun barely up two hours and William was hungry already. *It's your own fault for picking at your breakfast*, he scolded himself, mockingly. It was Ralph's voice he heard in his head. Guardian and murderer of guardians. Well, it was Ralph's job to worry and the Lord knew he had been rewarded handsomely enough for the responsibility for nine of the young Duke's nineteen years. Let him worry. William always lost his appetite on the morning of a hunt. If he had his way they'd be out in the forests at daybreak. How the rest of them could clamber onto their horses with all the food they'd stuffed into themselves, he'd never know.

Well, there would be venison enough later on.

The sound of hooves on the hard earth of the clearing betokened the return of the huntsmen. William signaled to his groom and mounted his horse with some haste. The mare twitched and jibbed beneath him, sensing the tension running through his body.

"Are the stirrups right, my Lord?" the groom asked. William swung his feet in them, stood in the saddle a moment, tentatively squeezed them towards the mare's flanks.

"Yes, fine," he replied.

"Only it doesn't take much spurring to make her fly," the groom added, lowering his eyes shamefully. William would have lowered his own had he not been Duke of Normandy. How many hunts had he returned from with two trails of blood running from his horse where he'd been over-eager with the spiked stirrups? He'd try to be gentler this time. Though when he caught sight of the stag and the fever of the hunt took over... It may be a vain hope, but he might as well try.

Though, of course, if it came to a choice between mastering himself, and mastering the beast, or another man, he knew which he'd choose. He checked the longbow where it was secured beside him, the quiver of arrows on the other side. It should all stay in place, but he wanted to be able to free the bow quickly when the stag was at bay. Neither did he want it clouting him as he rode.

The huntsmen, who had been gathered in a knot after dismounting, approached. Ralph and Grimoult, who had also mounted, nudged their horses over, and took their places either side of him.

"What game have you for us today, master huntsmen?" William asked, annoyance at the ritual tightening his jaw. This one dropped his eyes too.

"Three stags in the wood, my Lord," the first of the men said. "Would my Lord care to inspect the fewmets?"

Fewmets? Keep your damned deer turds to yourself, you filthy peasant! William collected himself, and unwrinkled his nose. "I... leave the choice to you, master huntsman."

The fear of unwanted responsibility brightened the man's eyes for a moment. He turned to his companions, and something unspoken passed between them.

"My Lord," Ralph muttered, "you ought to learn how to read the fewmets. Might I see, Master huntsman?"

William rolled his eyes. The huntsman cast a wary glance at him, no doubt fearing to become caught in a spat between his betters, before motioning the other three huntsmen forward. In a moment Ralph, Grimoult and the huntsmen were poring over handfuls of black, glossy pellets. Color... shape... consistency... odour. Ugh! William let his mind wander. It was a fine day. If only they could be out in it, pursuing stags instead of sitting here discussing the beasts' leavings.

"Ah, a fine hart we tracked to the West, my Lord."

William's attention snapped back.

"...Not far, and he will give good sport, I'll be bound," the huntsman added.

You will be bound if you're wrong. "Excellent. Lead the way," William said, yawning.

"Yes, my Lord."

Ralph and Grimoult shot him a glance. Grimoult's gaze stayed on him as Ralph turned back to the huntsmen, and William did not know quite what to make of it. Dried up old bore. He ought to have a bit more fun, with all the money and land he commanded. William did his best to maintain the baron's gaze.

"How old?" Ralph asked.

"Er, seven or eight," the huntsman replied. "A hart of twelve tines, perhaps? In full grease, my Lords."

"Good. We don't want to be hurtling after a folly or rascal, now. Do we Lord?"

3

"What? Oh, no. Let's trot gently after an aged creature that may die before we can shoot it, thus saving us the effort."

The chief huntsman looked close to tears. "He'll give good sport, sirs, on my life."

"Are your men and dogs in position?" Ralph asked him.

"Yes, Lord."

"Then what are we waiting for? West, you say?" With only the slightest pang of shame, William jabbed the spiked stirrups into his courser's flanks and hung on as the creature darted forward. Only by a supreme effort was he able to guide her round onto the wide droveway heading west out of the clearing, and chance a glimpse behind to make sure the others were following. Of course they were following, he was the Duke of Normandy! The wind was rushing through his hair and the trees were a blurred curtain to either side. He threw back his head and laughed.

A horn sounded behind him, warning the drivers they were on their way. Another sounded, distant, responding. He was outpacing the hunters, and reluctantly sat up, easing the mare's speed and waiting for them to catch up.

After what seemed an age, Ralph drew alongside, and the chief huntsman managed to edge his nag a little ahead.

"There's no need to hurry," Ralph huffed. "The hound masters will drive the beast toward us. We'll need some strength left when we catch the hart. And there's no sense in leaving everyone behind."

William glanced back. Neel, Viscount of Cotentin, and Renulf, Viscount of Bessin, followed clearly in a state of some disarray. Hammond, Baron of Creully, was struggling, even further back. Something must have caused them to leave in a

4

hurry. He smirked to himself, but reined his mare back to a canter.

The horn sounded again, a complex series of blasts, closer this time. The master huntsman replied with a different, equally complex phrase from his own horn. It was all William could do not to spur the mare to a gallop again.

The huntsman dropped back alongside. "We should take the fork to the left, Lord," he said.

William nodded his acknowledgement. The hounds had the hart on the move, but it might still be hours before they caught sight of the creature, let alone brought it to bay. His impatience flared once again. He increased the pace, just a little. They cantered on through the wide paths cut in the forest, occasionally taking a turning. At least the huntsman knew where they were. Occasionally, William became aware of the rising sun's light rippling through the foliage above, but he'd lost track both of the time and the direction.

The distant horn sounded again. William thought it was a different sequence of blasts but could not be sure. "What does that mean," he asked Ralph, still cantering along at his side.

"You should know the calls, my Lord," Ralph said, keeping his voice low enough that William could only just hear him over the pattering of hooves.

This again? William was about to laugh when he saw the set of his guardian's jaw. He exhaled. "Sorry, Ralph, I'll learn them." *Tomorrow.*

"It's important."

"I know. So what was it?"

"The relie. It means the tracking party has found more fewmets and the hart is close."

5

More deershit. Honestly, it seemed that some of the hunters cared more about the excrement than the animal. "All right. They sound a long way off."

"A league or more."

William sighed. This was going to take all day. They cantered on, moving in the direction of the hart, or as far as William knew, at any rate. Occasionally they heard other horns, from other parties out in the forest.

The distant horn blew again. Even William could tell this was a different call than any they had heard before.

"Blast it," Ralph muttered. He looked up. "I don't suppose you know what that means?"

William shrugged.

"The stynt. It means the hounds have overshot the hart. These creatures are clever. They can double back, jump sideways, cross streams. The hunt is a battle of wits as well as a physical sport, Lord."

William exhaled. If they'd kept up the gallop earlier, they might have caught up with the stag by now. By hanging around, they'd let the creature slip through their fingers.

They came to a fork. The huntsman vacillated before picking the path to the right, but William didn't think he seemed too sure of himself. The regular report of horn calls died away. Eventually another blast sounded. Way off to the left.

The huntsman pulled up his horse, looking desolate. "The forloyn, my Lord. One of the hunters has lost contact with his party."

"Damn him and his whole bloody family!" William spat. "How could any huntsman worth the name be so stupid?"

"They must extend the line to relocate the stag, my Lord." He took off his cap and mopped his balding head with a rag. "The forest is thick."

"Not so thick as your men's skulls, it seems." William could have thumped his mare, given that the huntsman was not quite close enough, but restrained himself.

"I am sorry, my Lord."

Hours seemed to pass, though it could not have been that long. Nevertheless, the sun was noticeably higher when the horns sounded again. They seemed closer than before.

"The rechace, Lord! They've located the hart. The lymers will push him toward us." The huntsman blew the acknowledgement, and they moved off at a trot.

"How far?"

"Half a league, perhaps? The beast may still give us the slip."

"You'd better hope it doesn't."

"Yes, Lord."

Just then, a crash of breaking twigs emanated from the forest somewhere ahead of them. It sounded again, then again. "What in God's name...?" William said, just as a powerful form bounded out of the foliage and onto the path in front of him. The stag's eyes locked with his own for a moment. Huge, brown, unfathomable. A second passed, perhaps two. Just long enough for William to realize he ought to be reaching for his bow. Just as his hand moved, the stag leapt away. Or rather, it must have done, for it seemed as though it had gone from standing to running with no intermediate step. The stag took what must have seemed the most obvious escape route – straight down the droveway.

William jabbed his spurs into the mare's flanks and hung onto the reins as she sprinted after the stag. Dimly, above the thunder of hooves he heard Ralph yelling "Duke William! Come back, that's not our stag!"

But what did he care? It was a stag, and they were stag-hunting and he was sick to the back teeth of trotting around listening to a conversation of hunting horns. This was what it was all for! The pursuit!

The mare was not gaining on the stag, but nor was she losing ground. William realized he had no idea how long a stag could run for. In the past he'd only seen the creatures once they'd already been run down, brought to bay, exhausted and so sick with terror the fight had gone from them. Still it had taken him so many arrows to kill that first one that Ralph had joked they were serving porpentine at the feast. Briefly he wondered if the others would follow – of course they would, he was the Duke of Normandy! – before casting the thought aside. He didn't care. It was between him and the hart. Only one of them would win.

The stag darted into a droveway that bisected the main hunting trail, and William hauled the mare round to follow. He caught a glimpse of the stag leaping high into the air and in an instant there were men on horseback around him, and something across the path... the mare bounded before William could haul the reins back, and as she hit the ground William realized it was a line of hounds they had just jumped. He laughed wildly. The stag had drawn him into their own party. Oh, if he could have seen the looks on their faces. Horns sounded frantically behind him, and possibly ahead, although they might have been echoing off the canopy for all he knew. He ignored them, and willed the mare on.

The stag didn't seem to be tiring. Well, it was running for its life. Once again it turned and for a horrible moment William thought it had jumped back into the thicket. But no, it was a narrow path through the trees, barely wide enough for a horse. Some forest warden's trail, no doubt. The mare shied slightly, but he gave her the spurs again, and she turned into the gloom of the forest willingly enough. The hoofbeats of horse and hart seemed to rebound off the trees, and his own breathing was loud in his head. The path was sinuous, darting this way and that, and the stag negotiated the bends with ease, though William realized he was definitely closer now. *Bless you, surefooted steed!*

A blaze of sun seemed to cut through ahead and William burst into a wide clearing. There were no paths out of it that he could see. The stag looked back at him, eyes wild, breath steaming in jets from its nostrils, and leapt for the forest edge.

At that moment, a horn sounded out of the wood directly ahead, and a line of men and dogs seemed to melt out of the trees. The stag feinted this way and that, but there was no way through. The silence of the lymer hounds was eerie. The stag turned back towards William, and in that moment, he thought the creature was going to charge him. It didn't. He remembered the bow again, too late, but the stag had run out of alternatives.

So had he. No time to dismount. The stag wasn't at bay, it was just trapped temporarily. Even with the cordon of men and hounds, in a moment it could leap for its life and be back in the dark and dense forest where no man could give chase.

His hands shook as he undid the longbow's fastenings, groped for an arrow, nocked it... The stag was still there, front hooves planted wide as if it were preparing for one last leap. As calmly as he could, he drew the bow back, aiming for the hart's chest. The string creaked as it reached the greatest tension. It was almost disappointing when he released it. In truth, he thought he'd missed. Nothing seemed to happen. The arrow could have disappeared into thin air. And then he saw that it had buried itself up to the fletchings in the very center of the hart's breast. The beast gave a brief jerk of its head, and then it was on the ground, as still as stone.

He realized his arms hurt. They were like rough sacks full of molten lead. He dropped the bow. The huntsmen raised a cheer, and one of them blew on that infernal horn.

What a beautiful sound it made!

CHAPTER 2

THE rest of the hunt had passed in a blur. William was now covered in blood after breaking the hart to share the meat among the huntsmen, as seemingly he was expected to, and all agreed how finely it had been done. Except that he knew damned well he'd shredded the poor creature and spent twice as long on it as he should have. It was obvious from the looks Grimoult and Hammond exchanged and hadn't even bothered to hide. Even before his mangling, there wasn't a great deal of flesh to be had.

"A young hart, four at most," Ralph had lamented when the others were out of earshot. "Only six tines. There was a hart of twelve out there for the taking."

The master huntsman approached, a grin all over his ruddy face. "Well done, my Lord, very well done! It was marvelous skillful how you did drive him towards the other party! You read the horns like a Lord well beyond your years. And to shoot him from horseback! If only I could have seen it, Lord!"

"Thank you, Master... er..."

"Ardfoot," Ralph muttered.

Ardfoot? What a ridiculous name. "Master Ardfoot. Thankyou. You provided for our hunt most satisfactorily."

"Thankyou, Lord, thankyou! I hope you will be able to come a hunting at Valognes again soon."

"As do I, Master Ardfoot."

The hunt master departed, wreathed in smiles. William watched him go. "It was a bloody mess," he said.

"Oh? And whose fault was that? My Lord?"

William sighed expansively. "Spare me the lecture. At least until this evening. I'm tired and hungry."

"Well it's your own fault for picking at your breakfast instead of eating it."

"Anyway, didn't I do well? The common folk all seem to think so."

"Yes, and lucky for you they do."

William didn't press that point. It was nice someone recognized his feat, even if they were the lesser folk. As for the so-called nobles, standing around and sneering down their noses at him... he'd liked to have seen one of them chase after a rascal through a woodsman's trail right into the path of a hunting party. All right, so the last part was pure luck. He'd no idea there had been anyone ahead of him, and he doubted he could have steered the hart one *pied* more to the left or right than he'd wanted to.

"We should head back to Valognes," Ralph said. "It will take us long enough, the state your horse is in."

William looked down. It was true. She was covered in foam, and still breathing heavily.

"You must look after your mounts better."

"Yes, Ralph."

News of the hunt appeared to have preceded them. As they rode back into the streets of Valognes in the early afternoon, it seemed as though the whole town had turned out to catch sight of the Duke who'd run down a stag virtually single-handed. William enjoyed basking in their adulation, though he noted that most of the Barons accompanying him were acting somewhat stiffly. Even frosty. Jealousy. It was an ugly thing.

The babble of conversation barely quieted as they rode beneath the gates of the castle. The bustle was perhaps unsurprising for a castle playing host to its Duke with a feast to be held that evening, but he fancied not a few of the hurrying servants and staff had caught a little of the excitement. He was alive with it. His heart was fit to jump out of his ribcage.

A ripple of feminine laughter pricked at his ears. He looked up. A gaggle of girls standing outside the kitchens. Commoners, of course, come to catch a glimpse of their stag-slaying Duke, no doubt, but he allowed his eyes to linger. Most of them turned away as they saw him looking, darted back out of sight, but one remained a moment longer, meeting his gaze. She was slender as a reed and her grace belied her class. Her eyes were large and bright, and if her skin was not pale enough for her ever to be mistaken for a woman of breeding, it was smooth as marble. It felt like a minute or more that they stood like that, but William knew that no servant or child of one of his men would dare such an affront. By the time she had bowed her head and moved away, his heart was beating almost as fast as it had on the hunt. "You," he called to his groom. "Who is that?" He pointed at the girl's retreating back.

"That's Helisande, Lord. Daughter of your Lordship's master of hounds." The boy's face reddened. William was not surprised.

"Is she married?"

"No, Lord."

"Good. Have her brought to my chambers after the feast this evening."

"Lord?" A note of panic entered the boy's voice. Either he had no idea how to go about it or he was in love with her himself. Probably both. "Should I speak to her father, Lord?"

"Good Lord no! Look. Find my écuyer, Bourdas. Tell him what I said, and he'll see to it."

"Yes, Lord. Thankyou, Lord."

William dismounted, catching, as he did so, the strong tang of horse blood. Sure enough, a thin crimson stream ran down the mare's flank and dripped off her belly onto the cobbles of the yard. He patted her, gave her neck a quick rub and turned on his heel. As he strode towards the keep, he heard the boy burst into tears, sobbing an apology to the horse for its ill treatment.

At the feast that evening, even William could not ignore the fact that the venison they were eating today was rather finer than the lean, stringy meat he had inexpertly butchered earlier. It seemed that while the commoners and the lower orders of gentry had been impressed with William's feats during the hunt, the nobles were not. He sighed. What on earth did he have to do before they'd acknowledge his right to sit above them? Grimoult sat a little further down with a face like a raincloud, pushing his venison round his plate. Renulf and Neel had not even touched their food but simply sat scowling at one another and avoiding each other's gaze by turn. William was not surprised at that – in truth he was more surprised the two of them had agreed to turn up at all, given that they'd been virtually at war with each other for months over some perceived slight or piece of land, despite his many commands for them to stop. Hammond kept baring his ridiculous teeth in a vile grimace. William sent Bourdas to tell the musicians to play louder, and throw in a few merrier catches while they were at it, then launched into the third telling of the chase.

It did little to mask the sour atmosphere.

On top of all that, it seemed that Ralph was in a lecturing mood. As if he was in any other kind these days.

"...The hunt is all life. You must see that. It's not simply a game for your indulgence."

William raised an eyebrow. *No? What else is it for?*

"All of life is brought together in the hunt, from your lowliest servant to your proudest Barons. All must work together to catch the hart, and each has their place."

It didn't seem like that today.

Ralph leaned over again. "Why do we hunt?"

"To catch the beast, of course."

"No. There are far easier ways of catching stags. Traps and snares."

"Ha!" William nearly spat his wine over the guests opposite. "Where's the fun in that?"

Ralph sighed. "Hasn't it occurred to you that the way we hunt is the most difficult, complicated way of catching a single animal?"

"I suppose so."

"It brings together the Lord and all his people. It reminds them of the natural order. And above all, it makes them see the sense of that natural order. What they saw today was you chasing off after the wrong stag and then making a mess of its carcass."

William rolled his eyes. "They saw me drive it into the path of the hunters and shoot it from horseback."

"Indeed. And no-one who didn't see it could be in any doubt after hearing about it for the tenth time."

He put down his knife and placed his hands flat on the table. "What's your point, Ralph?"

"There's more to the hunt than catching a hart."

"Really?" This was too much, even by Ralph's standards. "What? We hunted the stag. I caught the stag. Everyone went away happy." And what did it matter that everyone else was happy anyway?

"You caught a stag. If you'd caught the one we'd agreed to pursue we'd have more meat, and better quality, at the next feast."

"How do you know it wasn't the right stag anyway?"

"The fewmets-"

"Oh Lord, not the deershit again!"

Ralph sat back, and took a long draught from his goblet. William cast an eye at Bourdas to his other side, who was struggling to repress fits of laughter.

"Sometimes," Ralph sighed, "a hart has been known to find a younger, less guileful animal and push it into the way of the hunters."

"And you think that's what happened today?" A dumb animal switching a more likely victim? Preposterous.

"I cannot say, my Lord. That would suggest that you had allowed yourself to be outwitted by a wiser, cannier creature, who slipped away while you pitted yourself against another hotheaded youngster."

William snorted.

"You even sound like a stag today."

"Can't you allow me my moment, Ralph? I damned near killed myself hurtling after that creature and I didn't see anyone else hurrying to help."

"No. Don't you wonder why that was?"

What was Ralph getting at now?

"You broke that animal more like a boar than a stag."

"I don't see why I have to do that anyway. I have a kitchen full of butchers."

"That's not the point. You made a fool of yourself not being able to recognize the horn calls as well."

"I retain huntsmen. They have employment. Why should I buy a dog and bark myself?"

"Because you are the Duke, anointed by God to rule. It means you must be more than everyone you govern. It means that you must be a better hunter than the huntsmen, a better butcher than the butchers, and, if need be, a better dog than the hounds."

William shook his head. He'd heard all this before and it made as little sense now as ever.

"...because one day the Duke might have to ask the Barons and knights and huntsmen and dogs to follow him into more than a hunt. To die for him, perhaps."

"The Duke does not ask. The Duke commands."

Ralph looked at him through narrow eyes. William thought he was going to start up his lecture again, but he didn't. The rest of the evening passed in sullen silence. There was no-one else William felt like talking to – all the nobles seemed to be either blind drunk or in foul temper. He proceeded to emulate the former.

Some hours later, the feast stuttered to a halt. William slurringly thanked his guests and waited while they staggered out into the night. Hanging onto Bourdas he waded through the debris of the feast, which by now covered most of the floor, leaving the servants to clear it up.

The cold air of the courtyard hit him like a bucket of water, but rather than clearing his head, it just made things spin. The écuyer steered him towards the keep, where William's chambers were.

A crash reverberated out of the darkness across the courtyard.

"It's the stables for you, with all the other beasts, you drunkard!"

William stopped and willed his eyes to adjust to the gloom. Four, no five figures were moving about. One of them toppled away from the group and fell to the ground a few pieds from William's feet. The figure lurched to his feet, swayed. "Sorry sirs," he said, attempting a bow, before turning and rushing back at the others. "I'll teach you to say that about my Lord, you brigands!"

"If you were sober enough to handle a sword I'd duel you for that!" one of the others yelled, and the group degenerated into a cacophony of yells and thuds.

William took a step towards the mêlée, but felt Bourdas' hand on his arm.

"It's just a brawl, my Lord. Best stay out of it, eh? Look, I promised your guardian I'd get you safely to bed."

He looked into the murk, trying to work out what was going on. "I think they're knights."

18

"Probably. Anyway, there's plenty to keep you occupied in your chambers."

For a moment, William wasn't sure what he meant. Then, in a wave of clarity he remembered the girl. His heart started beating a little faster. Who cared about a bit of fisticuffs, even if the fellows were supposed to be gentlemen? He allowed himself to be guided away.

"Listen Bourdas," he said. "Ralph will tell you all kinds of nonsense about duty and honor. None of that matters. Take what you can. Whatever you would have, you must take, even if it already belongs to you. No man will give you a thing, and most of them will be trying to take whatever you have. There are two kinds of men in the world – those who take, and those who are taken from."

"Yes, my Lord. Like the Master of Hounds?"

William laughed, making his head pound. "He is my man, and his daughter belongs to him, therefore she is mine."

"What happens if... if she gets with child, my Lord?"

"Then she is fortunate indeed, for her bastard has every chance of becoming a duke."

CHAPTER 3

WILLIAM awoke from dreams about rushing through a forest, in which he was not sure if he was chasing or being chased. It was not morning. The chamber was wreathed in darkness, the pale sheets beneath him, slashed with the darker shadow of the girl's back were all he could make out. All was quiet apart from the sound of her breathing.

Something was wrong.

He blinked, desperately hoping for his vision to cut through the dark, and listened for anything that might reveal what had caused him to wake. Slowly, far too slowly, forms in the unfamiliar room began to take shape. Furniture. Scattered clothing. Just as he was beginning to think it was something in the dream that had wakened him, a cloak hanging on the wall detached itself and stepped across to the bed. Just as his mouth opened to yelp in surprise, a hand clamped over it, and an arm pinned him to the bed.

"Quiet, Lord, quiet," a voice said, so close to his ear he could feel the warm breath. "Don't you move. I'm sorry for this presumption, Lord, but there really isn't any other way. You need to listen to what I say."

William forced himself to relax his muscles – his whole body had stiffened when the stranger stepped out of the shadows. He tried to make an affirmative noise. The grip relaxed. "What's going on?" he hissed. "Who are you? Where are the guards?"

"My name's Gallet, Lord. I'm a knight, your man. But never mind that. Your enemies are coming to kill you. You need to fly."

William's head spun. His man? He didn't remember this fellow paying him homage... must have been years ago. And enemies? "Coming to kill me? What? Who?"

"Grimoult du Plessis. Renulf. Neel. That Hammond with the Teeth. Others. Rise, now. They mean to murder you and install Guy as the Duke."

"Guy... of Burgundy? My cousin? But I gave him Lordships? He swore-"

"I apologize Lord, but this isn't the time. They're on their way. I overheard them when they were gathering in the stables. I was.... sleeping off a little drink after a bit of a to do with some other men at arms in the courtyard."

"That was you?"

"Well, yes. But never mind that. I saw them, they're putting hauberks on and buckling swords under their hoquetouns, and they left me in little doubt what they were planning. Make no mistake, they're prepared for a fight and they'll kill everyone in their way. If they reach you, you will not see the morning."

There was a gasp from beside him, and before he knew what was happening, Helisande was grabbing at the covers and scooping them over her. "Please be quiet," William whispered to her. "There are men coming, to... to..."

"What should I do?" she said, voice muffled by all the cloth.

William marveled at how calm she sounded, under the circumstances. "Er...."

"We'll be leaving in a moment, Lady," Gallet said. "Probably best you leave the Duke's chambers with us. Do you know the castle?"

"Yes."

"And there's somewhere safe you can go?"

"Yes."

"Good."

William felt a little relief in amongst the panic that Gallet was dealing with it. He smelled like a wine cellar in a pigsty, but he had an air of calm about him. And although he hadn't had much thought for the girl besides the diversion she might provide, he did not want to think of her slaughtered on his behalf. He wasn't even annoyed at Gallet addressing her as 'Lady'.

"You'd better get some clothes on Lord, my Lady. You have only a moment, and you'll be as dismembered as that stag if you don't fly."

William and Helisande scrabbled at the floor finding whatever garments they could.

"Um, a short mantle, if you have one there, Lord," Gallet suggested. "Suitable for riding?"

Before long, they were at least covered. Gallet led them out of the servants' entrance and through the darkened back ways. Soon they were outside again, the challenge dying in the throats of all the guards they encountered when they recognized William. There was only one way in and out. William prayed they would reach the entrance before the assassins did. Mercifully, the guards opened the heavy, studded door without question and in a moment they were hurrying down the steps through the stone passage that led to the courtyard.

"I readied a palfrey for you, Lord," Gallet said, making to cross the yard, but stopped after a couple of steps and stood still for a moment. "Quick, this way," he hissed, bundling William and Helisande in the other direction, round the corner of the keep. They pressed themselves against the wall.

William heard the sound of boots marching on the flagstones, and chanced to peer round the edge for a second. Shadowy figures, seemingly dressed as gentlemen, but the metallic clink of mail and the rhythmic slap of scabbards against legs revealed what Gallet had said to be true. His heart competed with the thump of boots in his ears. More still were coming. He tried to work out from the sound how many of them there might be, but gave up. There were a lot of them anyway. Too many. The last of them disappeared up the entranceway. Faintly, William heard the gate open, and a challenge, then the sound of swords being drawn. A strangled cry. Suddenly William wanted to piss very badly. His thumping heart increased from a canter to a full gallop.

Gallet shook his shoulder and pointed. They hurried across the courtyard, William expecting at any moment to hear a shout from behind, and the armed party to return. For now though, they were unchallenged. Gallet gestured toward a post near the entrance to the inner bailey, where three horses were tied up. One of them was indeed saddled. It wasn't the finest mount, but it would have to do. "Here, take my cape," the knight added, sweeping it off and handing it over.

The cloak stank, but William was glad of it. "Will you see the girl to safety?"

"Aye, Lord." It didn't look as though he would have much choice. Helisande was clinging to his arm as though she would tear it off.

As William swung himself into the saddle, Gallet moved towards the gate a few paces, peered around and returned.

"All right. They haven't left a guard. They must not suspect you would be warned. Now, you've some water and a little food in the bags there." The knight lowered his voice. "I'd make for Ryes. It's on the road to Falaise, and Hubert's a decent sort, he'll give you shelter. And whatever you do, steer clear of Bayeux. But hurry. Even now they'll have found you gone. Oh, and Duke William?"

"Yes?"

"That was a beauty of a shot to bring the stag down like that! Finest I ever saw. Who cares it was only some scrawny rascal? Go safely now, Lord."

William didn't need further bidding. He gave a curt nod to Gallet and rode through the gate. No challenge came – the guard was already dead.

His mind spun. His vassal lords wanted to *kill* him! After all Ralph had said about the rightful order of things. Now which was the right road? He pulled the horse up briefly, facing the maze of darkened streets. The last thing he wanted was to be wandering around the houses of Valognes when daybreak came. Daybreak. He realized he had no idea what time it was, how much darkness he had left. *Come on William, think! Which way is it?*

All right. When we arrived we turned right into the castle. Left, then. He picked a route, hoping desperately it was the correct one, and spurred his horse to a canter. *Can't gallop inside the town*, he told himself. That was the best way to breaking the horse's legs and ending up on his head. It seemed like an age before the turrets of the East Gate came into view.

As he drew up his horse to ask the gatekeeper to open up for him, William swore he heard more horses' hooves behind him. Dear Savior, were they onto him to quickly? The bleary-eyed commoner swung the gates open and he darted through as soon as there was a gap big enough for his horse. He was about to command the man to bar the gate and not let anyone else through, but thought of his guards back at the castle. The gatekeeper just looked as though he wanted to get back into the warm. Those men would run him through if he resisted. Just then, William didn't have the heart to order the man to his own death. He hadn't seen a man killed since he'd woken in his chamber – what was it, eight, nine years ago? – to see someone slitting his guardian Osbern's throat. Without a word he gave his horse its head and galloped into the night.

For a good minute he thought he might have got away with it. That the conspirators, realizing he had left the town, would call off the hunt. Surely there was too much ground to cover? Too many ways he might have gone?

But that wasn't what he would do. If he'd raised his hand against his liege lord, he wouldn't stop until one of them was dead. And there was only one way he would go. Grimoult, Hammond, Neel, Renulf... they all knew he would have to head for Falaise. There was nowhere else in Normandy he could trust to his own safety.

The drum of hooves reached his ears even over the panting and galloping of his own horse. His heart plummeted in his chest. He leaned forward and urged his steed on, pleading and entreating. Every time the animal began to slow, he gave it the spur, feeling each jab of the spikes as if they had gone into his own side.

"Come on horse," he panted. "Come on. Just get me to Falaise... no, just get me to Ryes... and I'll have you a stable built... all to yourself... made of gold if you want... no need to carry another person again... and all the hay you can eat... come on, just a little further..." Just a little. *Oh Lord, Ryes must be four or five hours ride away.* His arms began shooting darts of pain up and down their length, and he realized he was holding them rigid. They were still sore from holding the bow yesterday. Good God, how was he supposed to ride for four hours when he was already tiring?

The horrible arrhythmic percussion of his horse's hoofbeats and its breathing, mixed with his own and the thunder of his heart filled his head with noise. Yet still he fancied he could hear a large group of horsemen behind. Heavy beasts, probably. Destriers, that could ride for hours and still keep on coming, never missing a beat. Saints and martyrs, they'd surely catch him, be it soon or be it late.

William momentarily wished that Gallet had been able to find a courser rather than this little palfrey, he'd outpace them then all right... but who knew how long he would need to ride for? Well, it wouldn't make any difference if those knights behind caught up with him. The gloom toyed with his mind. He felt the breath of horses on his back. He felt a gauntleted hand outstretched, about to grab him. Every so often, when the prickling in the back of his neck got too much to bear, he chanced a glimpse behind, but all was darkness apart from the pale streak of the road behind him, the occasional lighter patch of a wheatfield in amongst the green crops.

He passed through Carentan, which might have been deserted, so quiet were its streets, and pressed on. How long had he been riding? It felt as though it might have been all night. But he would have reached the ford of Saint Clement over the Vire before the end of the second hour, well before at this pace. Unless he had taken the wrong road somehow.

No! There it was! He was on the right road and had reached the river. The clouds thinned for a moment, and a glimmer of moon caught the broad strip of river ahead. The road began to slope, gently towards the ford. Hope burst once again in his breast.

But what if the river was in flood? The tide in? The flash of hope died as quickly as it had kindled. He reined the horse in a little. If they plunged headlong into a raging torrent... Was that any worse than what would happen if the horsemen behind caught up with him? He found himself wondering if any of the treacherous Barons were in the group behind. Curse it! He would not live to see the smirk on Grimoult's face! Better to drown.

The river was near now, and William could only hear a gentle swish and gurgle. He would not be carried away, thank the Lord! But the tide might still be in. Could this horse bear him, swimming? Doubtful.

He reached the edge, and urged the horse gently to walk into the stream. It did. Mercifully, the water came no higher than its fetlocks. Halfway across, the horse stopped, began to drink, and would not be persuaded to move on. William could hardly blame it. He was thirsty himself, and his head pounded, whether from all the riding or the wine last evening, he could hardly tell. He laughed, a bitter chuckle that was consumed by the shush of the river. After a few moments, the horse deigned to move on, and presently they were climbing the far bank. During the pause they had not been caught. William breathed a long sigh into the night air. He must have managed to put a bit of distance on his pursuers after all. He patted the horse affectionately, and urged it into the ambling gait that could enable palfreys to cover such great distances at a steady pace.

He sensed, rather than saw, the church just above the ford, a looming presence in the darkness, and remembered something Ralph was fond of saying—"God knows how to take in his keeping those whom he loves and whom it pleases him to defend". Well, let us hope so. William offered a brief, clumsy prayer of thanks to Saint Clement as he passed the church.

CHAPTER 4

ÆLFGIFA crouched beside a large oak chest in her mother's private quarters. A fold of finely woven wool cloth hung over the edge of the chest and the girl was small enough that unless someone was in fact looking for her, she would not be seen. In Ælfgifa's experience—the sum total of which culminated in nearly ten years' worth of child's wisdom—it was easy to make oneself invisible. Dimly, she was aware that her ability to get around unseen was due in large measure to others not wishing to see her.

Her mother, Gytha, was awake yet, pacing before the fire. She had removed her fine linen veil and her unbound hair was a dark, rippling gold in the firelight. Ælfgifa knew there were fine streaks of gray in that hair now. There had been ever since Wulfnoth had been born. From gossip and scraps of overheard conversation, Ælfgifa knew that her mother had been considered too old to bear children when Ælfgifa herself was born, a fact that had seemed validated by the state of the tiny female child. Five years later still, Gytha had gone on to bear a healthy son and the gossips had hushed. And Gytha was still fair. Not girlishly slender but still upright, tall, slim and strong. Other women had bodies like shapeless sacks, flaccid and bent after giving birth to fewer children than Gytha.

Ælfgifa shivered a little, wishing she could pull the woolen mantle down off the chest and wrap it around herself without giving her presence away. It was just past Midwinter and the season had been especially cold. It was not that she feared the swift slap of retribution her mother was likely to deal her if she was found, more that she saw so little of her mother – or rather her mother saw so little of her – that it had forced Ælfgifa to become creative if she wanted to see Gytha. She did feel a pang for her nurse – now Wulfnoth's nurse really. Beddwen was probably searching for her even now. She put the feeling aside. Ælfgifa had learned to be unseen even when she was not actively hiding. The household often forgot and talked incautiously in front of her. She had learned to eavesdrop, to spy and to sift conversation for nuggets of information. Hardly activities that were honorable or considered meet for a Jarl's daughter, though Ælfgifa did not see how she could find out what she wanted to know otherwise. Questions were often repudiated or ignored. She had learned to read faces and gestures, even those slight, unconscious expressions. It had fascinated her when she first realized that what was said was often at odds with what was communicated. And then it had confused and puzzled her, for truth was held to be a high virtue and virtually no one spoke the truth.

The talk of the moment was that her eldest sister, Ealdgyth, was to be married. From her mother's personal ceorls, Ælfgifa had deduced that this was not a match Gytha was favorably disposed toward. And there was something else. Something about the bride groom that suggested a lack.

Since the bride groom was King Edward, this puzzled Ælfgifa greatly. She had seen her mother exchange a certain look with her father when they sat at board earlier that evening. A look that meant they would talk in private later. Ælfgifa wanted to hear what was said.

Gytha stopped short and turned, causing Ælfgifa to draw back even further into the shadows. Gytha had not seen her however, she had merely heard the footsteps that preceded the chamber door opening and admitting Jarl Godwin. Ælfgifa relaxed a little at her father's appearance though she did not reveal herself.

"Well now, Wife. Here am I, ready for the lashing of your tongue." Godwin half-smiled.

"I would it were not a needful occurrence, my lord," Gytha replied. Ælfgifa noted the slight stress on the words 'my lord'.

She watched enthralled. Ælfgifa's parents never disagreed over any matter publicly and before this evening she had never dared to spy on them. She had watched serfs and thralls, ceorls and servants, even free men and women, play in this manner. Jesting when one or both were seriously displeased. It had never occurred to her that her parents indulged in such behavior, nor that the Jarl and Countess of Wessex were merely human, as well as being titled. It occurred to Ælfgifa suddenly, that her parents had less freedom than serfs in how they might publically act.

Godwin and his lady made a striking picture. Both tall, both fair. Ælfgifa thought that her father looked more worn and more aged than his wife, despite Gytha being several years his senior.

"You are not pleased by the honor the king does our daughter?" Godwin murmured. He had stepped closer and looped a waist-length strand of Gytha's hair out of her eyes. She brushed him off impatiently.

"I am not pleased to see our daughter, our first daughter —the greatest beauty of Wessex—wed to a man twice her age, who can have no proper use for a wife." Gytha's eyes flashed bright in the fire's glow.

"No proper use? What about to get heirs with? How is that not a proper use of a wife?" Godwin demanded. From her hiding place Ælfgifa noted that the fine crinkles at the corners of her father's eyes had disappeared. He was less hot in his temper than his wife, but when roused to ire he had a cold, creative way of slicing with his words that put Gytha in the shade entirely. Ælfgifa recognized the danger signs and her stomach clenched.

"You need not make such an argument with me as that, husband. Either our king has only an interest in matters of the spirit rather than of the flesh, or worse, a desire to appear so for some undisclosed reason. I would that Ealdgyth married another and Edward look elsewhere for his bride, if he must have one for appearances' sake. Were it not for the death of Edward's brother I doubt not that Wessex would have no need for such ties to prove loyalty." Gytha made as if to pace again but Godwin put out an arm to stop her.

"It is done, Gytha. We cannot withhold our daughter now without proof of viciousness in Edward himself. We must be the fools if we think that such an insult would have no consequences for ourselves, for Wessex, for the stability of the kingdom. Whatever your suspicions on the why of

Edward's conduct, he is neither vicious nor foolish. Besides, Ealdgyth is happy at the match."

"She is a foolish girl," muttered Gytha.

"She has been in want of a husband for these past five or six years! Be in your wits, Gytha, so please you."

"Why Ealdgyth? Cannot we offer one of our other daughters?"

"Who should we offer then? We are rich in sons. Less so in daughters. Would you send Gunhild? She is but fourteen and promised to the church besides. Or my little Blackbird? We'll marry our youngest to the king shall we? And hope she is old enough for the king to consummate the marriage before accident or misadventure nullifies it." Godwin frowned down at his wife. The light caught in Godwin's neatly trimmed beard turning the red-gold to copper.

"Would it were Ælfgifa. She would be a very proper wife for a man who cannot use one!" Gytha glared back at her husband.

In her hiding place, Ælfgifa had tensed at her father's pet name for her, then flushed with shame at her mother's jibe. Beddwen said once that those who peer at keyholes will see what they wish they had not. The same was true, it seemed, for those who listened. Ælfgifa did not entirely understand what her mother meant by being a proper wife for a king with no use for one. She did understand that her mother thought her only worth offering to a man she did not like or respect. The least of sacrifices. Flawed.

Godwin had gone very pale. When he spoke it was with great and measured control. "Enough. Have done with this now, Gytha. In God's name she is your own child."

Gytha did not blush nor did her gaze waver, but Ælfgifa thought that she detected a little unease in her mother's expression. Something like the guilt that Ælfgifa saw in her mother's face whenever she chanced to look up and catch her mother watching her.

"Well did you name her a gift of the elves," Gytha said, in a faintly mocking but weary tone. "Enough then. I'll not malign your favorite daughter. Even if you *will* give away mine." Finally her stance slackened, her head fell forward and she buried her face in her hands. "Edward is older than you, Godwin, her own father. How can she be happy with that? How happy in that pious household?"

"Ealdgyth has had some conversation with the king. I believe there may be affection there in time. It is strange that when the daughter should raise objections she raises a joyful countenance heavenward while her mother weeps. Come, your grandchildren shall be kings and princes." Godwin put his arm about Gytha's shoulders.

"I do not weep," she said with some asperity, but this time she did not shrug off his caress.

"Content yourself, wife. Your sons do well. Sweyn has held the Jarldom of Herefordshire for some time and given us a grandson. The king confirmed Harold's place as Jarl of East Anglia. Now our daughter shall be queen. It is naught to grieve over."

As they stood with their backs to her, Ælfgifa decided it was a good time to slip away. Silent as a cat, she slid out of her hiding place. Her bare feet made no sound on the rush strewn floor and the door was soon shut behind her. She padded up the hall to the rooms she shared with her nurse and her younger brother. It came as no surprise to Ælfgifa that Ealdgyth was her mother's favorite. They were very alike. The same height and slenderness. Their hair was within a single shade of being the same color, hanging in thick waves past their girdles. Ealdgyth was beautiful, like Gytha herself. Ælfgifa was not, nor could she ever be.

She had heard the whispers. How Gytha had borne her too late in life, which was why Ælfgifa, the third daughter, was so misshapen. What the explanation for Wulfnoth being brought to birth unmarked and perfect five years later was, Ælfgifa did not know. Some whispered that the Good Folk had played a trick and left a changeling in place of the Jarl's true daughter.

Ælfgifa, a name given by her father because he adored his youngest daughter.

Ælfgifa, a name agreed by her mother because with her usual sense of irony, Gytha had thought it fitting that the one imperfect child she had given life to, should be thought a changeling.

Under the flickering rush lights, Ælfgifa felt small and dark and loathsome. A creeping creature. Her face felt no different under her fingers than that of her brothers or sisters. But she looked different. She had a hare's foot mouth with a malformed upper jaw. She was small and olive skinned, dark as a Pict. Instead of gold, her hair was as dark as the wool of a black sheep. Her eyes were hazel and deep set under such strongly marked eyebrows that already they seemed the dominant feature in her face. Aside, that is, from the dark cerise stain over her left cheek, as though someone had split wine on her and forgotten to mop it up. A childhood fever had pock-marked her jaw and temples.

Ælfgifa had a face that was made to be forgotten.

35

Yet her mind was preternaturally sharp. Childhood curiosity made a further leap in her scrawny frame. That bright intelligence now prompted her away from the unending shame of being the beautiful Countess' unwanted, ugly daughter, and on to the snippets of information she had gleaned from her eavesdropping.

Harold is now a Jarl, she thought. She had not seen her brother for some time, but she remembered him. Everyone was tall to Ælfgifa but she thought he was an especially tall, well-favored young man, who laughed a lot but spoke sense. He had been kind to her. She thought he had the same red-gold hair as their father but she could not be sure. *He will want a wife soon too,* she mused.

Then there was Sweyn, the eldest, heir of Wessex. Ælfgifa remembered him less well but she pictured a man shorter than Harold with hair more dark, like her own . He had a hearty laugh but he had also pinched her and asked her when the Good Folk would fetch her back. He was hot-tempered like Gytha too, but hasty, less temperate in judgment. With none of her father's or Harold's natural kindness. She did not like him much and had been glad when he went away again. *Sweyn will bring misfortune,* she thought and then wondered at herself for being so sure.

And Ealdgyth will marry the king, she concluded. *At least she is happy about it. I do not think I should be if it were me. What is it that mother does not like about the king?*

"Mwyalchen? Where have you got to? Mwyalchen!"

Ælfgifa smiled the close-lipped smile she had learned that others preferred in her. Beddwen sounded furious. After the tension and strain of her parents' argument, a good scolding and then coddling by her nurse seemed welcome.

"Here, Beddwen," she called, before pattering in the direction of her nurse's voice.

CHAPTER 5

BEDDWEN was a stout Cymry woman, with ruddy cheeks and large, strong hands. She had a broad, kindly face. Not beautiful, but trustworthy and honest. Beddwen's eyes were dark and sharp like a robin's, and her smooth cap of brown hair and plump, short figure only increased her likeness to the little bird. Ælfgifa knew better than to suggest such a likeness to her nurse however. Those large hands might be deft and kind but they could also deliver a clout to make your ears ring. Nor was she so foolish as to actually call Beddwen *Wealas* as most people called the folk of Cymru. Ælfgifa knew that there was pain in the word for Beddwen. Perhaps her nurse was unaware of the sorrow that crept into her voice when she spoke of the land she had grown up in, but her charge was not. Thanks to Beddwen, Ælfgifa could speak the language of Cymru quite well and had spent many nights puzzling over why her own people, the Saxons, should call the Cymry 'strangers' in their own lands. It was a riddle that she had yet to solve to her satisfaction. But to call a woman who had cared for her, taught her, comforted her, loved her... To call Beddwen a stranger, even if it was considered apt? Ælfgifa just wouldn't do it.

That did not mean that Ælfgifa, gleeful on her fat, grey pony, did not find the sight of her plump nurse wobbling on the back of a sturdy mountain cob greatly amusing. She choked back a giggle. Beddwen eyed her charge, undeceived, and groaned about being too old for such capers on horseback.

The journey to Wintanceastre was well enough. There was a lull in the January snows so the tracks were passable. Ælfgifa had never left the family estate before and was excited to be out on an adventure. Everything was new to her. There were honeyed apples and millet cakes, and jugs of warm spiced cider. There was not much time to talk to her elder sister, Ealdgyth—who was in any case too much preoccupied with her forthcoming nuptials—and her brother Leofwine had said something cruel about pulling her veil down to cover all of her face, but still it was change. More importantly the thin crescent in which she had lived until now was waxing towards a full moon of experiences and knowledge. There had even been talk of her visiting the convent at Wilton, where surely Jarl Godwin would send her to be educated, as he had with Ealdgyth and Gunhild.

And then it had been time for the children of Godwin to wash, and greet their parents. Ælfgifa endured the zealous though mercifully brief scrubbing Beddwen gave her without complaint, though Leofwine and Wulfnoth yelled as if they were being disemboweled by *freets*. She sat patiently through the combing and pulling and plaiting of her hair into a heavy dark knot on the crown of her head, the loose strands, falling in fine and silky cobwebs over her shoulders. She rather liked the russet wool gown she had been given to wear, gasping in awe at the tracery of gold colored embroidery—a pattern of willows and hounds—at the cuffs and hem. Ælfgifa stepped very daintily and lined up with her siblings. Beddwen held Wulfnoth, who was so tired that he had fallen asleep on the nurse's ample bosom. Ælfgifa thought he looked rather sweet when he was asleep, all red curls and round baby cheeks, brushed by his long pale eyelashes.

Those of Ælfgifa's brothers and sisters who had yet to acquire or inherit lands of their own stood in order of seniority as if awaiting inspection. Ealdgyth looked especially beautiful in a dress of cream and gold. Dark-haired, stormy-eyed Tostig, now a man, came next. Gyrth, smiling and golden-haired. Pale, sweet-faced Gunhild. Then Ælfgifa herself. Godwin and Gytha entered the hall then to see their children before presenting them to King Edward. All might still have been well. Gytha bestowed a nod of approval on her sons and a kiss upon Ealdgyth and Gunhild. Then she saw Ælfgifa and her fury turned her white as milk, eyes glittering dangerously. Ælfgifa knew in that moment that her mother had not been aware Godwin had sent for her.

Her mother's voice to Beddwen was very cool. The north wind had more warmth in it. "I think we need not trouble the king with the younger children, Beddwen. See? Wulfnoth has fallen asleep. Take them away and put them to bed. Perhaps they shall sit up another night."

Ælfgifa allowed herself one mute look of pleading at her father. *Please don't let her send me away!* But it was in vain. He would not gainsay his wife on so small a matter in public. Godwin smiled wryly then kissed the top of Ælfgifa's head. "Bid me a good night then, Blackbird."

Ælfgifa bowed her head and said "Good night, Father. Good night, Lady Mother." All the while she forcing down the lump of rage in her throat. To swallow it, digest it lest it should escape her mouth and earn her a whipping. But it was Gytha's last words that cut her, uttered low so that Godwin would not hear or at least might pretend he did not. "And take that gown away from her, Beddwen. A waste of good needle work."

Ælfgifa allowed temper to conquer her for one of the few times in her life. She ran as soon as Beddwen's back was turned, seeking out the only company that she could be sure would welcome hers, or at least not mind her presence.

Spyrryd, her fat, gray pony munched on his hay, indifferent to the small girl concealed in his bedding. Ælfgifa had no intention of coming out of the pile of straw she was currently hiding in.

The russet gown now smelled strongly of horse and dung. There was a tear in one sleeve and some of the delicate embroidery was frayed. Straw poked out of Ælfgifa's crown of plaits and her face was smeared with dust and dirt. No tears though. She was not a child who cried. Gunhild could cry very prettily. Ælfgifa did nothing prettily. Besides, when she was wounded her first feeling was shame and her second rage. Sometimes one came so hard upon the heels of the other that she did not know which was which. So she lay in the straw, listened to Spyrryd's champing and boiled alive with fury.

"Mwyalchen? For the love of all the Saints! You will be coming out here this instant!" Beddwen sounded close to her wit's end. It would have taken more than that to make Ælfgifa move in her current mood.

Beddwen pursed her lips and blew a strand of hair out of her face. Despite the cold she was perspiring heavily and steam rose in little wisps from her rotund figure in the frigid air. "Very well then, Mwyalchen," she murmured. She pulled over a low stool used for milking the goats and sat. The wood creaked alarmingly but held. "Ælfgifa, I'm already knowing where you are. Come out when you're ready then, Mwyalchen."

Ælfgifa lay on her belly and glared down at her filthy hands spread in front her, working her fingers in the straw. Her fury was collapsing. *Mwyalchen. Blackbird.* Why did people call her that? Blackbirds were pretty and dark with sweet voices. *I should be called 'crow',* Ælfgifa thought mutinously.

Beddwen sang softly to herself. A sad song in the language of Cymru about a lady made of flowers and given to a great sorcerer as a wife, when she loved another. Beddwen's voice did not fit with her exterior. It was low and sweet and rich, putting the thrush to shame. It seemed to Ælfgifa that even the horses stood still to listen. And gradually, gradually the last coals of her resentment were doused and she found herself ere long, creeping from the pile of straw and curling up in Beddwen's lap. Without breaking tune, the nurse reached out to stroke the girl's hair. Ælfgifa relaxed further. Her fit of rage had left her wrung out and exhausted. Sleep now seemed not only possible but desirable. A cup of warm goat's milk and a bed with soft blankets.

Beddwen knew better than to try the normal platitudes and half-truths used on children. *Your mother loves you in truth. She did not mean it, she is tired and anxious for*

Ealdgyth. Ælfgifa would see through such pretensions instantly. Her trust was that of a wild creature who did not mete out second chances. And Ælfgifa was well aware that her mother did not care for her and had meant what she said. She simply didn't understand why. Was it not a strange thing to blame someone for the face that God had given them? How were they to help it? And if they strove with all their powers to be better in other ways, why, that deserved some credit, did it not? Yet it seemed that the more Ælfgifa excelled in Latin and Frankish, the better she read and, most unusually, wrote, the more she was shunned and despised.

She was clever, she knew she was. She could dance, although even she thought she would have little need for such a skill. She could learn anything the random assortment of passing monks and scholars could teach – and sit at it longer than any of her siblings too. But it was her needlework that ought to have garnered the most praise. She had soon outstripped what Beddwen could teach her. Her embroidery was finer and more original than Gunhild's. She was very nearly Ealdgyth's equal. Ælfgifa had a half-realized idea that if she could create something beautiful then one day she might present it to her mother and Gytha would see past her daughter's lack of personal charms. Would acknowledge her.

It had been a childish fantasy, Ælfgifa thought sleepily, lulled by the rhythmic stroking of Beddwen's hand on her hair. Her mother had been delighted with the exquisitely embroidered band of linen presented to her, until she had realized that it was Ælfgifa's work. Ælfgifa remembered how her mother's lips had drawn very fine and pale. Gytha had said nothing at all, and later Ælfgifa had found the band of linen, patterned with bees and meadowsweet, trodden into the rushes of the floor. At the time she had thought it must be an accident. Now she was certain it was not.

Beddwen persuaded the girl to go to bed. Ælfgifa saw her nurse take the russet gown away and felt ashamed of her temper. Beddwen had sewn the dress for her and one of the ceorls had embroidered it. A present, given with little ceremony to a favorite charge. It was Beddwen's way. In thinking to punish her mother, Ælfgifa had instead spurned a gift. That Beddwen would not call her to task for it somehow made it worse. *I must never let my temper rule me again*, she thought. *Certainly I must not let it snatch my reason over so trifling an occurrence as a hard word.* With that decided, Ælfgifa pillowed her head on one hand and fell into sleep.

CHAPTER 6

THE guards led William through the castle and he let them. Before he realized where he was going, he was in the great hall. Ralph was there.

"Are the extra sentries posted?" his guardian directed at one of the guards, who nodded. "Good," Ralph said. "Close the gates. Leave the drawbridge down for now, but prepare it for raising. Detail some more men to the gatehouse."

The guards confirmed the orders and left. Ralph turned to William.

"So, you're alive then?"

Through the fog of exhaustion William could tell something was wrong. He shrugged. "How did you get back here before me?"

"I flew as soon as I heard there had been an attempt on your life," Ralph said, "and came straight back here. Where have you been?" There was an edge to his voice. Anger that the Barons would seek to overthrow their Duke?

"Ryes," William answered.

"Ryes, eh?" Ralph glowered at him, his jaw muscles working. "You've done it now, haven't you?" he exploded. "You selfish, spoiled brat! There's only so much people can put up with but you kept on pushing and pushing and acting as though the world existed for your pleasure!"

William's mouth fell open. What did Ralph mean by this? The last hours swirled round inside his head. Surely he had misunderstood? The fog lifted like shutters opening.

"You're so keen on taking, aren't you? Well thanks to your selfish arrogance and not caring a damn for anyone in your Duchy apart from yourself, you've driven your Barons to take everything."

Had Ralph taken leave of his senses? Was he about to throw his lot in with the assassins? Beyond the odd sarcastic aside, he'd never been anything other than respectful to William. And now he needed help most... this? His chest seemed to clamp on to his lungs. Reason. He must appeal to Ralph's reason. "These men... my Barons... mean to rob me... Good God, they tried to kill me... and you stand here attacking *me*?"

"Yes, you pathetic swine. Idiot!" Ralph's bellow echoed round the hall. "Foolish! Little! Wastrel!"

William gave an involuntary start. "What do you mean by this, Guardian?" He heard his voice wobble.

"There is nothing you have that must not be earned," Ralph barked. "Nothing you can take that must not also be deserved. You think being the Duke is to be set above all men that you can go round plucking away what they've worked for? On a *whim*?"

William felt in sudden need of a seat but there was none nearby and he did not think it was the right time to ask Ralph. Yesterday the world was not so confusing. "I am the Duke. You make no sense."

"No. Nothing I do makes sense, because I've spent the last twelve years trying to make a Duke out of a... an ungrateful, unworthy *bastard*."

William felt the heat rising. He was the Duke! He had never been spoken to this way! And after a parcel of brigands had tried to murder him. "How dare-!"

"How dare? How dare? Oh, I dare because you've never heard a word I've said until now so why should I expect you to start today? Even if it doesn't go straight in one ear and out the other, it will have fallen out of your tiny brain by this evening!" Ralph's face was crimson now, and he was visibly shaking. How long had he felt like this? The guardian seemed to be fighting for control of himself. His lips pressed together into a white dash. His fists unclenched. "This is as important as any lesson I could give you. Only you won't learn it, will you?"

William opened his mouth, but no words would come. Just a thin wheeze of air.

"Your father, they called *'Robert the Liberal!'* That is how the chroniclers refer to him, and that is how he will be remembered in years to come. You know what they call you?"

Yes, he knew.

"'William the Bastard'. That's what you'll be now, forever. You could have been 'William the Munificent', or 'William the Wise'. Ha! Maybe even 'William the Great'. Lord, it would have been better if all your hair had fallen out, then at least you'd be 'William the Bald'. But no. You'll be forever remembered as your father's by-blow because you've never given anyone any other reason to remember you!"

There was the stag... shot from horseback... Probably best not to bring that up. William felt himself swaying. "I need to sit."

"Then sit. You're the Duke, as you're so fond of telling everyone."

William sloped to the edge of the hall and slumped down, sitting on the cold stone floor, back against the wall. To his surprise, Ralph did likewise, next to him. They sat like that for a while, saying nothing. The room gently tumbled around William's head, while his guts tumbled inside his midriff.

"How did you escape?" Ralph asked, eventually.

"A knight. Fellow called Gallet. Drunk, asleep in the stables, he heard the Barons planning to come for me. He sneaked away while they were arming and came to warn me. Then my horse was about dead, but Hubert de Ryes took me in, hid me when the rebels came by. Sent them on the wrong road. He insisted his sons accompanied me here. Three of them. He sent me all his sons..."

Remember that God gives honor and glory to him who dies for his lord, he'd heard the old knight telling his boys. *Not me,* he'd wanted to cry. But he had not. He had accepted their sacrifice. He would not have been able to look Hubert in the eye if anything had happened to them. The youngest was only sixteen. He must knight them all...

But Ralph snorted. "Oh? You still have two loyal knights then. Astonishing. You failed to make enemies of two of your sworn men. You'll have to try harder next time."

"Why did you become my guardian?" William's voice was almost swallowed up in the great hall. "If that's how you feel, why make the effort? If you hate me this much."

Ralph's voice was as soft as it had been hard moments before. "Do you really not know?"

"No. You had Gilbert killed, didn't you? Don't try to deny it."

"I never have. I had your guardian Gilbert killed, it's true. It had no connection with you, it was a matter of honor between Gilbert and me. But yes, I was responsible for his death."

"Osbern? Turchetil?"

"No, they were nothing to do with me."

"But why agree to be my guardian? If I'm such a worthless charge? If it's such a dangerous position? Why do it."

"Honor."

"What?" William turned to look at Ralph. Just now he looked very old and worn. "You are the Baron of Wacey. Was that not honor enough?"

Ralph laughed. The sound was bitter, harsh as it echoed off the flagstones.

"You don't understand. Why would you? You understand so little."

He put his face in his hands and spoke through them. "Then tell me."

"I was asked to be your guardian. Your uncle, Walter, asked me, before he died. I was given the role. I could not honorably turn it down, even at considerable risk to my own life, as you discerned. And my honor - my own, personal honor as a noble man, would not permit me to do anything but the best I possibly could. But I failed, didn't I?"

What could he say to that? William let Ralph continue.

"The world is a place of balance, William. We keep it that way. The nobles, from the King, down through the Dukes, Barons, Knights, beneath God... By being a good Duke, your nobles flourish, and in turn their vassals flourish, and the world flourishes. If there is a bad Duke, his nobles suffer, the commoners beneath them suffer, the wider lands and the King suffer. Unhappiness reigns and people begin to see how the world is turned upside down. They want to turn it right again. To remove the source of the illness."

William frowned. *Really? Is that really it? Is it not simply more power that they want? To take whatever they can get, whatever the rightful order of things?*

Ralph must have read the skepticism on his face. "Oh, they may have baser motives too. Those who move to overthrow a nobleman. But if the Duke is good, and his Duchy prosperous, no-one dreams of overthrowing him."

It made a kind of sense. What would his father make of it all? He had no idea. He barely remembered Robert. "I don't understand. The people at Valognes seemed happy enough." It came out reedier than he had intended.

"After the hunt, you mean? Oh, they were impressed by your cheap heroics, but that kind of thing doesn't keep anyone's belly full for too long. I've done my best, but I can't be the Duke for you. You needed to have done that yourself, if only you could."

"So what then? Do you think someone else would make a better Duke than me?" He didn't think that was how it worked. When his father named him as heir, when the Barons swore fealty...

"If there was a better Duke to be had, perhaps. But I swore to help you and protect you, and do whatever I could that you became the best duke. And I shall continue butting my antlers against yours until one of us dies or you become the Duke you could be. William, don't you see? If it hadn't been for one or two loyal knights, you'd be dead. If one more day had gone by, and you'd offended this or that fellow... This was your last chance."

Was that really it? Had he avoided disaster by such a narrow margin? He'd been congratulating himself for his escape, wondering what the bards might make of it. Like a sword pommel in the face, he realized he might still lose everything. And for the first time in his life he realized he might lose his lands, his wealth, and yet go on living.

It all seemed so complicated. Yesterday being the Duke had been hunting and feasting and wenching and drinking and doing what he wanted. He thought that there was nothing more to life than taking what it could offer while it lasted. In truth he had not really expected to grow to adulthood, to take over the Duchy himself.

But that was yesterday. Today, being the Duke was a matter of survival... and at the same time of somehow being responsible for all the land and people and animals and crops... He felt dizzy again and tipped his head forward. How could one person expect to look after all that? Oh, he knew what was expected of a Duke. Ralph had lectured him on it time and again. But now he began to absorb the slightest fragment of its meaning.

"Is it too late?"

"I don't know, William. I don't know." A wan smile crossed Ralph's face. "I'd been thinking of entertaining your cousin Edward here, if he could leave England safely. I'd hoped some of his good Lordship might rub off on you."

"Edward? The King?" Did Ralph mean the same Edward? That streak of piss with too much fondness for Mass and not enough for a good woman?

"Yes. Or sending you to see him. He has brought a measure of stability to that squabbling pack of Saxons and Danes and has made a prosperous country of England. Don't roll your eyes so – he had everything against him, growing up here in exile after the barbarous Danes seized the throne, and yet returned to make a success of his reign. There's so much you could have learned from him. Not that you would, I dare say."

Edward? The model of a good Lord? Now he had heard everything. The world was truly inside out and back to front. His mother, Emma, made a much more formidable Lord, and never mind the incidental matter of her sex. William had met her once or twice. He was still terrified of her and her enormous headgear. Edward, though?

"There's little enough we can do about it tonight anyway, Lord. Rest. Pray. With hard work, and God Almighty's blessing, tomorrow may bring better fortunes." He began to set out what they would need to do. Secure the lands around Falaise. Raise the levies, if there were any more levies to be raised. Find those nobles still loyal.

Ralph had addressed him as 'Lord.' That gave William more hope than anything else.

CHAPTER 7

THE convent at Wintanceastre had a beautiful, well-tended herb garden. The day had dawned cold and clear, scents of pine and woodsmoke interlacing with the sharper smell of herbs. Ælfgifa had donned her travel-stained gown and a warm cloak, shoving frozen toes into leather boots that had once belonged to Gunhild, before slipping from the room she shared with her sister. Gunhild had already left her bed and Ælfgifa supposed her elder sister to be at *matins*. The snow was crisp and pure but not deep. She enjoyed making a set of tiny footprints in the unblemished surface, though she might have taken one of the well swept paths the serfs had cleared. Ælfgifa had thought she might take a hard winter apple to her pony but the open door of the herb garden had beckoned to her. She moved daintily between the tidy herb beds. Some were laid with straw to shield the more delicate plants. Fruit trees had been tied up with hempen cloth to protect them from the bitter winds while the hardier plants drank in the weak winter sun.

St John's wort, she noted. *And crane's bill. Here's devil's claw—I wonder the nuns are allowed to grow that one. Do they call it something else? Those are stalks of woody nightshade. And there's foxglove and lady's bedstraw.*

She moved happily from plant to plant. Sometimes bruising a leaf and giving it a sniff. She was so absorbed that she did not notice the figure seated in a sheltered corner. Ælfgifa started with fright when she realized that the well-wrapped bundle in the corner was not another shielded plant but a woman—the oldest woman she had ever seen—well muffled against the cold. She stared, feeling an ugly flush rising in her cheeks, then cast her eyes down, lowering her chin. A habit that had grown throughout her childhood.

"No need to look away, girl, I'm not so important as all that." The old voice was surprisingly clear and full of wry humor.

"I beg your pardon, Lady," Ælfgifa began. "I know I should not be here but-"

"When one of my novices stammered that there was an Ælf in the herb garden, I thought it a poor excuse for a midwinter joke," the old woman interrupted.

Ælfgifa flushed harder. Muttered something polite.

"Ha. Don't like that then, girl? Come it is only the foolish who would truly think you anything other than human." The woman's dark eyes were very bright, almost hard. "Well, you're not nearly old enough to be Ealdgyth." Ælfgifa almost snorted at the idea that anyone might mistake her for her eldest sister. "And I know Gunhild and you are not she, though you share a look about the eyes. You are the third daughter. The one no one talks of but that everyone has heard of all the same. Speak up then, girl, you are Jarl Godwin's child are you not?"

"Yes, Lady. I am Ælfgifa," she said. Ælfgifa did not know quite what to make of this woman. She spoke as if she were highborn, certainly not a ceorl or even a thagn's wife. Yet she also spoke as if she had never had to be mannerly in her life. Ælfgifa was piqued and awed at the same time.

"An apt name, do you not think so?" The woman smiled, showing gaps where she had lost teeth.

"It is my name and that is all, Lady," Ælfgifa replied stiffly.

"You wear your hurt too openly, girl. Too openly and too hard. You present others with weapons to wound you," the woman commented. Ælfgifa did not see what more she could do to conceal it. "So you could not resist my garden, then?"

"It is beautiful. A piece of all the seasons in one place."

"You *are* an odd child," the woman frowned. "No not your face," she said as Ælfgifa raised her hands unconsciously to her mouth. "My Lord, if I'd seen no faces worse than yours, I should have had a happy career as a midwife! Your face is the least of you in any case. It will not stop you getting a husband when the time comes, though why you should want one I can't imagine."

Ælfgifa stared at her in shock. No one, not even Beddwen who loved her, had ever spoken as openly, almost callously careless, as this old woman. It was... liberating. And Ælfgifa didn't especially want a husband, but a home of her own would be welcome when she was grown. All her life she had been told she was not wanted, which had in turn become a constant refrain of 'no one will want you.' And yet this woman said it was not so. Ælfgifa was cautious but hopeful.

"I don't want a husband," she ventured. "But I must have land or money and I cannot yet see another way to get such things. I suppose I must not rule out the prospect until I know what I am to live on."

The old woman threw back her head and laughed. Her bared throat made Ælfgifa think of a scrawny hen plucked for the pot. "I heard you were a clever child—those gossips again. No one said you were wise. I suppose they haven't the wit to see it. It's a shame..." The old woman's mirth faded.

"A shame that I am so marked?" said Ælfgifa more fiercely than she intended.

"Nay, child. Did I not just tell you such things are of little account? Do you think beauty is a treasure you can take to the grave after a long and well-led life? Was I beautiful, think you?" She regarded the girl with a level gaze.

"I cannot tell. You may have been," Ælfgifa hedged.

"Or I may have been as ugly as an old boot. Who would know now? Behold your future, girl!" She laughed again. "I meant it was a shame that I would not live to see you become what you might become if you choose. No one can take away your mind save God and even he isn't that cruel."

"I may be sent here to be educated," offered Ælfgifa.

"Child, I will not live another turning of the moon. No, do not sorrow. I am glad. And more importantly, I am ready." She smiled faintly and leaned back as if tired. "Go now. Your sister, the queen-to-be, has sent for you. I thought to quiz you first. I am glad I did."

Ælfgifa curtsied far lower than was required for a Jarl's daughter. "Thank you, Mother," she said to the Abbess.

"You knew?" Her faint gray eyebrows lifted. "Farewell *Godwinsdöttir*. Remember my words. We'll not meet again this side of Judgment."

"I will. God speed you," Ælfgifa replied and left the old Abbess of Wintanceastre to her winter garden.

***

Ealdgyth was sitting patiently while her tiring woman, an exotic looking ceorl with gleaming black skin, finished dressing her long hair. Ælfgifa lingered in the doorway, suddenly aware of her dripping boots, stained gown and unkempt hair.

"There. I told you she would be out in the cold if she could manage it, did I not, Suela?" Ealdgyth turned to grin at the ceorl. Suela laughed, sloe eyes merry, and turned her mistress' head firmly back to face forward, so that she might finish the gathered rows of plaits on either side of Ealdgyth's head.

"I will change..." Ælfgifa turned to leave but her sister called her back.

"Sit. Please. I am not our lady mother to be annoyed by a speck of dirt. Besides, Gifa, you smell wonderfully of fresh herbs. Is that where you were?" Ealdgyth smiled and Ælfgifa tentatively took the seat her sister pointed to, wincing at the thought of her damp and dirty dress touching the fine wolf-skin that was flung over it. Ealdgyth seemed either not to notice or not to mind.

"We have had but little talk these past days," she said.

"You were much occupied," Ælfgifa replied, striving for a casual tone. In truth it had stung that Ealdgyth could forget her so quickly. Ælfgifa liked both of her sisters well but enjoyed the sharp-tongued and playful Ealdgyth's company far more than that of soft-voiced, quiet Gunhild. Ealdgyth was as likely to revile Ælfgifa for her appearance as she was to praise her for her quick wits but Ælfgifa had never sensed any malice in her sister. Ealdgyth was an autumn day, all surprises, sun shine and showers and the occasional howling gale. Although ten years her senior, Ealdgyth held a certain respect for Ælfgifa. It was becoming less and less unusual for her sister to ask Ælfgifa for her opinion or advice. And it was hard for Ælfgifa not to admire Ealdgyth who was tall and beautiful as well as clever, witty and well educated. She had Gytha's hot temper but Godwin's cool judgment. In a quiet corner of her soul, Ælfgifa had a painful hero-worship for Ealdgyth and would do much for her approval.

"Gifa, why do you not just ask what you really want to know?" Ealdgyth smiled conspiratorially. "You are wondering at my happiness over my prospective husband?"

"He is... a fine, virtuous man, they say," Ælfgifa said noncommittally.

"And yet?" Ealdgyth raised her fair eyebrows.

Ælfgifa darted an uncomfortable glance at Suela. "And yet there has been enmity between his house and ours. Also... he is *old*, sister!"

Ealdgyth laughed. "When you are a little more grown you will not think a man our father's age so very ancient, Gifa. As for the other, you raise a good point. It is on that and one other matter I wish to talk to you."

"I will try to assist if I may, sister," Ælfgifa replied, flattered by the attention and then annoyed with herself for being so easily handled.

"My marriage to Edward will, in time, end the enmity betwixt our families. At least that is our father's intent."

"I understand," Ælfgifa replied.

"I do not think our father is correct in this belief," Ealdgyth said, all traces of humor gone.

"What would make you suppose that?" Ælfgifa frowned.

"I have spoken to Edward. It is true he is in need of an heir or at least a wife. He needs to strengthen his position amongst the three greatest Saxon families. He came to the throne at a disadvantage having been raised to Norman ways and Norman thinking. Many of our people do not like that. So I am an ideal choice on many counts," Ealdgyth said unselfconsciously. There was no arrogance nor false modesty in her words. Just a cool assessment of what was. "And I am not wrong to think he likes me, despite our families' histories. While he was... diplomatic about Jarl Godwin, there is bitterness there. I believe Edward may well be a man to hold a private grudge. What say you, sister?" Ealdgyth leaned forward, her full attention on Ælfgifa. Even Suela now watched her gravely as if expecting wisdom.

"I cannot tell until I have seen you together," Ælfgifa pointed out. "But I have heard things that would make me uneasy to quarrel with such a man even were he not king. Ealdgyth, I do not believe our father greatly likes King Edward. Our mother goes a step further."

"I suspected as much but she would not tell me so. Do you know why?" Ealdgyth asked.

Ælfgifa thought of her mother's commentary on the king's lack of need for a proper wife and flushed. "I do not understand her reasons, and I will not guess." She met Ealdgyth's gaze. "What do you know of the king's dead brother?" She held her breath, sensing she was on dangerous ground.

Ealdgyth eyed her for a moment and then nodded. "It has been whispered that our father had a hand in Alfred's death. I know not the truth of it. But whether it was by design or mischance that Alfred was captured and killed whilst in Godwin's care, I fear Edward still blames our father."

"Cold murder is not... our father would not..." Ælfgifa struggled to fit the image of her loving father, who dubbed her 'Blackbird' and kissed her, with the picture she was building of her father's political stature. The two would not mesh.

"He might, Gifa. And he may well have done. You are too young to remember that the leading houses of Mercia, Northumbria and Wessex were not supporters of Edward's father. Our own father was raised to prominence by Cnut. Whatever happened to Edward's brother, I think we can safely assume that Edward will never fully trust Godwin. The question is how best to manage it." Ealdgyth tapped a finger to her lips in thought.

A new vista was opening in Ælfgifa's mind. It happened that way on occasion. A new piece of information would tumble into place and suddenly an entire perspective would shift. Perhaps if she had not spied on her parents so recently she might have had more trouble reconciling the idea she now entertained. But Ælfgifa had seen that Godwin was a different person when alone with her mother, so might her father not be a different person again when in counsel with other men? Who was he with her brothers? Who was he in battle? In judgment over disputes? Who was he to Ealdgyth even? It was like looking down from a great height after the mist suddenly cleared. Exhilarating and dizzying. With it came a new thought: everyone showed different faces in different situations. Which included Edward. Why, he might be an attentive suitor to Ealdgyth and a bitter enemy of her father with neither side of his personality holding dominance.

Ælfgifa felt sick with foreboding. She remembered her father taking her upon his knee and pointing out all the territories of Wessex on a map. It was a few years since, when Sweyn was first made Jarl. Ælfgifa had asked where her brother's Jarldom was and her father had shown her. Godwin had assured her that their family controlled the largest estate in England. At the time Ælfgifa had not understood the significance. Now she mentally fitted Harold's new Jarldom into the picture. *How would it be*, she thought, *to be king and yet to have one family holding almost all of the rich land of Southern England. To be king and have all your own estates separated from each other and harder to reach. To be king and have a Jarl who was richer and potentially more powerful than you were. So much so that open disagreement with him was too dangerous to risk. Were I king, I would marry Ealdgyth too. And I would watch and wait for opportunities to whittle away at my Jarls' power.* Ælfgifa shivered suddenly.

"Gifa? Are you well?" Ealdgyth said in concern. "Are your clothes still wet? Goose! You'll die of an ague!"

"Nay, sister, but a... a shadow crossed my heart. You must win Edward over if you marry him. You must make him depend on you. He must believe you work always for his ends."

"Gifa, you are shivering."

"You asked my advice. There it is. I cannot explain why I think as I do. I just... Edward must surely see father as a rival, no matter what." Ælfgifa felt almost faint.

"I do see. I will take your advice. But should you have a chance to see him with me, I would like to hear your further thoughts." Ealdgyth smiled but it was the smile of one who knew they were entering a dangerous arena.

"Gladly," Ælfgifa said. "I still think he is a terribly old man!"

Ealdgyth laughed again. "And now you sound all of your years and not day older."

Ælfgifa smiled, lips pressed together. At least Ealdgyth was not going in blindly. It was clear her sister wanted power and influence of her own. How much worse it would be if she were merely an infatuated girl? Yet Ælfgifa thought that Ealdgyth liked Edward. She mentally shrugged. If Ealdgyth could not captivate Edward then no woman alive could, or Edward was simply not capable of being captivated.

"You said you wished to talk of one other thing?" she asked.

Ealdgyth leaned forward again, corn-colored hair swinging over her shoulder and pooling in her lap. "What say you to being fostered at court after I am married?"

Ælfgifa was stunned. "I would like it very much but am I not to attend a convent?"

"I do not know, Gifa. But think on it? I will talk to Mother if you agree."

"I will. And I thank you," Ælfgifa said.

"Now, go and change into dry clothes and eat something or you'll be fainting away altogether!"

Ælfgifa smiled again and tripped lightly out of the room.

Before the door closed behind her, she heard Suela say, "She is the feyest child I ever laid eyes on. And such things she says! No child her age thinks or speaks so!"

"Have a care, Suela," Ealdgyth admonished. "You will not call her fey again. She is unusual, yes. But I like her the better for that. She thinks of things that others will not or cannot..." The door swung shut cutting Ealdgyth's voice off. Ælfgifa shivered, feeling once again as if she looked down from a great height and feared falling.

CHAPTER 8

IT was a strange sort of Conseil de Duc, and not just for being the first William had presided over that he remotely cared about. The hall looked half empty, as in truth it was. It was a pitiful haul of nobles who rallied to William's cause. When it became clear that no-one else was coming, his spirits sank even lower. Perhaps Ralph was right. Maybe he had thrown away his legacy.

Jean Bellin, Lord of Blainville was there, as was William's uncle, Mauger, Archbishop of Rouen. It was crucial that they had remained loyal, of course, but neither of them could fight. Bellin was too old, and Mauger... well, he didn't act much like a churchman except when it suited him. '*Alas, all the money was gone to the poor. There was none left to help raise arms.*' William's lip curled. Poor tailors and furriers and jewelers and whores, perhaps. '*I cannot fight, my Lord, I am a man of peace...*' Apparently, he kept his household strikingly loyal with the aid of a demon he reputedly controlled. Perhaps William could himself cultivate a devil who would strike down the disloyal. Ah well, it was a little late now. If only Mauger's friendly demon would fight with them, it might be of more use than the backsliding bishop himself.

Other than those two, his other cousins, William fitzOsbern, Roger de Beaumont, and Roger of Montgomerie were there, thank the Lord, another bishop, Lanfranc of Bec, and a smattering of knights and petty barons and vicomtes, all from Upper Normandy. Auge. Lisieux. Evreux. Caux. Roumois. Hyesmois. And Hubert of Ryes, bless his humble stockings. The reunion with his sons, Henri, Edward and Raoul had been a sight to behold.

Lower Normandy, it seemed, had gone over to Guy almost wholesale. Even with the few nobles left to him, it had taken William the best part of a week to get them all here. That was no great surprise—in a time of upheaval, with half the Duchy taking arms against another, no noble wanted to leave his lands for long. William realized that all of them would have had to make arrangements to protect their people and property before agreeing to come to Falaise, especially those nearest to the lands of the rebelling lords.

He drew his attention back to the council. It had not properly begun yet, but Hubert was explaining to the others how he had met the traitors on the road from Isigny and sent them in the wrong direction. It was a brave thing to do, and Hubert had put himself to considerable risk to trick the rebel lords. William found himself wondering what he had done to earn it. According to Hubert, Hammond with the Teeth had been in the party that had pursued him. It made him shudder to think about it. Hammond did not strike him as the type to show mercy to any that got in his way. A week ago, he would have laughed at his misgivings. What could a man, however menacing, do against his own Duke? It had been a very long week, and the world seemed very different at its end than it had at its beginning.

65

Ralph called the nobles to order. "My Lords, noble knights," he began. "You know we sit here through the grave and perfidious actions of traitors. My Lord William sent messages to the ringleaders, Grimoult du Plessis, Neel, Renulf, Hammond, Guy himself, offering forgiveness for their transgressions..."

His guardian paused. There seemed to be a commotion going on outside the door. Raised voices. A heavy thump. William's heart lurched—for a second he thought the rebels were here, that they were about to break in and murder him. Even as he thought it, he knew it was not so—the castle was prepared for defense and no-one could get in without warning. Even so, it was an unpleasant moment.

The door burst open, and in walked a filthy, scruffy form brandishing a pike, pursued by a guard missing his helm and bleeding from his temple.

"My Lord!" the guard said, "this caitiff insisted on joining the council, but... but..."

"...And I said you'd want me to be here," the form growled. "Here," he shoved the pike at the guard. "You'd better have this back."

"Gallet!" William cried. "What on Earth are you doing here?"

"Heard you were summoning loyal fellows," he said. "Was a bit disappointed I didn't get an invitation."

"You're welcome, of course!" To hell with decorum. William bounded up to the knight and embraced him warmly, ignoring the muttering from around the council table and the stench emanating from Gallet's clothing. "Take a seat," he added, gesturing to the table.

"Hubert," Gallet said, nodding at de Ryes, and shoved onto the bench between him and his eldest son.

"Gallet, you rogue," Hubert laughed. "I thought you were reduced to huntsman on the Ducal estates these days?"

Ah, so that was how Gallet had managed to be present at the killing of the stag! William smiled to himself. All life is in the hunt, after all...

Ralph cleared his throat. "May we continue with the council, gentlemen?"

Gallet bowed very prettily. "Proceed."

"Ahem. My Lord William sent messages to the ringleaders, Grimoult du Plessis, Neel, Renulf, Hammond, and Guy himself offering forgiveness for their transgressions, and in return for the destruction of certain keeps and fortifications that might be advantageous to any future uprising, to retain their lands and titles if they agreed to swear loyalty and pay homage to William once again. We have received the following by way of response, from Guy – I am assured it goes for all of them." He unrolled the scroll that had been sitting before him. William already knew the gist. Such things made him glad he had never managed to learn to read. "That haughty William who calls himself Duke, is a bastard and without rightful claim to the Duchy of Normandy. He did too much dishonor to the name of Normandy the day he became Duke."

Ralph let that sink in. A ripple of outrage, some of it genuine, passed around the hall, as he continued to read. "The son of a concubine. He has proved himself without nobility, insolent, vain and discourteous."

William felt the heat rising in his face, and knew, as it did so that a portion of his anger was at the truth in the words.

Ralph went on. "The rightful heir to the good Duke Robert is the son of Adelisa, true born daughter of his Grace."

Another wave of muttering rose from the nobles. Puzzlement. Disbelief. Anger. This was good.

"Should not those barons and gentlemen of Normandy cast off so humiliating a yoke? Thus do those loyal to the true heir make war on William, to dispossess by force the proud bastard. Only through his dethronement can Normandy free itself from ignominy."

"Goes on a bit, doesn't he?" Gallet muttered.

"Monstrous!" Mauger cried. "He thinks it right to descend through the female line? The insolence!"

"The wishes of the old Duke in naming his... natural born son as heir were proper and legal," Bellin added. "How dare the upstart declare he knows better?"

Ralph held up his hand. He was not finished delivering bad news.

"Further to this we have received intelligence that other Lords have joined, or are considering joining the rebellion. The traitors have begun to attack Ducal estates, and the estates of those who refuse to join with them. The lands are laid waste. Crops and dwellings have been put to the torch. The roads are choked with peasants driven out of their homes. Even in districts that Guy has not yet seized, rumors that William is dead or taken prisoner abound. It could be that many loyal subjects do not realize the Duke still lives."

William found himself clenching his fists. To be so powerless in his own lands. He may as well not be Duke. May as well be as dead as the rumors proclaimed him to be! The rebels evidently saw themselves as free of any vows of vassalage, and as such the people had no protection from rapacity and plundering. "How much of Normandy do the traitors hold?" he asked.

"More than half," Ralph answered, his voice dry and scraping. "Caen holds. We cannot be sure for how long, they had precious little time to prepare for a siege."

"How many men at arms can we raise?"

"Perhaps two score knights, and five-, maybe six-score soldiers on foot."

It was as though all the air had gone out of the hall. No-one wanted to look at anyone else.

"And how many can Grimoult, Neel, Renulf and the rest of them muster?"

"A thousand men. A quarter of them mounted knights."

The intake of breath from everyone seated at the council table told William everything he needed to know.

"What about Raoul of Tassin?" Bellin asked. "He commands forty knights by himself. Has he answered the call of his lord?"

Ralph rubbed his face. "Raoul has not admitted our messengers."

Oh, Lord almighty. They were finished then. It was over.

"...At least," Ralph went on, "I am led to understand that he has not entertained the embassies of Guy either. Yet."

"Ha!" Gallet snorted. "He's holding out for the best offer. Too smart for his own good, that one."

"It's our good I'm concerned with," William said.

"And in any case," Ralph continued, "unfortunately it is utterly impossible to consider collecting taxes and other revenues across the Duchy from Valognes to Caen. My Lord, in those districts you have not a penny. We have funds for a short campaign, but cannot consider any drawn-out conflict."

Nobody knew what to say to that. Starved of lands, men, funds... Had his father faced these travails? Had he simply negotiated them better? So much for Ralph's world of order and balance. "And what message from the King? Does he say nothing while his countryman rises up against his liege lord? My father defended Henri against his brother's revolt, didn't he?"

For a second time, the hall went utterly silent. Mauger appeared to be admiring a tapestry depicting a hunting scene. Bellin busied himself reading the scroll that had already been read out. Ralph closed his eyes. "My Lord... One must remember that Duke Robert's support was gained for a price—territory the Capets would not otherwise have parted with. The King..."

"Yes?"

"Our men in Poissy tell us that Henri has received Guy since the attempt on your life. We believe he has supported Guy with funds, arms, even men. In secret, of course."

"Of course." William's jaw was so tightly ground that the words came almost as a buzz.

"My Lord."

That was that, then. The Duchy of Normandy. His legacy. Created by his ancestor, Rollo, built to a thriving, prosperous territory by his father, Robert. And destroyed by the unworthy William. The bastard.

"Then what can we do?" *How can we set this great wrong to rights? How can we undo my mistake? Good God, let me face them with my sword and we'll settle it.* William looked at Ralph and suddenly felt a vast tide of guilt. The

Baron had put up with his wildness for years, and remained patient, tried to fulfil the promise he had made even while he knew it was impossible. A band seemed to tighten around his chest as if he were wearing the hauberk made for him as a child. He fought for a breath, then another.

Ralph continued, his calmness could have been an accusation. "Secure the lands that are left to us. Appeal to Henri for a settlement. In time, secure an alliance. You may still make a good marriage. One day we may be in a position to challenge to regain some of Upper Normandy."

"Appeal to Henri?"

The guilt washed away in a torrent of heat. William's chest felt as though it were filling with hot coals. He leapt to his feet. For all Ralph had spoken of the natural order... the cycle of virtue that spanned from God through King to Nobles and Commoners. He thumped the table in front of him, making Mauger start.

"And is he not a man of honor? Who accepted my fealty in good faith?" His voice reverberated off the hall's great stone arch. "Yet now he gives succor to my enemies! Where is the honor in this?"

The words circled round the hall, softened, died away, running into the cracks between stones.

Into the silence cut a voice, quiet, a little thin, even, but strong. "Do you think he would stand upon his honor, my Lord?"

It was the clergyman from Bec, who had remained silent up to that point. Everyone turned to stare at him.

William blinked. "What do you mean?"

"Would the King go against his honor?"

"Surely he already has."

"In the eyes of God, perhaps, alas. But not in the eyes of his vassals. His man, the Duke of Normandy is beset. His Grace regrets it in public, while doing nothing to stop it, and even helping the rebels in private. He regrets his father's loss of Rouen and sees a way to restore it, perhaps, even as he enjoys the benefits of *your* father's support in days gone by."

"Forgive me, bishop Lanfranc." For the first time, Ralph's composure threatened to slip. "We know this."

"Aye. But who has he sworn to help? You, my Lord. Guy is your vassal, not his. The oath of homage places responsibility on both parties."

William looked at Ralph, but his guardian seemed as mystified as everyone else. "Henri won't help, though, will he?"

"No?" The bishop smiled beatifically. "Have you asked him?"

The nobles around the table erupted into laughter. Only Ralph retained a straight face. Lanfranc smiled politely again, as if he'd meant it in jest and was pleased with the outcome. The rest of them roared and thumped the table like it was the best joke they'd heard in years.

"Asked him?" William said once the jollity had died down. "We know he favors Guy! We know he wants to take Norman lands back!"

"Yes." The bishop continued calmly. This was probably what he was like in the schoolroom with a class of rowdy boys. It was said his interest was more in education than with spiritual matters, after all. "...But only if his honor permits it," the bishop continued. "He is the King. His honor must remain unimpeachable. Or he is no longer the King."

Ralph began to smile. So that was it! Honor! After all this, still honor. It was obvious now Lanfranc had pointed it out.

"And an honorable man," William smiled, "when asked to stand upon his honor, upon an oath sworn in good faith, will not refuse. Must not."

"No, my Lord. And no honorable liege-lord may refuse the plea of his vassal for assistance in the hour of his direst need. Whether he actually wants to or not."

William sat again. "We ask the King for help. Good God, he might even provide it. At the very least he can't give any support to our enemies. Or risk humiliation before all his subjects."

"We have nothing to lose," Ralph sighed. "I'll prepare to leave immediately."

"No, Guardian." William stood again. "I must speak to Henri myself. I want to look him in the eye when I beg him for assistance. And then we'll see if he can find a good reason to upset the natural order of the world."

CHAPTER 9

ÆLFGIFA had little opportunity to observe Edward and Ealdgyth together until the night before the wedding. The opinion she formed as she watched the pair seated at board together, sharing a plate and goblet, just as Gytha and Godwin did, was that strategically the match had much to recommend it. Ælfgifa saw that Edward would marry her sister for political advantage, hoping to bring Wessex to heel. He was a calculating man—she supposed he could hardly have held the throne for so long without his being so. And yet there was a certain expression in his gray eyes when he looked at Ealdgyth. From her position seated further down the board, in the poorer lit area just above the servants but well below the salt, Ælfgifa watched her sister laugh and flush with color at the king's whispered words. Yes, he would marry Ealdgyth to stabilize his throne but he had a genuine affection for her. He smiled in a way that made him look much younger than his seven and forty years. For her part Ealdgyth was pleased by his attentions and, though careful to be maidenly, made no secret of her regard for him.

Ælfgifa felt very cold and clear. An occurrence that happened with greater frequency of late. It was as if she could step outside the moment and observe it. *They will be happy together*, she thought. *Well, if they can both keep their tempers.* There was certainly much to hope for from the union. Why then did Ælfgifa feel that shadowed sense of foreboding? She shook herself a little and sorted through the uneaten contents of her own plate—wood, not gold—and tried to take a few mouthfuls. She wanted nothing more than to slip away and be alone. There were too many intrigues and games here. It was exhausting to see everything, the probable outcomes, and then the outcomes after that... Her head was pounding. The cold, clearness was fading and Ælfgifa just wanted to sit with Beddwen a while and hold Wulfnoth, and then sleep. She forced herself to pay attention, lest Ealdgyth ask for her impressions later.

As far as she could see, the king appeared even-tempered —courteous to nobles, ceorls and serfs alike. Ælfgifa thought that spoke well for him as a man and a future husband for her sister. Yet there was something about him which failed to please her. He did not have her father's height or stature but Edward wore command well. He was clearly worthy of respect. On the surface he appeared pensive and calm. Ælfgifa had never been content with merely the surface appearance of things. She thought there was a curl to the king's thin mouth that in a lesser man might be thought petulant or even querulous. His mask was not so perfect that she didn't see the sudden flashes of dark rage that crossed his eyes from time to time. As for his supposed piety, Ælfgifa could not make up her mind. He ate little enough and drank far less ale and wine than might be expected. With unchildlike cynicism, Ælfgifa attributed his lack of appetite and thinness to some complaint of health. Edward's habit of folding his long white hands in front of him seemed to her to be an affected gesture. *If he does suffer*, she thought, *he is at pains to make the effects seem to be by design rather than affliction.* She was surprised to find herself privately agreeing with much of her mother's opinion of the king.

Two other things she had gleaned in the days before the wedding. One was that the king's men, whom she overheard talking in the stables while taking a treat to Spyrryd, held their king in awe and a little fear. For a man who made an effort to be known as godly and gentle, it seemed that the king had a fierce, unpredictable temper when roused. It was also apparent from the unguarded conversation, that Godwin was right. The king was far from being a fool and in fact his men regarded him as a shrewd commander and a decisive leader.

Earlier, she had asked Caedmon, the scribing monk attached to her father's household, whether the wedding would be like the weddings held by the ceorls and thagns. Caedmon had shaken his balding head and explained that the king would insist on a wedding 'in christiano', that is in the Christian style. There would be no ritual crowning with green wreaths or praise of the bride. There would likely be little carousing or dancing afterwards.

***

Ealdgyth wed King Edward on the twenty third day of January at Wintanceastre Cathedral. Ælfgifa was in attendance and almost wished she were not. With effort, she resisted the urge to yawn. She hadn't been prepared for anything so dull as this. The bishop droned on in fragmented

Latin and Ælfgifa felt a sharp spike of scorn. Why, she spoke better Latin than he did!

It was true that the sight was spectacular. Ealdgyth was radiant and attired like a queen already, with a fine cloth-of-gold mantle over her new cream wool gown. The gown had an embroidered band of crimson threads in a design so cunning that Ælfgifa itched for a closer look. Edward was attired as befitted his station as king but had clearly gone to great pains to appear plainly clad. No rich colors produced by expensive dyes, although his tunic was of that precious cloth called samite, usually reserved only for the making of altar cloths. *Has he donated a bolt to the cathedral as well?* Ælfgifa wondered, distracted once again.

She almost yawned, but the slight squeeze of Beddwen's heavy hand on her shoulder made her remember herself. She might well be in the shade here—as usual—but if someone saw her obvious boredom it would not be looked on favorably. *Then after all, who ever does notice me?* The thought contained neither the bitterness nor the shame it might have done once. Ælfgifa had started to think of herself differently since her strange conversation with the Abbess. Ideas were nebulous, neither firm nor fixed, but they were germinating. She glanced at Beddwen out of the corner of her eye. Her nurse squeezed her shoulder once more, then went back to watching the ceremony. If Beddwen had an opinion on the king or the marriage she had not voiced it, ignoring Ælfgifa's questions on the subject.

Ælfgifa could feel her attention slipping again and desperately sought a distraction. *Harold.* Her eldest brother, Sweyn had not attended the wedding, but Harold was newly confirmed as Jarl of East Anglia and paid his respects to the couple. He was very much as Ælfgifa remembered. Tall and, she supposed, handsome. By contrast, Edward was a pale streak of a man, dignified perhaps but lacking the ruddy good health and strength of her brother. Edward's hair was almost completely white now, too. It wasn't fair to compare them, Ælfgifa told herself. Edward had over twenty years on Harold. Still, it seemed to Ælfgifa that her sister ought to be marrying a man in his prime, as Harold was, rather than a man who had started down the path towards age and probable ill-health, even if he was king.

At that moment Harold glanced up, his flashing blue eyes meeting the startled gaze of his youngest sister. Ælfgifa froze. Her curiosity was never welcomed and rarely tolerated – which was why she made efforts not to be caught. Harold flashed a swift, surprisingly boyish grin at her before turning away again. *Why, he might be as bored as me!* Ælfgifa thought, suppressing a smile of her own. Harold, it seemed, remembered her and still thought of her with affection perhaps.

The last slurred Latin phrases were uttered and with a sigh of relief, the congregation parted to let the new husband and wife by. Beddwen grabbed Ælfgifa's hand and they joined in towards the end of the procession. It did not surprise Ælfgifa when Beddwen led her away from the wedding party. Gytha had not glanced at her all morning and she supposed it was on her mother's instructions that she and Wulfnoth were being banished early. Ælfgifa felt some of the customary pique but it was overshadowed by annoyance. She had wanted to see Harold and speak to him. She had wanted a last word with Ealdgyth and a kind word from her father. She would have most liked to see the bride and groom together at the wedding feast. To see if Edward would eat more on his wedding day, or whether his mask might slip more now that he and Ealdgyth were legally bound.

She made no protest however. Beddwen was tired and Ælfgifa had no intention of staying in their chamber all night.

***

Ælfgifa slipped silently along the corridor towards the muted sounds of revelry. There was a convenient wall hanging—showing embroidered hounds holding a stag at bay —over an inglenook in the great hall. She was confident in her ability to slip in and get behind it unseen. She had donned her darkest gown and walked barefoot to aid her in blending in.

Having secured a hiding place for herself, she gazed out on the proceedings with interest. Ealdgyth and Edward headed the board, sharing plate and goblet as they had before. Ælfgifa thought her sister looked happy and noted how she fed delicate, choice morsels to her husband who seemed willing to accept them from her hand. A fatling had been killed and roasted, and there was boar and baked apples and turnips. There were sweetmeats made of millet seed and honey with hazelnuts. Ælfgifa's mouth watered at the scents. Still, the king was only eating the delicate white flesh of some fish that was not served in common and perhaps some roast fowl. She was willing to wager that the goblet they shared contained very well-watered wine rather than ale or mead. *He cannot eat unguardedly,* Ælfgifa decided, *Ealdgyth knows this and is serving him accordingly.* If her sister was nervous about the forthcoming 'putting the couple to bed' she did not show it, turning away the most ribald jests with a smile and a witty word. If anything, it was Edward who seemed to pale at such natural jests though whether with anger or some other emotion, Ælfgifa could not tell.

She was so absorbed in watching that she didn't notice a tall figure approaching the tapestry she was hidden behind until it was too late.

"Will you come out, little owl? It looks most strange that I should converse with a condemned stag—in truth it never looks well to talk to needlework—and there is altogether too much of me to join you in there." Harold lifted his goblet as if in toast but Ælfgifa suspected that it hid his grin.

"I daren't, brother." She whispered, hot with embarrassment at being caught.

"You have not grown so shy these past few years, have you? I remember you as a bold, hardy thing."

"Gytha does not wish me here, brother. I was sent to the nursery with Wulfnoth," she replied.

"Ah so not only a spy but a disobedient one at that," Harold said. The light from the fire and the lamps made his hair glint even in the smoky air.

"I am only disobedient when it is against my own interests and inclinations," she retorted pertly.

Harold laughed. "Simpleton. It would not be disobedience otherwise. Very well, as punishment for making me talk to this stag—which even now rolls its eye most alarmingly at me—you must tell me what you see."

Concealed behind the tapestry, Ælfgifa grinned, something she never did where anyone might see. "See the Bishop?"

"I do," said Harold taking a draught from his goblet.

"Watch when next he is served the boar. I fear he does not taste it often." Ælfgifa had never felt more impish.

She could feel her brother's puzzlement but he did as she suggested. After a moment he coughed out another laugh. "By God, he is stuffing the pockets of his cassock!"

Ælfgifa sniggered.

"What else do you see?" Harold demanded, not teasing any longer.

Ælfgifa hesitated. It would be no betrayal to tell Harold what she had observed would it? He was a loyal son of Wessex and her brother after all.

"Ealdgyth is already fond of her husband, and he of her. Our king is weak of digestion—see she panders to his dull appetite? And there, our mother is not pleased with this match and has still not reconciled herself to it. She eats but little and her smiles are forced. She has twice now stopped our father from rising to make a speech. Godwin has drunk too much tonight I think. See there, again." She paused and it seemed Harold hung on her every word. Thrilled she went on. "Tostig seeks to win the favor of the fair ceorl with red hair. Perhaps he does not know that she is married? And there, Leofwine has been seated with the fourteen-year-old daughter of a thagn and is too self-conscious to speak. He will spill wine on himself in a moment, I think."

"Gifa... you have astounded me. I would I had a sword so sharp!" Harold half-laughed but he was in earnest, she could tell. She warmed under the rare praise. "Why are you not at this feast? You are not such a baby, I think."

"I... I do not wish to speak ill of our mother. But I think she does not like me to be seen in company." She swallowed and forced herself to say, "Doubtless she has a good reason and only my best interests in mind."

"Ah," Harold replied noncommittally. Then as if he knew the subject must be painful to her, he changed the subject. He told Ælfgifa about his Jarldom and about a certain noble lady on whom he had his eye. Ælfgifa listened enthralled. Her brother had an easy manner and a gift for speaking well. She would have liked to speak with him on more complicated matters—why Edward had married Ealdgyth and whether Harold thought it would bury the enmity between their houses or whether Edward would cherish his grudge against Godwin in private, for instance. But she felt too shy, so instead she asked him more about his lands and about his lady.

"Do you mean to marry this Lady Edith?" she asked, unaware of how blunt she sounded.

"I have met her but twice, Gifa. It is a little early to say." His teeth flashed white in a grin. "Still, she is tall and fair. And heiress to great estates that share borders with mine."

"Have you checked her teeth too, brother?" Ælfgifa asked a little waspishly.

Harold laughed. "She is also young and healthy and sufficiently accomplished. It is most strange to discuss such considerations with you, little sister."

"I hear that often of late," Ælfgifa grumbled.

"You are... what? Twelve now? Will not our father seek a marriage for you in a few years? In fact surely he would begin negotiations now." He looked towards Edward and his bride. "Ealdgyth waited overlong to marry, I think."

"By her own choice, brother. And I am but ten years old. There will be no marriage for me, even if Gytha would allow it. Cannot you see how impossible such a thing is?" Ælfgifa spoke without bitterness. She did not feel she was losing anything by relinquishing a faceless future husband.

"Gifa, we do not marry as our fancy directs us. You are a Jarl's daughter. If Gunhild does enter a convent then you will be Godwin's only unmarried daughter. There will be suitors enough, believe me."

Perhaps her brother meant to be comforting but Ælfgifa was annoyed. "I will not take a man who will hate and resent me but marry me anyway for connection to our family," she said.

Harold nodded, eyes shrewd. "Forgive me sister. I meant no offense. Perhaps you are right. Or perhaps your suitors will surprise you. You are too young now in any case." He risked a glance back through the tapestry. "Have you supped? Shall we see if I can be as deft at making food disappear behind cloth as our good friend the bishop?"

Ælfgifa giggled as Harold casually slipped slices of boar and beef, cheese and baked apples behind the tapestry. He even managed a small cup of mead. Ælfgifa was munching happily when she saw her mother approach and froze in fright.

"Do not fear, little owl. I will draw her off. Look then that you make your escape. And good night, sister."

"Goodnight," she whispered back before Gytha drew close.

"And how is it with my second boy?" Gytha said to Harold.

"Well enough, Mother," he replied.

"Then come and speak to the guests. You have been standing by this old hanging in the strangest fashion."

"It is uncommonly fine workmanship," Harold grinned but allowed Gytha to lead him to a party of pretty, eligible young women.

Ælfgifa waited a moment and then slid out of her hiding place, gliding through the smoke-wreathed air and out of the hall. She was giggling, sure she had got away with her sneaking and spying, until she found Beddwen waiting for her at their chamber door. The nurse eyed the grease spots on the girl's gown and took in her sticky hands and filthy, frozen feet. Ælfgifa braced herself for a scolding but Beddwen merely sighed and bustled her into the chamber.

CHAPTER 10

FOR all the need for haste, it was nearly a month before William was able to leave for Poissy, where the King then had his court. The country was too much in disarray, the roads too uncertain. There was too much to do to prevent further lands and people slipping away to Guy. Much of the time was spent in proving to minor gentry he was still alive and free. The arrangements for the trip itself were not simple. He did not want to make the journey without Ralph by his side—after everything that had happened, William was prepared to admit to himself that his guardian knew a good deal more about the business of being a Duke than he did. And yet someone trusted and capable would have to remain to hold Falaise and stop the remainder of Normandy collapsing. There were other considerations too. A second council was held to discuss arrangements for the Duchy while William was away. Archbishop Mauger offered very generously to look after the Duke's lands for as long as it might be required. William, sensing reluctance on the part of Ralph, hedged.

Sure enough, Bellin sought him out after the council and after what felt like half an hour of dancing around the

85

subject, confided that his neighbor had been heard privately expressing rather too much sympathy for the traitors, and making plans to take advantage of any confusion by enlarging his estates at William's expense. Purely to protect them from anarchy, of course. William rolled his eyes, thanked the nobleman and found Ralph.

"We'll have to bring him with us," Ralph sighed. We can't leave him here if he's stirring up trouble, and we can't arrest him—he hasn't been proved to have acted against you."

"That'll slow us down," William complained. "I'd hoped to take a handful of knights and rely on speed to get us through."

"A wise plan. But I want Mauger where I can see him."

"Between him and Lanfranc I wonder that there are any churchmen in Normandy who have any interest in the Lord."

Ralph laughed. "Your mistake is thinking of the Church as predominantly a Church, my Lord. In any case, I recommend we bring six knights. Enough to make something of a show but not slow us down, or give Henri any excuse to suggest we're trying to threaten him. Is there anyone you would like to bring?"

"Gallet."

"I thought you might say that. I vaguely remember him, you know. He was dismissed from your guard for drunkenness. It was only just after you'd become Duke."

"I can't say I'm surprised. But I'd rather have Gallet drunk than two of the others sober. He saved my life."

"Indeed. Well, I thought you might say that, too, so I asked him. He said he has a condition, would you believe, but I can't imagine it's anything that might give us any trouble."

"Oh, he did, did he? I admire his confidence," William chuckled. Gallet was cocky for a fellow who looked and smelled like a dunghill, but he was capable too, and William couldn't help liking him.

"Quite. Anyone else?"

"Hubert of Ryes' eldest, Raoul. He was steadfast and resourceful on the road."

"Agreed. Also your cousin William fitzOsbern. Odo of Evereux. Richard Beaumains, perhaps? Baldwin le Chien."

"All right."

"And you can have a squire if you want, but the knights travel by themselves."

"Mauger will want an entourage."

"He can have two servants. I'm not putting up cloth-of-gold pavilions whenever we stop."

"He won't like that at all." William couldn't resist a smirk. "If he kicks up a fuss I'll just tell Gallet to truss him up and we can carry him there like a deer carcass slung over a horse."

Mauger was predictably outraged. William explained the situation with as much flattery as he could muster, insisting that a having a cleric of his standing there would do their cause nothing but good. Mauger tried numerous means of extricating himself, but even he could not give a flat refusal to a command from his lord. And then, naturally, he wanted to bring half of Rouen and summon chests full of ecclesiastical garb from the cathedral, and nearly wept when William told him he was to bring two men and only a minimum of baggage. He would just have to remain apart from his concubine and finery.

William reflected that not so long ago, he would have enjoyed baiting Mauger. But then not so long ago he would have passed that unpleasant audience to Ralph, so he hadn't really lost anything important. They left Bellin in command. If William was unsure of his energy, he was at least sure of his honesty. And that was not a commodity to be valued too lightly in these days.

On that subject, William summoned Gallet, wondering what the knight wanted in return for pledging his own loyalty. Lands no doubt. A title or two. It was disappointing. William had genuinely thought the man had a liking for him. That was not how the world worked, as he was finding out.

To William's surprise, when the knight appeared, his usual brash confidence seemed to have fallen away. He shuffled his feet and seemed unwilling to make eye contact.

"What is it Gallet?" William asked. "I understand you have a condition for your support on our little trip to see the King."

"Yes, Lord. I'm sorry, my Lord, only I wanted to make sure, and I promised..."

"Promised? Promised what?"

"I would like your permission to marry, my Lord."

"Marry? You want my permission..." He felt his lips twitching beyond his control, tried to maintain a mask of composure, and failed. Once he had started laughing, he could not seem to stop. Some moments later, he managed to get a grip on himself, wiped the tears away. "You don't want a castle and a fat estate and an income from my own coffers?"

Even beneath Gallet's shaggy hair and thicket of stubble, William could tell he was crestfallen. Only for a moment, though. The big knight threw back his head and laughed too. "Oh, you thought I wanted to screw a bribe out of you? Oh, Lord, what must you think of me?"

"That you are a man, and a Norman."

"Well, yes. But can you imagine me as a lord?" He chortled to himself. "Vicomte Gallet! *Hahahaha!*"

"Of course you can marry. Marry whomever you like. You can do it here if you like, I'll get Mauger to officiate. Oh Lord, not him. Lanfranc, how's that?"

"Thankyou, my Lord."

"Who is it, anyway."

The confidence left Gallet again. "Well... you see..."

"Go on."

"It's Helisande, my Lord. Your master of hounds' daughter. And who... um..."

"Yes, I remember." He felt the blood rush from his face. "Oh! She's not... is she...?"

"Er, no, my Lord."

"Oh. Good, good..."

"It's just that... well, she's a lovely young lady and I've taken quite a shine to her. And seeing as she doesn't seem to mind me so much..."

"Really? Of course, I mean. Well. Go ahead. I give my permission."

Gallet exhaled and his shoulders relaxed. "Thankyou, my Lord. Only I wanted to speak to you, in case... in case you... might..."

Oh. In case he had further designs on the girl. Well, she was a beauty, there was no doubt about it, and good company besides... and she had kept her head when the barons had come for him. Still, he realized he hadn't given a moment's thought to female companionship since that night. It seemed he had enough to think about. If she was able to be wed, and to a knight—even a knight like Gallet—it might resolve a number of matters, and he might escape having his own hounds set on him the next time he visited Valognes.

He smiled. "I have no further thought of the girl. Marry her and be happy. And I trust she'll give as good as she gets."

"Yes, my Lord." The grin and the self-assurance were back in an instant.

"I have one condition of my own."

"Anything, my Lord."

"Keep an eye on Mauger, when we're at Poissy. I want to know who he sees, who he speaks to."

"Aye, my Lord. He won't be able to take a shit without you knowing about it."

"There won't be any need for that. He isn't a stag, after all."

"A shame, I'd be happy enough to shoot him."

At least the journey would be more interesting with Gallet around, William reflected. With all the loose ends tied, there was nothing else to prevent them from leaving. The journey was seventy leagues, and should take them no more than two days.

Through Mauger's foot dragging, it took them four. William felt horribly exposed on the road, no doubt partly as a result of the last time he had ridden any distance in the company of only a few men. Every so often he felt the hairs on the back of his neck standing up, and felt compelled to look around, expecting to see anything from a feather of dust on the road behind suggesting a distant pursuit, to a gauntleted hand inches from his collar. He was delighted when they reached Poissy and could get on with obtaining the King's support.

But after they arrived, it was a further four days before Henri deigned to see them. His Grace was indisposed. His Grace was unwell. His Grace was hearing Mass. His Grace was fasting in honor of some saint or other. His Grace was in Council with his nobles. It went on just long enough to avoid being an obvious snub. Long enough to hope that William would get bored and leave.

The old William might have done.

The new William realized that Henri was a little desperate to impress. He'd been to the castle at Poissy once before, when he had sworn fealty to the King after his father's death, but the situation then had been overwhelming and he hadn't really noticed how small the palace was—little more than a big, walled hunting lodge. Falaise was far grander. Perhaps the Kings of France were in decline.

Nevertheless, while they were kept waiting, William's instinct was to quest after entertainment. Oh, for music, or dancing, or a woman, or a good, honest hunt. The one thing he was not used to was boredom. But in his gut he knew that the meeting with Henri was crucial. If he erred and offended the King in some way, he would lose any chance of his support. Alternatively, it occurred to him that Henri knew he was desperate, and might exact such a price for his assistance that William might as well have let the Barons take what they wanted instead. To Ralph's apparent surprise, William insisted on shutting himself away with his guardian for several hours every day to prepare as well as he might for the audience. They trawled through every possible outcome.

Ralph coached William on his words and comportment. He felt his frustration building.

"I don't see why I have to have my nose rubbed in it," William said after he had practiced prostrating himself elegantly but respectfully for the hundredth time. "Look at this place. He's poorer than we are. In better times we could probably take all this for Normandy."

Ralph looked sidelong at him. "These aren't better times, in case you hadn't noticed. You're not thinking of it the right way. This is not a man-to-man matter, it's God's holy representative in France deciding how to help his sworn servant. He made promises, William, but so did you."

Finally, the audience was granted. William took Ralph and Mauger with him into the throne-room at Poissy, hoping that the latter would keep his mouth shut. The room was small, illuminated only by a few arched windows that did not succeed in making the space seem any bigger. Neither did the rich but slightly tatty decoration. Henri had stuffed the room with nobles, and had a couple of bishops of his own too. William felt constricted rather than intimidated, and tried not to pay much attention to the way they all seemed to be looking down their noses at him.

He walked the few paces to the space before the throne and prostrated himself as he had practiced, for as long as seemed appropriate when it became clear that the King was not going to tell him to stand. He picked himself up and bowed his head. "Many days of happiness befall thee, my gracious sovereign and loving liege." The words felt like oil running out of his mouth.

"We thank you," Henri replied. "We understand you come before us with grave tidings from Normandy."

William fought not to roll his eyes. Ralph had told him about the monarch's habit of referring to himself in the plural, as if he had to emphasize that he acted with God in all things. And as if he didn't know what the tidings were from Normandy. God hadn't done anything to prevent Henri's physical decline, at any rate. Since William had last met Henri a decade before, his hair and beard were now more gray than their previous reddish blonde, his cheeks were hollow and his face was deeply lined.

"Sire," William said, "I no longer trust in aught but God and you. All my vassals are in rebellion against me. They no longer do me homage. They have taken my lands, they ravage and burn all my domains. Soon I shall have nothing left." Well, that was something of an exaggeration, but he might as well play the King's game. "Sire, I appeal to you most humbly not to abandon me. My father made me your vassal, when he went to the Holy Lands to restore them to Christian lordship. Your vassal am I of Normandy, and I call upon the oaths of vassalage to defend me well. My father formerly restored France to you. When your mother Constance tried to disinherit you, you came to Normandy with but a small company. He recognized you as his lord, received you with great honors, helped you in your need, and gave you back all the land of France. Give me then, I beg and require you, for this service, a just reward. Come to Normandy with me and avenge me on the disloyal traitors who have sworn my death. If you do this, full well will you act, and I will be your vassal all my life."

Well, there it was. That was all he could do for the time being. William resisted the urge to turn around to look at Ralph to see if he had delivered the words properly. This was all down to him now. Unless... there was something he had missed. Guy may be a Frenchman, he may be a cousin of William's, but he was of a different Royal house... That of Henri's brother, Robert, who, William imagined, would very much like to take the throne for himself. Wait! That was important. "...And should Guy take Normandy," he added quickly, "even part of the Duchy, Sire, then the Royal demesne would find itself locked between Burgundian territories."

The King looked down at him, inscrutable. But had there been a twitch when he mentioned Burgundy? Then Henri leaned back to whisper in the ear of one of the barons crowded around him.

It was a gamble, to remind Henri of the embarrassment of the past, when Robert had virtually handed Henri his kingdom back, and to frame his request as a return of services previously rendered rather than hinting at offers that might be made now. But it was much too late to tread softly. All of Normandy was at risk. Through his own folly. Nothing less than the total defeat of the traitors would now do.

Henri had finished conversing with his nobles. The expression on his face was like that of a man who knew he was being cuckolded and had just found out it was by his brother. He simply sat, looking down at William for what felt like minutes.

"William. Thou hast spoken well," the King said eventually. "We are moved by the dire misfortune of our vassal, whose father rendered us some assistance in the past, but who has come to desperate straits deserving of only the lowest and most insolent varlet."

Ralph had warned him that securing the help they needed might require swallowing some not-very-veiled insults. It didn't make it any easier. He felt the color rising in his cheeks.

"...To find yourself beset by vermin, accusing you of all manner of filthy crimes that it offends our ears to hear. We sorrow to hear of our vassals brought thus low. The more fair and crystal is the sky, the uglier seem the clouds that in it fly."

Oh Lord, bad poetry now. This was torture.

"To traitor and miscreant lords we say, thou art too good to be so, too evil to live."

Yes, yes. Get on with it.

"To our young vassal, who twelve years since we promised to help and protect..."

Really? Then where were you when three of my guardians were murdered?

"...We now promise to deliver from his despair and ruin, and take him from the unclean earth to lift him up where noble blood mingles with the Holy Spirit..."

I wonder what meat we'll be served this evening?

"...help in any way possible..."

Not sure what the beef is like in this district. Have to ask Bourdas to look into it.

"...false traitors... injurious villains..."

Or is it pigs they are famed for around these parts?

"...raise all the armies of France in your support."

What? All the armies? It was better than they could have hoped. Far better! "Sire!" he cried, and prostrated himself again, trying to ignore a face-full of dust.

"...When it is possible to bring them to the field," Henri concluded.

There were the usual sycophantic phrases to babble before they could escape, but unless Henri managed to find a way to go back on his word, they had what they'd come for. And not just that, but Henri had been so intent on insulting William that he had somehow managed to forget ask for anything in return. There was a long way to go, but for now, blind hope had some realistic expectations for company.

CHAPTER 11

JANUARY gave ground to February with ill grace. Tiny shoots of brilliant green thrust through the crust of snow, before blooming into the drooping white bells of snowdrops. There was a smell of rising pine sap. Spring was on the way. Ælfgifa gritted her teeth in concentration as she wielded the tiny knife. She had three crow's feather quills made already to Caedmon's exacting tastes and a fourth nib was shaping under her fingers.

In the weeks since Ealdgyth's wedding to Edward, Ælfgifa had heard little of her sister. It was not greatly surprising since she was back at her father's main estate. A freak snow storm had blown in just after they arrived home, shutting them off from all but the most urgent of messengers. Ælfgifa fought herself daily, missing her sister and now Harold— whose renewed interest in her had sparked corresponding affection—feeling stifled and excluded from the dangerous but seductive adult world she had had a glimpse of. Much as Ælfgifa loved Beddwen, she wanted more than nursery tales and songs now. Her agile mind ached like a cramped muscle. She wished that Ealdgyth might send for her to be fostered at court soon, little realizing the negotiations that would be involved. In the meantime she set herself to acquiring knowledge with a drive that privately frightened her teachers.

She had practiced writing in Latin all morning and would have continued into the afternoon if Caedmon had not stopped her and set her to trimming quills, and grinding and mixing ink. Ælfgifa could already write well in Anglish, and the old monk, seeing that it was not enough of a challenge for her on a day when she felt so restless, had set her to copying passages from Roman philosophers. Ælfgifa occasionally forgot herself and exclaimed aloud at what she thought were particular pieces of folly, as she traced the words in a tray of fine sand. Then Caedmon had unrolled part of a scroll that held the thoughts of a man called Marcus Aurelius. It was a strange name—most of the Romans had strange names—but the scroll was fascinating. Ælfgifa had felt she was tracing the words into her bones as well as the sand. Occasionally Caedmon would gently correct her and she would adjust her hand or smooth out a word and repeat it correctly, never taking her eyes from the scroll.

Caedmon had finally rolled up the scroll right under her sharp little nose, having tried in vain to get her attention. Ælfgifa had made a soft whimper of disappointment but had not whined as another child might have at having to leave off a plaything or being denied a treat. If one could think of the teachings of an old stoic a treat, that is.

Now, as she set her fourth completed crow feather quill to one side, Ælfgifa studied Caedmon. He had once been a monk and still tonsured his hair. It was odd though because Ælfgifa had seen other monks at Wintanceastre and thought that they part-shaved their heads differently. She wasn't sure how old Caedmon was either. Ten years older than her father? Twenty years? Perhaps more. His face was almost unlined and brown as cut peat. There was little white in his dark hair and his eyes were gray and disconcertingly direct. Caedmon was clearly no warrior. He was a small, thin man, unprepossessing on first glance. Yet he was straight-backed and hale as an oak. Hardier than many real warriors. He was a mystery and Ælfgifa loved mysteries. She had pestered him into teaching her four years ago. Ælfgifa guessed now that he had taken pity on the least regarded of Godwin's children. Perhaps he had thought a little attention could do her no harm. She had heard him murmuring to Beddwen once, that his pupil sucked up learning with such frightening rapidity that he wondered whether it was actually attention she was starved of.

"Caedmon," Ælfgifa began softly, "will you teach me the *futharc* as well?"

"Latin, Irish, French, reading, writing. Now the runes? Will it never be enough, Gifa?" Caedmon asked mildly.

"I don't think it's possible to make learning a gluttony," the girl mused.

Caedmon smiled wryly. "Man can make a gluttony of anything, child. Wealth, power, land, desire. Gluttony is a void that grows the more you feed it."

"Then let learning be my gluttony. It is a harmless one. Will you teach me? I know you know the *futharc*. I've seen you reading them."

"Firstly, girl, it is what one is willing to pay to feed a gluttony that makes it dangerous. Secondly, it is what one does with learning and knowledge that makes that dangerous —remember the stories of the Norse god Woden? Hmm? Knowledge without the wisdom to use it is always dangerous," he paused and then sighed. Ælfgifa watched him, hazel eyes wide in her sharp, marked face.

Caedmon gave her a strangely tender look and relented. "I ought not to teach you. The runes were outlawed by King Cnut decades since."

"But you will?" Ælfgifa said eagerly.

"On condition that you keep it to yourself. I doubt anyone will think to ask you if you can read the old language. Few remember it, fewer can read it." Caedmon looked down at the manuscript he was working on.

"Why did King Cnut outlaw the runes?" Ælfgifa frowned, her strongly marked brows drawing together.

"King Cnut was concerned with appearing to be a good Christian," said Caedmon. "You know there are several forms of Christian mass?"

Ælfgifa shook her head. This was new. "Like how Ealdgyth was married 'in christiano'?" she asked.

"That's part of it. In Rome, the pope is the head of the church—of all Christians—or so he would like us all to believe. The Latin Church wants all Christians to worship God in the way they deem correct. But England, Britain in fact, has been settled by many people. They've intermarried and their children and grandchildren remember older rites. Still Christian but not approved of by Rome."

Ælfgifa stared at him, willing the old monk to go on.

"Did you visit the convent at Wintanceastre when your sister married the king?" Caedmon asked abruptly.

"Yes, Beddwen and I stayed there. My brothers stayed in the male quarters with the monks." Ælfgifa could not see where this was going.

"And from your observation, who would you say was in charge of the convent and the monastery? Oh they'll have had both a Prior amongst the monks and a Mother Superior amongst the nuns, but one will have deferred to another. Who was it?" Caedmon's eyes were very sharp.

"The Abbess," said Ælfgifa still confused.

"That is how it has always been. Woman, man—both are considered equal in the eyes of God here on earth as in heaven. But if a decision needs making, it is the senior female, in this case the Abbess, who will have the final say. Before we knew of Christ and his teachings, our people always deferred to the priestess, the wise woman, the cunning maid, the head woman of the tribe, in all matters of the *spirit*, and we still do today." Caedmon gave her a wry smile. "Women guard the secret of life and death."

Ælfgifa wondered if he meant that women could have babies so they were closer to the creative power of God, and would have asked him but he had taken up the thread of his narrative.

"Rome does not like this. They do not believe that women should stand equal with men. They believe it is a woman's lot to be subject to a man, to hold any position or power only under a man's guidance and often not to wield power at all. They believe a woman must submit."

I would love to be a sparrow in the roof beams if anyone ever tries to explain that to my mother! Ælfgifa thought with some amusement. She couldn't imagine Ealdgyth taking such news well either. Nor even gentle Gunhild – who might be quieter by nature but was still very much mistress of her own mind.

"I think few women would agree with anything so stupid," she said aloud.

"Gifa, they do agree. Whether because they are not allowed to learn or taught not to think, or whether they are terrorized..." He sighed. "Rome wants to control the hearts and minds of all her children. The current pope has been discontented at the way we worship God here in Britain for some time. He would like to see a more firm turning to Mother Church."

Ælfgifa thought for a moment and then pointed out, "But he is all the way in Rome. It is out of his hands."

"Gifa, he need only wait for a dispute big enough to cause men to war with each other. You cannot imagine what men will do if they think that God and Right are on their side." Caedmon looked sad, as though he remembered things that pained him.

"You mean that if the pope wanted to influence Britain then he would only have to lend support in the right quarter? That he might say that God was with them?" Ælfgifa felt troubled but could not quite grasp why.

"Edward is childless. If he dies who will be king?" Caedmon asked softly.

"Who... whoever the *Witenagemot* deems most fit, I suppose," Ælfgifa frowned again.

"And what, Gifa, if there are several contenders—none more worthy than another—who all believe that they should have the throne?" Caedmon searched her stricken expression. "There child, I only meant to explain a little, not frighten you. It may be that no such deciding conflict will happen in my lifetime nor in yours. Indeed it may not happen for many generations. Edward is not so very old yet and your sister is well able to bear him heirs. Rome is not so very well organized and will have to endure our ways."

Ælfgifa did not think he really meant what he was saying. "Caedmon, is that why King Edward tries so hard to appear pious?"

Caedmon stared at her, shocked by her deduction. "Gifa, while you may be right, I want you to promise me that you will not voice such an opinion where anyone else will hear it."

Wide eyed, Ælfgifa nodded.

***

Wulfnoth was only five years old and when he was not clinging to Beddwen, he trotted in Ælfgifa's footsteps like a faithful hound. Beddwen had sent the girl to pick herbs in the kitchen garden and Wulfnoth had run after her.

"No, Wulfnoth. It's too cold. Go back to Beddwen," Ælfgifa said, a little exasperated, although she knew her brother was bored with sitting in the still room while their nurse made tinctures and tonics.

"Want to be with you, Gifa," the boy whined, kicking icy slush and thawed mud everywhere in his haste to catch up with her.

"You should have a cloak." Ælfgifa gave in and smiled.

"Don't want a cloak." Wulfnoth sounded so aggrieved at the slur on his manliness that Ælfgifa laughed.

"Very well, but just for a few minutes." She took her brother's hand and they trudged through the half-melted slush. Wulfnoth wanted to be chased so Ælfgifa good naturedly ran after her brother, pretending that he was far too fast for her too catch until he was giggling and breathless. She caught him and swung him in a wide circle that made the boy squeal with delight. Ælfgifa laughed so hard that tears ran hot down her cold cheeks. Their breath rose in plumes on the frozen air, like the smoke from a great *wyrm* in a story. Finally, out of breath and starting to feel the cold, Ælfgifa set her brother on a stone bench and quickly cut the herbs Beddwen had asked for. Her hands were reddened and stiff with cold.

"Gifa, are we going back now?" Wulfnoth rubbed his knuckles into one eye. Ælfgifa was alarmed at the blue tint to her brother's lips.

"I told you, you needed a cloak," she said, annoyed with herself. She wrapped her own cloak around the shivering child. Wulfnoth didn't protest, just snuggled into the thick wool warmed by the heat of his sister's body. This worried Ælfgifa even more. *I must get him back*, she thought. *Beddwen will know what to do. Maybe he needs a posset.* She picked her brother up and staggered a little under his weight. Nestled in her cloak, Wulfnoth put his arms around her neck and laid his head on her shoulder.

Beddwen exclaimed at the sight of them, hurrying to take the boy from Ælfgifa who was now shivering herself. The nurse bustled them out of the still-room—Ælfgifa left the collected herbs on the table—and back to their own chambers where she sent the girl to change into dry clothes. Warm and dry once more, Ælfgifa joined them before the fire. Wulfnoth was a natural pink again and had fallen asleep. Perhaps she had over-reacted.

"Why did Wulfnoth not have his own cloak?" Beddwen asked softly.

"He didn't want it Beddwen, and it didn't seem so cold when we were playing," Ælfgifa said, a little shame-faced. Beddwen nodded.

"You'll be making him wear it next time, if you please," Beddwen said. "There is more sickness at this time of year than at any other. Spring's not here yet but people think it is and forget their warm clothes."

"Yes, Beddwen. Sorry."

"No harm done, girl. The boy is just worn out."

Ælfgifa thought that was an end to it but after supper, Gytha called to her as she was leaving the hall.

"Ælfgifa, come and speak to me in my chamber." Gytha turned and didn't bother to look back to see if Ælfgifa was following. Ælfgifa wanted to ignore her mother and go back to her own room but long habits of obedience made her drag her feet after Gytha. It felt as though her heart had fallen into her stomach.

Gytha shut the chamber door then stood looking down on her daughter for some moments. She took no pains to school her expression and it was plain to Ælfgifa that her mother was displeased with what she saw. She looked down at the floor, wishing to disappear into the fresh strewn rushes.

"You were in the garden today," Gytha said at last.

It was not a question yet her mother plainly expected an answer. "Yes, Mother, I picked rosemary and other herbs for Beddwen." Ælfgifa resisted the urge to shuffle her feet.

"Why was Wulfnoth with you?" Her mother demanded abruptly.

Ælfgifa did not understand. Wulfnoth was often with her. "He wanted to come outside." It was the best answer she could give.

"He ought to play with his brothers, not be trailing your skirts. And you should be making yourself useful," Gytha admonished.

Stung by the unfairness of this, Ælfgifa answered without thinking. "Wulfnoth is only five! Leofwine and Gyrth don't want to play with him. He likes being with me. And I was helping Beddwen. I *was* being useful!"

For a moment Ælfgifa thought her mother would slap her, but then Gytha's raised hand slowly lowered. There was disgust in her eyes. *She cannot bear to touch me, even in anger*, thought Ælfgifa. The shame was so familiar that it was only half intelligible. Indistinct and crushing.

"No more," said Gytha coldly. "He will grow up a man, which he cannot do if he is always surrounded by women." She nodded once, coming to a decision. "You are too old for a nurse. You will move into another chamber. I will speak to the steward."

"I was not too old to be sent to bed straight after Ealdgyth's wedding," Ælfgifa said hotly. She was in a confusion of rage and shame and frustration. Gytha's words, her treatment were so arbitrary. There was no reason, no justice. Had she seen Wulfnoth and Ælfgifa playing and laughing? Had that irked her so much? Ælfgifa did not even know why she was arguing. A day ago she would have welcomed a room to herself, or to even to share Gunhild's chamber.

"Get out of my sight," Gytha said in a voice that snapped with menace. Her beautiful face was a frozen mask and she spoke through her straight, white teeth.

Ælfgifa stood for a moment, shaking and sick, hands clenched, breathless. She felt fever hot and as if she no longer knew how to get out of the chamber. A cornered animal. A trapped weasel. Then a cold clarity took her and set her towards the door.

"Go and tell your father you were disobedient and ask his forgiveness," Gytha said as the door closed.

Ælfgifa stood outside her mother's chamber for a moment, mastering herself. One thought rang with utter clarity in her mind. *Your mother will never love you. Your nature and your visage offend her. This is something you cannot hope to change.*

***

Beddwen's lips went so thin as to be almost colorless when Ælfgifa explained that she would not be sleeping in their chamber anymore. The nurse's normally ruddy face was as blanched as good vellum. Ælfgifa thought Beddwen was restraining herself from speaking against Gytha with some difficulty. It didn't matter. When she had gone to her father as Gytha ordered, Godwin had ruffled her hair and said "What, in trouble again, Blackbird?" and grinned at her before saying that as she was growing up, she would be glad to leave the nursery in any case. Ælfgifa hadn't felt equal to trying to make her father see that Gytha was trying to stop her associating with her own brother. The clarity of thought that had come in the wake of her argument with Gytha had faded, leaving her feeling low and oppressed. Uninterested in further conflict.

She had thought that she would be moved into the chamber Gunhild had shared with Ealdgyth until her wedding. It was with some surprise that she found herself being led to a small room with one tiny window and no fireplace, just off the still room. There was a raised pallet bed of bent ash wood with lashed animal hides as a base. It was padded with dried heather and ferns, spread with a single sheet. There were two thin wool blankets folded on top of the only other piece of furniture in the room, a single small, oak chest. It was a postulant's room. A serf's bed. Less so, for the serfs were valuable and provided with fireplaces. Ælfgifa dully wondered if her mother wished her to freeze to death.

Beddwen came in then and exclaimed in horror. She ran out again immediately, leaving Ælfgifa bewildered and alone. Beddwen returned in a few moments with two more blankets and a good fur—clearly purloined from storage—as well as a jug of spiced cider and a platter of honey cakes.

Ælfgifa fingered the fur. The wolf had been a huge, silvered beast and the hide was cured to a supple softness. "I cannot keep this, Beddwen. The blankets I might explain, but you must take the fur back."

"Mwyalchen, you will die of cold in this..." Beddwen could not seem to think of a word that adequately expressed her opinion of the chamber.

"Please, Beddwen. What if Mother sees it? If you are sent away who will look after Wulfnoth?" Ælfgifa wanted the fur. She wanted a heap of furs. If Beddwen didn't take it away right now...

"Your Lady mother will not be sending me away for doing my task and tending her littles!" Beddwen's dark eyes flashed.

"I'm not your task anymore, Beddwen. Mother said I am too old for a nurse." Ælfgifa swallowed against a lump in her throat. "Take the fur back," she said, trying for the tone of a Lady addressing a ceorl and hating herself for it.

"You should be complaining to Jarl Godwin about this," Beddwen said, picking up the wolf skin. "Unbecoming to a Jarl's daughter, this is! He would not stand for it."

"No!" Ælfgifa cried. "No, Beddwen," she said more softly. "I would not have him told." She twisted her already crooked, misshapen mouth into a mulish expression.

"As you are my charge, as I love you as a daughter, I ought to complain, no matter what you say," Beddwen replied thickly. "But I can see you will not be having it."

Ælfgifa felt a pang of guilt but smothered it. It was as if someone had lit a fire in her head and heart. With a single kind word, Gytha might have made her biddable. With this deliberate cruelty, she had earned Ælfgifa's stubborn disdain. The girl resolved to pit her will against her mother's. Gytha would see that those who yield are not always weak. Her mother would learn in the fullness of time just what mettle her daughter was made of. But even Ælfgifa, with her knack for predicting logical outcomes long before circumstance brought them to fruition, did not see what some of those consequences would be.

***

Beddwen, as a skilled healer and midwife, had been in great demand over the winter—the wife of one of the thagns had had a difficult pregnancy, and the cold, wet spring had brought a greater number of patients with agues and injuries to the still room door. Until Gytha's interference, Wulfnoth had been left more and more often in Ælfgifa's care. It was to

109

his sister Wulfnoth ran with small treasures—a shiny stone, a sleek feather—it was 'Gifa' he cried for when he grazed a knee or had a bad dream. Ælfgifa had been surprised to find that she enjoyed caring for him. Wulfnoth was bold and mischievous as well as roughly tender. He would disobey just to see what he could get away with and then charm his way out of a scolding with a huge, dimpled grin that Ælfgifa could never seem to resist.

Now Ælfgifa was almost always alone, save for the time she spent learning with Caedmon. She missed her brother. It made no sense for her mother to order her away from Beddwen and tell her she was not to mind Wulfnoth.

Her new chamber was bitterly cold. The shutter did not fit the window well and a draught always blew through the room. On stormy nights, the wind unerringly found the cracks under the shutter and howled through, bringing sleet and rain. Beddwen continued to beg Ælfgifa to go to her father. She always refused. This was between Gytha and herself alone. She hardly knew what outcome she hoped for. Her mother was unlikely to acknowledge her fortitude or strength of mind, just as she had been blind and deaf to Ælfgifa's other qualities. It just seemed to Ælfgifa that she must hold on. From the way she caught her mother watching her at board from time to time, she felt sure that Gytha was waiting for something. Some sign of weakness, of a faltering resolve. It made Ælfgifa even more determined to hide her discomfort. To appear as stone, as if her mother's words and treatment affected her not at all. She had learned to pass unnoticed out of necessity, now she was learning to let others see only what she chose to share.

Yet Gytha was a puzzle. Forcing herself to be objective, Ælfgifa could see that her mother was a loyal and loving wife, a kind but firm mother—to her other children at least. Gytha had a knack for sizing a situation up in a few moments and acting accordingly. She was a clever manager of the household, which was large, and of the immediate farm. She knew the names of all the serfs, not just her personal slaves, and ensured they were fairly treated. The ceorls, male or female had not a bad word to say of her. She made the thagns' wives and daughters feel valued without ever losing her authority, which she wore lightly. Her judgments were fair, as far as Ælfgifa could see, and while Gytha had fits of passionate temper, it was rare for any of the household to bear the brunt of them. Ælfgifa was forced to concede that her mother was in general, kind, just and strong-willed. Nothing, it seemed, happened to any of her household, that Gytha did not know of almost immediately. The only exception was Ælfgifa herself, and she wondered if that was not because her mother refused to notice her.

Gytha was a contradiction, Ælfgifa decided. She was sure that her facial deformity would merely raise Gytha's pity in another. If Gunhild had shown such a propensity for learning, she would have been praised. If her brothers had displayed precocious wisdom, Gytha would have rewarded them.

"What is it in me that she so dislikes?" Ælfgifa asked herself. It was nearly ten days since she had been removed from the nursery. She could not sleep, even piled in the extra blankets Beddwen had pressed on her, she was too cold, her body too small to warm her bed quickly enough. The wind howled, wolfish and hungry, and her single rush-light guttered, almost died. She shivered, considering throwing her cloak around herself too. There was a faint whimpering noise. Ælfgifa froze. *Not the wind. There's something outside my door.* She realized that she had been hearing it on and off for a while, but it had been swallowed into the general noise of the storm. Had one of the dogs got into the house proper and found its way to her room? Ælfgifa was tempted to let the poor beast in. It would be another warm body at least.

Biting back a yelp as her bare feet touched the thin skin of ice on the floor, Ælfgifa padded to the chamber door and drew it open. She could not see a dog, nor anything that might make a whimpering sound. Had it merely been the wind after all? And then a tiny, cracked voice whispered, "Gifa...?"

"Wulfnoth? What are you doing here?" Ælfgifa cried, seeing her brother curled against the wall outside her room.

"Want you... wind calling my name..." her brother murmured.

Ælfgifa gathered him up in her arms. He was frozen. Pale, blue-white. His little hands clawed and unable to straighten. He had no shoes, no cloak. Only a thin night-shirt on his scrawny body. "Wulfnoth, how long have you been there?" Ælfgifa half-sobbed.

"The wind... calling me..." Wulfnoth's eyes were glazed. He wasn't seeing her at all. Badly frightened, Ælfgifa wrapped him in a blanket from her bed. His hands and feet were like ice but his forehead was scorching to the touch. Ælfgifa watched as his eyes slid shut. On some unconscious level she knew her brother had reached the dangerous stage of chill where he was not even able to shiver. Grabbing another blanket to swathe him in, she hauled him onto her

hip and carried him back to Beddwen. With every step she felt her brother's rising fever burn against her own skin.

CHAPTER 12

HENRI had made the promise, and could not now go back on it. Even so, it wasn't quite as simple as raising an army and going to kick the traitors into La Manche. The weather broke while William and his representatives were still deep in negotiations with Henri's councilors, and weeks of torrential rain gave way to snow. Before any army had taken a single step, Christmas had been and gone, and all thoughts of fighting vanished from all but William's mind, it seemed.

The wedding of Gallet and Helisande was one bright spot in an otherwise grim span of months. William could not imagine two people more oddly matched than the bear-like, often filthy knight and his pretty, graceful bride, and yet they seemed utterly devoted to one another. One could only hope their children took after their mother.

As January gave way to February, and February to March, the ground unfroze, and turned to mud beneath a deluge of freezing rain. Henri sent messengers putting off the campaign, once, twice. William's hopes for a Spring assault began to waver. He even found use of his chapel to pray for better weather, and that Henri's resolve would remain strong, though he wasn't sure how much good it did. For all the preaching of fellows like Mauger and Lanfranc, he could

not help but see God as a distant, uninterested deity who largely left his creations to fend for themselves.

It became apparent that Gallet had brought Helisande and her family away from Valognes not a moment too soon. As the months wore on, more reports came in from the lands overrun by Guy and the renegade barons almost by the day. Of the strengthening of Caen against siege on the one hand, the plundering of William's castles and lands at Isigny and Valognes on the other. The displacement of serfs in lands the traitors did not control, but William could not defend. Every week more people arrived at Falaise hoping to find safety there, shelter and food. More than once he had stormed to Ralph insisting on gathering a force of knights to prevent more pillage, and avenging that which had taken place. Ralph had been implacable in his opposition to any such schemes. "I know you're stinging from the insult," he said, "but we must let them go on ravaging the land. Then, in time, we can stop it. If we attack before we are ready, far more may be lost."

It was barely tolerable, but William resolved to do so if he could. The thought of that awful grimacing Hammond riding around the once-rich districts, burning, destroying, killing... William discussed tactics with Ralph, who had been in charge of Normandy's armies for twelve years, though heaven only knew which tactics they should focus on. When and if it came to a fight there was no way of knowing what kind of battle it might be. Even so, the young Duke trained in the courtyard with sword and bow, on horseback and off, roping in as many armed men as he could to practice hand-to-hand fighting. Gallet threw himself into the preparations with enthusiasm. William sensed he would welcome the opportunity to get at Grimoult, Renulf, Neel and Hammond in person with a lance, sword or his bare hands if it came to it. Every day, the food stores and money reserves ebbed away. If this went on too much longer, there would barely be a Duchy to fight for.

Finally, the sun returned. The rain receded. The earth began to dry, or at least harden. Leaves returned to the trees, and bluebells began to carpet the earth in the forests and woods. William sent messengers to Henri, and they returned with noncommittal responses. He sent more messengers, bearing polite, courtly but firm reminders of the King's commitment. If Henri hoped William would accept the situation, or through circumstances beyond his control be forced to accept it, and reach a settlement with Guy, the King would surely be disappointed.

The rebel lords, it seemed, had also accepted that one way or another there would be a battle. They had begun to assemble, with all the men and arms they could muster. Of the actual numbers arrayed against him, William had frustratingly little idea. Reports of military preparations in Bessin and Contentin from spies, traders and travelers arriving in Falaise varied wildly. There might be everything from a thousand to ten thousand men bearing arms. Disentangling rumor from fact was next to impossible.

In the second week of April, a messenger arrived from Poissy while William was sparring with Raoul de Ryes. He quickly summoned Ralph and they met in his private chambers.

It was the message he had begun to fear would never arrive. Henri had assembled his army, at last, and was already moving on Caen!

"There's not a moment to waste," Ralph said, his brows knitted. "After all this waiting I had hoped for more warning than this. We'll need to assemble the Cauchois, Roem and Roumoiz as quickly as possible. I wonder if we can pick up the men from Auge, Lievin and Evreux on the way?"

"Why don't we muster in Oismeiz?" William said. "It's closer for nearly everyone and the roads are more direct."

"Good idea. We'll send messengers right away. We'll have to move fast if we're going to prevent the traitors bringing all their forces together."

"I'm more worried about them holing up somewhere or avoiding battle. We need a quick victory."

Ralph frowned. "Better a drawn-out partial victory than a rapid total defeat."

"Come on Guardian." William clapped Ralph on the shoulder. "Not so glum. We have God and my right on our side, don't we? After all this sitting around aren't you ready for a good battle?"

Ralph smiled wanly. "I fear there are few that die well in battle, and when they assemble at the latter day, the lord that brought them to it will have a heavy reckoning to make before the Almighty. It will be a black matter for that lord if the cause was not good."

"You think about things too much. The sooner we split the pate of a traitor or two the sooner we can get things how they should be."

"And how is that?"

William's smile faded. "As you describe, Guardian. A prosperous Duchy under a good lord. I swear it."

They marched North East for the muster at Oismeiz, which went as smoothly as could be expected. Still, they had fewer men than they might have done. When the force was ready to march North East towards Caen they had sixty mounted men and another two hundred or so on foot—the muster varied each time it was taken. Some slipped away while others joined, but in the main, the force held together well enough. No word had arrived from Raoul de Taisson. There was no point in waiting any longer.

They had not been on the move more than an hour, however, before a tang of smoke could be tasted faintly on the air. And then another smell. Something sharp and thick that forced its way into William's nostrils and throat.

A cluster of houses, barely worthy of the name of village—indeed, no-one seemed to know the name of the settlement—straddled the road as it dipped into a hollow. At least, they had been houses. The thatch of the roofs had burned almost completely away. The walls were smashed and stained. The residents had, it seemed, been dragged into the road and killed where they knelt. The men, at any rate. A dozen lay in a loose group, throats cut. A few had fought, it seemed. One was covered in so many slashes and cuts that his own mother wouldn't have recognized him. Another's entrails had been torn out, and lay around him like gigantic, grotesque earthworms. The women were scattered around, bloodied, twisted, violated.

"Guy." William almost choked on the word.

"It can't be helped," Ralph said.

"Why? He doesn't even claim to control this area."

"*Because* he doesn't claim to control it," Gallet growled. "Anything he can't get his hands on, he'll destroy. This won't be the only place. He'll have had his raiding parties tearing up villages and hamlets wherever he can. If he can't have it, you can't have it either."

"This isn't war," William breathed. He fought down bile as it rose in his throat. Dear Lord, the stink.

Ralph snorted. "That's exactly what it is. He means to hit you wherever and however he can. You have to ignore it. Reacting to this won't help you recover your lands."

William whipped round, a bellow of rage unformed in his chest, which died as a cry went up from an outrider. They looked up, to see a scout from the distant picket riding back towards the army, at the foot of a great plume of dust.

"It's Guy," the scout panted, while his horse did likewise beneath him. "He's wheeled right from Caen and he's marching right toward us."

"Where is he now?"

"Barely two leagues West of here. A little North of Secqueville."

"How many?"

"Three hundred horse. Perhaps a thousand on foot, maybe more. I saw a large group of common folk following behind the infantry, bearing arms."

"They have commoners fighting for them?" William cried. "We'll cut them to pieces!"

"We need to turn West," Ralph said. "And march with all haste. Scout, did you make contact with Henri?"

"No, my Lord."

Ralph turned to William. "We need to find Henri and link up with him as quickly as possible. It may be that Guy knows we are separated from the King at the moment and is trying to destroy us before Henri can get here. Based on our last reports, I suspect he'll be coming from the South, towards Navarre. We'll aim to join with him there."

Ralph sent the scout back to keep an eye on Guy's army, and dispatched further men on fast horses out towards Billy and Navarre, in case the pickets should miss Henri. William watched him closely. He was a general with experience, and wanted to leave nothing to chance.

"We should take the chance to arm ourselves," Ralph said. "But quickly." There was a cacophony of clanking and scraping as armor was buckled on, helms were laced, lances passed up. The scene took on a blaze of color as each knight secured a gonfanon bearing his or his liege lord's coat of arms to their saddles, should they be needed to rally men to them in the confusion of battle. William noticed Bourdas' hands shaking. This was his first time squiring for William, and it was the most important occasion imaginable. Most squires got to start out with a tourney or two... Once everyone was ready—and still no sign of de Taisson—they set off at a punishing pace for the men on foot, especially armed and wearing hauberks. Within minutes, everyone was feeling the weight of their mail and sweating despite the air being far from warm.

"We have no choice," Ralph explained as they rode. "If Guy catches us on our own, with his numbers, without de Taisson, we're done for. And with him still on the move, today will be a contest of horse, I expect. If only we had more mounted knights."

"Why would he bring common folk?" William asked. "If he were not desperate?"

"He is desperate, but that's what makes him dangerous. He needs to win today, or everything is lost. You or Henri are unlikely to lose everything today, but Guy can. So that means he's going to fight like forty leopards."

"Can common folk even wield a sword?"

"Probably not, and in any case they don't have the right. But they'll have staves, clubs, knives. One of those will kill you just as much as a sword or a lance will."

Good God. The thought of being killed by a peasant with a stick. "We'd better make sure we defeat the cavalry outright, and the commoners don't come into it."

"Quite. The battle will most likely be on open land, and Guy will not have had time to build fortifications."

"So it will be down to the maneuvering of cavalry?"

"Yes. Depending on where we join battle. If Guy is clever, or has good advisors, he'll still be able to choose ground where he can move freely but we're restricted."

"What happens if he catches us?"

"Honestly? If we've established where the King is, I recommend we flee in his direction. If not? Withdraw on Falaise and hope he doesn't outrun us."

William fell silent, and became aware of the drum of the horses' hooves, the clink of armor and weapons, the thud of marching feet, the panting of tired men and horses.

Before too long, a cloud of dust was seen on the road ahead. William's heart lurched. Had they been cut off? No, it was only two horses. The scouts had returned.

"My Lord," the leader reported when they had approached. "The King is encamped near Beneauville"

"He has not yet broken camp?" Ralph cut across William before he could question the men.

"No, Lord. When we left, the King was still hearing Mass."

"Mass?!" both Ralph and William shouted.

"Yes, Lord. At the church of Saint Briçun de Valmerei. I understand he had been there some hours."

William and Ralph shared a look. It did not do to say anything disparaging about their monarch in front of others. William was aware of what Ralph thought of Henri's piety at that moment.

"Any news of Guy?" William asked.

"Yes, Lord. He has established his force at the hill Malcouronne on the plain at Val es Dunes."

"Hmm," uttered Ralph, and dismissed the scouts.

"What is it?" William asked.

"It appears that Guy is clever, or well advised."

CHAPTER 13

WULFNOTH did not improve. Ælfgifa and Beddwen had put him back to bed, piling blankets on him and building up the fire. The room was so hot that Ælfgifa felt sweat trickle down her spine.

"He is not so cold now," she said hopefully, massaging one of her brother's tiny hands out of its frozen claw.

Beddwen made no comment, other than a noncommittal grunt, and added shredded leaves to a pot of water boiling over the fire. "Beddwen?"

"The cold is not being the danger, Mwyalchen. It is his fever, see? That's dangerous hot, your brother is." Beddwen looked grim.

"But then why are we making him hotter?" Ælfgifa cried.

"It's still early, and if we don't warm him then he'll not be having the strength to fight the fever." She dipped a cup of hot liquid out of the pot and blew on it to cool it. "See if he'll take this."

Ælfgifa raised her brother against her arm and tried to coax him to drink. He swallowed half a cupful before knocking the cup from her hand, but she still felt encouraged. She recognized the sharp scent of willow bark mixed with the warm smell of hops and yarrow. Beddwen still looked severe. "He'll be alright now, won't he?"

"We'll see if his fever breaks. There will be a long road ahead of Wulfnoth if it doesn't." Her expression softened. "Climb in with your brother. Looking like a wraith, you are, girl. There's nothing more we can do for him yet."

Yawning, Ælfgifa slid under the blankets and put an arm around her brother. *He does seem to be resting easier*, she thought as a black tide of sleep dragged her under.

Her awakening was less calm. Sharp twigs twisted in her hair, close to the scalp, and she was yanked from under the blankets, hitting the cold floor with a gasp. For a moment she could not make sense of where she was or what was happening. This was not her little chamber. Then the tall and terrible figure standing over her, resolved itself into her mother. Gytha was white with fury. And with fear. And she wasn't looking at Ælfgifa but down at the bed where Wulfnoth lay.

Ælfgifa lurched to the side of the bed, calling her brother's name, but Gytha's fingers bit into her shoulder and thrust her aside.

"What is the meaning of this?" Gytha demanded, ignoring Ælfgifa as she pulled herself to her feet again.

Beddwen's face was a bland mask. "I was calling for you as soon as Wulfnoth became worse, Lady." And laconically, Beddwen laid out what had happened. How Ælfgifa had found the little boy at her door and carried him back. What they had done to treat him.

Ælfgifa barely heard her. She strained against her mother's iron grip, frantic at the sight of her brother lying so still and pale in the bed. There was a hectic flush to his cheeks and a light sheen of sweat on his skin, but otherwise he might have been a corpse. Ælfgifa's heart stopped in her chest, then Wulfnoth gave a feeble moan and moved a hand weakly as if searching for something. Gytha let go of her and sat at Wulfnoth's side, holding that questing hand and stroking his sweat-darkened hair off his forehead.

"My Lady," Beddwen went on, "This fever is dangerous. The willow is not touching it."

"What else has been done?" demanded Gytha in a passion of fear and unfocussed anger. "Has he been bled?"

Bled? Ælfgifa thought, horrified. Did they mean to cut Wulfnoth?

"He is too young. Not strong enough for that, Lady," Beddwen replied and Ælfgifa felt a wave of relief.

"What then? Mugwort? Mandrake?" Gytha said, in tight control of herself once more. Ælfgifa was surprised at her mother's knowledge as much as by her ready acceptance of Beddwen's skill.

"We will keep trying him with the willow and yarrow. If there is vinegar and birch leaves in the store room that would help. If I can be getting him to swallow enough water, we might be trying a mugwort plaster later." Beddwen nodded towards Ælfgifa. "Your girl there is best at coaxing him to drink."

For the first time since she had seized her daughter's hair and yanked her from the bed, Gytha turn a cold gaze on Ælfgifa. "And whose fault is it that my youngest child is now so sick he may never recover?" Her voice was as scorching as her gaze was icy. Ælfgifa felt herself becoming something small and loathsome under her mother's scrutiny. She had been struggling against guilt already. It was her fault

Wulfnoth had been in the hall so long. It was her fault that she hadn't understood or heard his cries earlier. Gytha was right, it was her fault Wulfnoth was sick. If he died that would be her fault as well. She shivered, still dressed only in her shift, but it was only partly from cold. There was a creeping sick feeling in her belly, spreading out into her throat.

"You cannot blame the girl, Lady. How was she to know the child would creep down to her chamber? It is me you should be blaming, for he slipped away as I slept when I had charge of him," Beddwen said with heat that matched Gytha's. "Do not let your anxiety make you say something incautious-"

Gytha held up a hand and Beddwen stopped. "You have always been a good nurse to my children, but you go too far. Wulfnoth is not a disobedient child. The girl encouraged him somehow. She is a slinking, sneaking thing and has been teaching her brother the same ill-behavior."

Ælfgifa felt as if her face had gone numb. She knew her eyes were open but she couldn't feel her mouth at all. Her hands tingled. She should say something. She knew she should. But it was as if her mother's antipathy had frozen up all the words she knew. Had stolen the life from her, almost, until all she could do was stand and think and feel, but not act.

"Go now and dress," Gytha ordered. "Find something useful to do. And stay away from your brother-"

"Oh, but please! Don't make me leave him. He will want me here!" Ælfgifa cried finally finding her voice.

"Get out!" her mother almost shrieked. "He will not want you here, and I do not! You are not to come back. Would you had been a dutiful child in the first instance, your brother might then not be sick." Gytha caught Ælfgifa's upper arm and thrust the girl out of the chamber, closing the door in her face. Ælfgifa stood, staring at the door for a moment, unable to believe what had happened. Wulfnoth *would* want her. She knew he would. It was no use returning while her mother was there, however.

She made her way to her chamber and dressed quickly, her breath hanging in the chill air of her room like silver thread. The still room needed reorganizing and there would be herbs that Beddwen would want prepared, so Ælfgifa busied herself with that. The morning passed and she realized that she had had nothing to eat. Putting the millet broom back in the corner, she left the packets of prepared herbs where Beddwen would find them and went to purloin food from the kitchen. *Later*, she told herself, *later Beddwen will send for me or Wulfnoth will ask for me and then even Gytha will have to let me see him.*

No one sent for her that day. Nor the next.

***

Ælfgifa had grown tired of waiting. She had seen Beddwen once since Gytha had banished her from the sick room. The nurse was flushed and harried, her normally neat, dark hair falling out of its knot. The nurse had been able to tell her nothing except that Wulfnoth was no better and they might have to try the mandrake after all. Ælfgifa knew that it was very strong, a last resort for fever and never used on someone who was already weakened. She had continued to prepare and mix herbs, but it galled her to be kept away when she could help.

When Gytha's absence at board in the evening was noted on a third night, Ælfgifa made up her mind. She would find a way to see Wulfnoth. It would just have to be a way that would not get Beddwen into trouble. There was a subdued air to the household. Everyone waited, hanging upon the fate of the youngest of Godwin's sons.

It was very late when Ælfgifa made her way through the thickening shadows to Wulfnoth's room. She knew that Beddwen had left for more water and herbs, perhaps even to hastily eat a bowl of gruel. The door was ajar and it was the work of a moment for Ælfgifa to slip inside and conceal herself between a table and a chest. There was only the light of the fire and a single, tallow candle burning on the stand near the bed. The room was warm and dark. Ælfgifa did not care about any trouble she might find herself in, but she did not want to be caught and thrown out before she had a chance to see her brother.

She started from her hiding place then cursed under her breath. Her mother was here. But as Ælfgifa watched she realized that Gytha's head was resting on her arms on the bed, fair hair falling in tangles around her. Her breaths were deep and even. She slept. *Dare I?* Ælfgifa remembered that Beddwen would be back soon. This might be her only chance. She crept out of her hiding place and approached the bed, careful lest her shadow fall on her mother and somehow wake her. Crouching on the opposite side of the bed to Gytha, she peered down at Wulfnoth. For a moment she did not recognize her brother. Gone were the chubby cheeks and healthy roundedness of his limbs. Gone the ruddy good health. He was still and waxy pale. And so thin, the fever had stripped his flesh from his bones. So fragile. Like a sheet from an ancient manuscript, worn thin with time and faded. Except that Wulfnoth was a blank page. If he died nothing would ever be written upon him. Ælfgifa wavered in her anguish. She wanted to gather him up in her arms, and dare Death to try and take her brother.

She took a step forward and Gytha stirred in her sleep. Ælfgifa froze and her mother was still. But she could see the pallor of her mother's face now, and the puffy redness of her eyes. Ælfgifa had once or twice seen Godwin shed tears—for a fallen comrade or a good servant—but never her mother and it was clear that Gytha had been weeping.

A noise at the door sent Ælfgifa scrabbling under the bed. She lay on her back in the dust, trying to breathe silently as her heart punched her ribs.

She heard Godwin say, "How is it with the boy?"

Gytha shifted and replied thickly. "Very ill, my lord. His fever will not break. I have sent Beddwen for the mandrake." She paused and from the shifting play of shadows, Ælfgifa thought that her father had moved first to look down on Wulfnoth and then to rest his hands on Gytha's shoulders. "It may kill him, my lord, but if we try nothing he will not recover."

"Then it must be tried," Godwin said. Then more softly, "Do not blame yourself, Gytha, children sicken. It is a wound to my heart to see him so, but the midwinter death took so few this year... can we wonder if it makes a last snatch for the lives of the very young and old?"

"I would not have it take my son! And I do *not* blame myself. I blame that wretched girl!" Gytha snapped.

The shadows shifted again. Ælfgifa thought Godwin must have moved back a pace from his wife.

"You speak of my Blackbird," Godwin said heavily.

"What a pet you have made of her," Gytha said bitterly.

"Your grief makes you speak so," Godwin said tightly. "Nay. I will hear no more. Ælfgifa is not to blame. And I hear from the gossip of ceorls that you sent her from her nurse and brother into a chamber where you would not keep a dog!" He took a deep breath as if reining in his temper and Ælfgifa shivered in her hiding place. "Were I a cruel man, I might ask if it was intended that your daughter should be wasting away under this fever, rather than your son. As it is, Gytha, I cannot reason out your actions. You are famed for good judgment. Was the girl really such a bad influence on her brother?"

Gytha made no answer but Ælfgifa could imagine the proud tilt of her head. The refusal to back down. Her gaze would be unflinching, Ælfgifa knew. Her mother never felt shame. Never showed remorse. Would never admit that she was wrong.

"Done is done," Godwin said finally. "It may be that God will spare the lad yet. Perhaps he was already sickening. It seems to me more likely that, feeling ill, he would seek his sister out for comfort. A night in a chill corridor worsened his illness, rather than caused it."

Gytha replied in a small, tight voice. "I would she were gone, Godwin."

"Ælfgifa is scarcely more than a child!" Godwin exclaimed. "And you are not to blame for Ælfgifa, either, wife. Indeed, while Blackbird is ill-favored in feature, she is quick in wits and kindness. She is a credit to her mother. I cannot understand you, Gytha."

Gytha gave a bitter little laugh. "If I had only borne an ugly child that would be a sorrow. But she is not merely 'ill-favored,' she is deformed. Even that might be a cause for pity but she is not right. Ælfgifa is something *not right*. She looks at me, at anyone, as no child in the world. She speaks as if an old being inhabits her body. She always knows too much and she is silent, as if she is storing up your secrets..." Gytha trailed off. The silence was uncomfortable as if she had never meant to say so much.

"You can hardly believe," Godwin began, voice soft with outrage, "you cannot give credence to our daughter actually being a changeling, Gytha?"

"I do not. And yet for all that she is no child, whatever she appears. And I mean this truly, my husband, Ælfgifa must go. She must be sent away to a convent—for good, not just learning—or she must be fostered elsewhere. I will not suffer her here longer. As soon as the roads clear, Godwin. Heed me."

Godwin moved toward the bed again. "You are overwrought, Lady. Nay, hush. We will talk of this another time. You have neither eaten nor slept. Come now. See, here is Beddwen. She will send for you if there is any change."

By dint of coaxing and command, Godwin persuaded his wife to leave the sick room. Beddwen shut the chamber door and set a steaming pot on the hearth to keep it warm. Ælfgifa wondered how exactly she was going to make her escape, then Beddwen sighed and said, "Come out now then, *Mwyalchen*." There never had been any fooling Beddwen.

She emerged, smudged and rumpled. The nurse shook her head but did not chide her charge for spying as she would have done normally.

"Come then, you'll be making yourself useful since you're here. See if you can get your brother to take some of this. It'll make swallowing the mandrake easier." Beddwen handed her a cup and Ælfgifa once again recognized the scent of willow.

"No yarrow?" she asked.

"Not strong enough, is it. Little good the lesser plants have done. But he can swallow nothing while he is hurting so get him to drink that and we'll see about something stronger."

Ælfgifa lifted her brother, quietly shocked and frightened by how light he was, how insubstantial. He might already have blown away like wood smoke. She could not get him to drink. His teeth seemed locked together and more and more of the liquid ran down Wulfnoth's thin cheeks, wetting the bedclothes. Ælfgifa found she was shaking so she set the cup down and took a deep breath. She felt Beddwen's eyes on her, sympathetic and anxious. There had to be a way to reach Wulfnoth. Ælfgifa started to speak to her brother, low and soft. Telling him of the fun they would have when he woke up, only he must be a good boy and get better so that he was strong enough. He must drink what Ælfgifa gave him even if it did taste nasty. She ran on, nonsense and rhymes and stories until her tongue felt as if it would glue itself to the roof of her mouth. She stopped and found Wulfnoth looking at her with glazed, feverish eyes. "G-gifa..." his voice was scarcely even a whisper.

"Drink this, Wulfnoth," she said striving for calm when she wanted to cry. Obediently he swallowed a few mouthfuls and then his eyes drifted shut once more. "Beddwen?" She said in panic.

"He's not gone, girl, not yet. Give him this while he's strong enough." The bowl Beddwyn passed her was full of a dark, thick, pungent liquid. Ælfgifa eyed it warily and then looked at her brother.

"He cannot swallow all that," she said. "Is there a rag?"

"Feed him like a babe, you mean?" Beddwen handed her a clean piece of cloth. "Aye, it's the only way I've been able to make him drink at all until you came."

Drop by drop, Ælfgifa fed her brother the dark mixture, dipping an end of the rag in the bowl to soak it and letting the liquid trickle from it down his throat.

The mandrake brought on a profuse sweat and a shivering that had Ælfgifa shaking in sympathy. They piled more blankets on Wulfnoth and kept up the fire. His breath wheezed in his chest with a horrid, phlegmy rattle. Ælfgifa had never been so afraid.

Sometime after midnight, Wulfnoth's fever broke. He was bathed in sweat but underneath the sheen, he was cool. Weak but alive. Beddwen cried as Ælfgifa held her brother's hand. She slipped under the bed again when they heard Gytha's footsteps in the corridor and Beddwen didn't protest.

Gytha gave a cry and ran to her son's side.

Wulfnoth opened his eyes sleepily and half smiled. "Gifa? Want Gifa," he said before falling into a deep, healing sleep.

CHAPTER 14

THE moment Henri's army finally came into view was one William would not lightly forget. As they breasted a rise and the walls of Caen appeared as a gray line on the horizon, punctuated by church towers, they came upon row upon row of infantry, with two rows of cavalry at the head. A forest of pikes and a dozen banners fluttering over their heads. From here the force looked huge. William's confidence ebbed a little when Ralph estimated the size of the army at no more than eight hundred and fifty, barely fivescore of them mounted. If the estimates of Guy's army were true, the traitor lords still had them outnumbered.

"Where is Guy?" William asked his guardian.

Ralph pointed somewhere to the North. "He's drawn up on the hill there."

William surveyed the scene. The 'hill' of which Ralph spoke was barely worthy of the name. A slightly raised patch of ground some half a league distant. Circular, with a fringe of trees around the flanks, but bare on top. He smiled, realizing why it was known as 'Malcouronne' - it looked just like a monk's tonsure. "I don't see them."

"They'll be in the tree-line."

"Won't that be hard to attack?"

Ralph looked thoughtful for a moment, casting his eyes over the field. "Only if they decide to dismount and fight a defensive battle," he said, eventually. "Guy has a slight advantage in horse, so I suspect he'll try that first. There's no honor in fighting on foot. We're not Saxons."

William laughed. Ralph just looked at him. Wasn't the point to win?

"Anyway," Ralph went on. "We'd better ride ahead and see Henri. How we fight the battle will be up to him. Oh, and you'd better do the talking."

They spurred their horses into a trot and made for the cluster of gleaming knights on destriers standing before the leading row of cavalry, the Capet standard snapping above them. William and Ralph were permitted to approach the King's person.

"Good day to you Normandy," Henri said. He certainly seemed enthusiastic about it, William reflected. It made a difference from their last meeting. Perhaps the idea of having Burgundian lords either side of the French king's remaining domains had lost its appeal. "Wacey," Henri nodded to Ralph. "An excellent morning. We have shriven ourselves and are ready to take the field with spotless souls."

"How may we serve Your Grace?" William asked, bowing his head.

"You may form your forces up on our right flank. I'll make the first charge. You will act as our reserve."

Reserve? They had come all this way to act as a reserve? In the fight for his own Duchy? Good Lord, the insult. "Sire," he said, bowing again in the hope that Henri would not see the fury on his face.

"Well, we might as well make a start. I see Guy is ready."

William looked over his shoulder. A line of banners could now be seen against the trees. He tried to make out which belonged to each of the traitor barons, but they were too far to distinguish.

"When your men have formed up, we'll make the first charge," the King said.

"Yes, Sire."

"We will send a messenger if we require your assistance."

"Thankyou Sire."

"Pray tell me, who is that and for whom does he fight?" Henri gestured to his left. On a fold of ground, another division of cavalry sat, as if it had risen up out of the earth roughly half distance between the two armies. William squinted, trying to make out the banners.

"Raoul de Taisson, your Grace" Ralph said, before William could answer.

"Ah. Is he with us, or with Guy?"

That's what we'd all like to know. "He has no cause for quarrel or enmity with me, your Grace," William said.

"Ah. Good."

As they rode back to their own ranks, Ralph leaned over to William. "You may curse, Lord," he said, "but I advise you wait until we are further away from the King."

William laughed, despite his anger. "I imagine we'll be needed. Guy has numbers on his side."

"Yes. And position. We'll be going uphill, although there's not much of a slope. It's the room to turn I'm concerned about. Look," Ralph pointed. "They have lots of space. We're caught between those marshes and rough ground."

It was true. The water in the marshes formed a shining sheet off to the right. Anyone who ended up in that would have a very bad day. To the left, the ground seemed to ruck into tight folds that it would be impossible to maintain speed and formation over. Beyond, towards Guy's army, the fields broadened out into a flat plain.

"Who do you think Raoul will fight for? With all his knights, he could swing the battle."

"Yes. If I know Raoul, he will have a deep and unshakeable commitment to whichever side looks as though it has gained the upper hand."

They drew up their paltry assemblage of men to the right of Henri's ranks, and William's guard lined up on either side of him. Gallet, Raoul of Ryes, and his cousins. At least he'd spent a bit of time with them, and could attest to their honesty and steadfastness. He only wished he knew the rest of them a bit better. Well, there'd be time if they won. If they lost, it didn't really matter.

"Sorry, gentlemen." He clenched his jaw. "We're to act as the King's reserve for the time being."

The knights around him broke out into a flurry of obscenities, which passed like a wave through the ranks behind as they realized what was going on. They were reduced to watching as the King's cavalry began to move off at a walk.

"It looks as though we have some company, my Lord," Ralph said, and gestured to their left. A small group of horsemen were crossing behind the King's infantry and making towards them. "Raoul de Taisson wants to wish you a good morning, it seems."

"I'm glad someone does."

The horsemen slowed to a walk and crossed to where William and his guard stood. "My Lord!" one of them said, bowing a little.

"De Taisson," he replied. "Glad you could join us." For some reason, Raoul was only wearing one gauntlet. Had they been caught in some disarray?

Raoul drew up his horse beside William.

"I'll be honest, Lord," he said. "Those viscounts over there have promised me a great deal for my help. Land, gold, titles and suchlike."

William raised an eyebrow. "They are generous fellows, with other people's property."

De Taisson laughed. "Indeed they are. I'm afraid I made some promises to them."

"Really?" *Avaricious swine.* "That I find... disappointing."

"But when we arrived, I asked these good fellows here," he gestured to his guard, "whether we were doing the right thing. To a man they said I really shouldn't make war on my lawful liege, and I should do my duty to you. And as you are my natural lord..."

William clenched his jaw and attempted to ignore the emphasis Raoul had placed on the word *natural.*

"...to whom I paid homage before your father and your barons... the man who fights against his lord has no right to fief or barony."

If that were true, there were an awful lot of barons who had no right to fief or barony, and not a few of them were on this field.

De Taisson continued, "'Your advice pleases me', I said to them, 'you say well, thus will I act'."

"It delights me to hear it."

"There is one problem, though. Those promises I made on all the Saints of Bayeux." At that, he slipped the velvet glove off his ungauntleted hand and swiped it lightly at William's shoulder.

William gaped, and heard Gallet growl, then a rustle of mail and leather as hands moved to weapons.

"Sire, what I have sworn, I am doing," Raoul said, chuckling. "I swore I would strike you as soon as I saw you. To accomplish my vow, I have struck you. Well, you wouldn't want a perjurer as your vassal, would you?"

"No," William answered. "Most assuredly not." He also did not want vassals who struck him, and attempted to play his enemies off against him. It took all his strength not to draw his sword and swing it at Raoul de Taisson's neck.

"Don't worry Lord, I only struck you with my glove – with my good sharp sword I'll pierce a hundred of your enemies."

"I thank you," William said, through gritted teeth.

Raoul and his guard spurred their horses back to their own lines. "That was well done, William," Ralph said when they were gone. "I'm sorry to say we need him."

For now. "Watch him like a peregrine. And fall on him if he makes the slightest hint of a move against us."

"Aye, my Lord."

The King's cavalry had, in the meantime, broken into a trot. As William watched, the trot became a canter, and eventually a gallop. From the hilltop, Guy's cavalry could be seen to move. Which banners were which? Oh, if only they could save Hammond for him. It would be a pleasure to knock those teeth out with his lance. After a minute, the king's two ranks of horse had become a dark smudge at the head of a great wedge of dust rising into the air, sometimes slashed with color and sparking with light flashing from armor. The sound of hooves was like a distant rushing river.

"Magnificent," he breathed. The men around him chuckled.

Just then, the dark mass seemed to fracture. Most of the knights pulled up to a trot, and a small group raced on ahead. It seemed Guy's army had done the same.

"What are they doing?"

"My Lord?"

"Why aren't they all attacking?"

"You don't want to commit your whole force at once, Lord," Gallet muttered. "You probe a bit and see who's looking stronger on the day."

"Well they're stronger, obviously!" William hissed. "They have greater numbers and the high ground!"

"I know, Lord, there's nothing for it."

There must be something. No position was perfect. Ralph's words at Valognes came back to him. He needed to be seen to be a better hunter than the huntsmen, a better butcher than the butchers. A better soldier than the knights. So he needed to think, and see something nobody else had. It was no easy business being a Duke.

"When will Henri call us to come in, do you think?"

He was answered with silence. Everyone avoided his gaze.

"He will call us in, won't he?"

"If it looks as though victory can't be gained, maybe not." Ralph's voice was heavy with apology. "Withdrawal without dishonor."

So that was it! The king would make a bit of a show before retreating. *Well, everything was against us. They were too strong. We will negotiate a settlement.* Everyone's honor intact but William's. God curse it! Was Henri just playing his upstart neighbors against one another? Were there no honest men in the country? His hands gripped the reins. His face felt hot, and his scalp itched under his helm. *Damn them all! Cowards and traitors!*

"Sometimes you have to wait," Ralph said, seeming to sense William's impatience. "And sometimes it's better to wait. We're lucky—today, both are true." William grunted. He was not convinced by the argument.

The two leading groups of knights appeared to have come together and separated again. It didn't look as though anyone had been unseated. "Is this a battle or a tourney?" William growled. The two small leading groups wheeled around and merged with the main forces, which had withdrawn a short way. The mass of dust above each force began to dissipate into a flabby cloud.

"They picked a good spot all right," Gallet said brightly. "We can't maneuver much to the left or we'll get tangled with the King. He won't thank you for that. And there's bugger-all movement to the right with those marshes there."

"True," Ralph observed. "Perhaps it's best we stay out of it."

"Perhaps," William conceded. If they ever were called upon to charge it would be a rush up the edge of the field with precious little room to turn. And if they tried to withdraw, the battle could quickly become a rout. Everyone seemed so impressed with the way Guy had chosen the field. In future, William resolved, he would choose the ground on which he fought.

"At least it's a nice day for a swim," Gallet added.

"What do you mean?"

"If we're driven back to la Muance we won't have much choice." He smiled grimly.

Oh Lord. Yet another problem. "No," William answered, more to himself than anyone else. It was true. The river stretched behind them, no ford for miles. An entire army could be driven into the stream. Armored knights faced with a choice of drowning or slaughter on the bank.

But the Muance was not the only river in these parts.

"No", he repeated. "The Orme is what, a league? Two leagues that way?" He pointed beyond Guy's army.

"Yes, my Lord. Why, is the swimming better in the Orme?"

More chuckling from the knights behind. William gripped the reins and his knuckles whitened.

"For Guy, perhaps." That was the Barons' weakness. They'd chosen a position for its advantages in battle, not its options in defeat.

"My Lord?"

"If we have no escape, neither have they. If we break them, they can't fall back and re-form. They can't withdraw toward Caen, or they'll be caught between us and the walls. They can't come through us. The only other way out is that way."

Gallet smiled. "And into the Orme they go."

"Yes!"

"Someone should mention it to Henri," Ralph said.

More laughter. Good God, if one more man laughed he would have his tongue ripped out! The armies had reformed and seemed to be trotting round in wide circles. The banners cracked and snapped.

"I'll tell him after the battle," William said. "When we've won it for him."

"My Lord?"

"Form up. We charge. And none of that nonsense with advance guards skirmishing and pulling back. We go in all at once."

"My Lord," Ralph leaned forward, voice rasping. "If we fail we'll have lost your entire cavalry in one charge! It will be a disaster. Please, leave this to me."

"We won't fail. If they're expecting us to piss about like Henri we'll be through them before they know what's happening. Now form up or I'll send you on your own."

"Yes, Lord." He actually smiled before he turned to the leading rank. "Form up knights, one line! We're all the advance guard today."

"So pick your man and make sure you knock him flat on his arse," Gallet added.

William felt a thrill run through his scalp as he loosened his sword in his scabbard, and called for Bourdas to bring him his lance. He checked the gonfanon was attached firmly to the saddle, and secured his shield to his arm. This was it. The moment his life had led towards. From now on, things would be different. He would be the Duke, as his father had been, as Rollo had been. Or he would die.

The cavalry, now in a single line, moved forward as one. William let Ralph set the pace. He'd done this before. The big destriers were best brought up to a gallop gradually, building up a formidable momentum as they did. It seemed to take forever to close up on the King's right flank. The ground began to slope upwards, but the horses had built up speed now.

Perhaps they were not too early. In the middle of Henri's front rank, a banner went down and the line seemed to collapse. A collision, perhaps, several men unhorsed. The French cavalry suddenly seemed to clump towards the spot.

"The King has fallen!" Ralph shouted, though how he knew that, William had no idea.

"Aid the King!" he shouted, but just at that moment spotted Renulf's banner and kept the line directed at Guy's left, yelling the Norman battlecry, "Dex Aie!"

"Dex Aie!" the others took up the call, "Dex Aie!"

Renulf and his knights had fallen a little way back from Guy's main lines, as they were off to one side of Henri's force with no-one to engage. William could tell the moment they had been spotted coming into the fight, as a small group of horses broke into a gallop. A battle cry of *"Saint Sever! Sire Saint Sevoir!"* drifted down from Renulf's knights. William noticed with admiration how the line closed up behind the leading knights, but Renulf was clearly expecting a probing joust as Henri and Guy had engaged in. He was going to be disappointed.

William couched his lance and picked a knight, hoping it was Renulf himself. The air was filled with the thunder of hooves and choking dust. For a moment there was nothing else but him and the knight as they bore towards each other. Just then the vanguard realized it was facing William's entire cavalry alone. The knight William was facing pulled up a little, let his lance drop. He was struggling to couch it again when William's lance hit him in the shoulder and he tumbled, spinning in the air before thudding into the ground.

The kick up William's arm was immense, and he nearly fell himself, but managed to hang onto the rein. He had aimed for the chest, but shoulder wasn't bad. He chanced a look to either side. His cavalry had ridden down Renulf's vanguard as if it were no more substantial than smoke. The main rank had only just realized it was being charged, and only just had time to raise their lances, spur their horses to a gallop before William was on them.

He'd barely had time to choose his man this time, and the lance glanced off the shield. The shaft wrenched at his arm and he dropped it. Damn. The impact had thrown the two leading ranks together into a mess of curvetting, jibbing horses. William grabbed for his sword hilt, fumbled it, grabbed it again firmly this time and drew. By this time the second man he had hit had gone. He spurred towards a knight who had pulled up in front of him – then realized it was one of his own men. Through the steel of his helm, the echoes of shouts and clashing weapons reverberated.

"Dex Aie!" he yelled again. A flash to his right drew his attention and he just had time to raise his sword as another blade swung down at him. The blow sent a shock through his shoulder, and he twisted his sword to shove the other blade away, finding himself face to face with a surprisingly young knight. Dully, somewhere in the depths of his mind, he realized the fellow was familiar. A nephew of Grimoult. Hardé? Bardon? They'd hunted together.

The brief pause gave William time to swing his shield over to his right just as the knight's blade slashed at him again. It bit into the wood and caught for a moment, just long enough for William to twist his own sword round. No room to swing it. Instead, he stabbed roughly, throwing as much weight as possible up from the hilt. The tip of the sword plunged into the knight's throat just at the base. William felt the blade scraping against the top of the collarbone. He shoved again. Dark liquid streamed over his hands. The knight's eyes looked surprised, then nothing at all. William put his free hand to his opponent's chest and pushed, yanking at his sword. It caught for a moment, snagging on bone. God, he was vulnerable. The other slumped, and toppled back, almost pulling William's sword out of his hand, but one last pull freed it. His whole arm was covered in blood. The other knight—Bardon, definitely— slipped from his saddle. The last William saw of him he was dragging along the ground, one foot caught in the stirrup, as his horse fled the battle.

Everyone around him seemed to be engaged. Little knots of men hewed at each other with swords, a few with axes. For a moment he thought the infantry had come up, but realized the men fighting on foot were knights who had been dismounted.

Just beyond the nearest press William spotted a gonfanon attached to a lance waving in the air. Renulf's arms! He spurred his horse around the fighting clusters and there was Renulf, alone, not waving the banner – just holding it and letting it sway. He looked up and his eyes locked with William's. William raised his sword and yelled "Dex Aie!"

Renulf dropped the lance, turned his horse and bolted.

William heard a bellow of rage and realized it was coming from him. He spurred his horse but had taken no more than a few steps after the retreating baron before an instant of clarity made him pull up. The battle was the important thing,

not one fleeing traitor. He guided his horse into the nearest
mêlée, looking for a gonfanon or ensign to identify an enemy.
A knight bearing Renulf's coat of arms backed towards him,
slashing wildly with his sword at another knight who was
advancing slowly with lance levelled. William realized the
knight with the lance was Ralph. He rode towards them, but
Ralph had darted at Renulf's man and in the clash they were
both unhorsed. The baron's man was up first, and he had
kept hold of his sword, but let his horse go, while Ralph had
hung onto the reins of his own steed and was trying to steady
it as it jibbed and pulled. Renulf's man took a lurching step
towards Ralph so William spurred at him, loosened his wrist,
keeping his movements fluid, and using the blade's own
momentum, swung it back, around and down on the crown
of the knight's head. The edge of his blade sliced into the
steel helm, not deep, but enough to catch in the cut it had
made. William managed to pull the horse up and wrenched
at the sword, yelling in panic. Christ, he was vulnerable now!
But the man was dead or unconscious from the blow, sagging
to the ground. William wrenched again, heaving his sword
out of the cleft in his opponent's helm. The grating of metal
on metal seemed to cut right through him and he tasted bile
once again. Once he'd steadied himself and his horse, he
called to Ralph. His guardian had managed to still his horse,
and turned to hear his name.

"Ralph, take my hand," William said, reaching out. For a
second, Ralph looked at him with confusion. A huge purple
bruise like a wine birthmark had bloomed on the side of his
head. William winced to see it. "Give me your hand," he said
again and this time Ralph comprehended. He took William's
gauntleted hand in his own, put a foot in the stirrup of his

own horse and pulled himself up onto the saddle. The wrench on William arm sent pain shooting through his shoulder and he winced.

"Are you all right my Lord?" Ralph said, his voice a dry scrape.

"Fine. And you?"

"Took a knock. I'll be alright." He narrowed his eyes at William's sword arm.

"Oh, this?" William nodded at all the blood. "Not mine, don't worry." A cloud seemed to lift from his eyes and he saw the sheer bone-weariness on Ralph's face. "Look, you've done your part. You should withdraw, rest."

"I'll be alright," he repeated. "You should rally the cavalry, see if we can get another charge together."

William glanced around. The hand-to-hand struggle was still raging, but there did seem to be a few disengaged men now. He realized that several of the knights were fleeing after their lord. "Saints' bollocks! Are we winning?"

Ralph laughed. "I think we might be, but don't start sewing the victory banners just yet. Wait, what's that?" He pointed to the left flank. A line of cavalry was rippling down onto the plain from a slight rise.

"Thury! Thury!" yelled the charging division.

"It's Raoul!" William cried, recognizing the battle cry. "He waited until now, damn his sneaking hide!"

"Better late than never. And he's going for Guy's men. Quickly, my Lord. Rally, and we can trap them in closing jaws."

Ralph called to a man on foot to pick up a lance—there were plenty lying on the ground, he saw, and some were still intact—and hand it to William, then untied his gonfanon from the saddle. With trembling fingers, William sheathed his still gory sword and attached the banner to the head of the lance, hoping fervently that it would not come loose.

"To me, Normandy!" he shouted. "To me! Dex Aie! Dex Aie!"

All who could break free converged on his banner, assembling into a scrappy line. He noticed some of Renulf's knights grabbing the chance to turn their horses and retreat on their infantry.

"Charge!" he bellowed, and urged his horse to a canter, then a gallop, directing the line as best he could at Guy's left flank. In a mirror image, Raoul's force was thundering at Guy's right flank. William lowered the lance with the gonfanon still fluttering at its head, couched it to the left across his horse's neck, and picked an opponent.

The two main lines, Guy's and Henri's, had more or less kept their shape after the initial clashes, and were for the most part fighting hand to hand. It was easy to make out those knights who were a little more timid, more cautious. They were the ones a bit further back or to the side, not really getting involved. They were the first to turn and see William's cavalry charging in from the side. Some held their ground, attempted to form a line, level their lances. Most broke and ran.

The cavalry plunged into the side of Guy's line and it rolled up like a carpet. Those men who did not tumble before the onslaught began to back away, move aside, flee. William unhorsed a man who tried to turn at the last moment. William lost his grip on his lance, which clattered to the ground, but he just kept roaring "Dex Aie!" until nothing came out but a croak. There was a stream of men and horses running back across the plain. He shouted to those men nearest him and turned his horse after them and fumbled for his sword.

There was a row of pikemen up ahead, and for a moment or two William thought they might have another fight on their hands. One thing fighting mounted lancers, another charging at men holding pikes driven into the ground... But long before they arrived, the infantry had abandoned their pikes and turned tail. Fools. They'd have a better chance standing their ground. Now they'd just be cut down like straw.

It was a slaughter. William lost count of the number of men he'd ended with a stroke of his sword. As he'd predicted, the only way the fugitives could go was into the river Orme. When they reached its banks, some were crowded by the stream pleading for mercy. They received little. Others had tried to cross. The edges of the water were already choked with those who had failed and washed up in the mud. A few were struggling midstream, fighting against the weight of hauberk and boots, failing. One or two mounted men had succeeded in getting across, William saw, hanging onto the reins of their horses as the beasts swam. If only they had archers. A few would do.

In the final reckoning, Guy had escaped, it seemed, for his body was nowhere to be found and captured knights said they had seen him making for the river near the end of the battle. Neel had also escaped. Hammond had succeeded in unseating the king and had been killed by Henri's guard. Renulf was either dead or had escaped, it was unclear which, but only Grimoult, of all the conspirators, had been captured.

As he was brought before William, unbound and unshackled as befit his station, his eyes seared with hatred.

"You fight with no honor!" He hissed. "You fight like a Saxon! No grace. No nobility. Just attack!"

"Take it up with God," William replied. "He has seen fit to deliver me victory, despite my lack of honor. I will take His judgment over that of a traitor and an oathbreaker. Take him away. Lock him up. But not to Falaise. I can't bear his stench. Rouen, take him there. Find a cell befitting his crime."

As Grimoult was led from the field, William could make out very little of his screaming rant, although the word 'bastard' was discernible and repeated several times.

CHAPTER 15

WILLIAM usually experienced a pang of disappointment on seeing the keep of Falaise poking above the horizon as it meant the return home and the end of another adventure. While this was, he supposed, still true, he found himself yearning for the comfort and security of home. He had survived his first battle. Winning it almost seemed incidental. The last leagues over the familiar roads felt like the hardest ride he had ever undertaken. Every step jarred his spine. His arms felt as though they only had a few spindly muscles left in them, and those that remained were screaming in pain. He could barely hold the reins.

By the end, the sight of burned villages and dead serfs had become almost normal. The smell, however, never would.

When they finally walked through the gates into the inner bailey and were able to dismount, all he wanted to do was fall into bed and sleep for a fortnight, but there was business to attend to. Ralph called a Conseil de Duc immediately—as good as any other reason being that many of the most powerful lords were already at hand. There were terms to be hammered out with the defeated lords. They would be ordered to hand over hostages. Their castles near the border with William's own territories would be torn down rather than allow the traitors to wage war on him in the future. Guy had managed to avoid the patrols he had hastily dispatched over the country, and had returned to his castle at Brionne, or so it was reported. There would have to be an army sent to invest the castle, or bring Guy to terms. William was not interested in any terms that did not involve Guy's head on a pike, but he recognized the reality. It meant a lot of details had to be established, orders drafted, signed and sent out. Someone would need to lead the army. Someone trustworthy, experienced, of sufficient nobility. William would have to show his face at the front, but he'd done enough to prove his military prowess for the time being. They settled on William fitzOsbern, who willingly took Gallet along. The knight was proving invaluable. To think it hadn't been that long since he'd been scraping a living as a huntsman, and sleeping off drunken stupors in the stables at Valognes...

Eventually, after several hours, it was all done. It was just as well. William had been forced to jab the point of his knife into his thigh beneath the table just to stay awake. How the rest of them were able to keep their mind on the business at hand, he did not know. It would be a long time before he really felt like a Duke. But he had taken a step towards it, at least.

His councilors took their leave. Ralph remained.

"Well, Guardian. What a week it's been," William sighed. "It seems so strange. A few days ago we were fighting for our lives. Now the most important thing seems to be parchment and ink. I almost wish I knew what those squiggles mean."

"A lord's work is never done."

"I thought that council would never be done. Please tell me that's everything. I couldn't cope with another matter to be debated and decided."

"There is... one more thing, actually. A favor I would ask of you."

Good heavens. He hadn't done a thing to thank Ralph. Wasn't that what a good lord should do when he'd been through an ordeal like that? "Guardian! You have only to name it. I owe you my Duchy. Probably my life." He needed to think. What rewards should he bestow on his loyal followers? There would be land, now, that should be stripped from the rebels...

"I don't know that that's true, but your words are most welcome," Ralph said. "Most welcome. My request is this: I would like to go back to Wacey, Lord."

Was that all? No lands? Wealth? Honors? He caught the look in Ralph's eye. The baron did not want baubles. He wanted something simpler than that, and perhaps more real.

"Good idea," William replied. "I've kept you with me for too long. I didn't appreciate how much of a wrench it would be for you. You must have seen far too little of home these ten years. I was thinking only of myself, of course. Go home, re-acquaint yourself with your castle and lands. Hunt. Ride. Take as long as you like, and come back here refreshed when you've had enough of the comforts of home."

A flicker of dismay passed across Ralph's face. He looked at his feet for a moment, and back to William. Even with the ugly purple bruise still splashed around his eyes, the regret in them was obvious.

"My Lord. I am sorry... There has been no great sacrifice. My wife has been dead these four years and I have no living children. But I... I wish to return home permanently. To leave your service."

No! It could not be! The thought of acting as Duke without Ralph here to guide him... He'd only just come to appreciate everything his guardian had done, all the knowledge and experience he had. Without Ralph, William realized he would have been deprived of Normandy years ago. The words wouldn't come. He would command him to stay! Give him Rouen! Let him marry William's mother!

"But Guardian!" he spluttered when his ability to talk had more or less returned. "I need you! I've just taken the first steps. I made so many mistakes, I have so much to put right. I can't do it without you."

"You'll have to if you are to be the Duke I know you can be." Ralph smiled wanly. "I tried so hard. I've done everything I can do."

"I know. You've done so much, and I was a dreadful ingrate—never listened and didn't care. I've only started to realize how wrong I was about everything and you were right the whole time." Could a Duke fall on his knees before his vassal? William was prepared to. "I don't know how you managed to stay with me all those years. What have I done to offend you? I know I make mistakes, I know I'm foolish, but that's why I need your help."

Ralph looked away. William thought he had given offense again. Shown his weakness. Unforgiveable. But what could he do? When his guardian turned back to him, there were tears in his eyes.

"I could not leave you before," he said. "Not until you were on the right path. You must see, I can go home now because finally I see in you the true successor to your father, and his father. You don't need me any more."

Oh, Ralph. If only you knew how untrue that is.

Ralph folded his arms and leaned forward. "You must see," he said, "at the final reckoning I cannot tell you how to be Duke. You must be your own Duke. I have given you what lessons I can in good lordship, but as I said to you once before, I cannot be Duke for you. I see it this way – now you're on the right path, the longer I act as your guardian the more I will be holding you back. There must come a time when you stand up on your own. You've secured the support of your king. Won a victory on the field. The time might as well be now."

It was true—those had been worthy achievements, and they had been his achievements in no small part. But William could not help but feel they had been more the result of luck, or blind tenacity. Maybe his own abilities had played a part... and yet most of the time he felt he was riding circumstances as though they were a bolting horse and he was just trying to stay in the saddle.

Could it even be that God was on his side?

"I may not need a guardian any more, but I need advice. There's so much I don't know."

"You don't need me for that," Ralph smiled. "There are plenty of men who can give you advice. I'll help you choose them."

What if I don't like their advice? What if they can't persuade me? What am I going to do? William felt lost in a way he never had when his father had died.

CHAPTER 16

ÆLFGIFA was riding away from her childhood home for the second time in her life. This time she was with her father and the Jarl's men. Gunhild rode next to her and they were chaperoned by a ceorl their mother had assigned to them. Ælfgifa already missed Beddwen desperately, almost as badly as she ached at having left Wulfnoth behind. Yet her eyes were bright and her cheeks flushed. It was an adventure and this time she wouldn't be returning home.

Ælfgifa had had time to think about everything she had overheard while hiding under Wulfnoth's bed. Perhaps Godwin had been right and Gytha had been speaking out of the depths of her grief. Ælfgifa was more inclined to believe that Gytha had been less guarded in her anxiety over Wulfnoth and had spoken more truth than she would ever normally give voice too. Strangely, it brought Ælfgifa a measure of peace. She knew that part of her might always hunger for her mother's approval, which was irksome, but it was a part that could be shut away now. Ignored. Isolated. Ælfgifa could look at the situation objectively. She had always felt a measure of guilt that she could not love her mother as she loved her father. Gytha's admission that she had no love for Ælfgifa, while naturally painful, freed the girl to admire Gytha as a person of influence and intelligence, and rather pity her for needing her daughters to fit a certain mold. Ælfgifa would no longer twist herself in two trying to gain her mother's affection. Beyond duty and manners, she would be herself and nothing less. Others might love, hate or fear her as they would. It was a bold idea. Ælfgifa did not yet realize that survival might require a little careful play-acting. For now, it was enough that she had put her childhood behind her, in mind if not yet in body.

Spyrryd snorted and tossed his head, prancing a little. Ælfgifa smiled to herself and reined him in, keeping pace with Gunhild. Her sister was quiet but that was not unusual. Unlike Ealdgyth, Gunhild had a soft, bland prettiness, the same flaxen hair and blue eyes but muted somehow. She had none of their elder sister's fire and ambition, nor the sharp and analytical mind of Ælfgifa herself. Of the three girls, Gunhild might have made the better wife, Ælfgifa mused. She was by far the most sweet-natured and better at most domestic tasks. But Gunhild had cherished the idea of joining a religious order since she had been younger than Ælfgifa was now. A resolve only strengthened by her education at Wilton Abbey. Gunhild had proved uncharacteristically intractable and stubborn when Gytha had raised objections to her daughter joining a convent. Finally Godwin had been persuaded that a daughter who had every capacity to become an abbess in her own right was just as much a political advantage as one who was marriageable. Reluctantly, Gytha had agreed. They travelled now to attend Harold's wedding to Edith Swannesha, and would leave Gunhild at the Abbey at Cnobheresburgh on their return. Ælfgifa was unsure about herself. She thought it might be time that she was sent to Wilton Abbey herself. And yet nothing definite had been said. Her father, normally so forthright with his children, had given her an indirect answer to her question that left her with a queasy feeling of uncertainty. All Godwin would say was that she should be prepared to stay from home for some time.

Far worse than the uncertainty or the prospect of a long journey was how betrayed Wulfnoth had looked when she had crept in to see him. She had told him she was going away for a while but had not been able to say for how long or even to where. She had had to make do with telling him about Harold's wedding and then saying that she thought she was being sent to a convent for learning. Wulfnoth had not been impressed. He did not remember their brother, who was twenty years older than Wulfnoth in any case, and he did not see why Ælfgifa should have to go away to become educated when as far as he was concerned she knew everything already.

Wulfnoth had improved greatly after his fever but his lungs were still weak and he had not gained the weight he should have. He was still very thin and took cold easily. Beddwen had said she thought he would take a long time to recover fully and must be built up slowly. It made him peevish and only Ælfgifa's company helped. Not that she had been allowed to spend time with her brother—Gytha absolutely forbade it—but Beddwen and even Godwin had turned a blind eye, and she had snuck in as often as she could. It hurt to leave Wulfnoth behind but she was looking forward to seeing Harold again, and in some secret part of her soul, she was glad to be away from her mother.

An Argument of Blood

***

Harold had set up his homestead at Deorham, which, although Ælfgifa found the estate beautiful, seemed an unlikely base for a Jarl at first glance. There was time to rest before greeting her brother. Harold had led a fleet of ships sent against Magnus the Good of Norway and was even now on his way back. She was pleased to hear that he had been successful and was unharmed. She could not quite feel easy here, however. The ceorls and the serfs stared at her. Ælfgifa felt self-conscious in a way that she had not at home. For all the whisperings that the servants thought bypassed her, but of which she was so keenly aware, they were at least used to her in Godwin's household. She saw at once that it would be harder to go unseen here, where the people would actively watch for her. At least until she ceased to be a novelty. Ælfgifa doubted she would be here long enough for that.

With some relief she retired to the chamber she was to share with Gunhild. They rested, then helped each other wash and change before supper. Gunhild held out the blue gown their mother had packed for her with disdain.

"It is not that I am not grateful," she said, eyeing the embroidered bees and heather at the hem and sleeves, the silk ribbon lacing the bodice. "It is just that I wish my clothes to be plain. Mother knows this so I think she must be hoping I will catch the eye of a likely suitor here before I can escape to the convent."

Ælfgifa covered her mouth with her hand to laugh. It would be just like Gytha to do such a thing. She pulled a gown of shapeless, plain homespun from her own saddlebag and shook out the creases. "You might cover your hair,

Gunhild," she suggested. "I think it is your hair that catches the eye first. It is so light—like honey."

"You are right, Gifa," Gunhild cried. "Quick, help me to braid it up."

Wear it up? Maidens did not wear their hair up until they were married. Even then, they rarely wore their hair up if they had a good head of it. Only graying matrons or nuns hid their hair or cut it. Ælfgifa shrugged, and deftly brushed out Gunhild's waist-length tresses, nimbly plaiting it into a tight, corn-colored rope. "You look most strange," she offered, as at Gunhild's direction she coiled the heavy length about her sister's head.

"I would cut it off if it were not Harold's wedding!" Gunhild said. "Besides, I shall wear a veil as well. That will hide it."

"They will still notice your face," Ælfgifa said doubtfully. *You can't hide that,* she thought. *I've tried.*

"Let them," snorted Gunhild, more fiery than Ælfgifa had ever heard her before. "I'll wear no jewelry and if anyone asks I'll say I am bound for Cnoberesburgh Abbey. If only I had a plainer gown, I might pass for a nun already." Her eyes lit on the length of unadorned homespun that Ælfgifa had not yet donned. "Gifa! You must let me have your gown!"

Ælfgifa giggled before she saw that her sister was in earnest. "What? You can't wear that. It's not... fitting."

"You are the daughter of a Jarl too, is it more fitting for you? Come, give it to me."

"But Gunhild, what will I wear?" Ælfgifa was starting to feel panicky. She'd never seen Gunhild like this. Her sister had always seemed so biddable and quiet. And she was, until anyone tried to dress her like a doll or a Jarl's daughter, she realized. Gunhild not only had little personal vanity beyond cleanliness, she abhorred show.

"Wear the blue," Gunhild said, holding it out to Ælfgifa.

Ælfgifa stroked the nap of the fabric. So soft. A pretty color, that matched Gunhild's eyes. She sighed. "Gunhild, you are two handspans taller than me. I will be falling over it all night. I'm not sure my gown will fit you. It might be too short."

"Let me try?" Gunhild begged, dragging the homespun over her veiled head. "Well?"

It didn't look too obviously ill-fitting, Ælfgifa conceded. "Well if you wanted to look like you haven't a figure at all, you've succeeded. Will you at least use a girdle?"

"Very well, but loosely. This must have been very big on you Gifa. I'm barely showing my ankles."

Ælfgifa shrugged. "I'm a child. No point in my having gowns that fit too well," she said flatly.

Gunhild frowned a little but said nothing. *Doubtless she knows what Gytha thinks of me*, thought Ælfgifa. *It was no great secret.*

***

Harold joined them three days later bringing his lady, Edith Swannesha with him. Ælfgifa could easily see why she was known as Edith the Fair. She was probably the most beautiful woman Ælfgifa had ever seen. Tall and supple, with hair that fell thick and dark and shining to her knees. Her face was serene, her skin pale but not wan. More the color of fresh cream. Ælfgifa thought at first that Edith's eyes were black—like those of the swan she was named for—it was only later she saw that they were a deep, clear violet, darkened by the thick black lashes that surrounded them.

Wryly, Ælfgifa noted a good set of white teeth when the lady smiled at her new family. Harold had certainly made a fortuitous choice if the lady was half as wealthy as he had said. She was well educated and conversed with wit in a gentle voice. Altogether she seemed as if she ought to be in an old tale of gods and wyrms, not standing in a Jarl's rich but ultimately mundane hall, calmly conversing with guests. But as the evening meal wore on, it seemed to Ælfgifa that the lady was more human and less legend than she appeared. Her humorous comments were delivered in such a way as to avoid any offense to the target, but Ælfgifa noted a certain sharp edge to many of them. And then Edith's mouth would curl, very slightly, as if taking pleasure in her own dry wit. There was no malice in what she said. She was not cruel. Ælfgifa had the impression that this was a lady who would display no temper but of whom one should take great care not to cross. *She and Ealdgyth would not get on at all,* Ælfgifa thought, watching Edith. *Both like to have things their own way, to their own exacting standard. But my sister is hot-tempered and forthright and the Lady Edith is cool-headed and subtle.* The idea of two acknowledged beauties sharing a room and the attention therein amused Ælfgifa. She smiled, close-lipped, behind her goblet. Then blinked, startled to find Edith's clear, penetrating gaze on her.

There was no judgment in that gaze. Frank appraisal, curiosity and perhaps self-deprecation, as if she knew what Ælfgifa had been thinking. She flashed a smile at Ælfgifa, which, though brief, was also warm and genuine. Ælfgifa decided she liked Edith the Fair.

Harold was calling for a toast to his future bride. He swayed on his feet and Ælfgifa guessed that her brother had begun celebrating before his guests. When he started to wax lyrical and long on Edith's virtues, she smiled and placed a small white hand on his arm. Only Ælfgifa noticed the strength of that grip. Harold broke off, smiled down at his bride-to-be and raised his goblet. *Yes, thought Ælfgifa, Swannesha—the gentle swan—is more likely known for her wingspan and her sharp, dark eye than for any seeming gentleness. There is a swan with a sharp beak and not much gentleness if one looks below the surface! She should suit Harold very well. They look well together. Their children will be stunningly beautiful.*

She sipped the small-beer in her goblet and continued to watch. Here was a new household, with new intrigues and power plays, new secrets. *If only, Ælfgifa thought, I was staying a few more days.*

***

Ælfgifa was woken before dawn by her sister Gunhild trying to be quiet as she dressed and left for *matins. Is there anything in the world louder than someone* trying *to be quiet?* Ælfgifa thought irritably. She was still tired and the bed was warm. A blackbird began a fluting song from the branch of the cherry tree outside the window. As if the first call had been a signal, all the birds joined in. Finches. Sparrows. A wren. The pale beams of light that snuck through the shutters were a faded gold. Ælfgifa flung back the blankets and dressed.

She slipped through a door into the kitchen snagging a treat for Spyrryd on her way out. Once in the garden she lingered. There were few people about, no servants to point at her, no serfs to stare and pull their children away from her. She tilted her face up to the fresh breeze and enjoyed the morning.

Ælfgifa came across Lady Edith Swannesha in the orchard. She stopped short in the long grass, the hem of her gown soaking with dew. Should she approach her brother's bride or slip away? Edith looked up and fixed her with that penetrating gaze, then smiled. "Will you walk with me, sister? I see you are an early riser also."

"Yes, Lady," Ælfgifa said falling into step with the tall woman.

"Please, call me Edith. We will be family soon," She stooped a little to look into Ælfgifa's face. "You are not unhappy are you? You do not mind if I call you 'sister'?"

"Not at all, La- Edith," Ælfgifa corrected herself, feeling a little overawed.

Edith smiled again. "Good. I never liked my half-sisters much. Dull-witted, bland creatures. I shall be glad to have you for a sister. Harold tells me you are clever."

Ælfgifa wasn't sure what to say to this. "You're very kind, Lady Edith."

"Cautious as well," Edith replied with a laugh. "You are quiet, Gifa—do you mind me calling you Gifa? When Harold speaks of you, it is what he calls you and now I think of you the same way—well then, Gifa, you are very quiet and Harold says you are not shy, only watchful. Have I made you uncomfortable?" She looked genuinely anxious for a moment.

"No, La- Edith, it is only that I wonder what my brother can have told you? I have seen him but little these last years," Ælfgifa said a little anxiously.

"Harold said that you had the most perfect disguise of anyone in England. That you looked like a child but you had the designing mind of a warlord's advisor or a sage." Edith grinned. "He may also have mentioned that you were an adept little spy as well."

Ælfgifa flushed. It wasn't kind of Harold to malign her behind her back like that.

Edith grew sober, her mirth faded. "Truly, he meant it as a compliment. Harold is quick of wits himself but he said he could scarce keep up with you."

"That last is an exaggeration, I think!" Ælfgifa scoffed.

"Not much of one," Edith promised. "Now, I hope this will not offend you, sister, but I could not help but notice that you are in need of a new gown. I'm sure your mother was very busy or doubtless she would have seen to it."

Heavens, Ælfgifa thought, *am I to be surrounded by intelligent women who relentlessly pursue matters of dress to the exclusion of all else?* Then she felt annoyed and a little ashamed of herself. Edith was being very kind, after all.

"I have one which I think will suit you exactly. I wore it when I was a girl but it would not fit me now," Edith went on.

"You are very good, Lady Edith," Ælfgifa murmured. Whether the dress looked well or not, Ælfgifa knew *she* would not. But it was a gesture of friendship and Ælfgifa was inclined to take it as such. A cool, clear part of her seemed to take a step back, watching Edith and assessing her motives. Did she think Ælfgifa a favorite of Harold's? Did she hope to curry favor with him by making a pet of Ælfgifa? Madness. Anyone with half Edith's appeal and wealth could hardly be in need of means to secure her husband's affections. Perhaps it was genuine kindness.

"Will the priest be coming from Northwic, Edith, or will you have your household priest perform the ceremony?" Ælfgifa said by way of changing the subject.

"The priest?" Edith's fine dark brows drew together in puzzlement.

"For the wedding?" Ælfgifa replied.

"Oh! No, we shall not need a priest for that," Edith laughed. "It is not a *Christiano* ceremony but a *Daneco* one."

"In the Danish style?" Ælfgifa confirmed, looking puzzled in turn. "La- er Edith? I hope you will not take this amiss but I thought the Roman church did not recognize such a union?"

"Nor do they," Edith smirked. "If I cared what some prating fool in a white dress, lying on more gold than the rest of Christendom put together thought of me, then I should be greatly cast down! As it is, a *more Daneco* match suits us much better."

"I'm not sure I really understand the difference," Ælfgifa confessed.

Edith smiled. "If Harold were to marry me *in Christiano*, he could not then put me aside save in a case of infidelity. And he would need the Pope's approval to do so. What if I should prove barren? I've no reason to think I will, but it is a consideration. Marrying, or handfasting under Danelaw allows Harold to take a second wife if need be."

If Ælfgifa had been confused before, she was bewildered now. "But what would happen to you?"

Edith shrugged, a pretty movement that made her loose hair ripple. "I would be put away for a time. Run a lesser estate perhaps, foster his cousins or perhaps some of his illegitimate issue."

Ælfgifa had no silly, romantic illusions about marriage but to hear Edith's casual discussion still shocked her. "And this sits well with you, Lady?"

"Edith! And yes. It was my idea in fact," she gave Ælfgifa that wry little crook of her mouth that meant she had done something clever. "Can you see no other advantage in such a match, Gifa?"

Why, she is testing me, Ælfgifa thought. "Harold would have secured an alliance with your family and with your ceorls and thagns. Valuable, since Harold is new to these lands while you have grown up here." Ælfgifa met Edith's gaze steadily and continued, all the game pieces revealing themselves on the board in her mind. "Harold is valuable to you for in one stroke you become the countess of East Anglia, which increases your already vast holdings as well as gaining you political power and influence. In England, Harold would be considered both wed and available. Your children will be considered legitimate. Abroad my brother would be known to have an official concubine. In either matter he would be considered an eligible match, should the need arise for an alliance with another house or even a kingdom." She half-smiled at Edith. "You both drink beer and store it for winter, Lady. It is cleverly done. And of course *you* need fear no competition for my brother's affections even if he were to wed another."

"Very good, Gifa," Edith breathed. "How old are you, may I ask?"

"Near eleven."

"I think Harold is right. You will be formidable someday." Edith paused pensively. "Will you believe me when I tell you that for all the advantages on both sides, for all the power and influence, that I esteem and respect your brother? That he has a great hold upon my affections?"

"Yes, Lady Edith," Ælfgifa said. "For if you did not care for Harold, you would have told me so."

***

No one saw Ælfgifa slip into one of the smaller receiving rooms. They were an oddity. Halls and gathering areas tended to be large and rounded, or long and rectangular. Smaller apartments that didn't have a specific purpose were unusual. Beddwen had entertained her with stories about secret passageways and concealed entrances in the great halls of the Kings of Cymru. Dinefwr or Rhosyr, perhaps. Some were even built of stone which seemed fantastical. Few buildings were made of stone unless they were churches or monasteries. Timber was cheaper, quicker and required less skill and time. Still, despite the strangeness of this chamber, with its three deeply recessed windows, each hiding a broad wooden bench behind a finely embroidered curtain, Ælfgifa had come here often in the last few days. It was hard to find anywhere to be alone in this household and the constant staring and murmurs of serfs and ceorls grated on her nerves. She had noticed that this chamber was rarely used and it had become a favorite retreat.

She settled herself in the window seat furthest from the door, allowing the embroidered curtain to swing partially closed. The light was good and she had brought some embroidery of her own to do. There was a particularly cunning stitch used on the birds depicted in the curtains that she wanted to try. Ælfgifa was feeling the strain of constantly being the source of attention that was not especially welcome or kindly. Harold and Edith had been handfasted yesterday. Unlike Edward's wedding to Ealdgyth, the ceremony had been short and heartfelt. A length of cloth embroidered with the signs of both their houses had been wrapped around their joined hands and circlets of greenery placed on their heads. Hawthorn and apple blossom for Edith, oak and holly for Harold. The celebration that came after had been anything but short, and Ælfgifa had wanted to hide long before it was polite to leave. Her head throbbed with the aftermath of tension. Calligraphy or Latin would be too difficult today. There was little to do in the household's still room—a ceorl always shooed her out and told her to play elsewhere anyway—and she desperately wanted to be alone. She tucked her feet up under her skirts on the bench and unfolded her needlework.

The door of the chamber creaked open, making her jump. She heard her father's voice:

"...had thought to speak to you before this, Harold, Lady Edith, but there was little opportunity." Godwin sounded almost diffident.

Ælfgifa could imagine a look being exchanged between her brother and his wife. Honorable behavior demanded that Ælfgifa declare herself, but listening unseen had become a habit for her.

"It is about your sister," Godwin said, coming to the point. "She cannot stay at home any longer. I am asking you to take her into your household."

There was a long, heavy silence in which Ælfgifa found herself hot with mortification.

"She is of an age for fostering, broadening her understanding," Godwin went on. "Indeed perhaps I should have sent her from home before this..." This last seemed more to himself than to Harold or Edith.

"Might I ask why now is such a meet time for so great a change?" Lady Edith asked, an almost undetectable hint of criticism in her sweet voice.

Harold was less delicate. "This is Gytha's doing." He sounded angry but Ælfgifa could not tell at whom. "If she is of an age for learning, is she not of an age to go to Wilton as Ealdgyth did?"

Godwin sighed. "I would not send her to a convent. Or indeed anywhere she will be unhappy."

"But surely if it is just for a few years while she gains learning..." Harold began.

"You do not anticipate Gifa's return to your household, do you my lord?" Edith said softly. "You would send her to Wilton readily for learning but you think her change of abode permanent."

"You are perceptive, daughter-in-law," Godwin said. "I fear that shutting Blackbird up in a convent will have one of two outcomes. She will be bored—she already knows more than many who would be teaching her, a sure way to become unpopular and subsequently miserable."

"And the second?" Harold asked, voice deceptively bland.

171

"That she would grow to love a convent's walls. The rigors and routines. She might not want to leave," Godwin sighed. "I am about to give one child to the church. I will not give my Blackbird also."

"What if Gifa wanted it?" Harold said.

"Then let her tell me so when she is fifteen and has lived in the world for a time." Godwin sounded irritated now. "Will you have your kin here or no? She is unprepossessing to say the least, but she is biddable, good with children and not unskilled. You might in time find a husband for her, who would value her, Lady Edith."

Behind the curtain, Ælfgifa burned with humiliation. *No one wants me*, she thought. *My mother wants to be rid of me and has made my father agree.* Harold would not want an uncanny child like her when he was but newly wed. Edith may be kind but doubtless she had hardly thought of her husband's malformed younger sister as being a permanent addition to her household.

"That is as may be, my lord, but I doubt I will find a man who could deserve Gifa." Edith had a slight smile in her voice. There was a barb for Godwin in her words but it was hard to discern. "Well, I would gladly have Ælfgifa here. She is refreshing company. You do not object, husband?"

"No, I will be happy to see her here, especially if it pleases you." The smile was in Harold's voice now.

"Then it is settled," Godwin said, sounding relieved. "I could take a cup of ale."

"Do," said Edith. "And then you must tell my new sister her fate!" She laughed a little and the two men uncomprehendingly joined in.

Ælfgifa stood clutching the curtain for a long time afterwards, her mind whirling and a sick feeling of dislocation in her belly.

CHAPTER 17

AS the Eastern sky began to pale, a thin trail of smoke could be seen forming a vertical scar across its face. William exchanged a look with his guards, and they increased their pace. As they arrived outside the camp, they were challenged by a man who sounded terrified. William had to lower his hood to prove his identity. They drew closer. Part of the wooden rampart was black and issuing smoke, with a shattered breach gaping at its center. There were bodies lying in the mud. The bulk of Brionne castle loomed in the distance, solid, impassive, insulting.

The shaken soldiers manning the perimeter eventually managed to impart that fitzOsbern was out checking the pickets, and Roger de Beaumont had been left in charge of the camp. William found him trying to steady the men and supervise repairs to the fence. There were cinders in his beard and mud on his boots, no doubt from the water they'd had to bring up from the river to put the fire out. William was already ankle-deep in it.

"If I might just finish with the defenses here, my Lord," Beaumont said ruefully, "and I'll take you to see what we're up against."

As they left to see where Guy was holed up, Beaumont explained that there had been occasional raids, just pinprick efforts, in the previous months, but last night the Normans had suffered a major assault. The enemy had attacked in numbers, and burned everything they could get a torch to. "We felt as though we were the ones under siege," Beaumont admitted, ruefully. "Well, here it is—Brionne castle."

William had to admit, it was a formidable place to try and outlast your enemy. Falaise was by no means insecure but if it had half the natural defenses that the castle of Brionne enjoyed, he could be secure as Duke there should all of Normandy rise up against him. For a time, at any rate. Beaumont had brought him closest to the walls to the South bank of the Risle, no doubt to impress him with Brionne's particular qualities.

Well, he was impressed.

The castle was built on a small island in the river. Just across the bank from where they stood, the South flank of the islet rose almost vertically from the stream for more than twenty pieds, and the curtain wall right at its top added almost the same. The river ran fast and deep, as the Orme had back in the Spring. And while at Val es Dunes the rains swelling the rivers had cemented Guy's defeat, here they aided his defense.

"We should move away, Sire," Beaumont said. "We're within range of their archers."

"All right." William took once last look at the scene, entertaining a vain hope that a weakness would present itself.

"They've been saving their arrows," Beaumont added as they rode away for the Norman camp. "But if they realized it was you scouting their walls it would probably be worth taking a pot-shot or two."

"How many men did you lose last night?" he asked.

"Twenty."

"In one assault? That's not very encouraging. Did we get any of theirs?"

"No, Lord."

Saint Peter's cock! "What have you done to prevent another occurrence?"

"Increased the pickets, and moved them further from the camp. The trouble is, Guy's men know the territory here with their eyes closed. It's proved hard to prevent them from finding weaknesses in our perimeter. We're going to start building a ditch later."

"Don't," William said. "I don't like where the camp is situated. I think we can do better." He stopped his horse and surveyed the scene – the river curving around, skirting the open lands that had been cleared assiduously of trees. The wall up at the top of the bank. There did not appear to be a stone keep, at least, but that did not matter. It would take more men than he had to storm that wall, and so very easy to run out of them before it had been breached. Was it worth ordering the camp moved back to the tree line? It would be easier to defend. No, too easy to ambush.

"We think they may have brought supplies into the castle by boat while the attack was taking place," Beaumont added. "They seemed to pull back as one on a signal from the castle. We tried to pursue, but they covered us from the walls. I think we must have been nicely silhouetted against the flames for their archers."

For a moment, anger pulsed through William's chest and he had to restrain himself from bellowing into the air. He had won on the field, and now to be subjected to this! If they would only come out and fight he would show them what honor meant.

"Here's what we'll do," William said, after he had sketched it out in his mind. "Build two earthworks—one upstream on the North bank, the other downstream on the South bank."

"Hmm. It will mean splitting our forces, and we don't have that many men to begin with."

"Well, the curve of the river means we can position the earthworks in line of sight, so you can signal between them. You can cover the approaches from both sides, and both banks. And I'll send more men. Think it through and let me know how many you'll need."

"Yes, my Lord."

"Finish the fortifications first, then palisade them. You aren't short of wood, at least. If Guy can shut himself up in his fastness, so can we, and we can cut off his supplies. At least you can mount regular armed patrols without them being too far from safety should Guy decide to try a sally."

"Very good my Lord."

"I think I'll stay until you're established. Then take Fitz and Gallet back with me to Falaise, if you can spare them."

"Hmm. Gallet's a useful fellow to have around, but once we're dug in we should be all right. And you know Fitz, he's not entirely useless in the field, but he does miss the comforts of home."

Don't we all, William thought. "It's going to be a long haul here, I fear. There will be no way to actually assault the

177

castle. Our main hope lies in preventing relief from reaching Guy, and stopping him escaping to somewhere beyond our reach. We'll get him. We just need to be patient."

"Yes, Lord."

William sighed. "Just once, it would be nice to attack someone who isn't up a hill."

***

For a second time, William experienced mixed feelings on seeing the bulk of Falaise castle rising above the gently undulating fields of Normandy. It had been a long six months since the battle at Val es Dunes. So much had happened, and so little had changed. A month he'd spent with the army encamped around Guy's castle, but Guy had proved better provisioned than anyone realized.

William had hoped that some opening would present itself for an attack, that some idea would come to him as it had facing the plain at Val es Dunes. But good generalship was, it seemed, a matter of more than just the occasional timely revelation. When the earthworks were built, he and his commanders had discussed a dozen different schemes for an attack, none of which had much chance of success without incurring horrific losses. Mining the walls might take years. They had attempted to open negotiations, but Guy declined every offer that was made, throwing in a few more choice assessments of William's parentage. Reluctantly, William decided to return to Falaise, bringing fitzOsbern and Gallet back with him. They left Beaumont in charge of the besieging garrison, half hoping that his rapidly growing beard would scare the traitors out, and rode for home. Nothing had been achieved, at great effort and expense. At least incomes were starting to arrive from Upper Normandy again.

He knew, however, that on his return to Falaise, the question of justice regarding the rebels would arise once more. William would very much have liked to submit all the treacherous barons and their supporters to his justice, but unfortunately, only Grimoult du Plessis was available. Given that the early attempts to dislodge Guy had proved fruitless, Neel was out of reach in England, and the others were dead, it would have to do.

After dealing with the immediate business that had been waiting for his return—petty disputes between vassals, late taxes, envoys bringing messages of respect and kinship from other Lords, and a thousand and one other things—he travelled with his court to Rouen, where Grimoult had been imprisoned. It would mean spending Christmas in Rouen, and far too much of his uncle, Mauger. Such were the penalties of lordship.

The hall was crowded for Grimoult's trial with nobles, knights and freemen. As if Mauger wasn't enough, his brother, William of Arques had turned out. William did not need reminding that his other uncle had tried to have him declared ineligible to inherit the Duchy when his father had died. William smiled pleasantly at his uncle and ground his teeth. The nobles must expect Grimoult's trial to be high entertainment.

Even this, though, would be an anti-climax – a messenger came in just before the prisoner was due to enter and told William that du Plessis confessed to everything. The trial would just decide what happened to him and his estates. William was placed in a stout chair in front of the bench containing his councilors and retinue, feeling horribly exposed.

"Bring in the Baron."

The doors were thrown open and the prisoner entered, guards before and behind. For a moment, William was about to ask who the old man was who had been brought before him, and where was the traitor lord. The prisoner was not bound or chained, but his movements, stiff and uncertain, suggested he had not long been out of shackles. He was thinner than the Grimoult William remembered, and the pale, hollow face was not the broad red visage he expected to see. The man who was led out had iron-gray hair, not Grimoult's black curls. It had only been six months since the battle, and yet Grimoult might have aged fifteen years. It was only when the prisoner looked up at him that William recognized the lord—the hatred shining in those eyes could belong to no-one else.

"Grimoult de Plessis," William said. "You stand accused of bearing arms against your sworn lord. Of seeking to overthrow him and replacing him with another. Of... oh, we all know what you did. Do you deny this?"

"No. Lord. I have confessed all my... *transgressions*." Grimoult's voice was quiet. Halting. Dripping with poison.

"Good. And will you name those who acted with you?"

"Yes. My Lord. They are Guy of Burgundy. Neel, Viscount of Cotentin. Renulf, Viscount of Bessin. Hammond, Baron of Creully..." He named a few others. Knights in his households of the barons. He dropped in the name of Bardon, who William had killed, which made William shuffle uncomfortably, but the list went on and he had almost stopped listening when Grimoult added "Salle, son of Huon de Gornai, Knight."

"He lies!" A young man near the back of the hall was on his feet. He turned to William. "I am loyal to you, My Lord! I had no part in the attempt on your life, nor the revolt. I was here in Rouen!"

"I speak the truth," Grimoult said, his gaze flicking to William's left for several moments.

Look at me, damn you. "What part do you claim he had in the affair?"

"He planned with us to come to Valognes and there to murder you." That glance to the left again. "He fought with us at Val es Dunes and struck down many a Norman knight."

"None of it true, my Lord!" Salle shouted. "I swear it!"

"You would swear an oath that you were not involved?" William asked.

"I swear upon the Holy Bible, all the Saints of Bayeux and the relics of the faith that I speak the truth!" Grimoult shouted, before Salle had a chance to respond.

An expression of horror passed across Salle's face. He took a gulp of air, then sat. Grimoult may have sentenced him to death. No-one would swear such a powerful oath without good reason, surely? Salle simply shook his head.

"Is there anyone here who can attest to your accusation?" William asked Grimoult.

"I need no witnesses," Grimoult said, his voice cracking. "I have sworn a sacred oath."

You swore an oath to support your lord and not try to kill him. To uphold the law and act with honor. What difference do a few bits of bone and wood make? "Is there anyone who can attest to Salle being in Rouen when the traitors came to take my life? Or fought against their lord and king at Val es Dunes?"

Salle looked around the hall hopefully, but no-one stood or spoke up. He slumped further in his seat.

"Bring Salle up," William said. "I'd like to hear what he has to say." He turned to the bench behind him, looking for Gallet. Fortunately, the knight was there. William gestured him forward.

"My Lord?"

"Do you recognize this Salle from the stables that night?"

Gallet studied the youth, cocking his head to one side. "No," he said eventually, "but it was dark, and I was pissed as a newt. I wouldn't like to swear to it."

"Really? Everyone else seems desperate to swear to something today."

Gallet laughed. "I wouldn't want God to strike me down. He's managed to miss me so far, but I don't want to push matters."

"No. All right then. I thank you."

Gallet returned to his seat. Salle had been led before him. His expression was alternating between shocked disbelief and venom directed at Grimoult.

"Do you deny the accusation?" William asked.

"I do, My Lord, most fervently, I do."

"Do you know why Grimoult might choose to bear false witness against you?"

"My Lord!-" Grimoult cried, but was silenced by a look from William.

"No, Sire," said Salle. "But it is a monstrous falsehood. I..." his voice wavered. "I insist it is withdrawn."

"Grimoult?"

"I speak truth," Grimoult said, speaking to the floor.

Great God, will you not look at me! William sighed. An intractable problem. If only Ralph were here. He'd know what to do. At that moment, he wanted nothing more than to cast off the responsibilities of lordship and go hunting. But those times were all gone. He had no-one to make those decisions for him any more. *He had never felt lonelier. A mote, spinning through the empty cosmos. For what does a Duke have that a common man does not, save ceremony?*

Choices. No, there was no time for self-pity or indecision. What would he do if he were falsely accused? Fight with every last drop of his spirit to prove it otherwise. "Salle, will you stake your life that you are telling the truth?"

"I will, Lord." Not a hint of a hesitation. Good.

"And you, Grimoult?"

The baron raised his eyebrows for a moment, that flick of a glance to one side again. "Yes, Lord."

"Then it is settled. A trial by combat. Tomorrow morning."

"Thankyou Lord!" Salle bowed. He looked at Grimoult, removed his glove, and tossed it at the baron's feet.

Grimoult did nothing, said nothing, but all the hatred seemed to have disappeared from his eyes. They had taken on a haunted look. Slowly, he bent down and, with some difficulty, picked up the glove.

"Very well. Have Grimoult taken to comfortable lodgings tonight and give him what he needs to prepare for his trial."

There was a sound of a throat being cleared behind him. "Ah, Duke William, is it not customary to ask for any pleas in support of the accused?" The oleaginous tones of Bishop Mauger.

William turned. He had not forgotten the bishop's double dealing, and having to drag him to Poissy just to keep an eye on him. What was he playing at now? He did not like the look on Mauger's face at all, though that was nothing new. Arques just sat there next to him as if this was all in a day's work. "The accused has confessed," William sighed. "And tomorrow he will face trial by combat. Do you propose to fight in his stead?"

There was a ripple of laughter from those nearby.

"But when it comes to passing sentence, Sire. It is customary that the court hears testimony in the prisoner's favor, if there is anyone to give it."

William glanced at Lanfranc, who nodded.

"And is there? Anyone to speak up for Grimoult?"

"I know the accused, Sire," Mauger said, "and would consider it my Christian duty to tell the court of his virtues."

What a surprise. William sighed. "Very well." He gestured to Mauger to take the floor.

The bishop delivered such a convoluted and elaborate encomium to Grimoult that even the baron himself must have wondered what, or indeed, who, the cleric was talking about. His honor and truthfulness were praised to the skies, as was his willingness to serve, his only failing in Mauger's eyes being that he had proved too trusting of unscrupulous wretches who had poisoned his unsuspecting soul against his liege lord. After what seemed like hours, the bishop concluded, "...and I should add that the accused, in all Christian goodness, has agreed that if he is spared and his lands returned to him, subject to justifiable penalties to the Duchy, of course, he will give over two hundred arpents of land with all its incomes to the Church, and to have two new churches built. Such a gesture of faith should not be rejected, my Lord."

So that was it. Mauger was trying to stitch things up with Grimoult, was he?

"...And therefore, my Lord, I see no reason why the accused should suffer the indignity of having his honor impugned with this trial by combat. Have mercy on your vassal, Duke William, and he shall be a good servant to you all your days."

William looked at Lanfranc, who simply shrugged. Time to play the Duke. William raised his chin and pushed his shoulders back. "Your... kindness to Grimoult does you credit, Your Excellency. but I have two subjects before me, and one of them is guilty of treason, for he is prepared to falsely swear before his lord. In spite of your... excellent arguments, which I take full regard of, Grimoult is an avowed traitor. I cannot arrest a knight on his word alone, when that knight is also willing to swear to his innocence and defend it with his life. There is no other way for it."

"My Lord!" Mauger's voice had taken on an edge. "Have the prisoner transferred to my care. I will stand for his good behavior." And then, almost sharply, "I am the Archbishop or Rouen!"

And I am your Duke! William thought. "Either he withdraws his accusation or he fights tomorrow. I'm sorry, Excellency, but the law is clear."

A look of such fury crossed the bishop's face that William almost stood and struck him. But that would not be a seemly action for a Duke.

Oh, Guardian, why must you leave me with all this still to deal with?

A horrible realization struck William just then, like a blow to the stomach. This was what it must always be like.

But Ralph trusted him to deal with it. His father had seen something worthy in him to nominate him as his successor. And he was in no mood to let anyone down again. It wasn't as though anyone was arming in the stables to come and kill him, or charging at him with a lance.

No, he would deal with this, and deal with it well. Now he thought of it, trial by combat was an excellent way to manage disputes by his vassals. A shame he hadn't thought of it earlier. He called William fitzOsbern to him, and they went over the details for the combat the following morning. A squire would be needed for Grimoult, and it wouldn't be easy finding someone who wanted to associate themselves with a known traitor. Perhaps William of Arques would have someone in his retinue who could fulfil the task. He and his brother Mauger seemed to be on good terms these days. They sent a request to the Count.

FitzOsbern suggested shields and staves rather than swords. William agreed. There was no sense in either of them actually dying over it. Given the state Grimoult was in, William could not see that he had much of a chance of victory, but what he lacked in strength he might well make up in guile. In any event, it was highly unlikely he could manage a lance in his condition, and though he might manage a stroke or two with a sword, William did not think that he could keep up with even the shortest bout. Even in his weakened state, Grimoult should be able to hold a staff, though.

"Shall I tell the accused?" FitzOsbern asked. "Let them prepare at least."

"No," William answered. "I want Grimoult to sweat a bit first." Naturally, as Duke he was supposed to be neutral, though even if he had taken steps to ensure du Plessis came out of the bout alive, it did not mean he wished the baron well. In fact, he could not help hoping Salle won. It was not simply that Grimoult had tried to kill and then overthrow him, though that was undoubtedly part of it. He sensed that Salle was being used as a piece in someone else's games, and the thought unsettled him. A young squire who might end up dead before he came into his prime because of the machinations of calculating men.

There was more than he might have thought to arranging a simple combat between two men, and by the time all the arrangements had been made and decided upon, he was exhausted. William passed the last instructions to Bourdas and decided to retire to bed. Combat was to begin shortly after first light, and he wanted a good night's sleep. But the trial of Grimoult and the odd business with Salle kept swirling around his head. No sooner had he put it aside than some new suspicion crowded in. It seemed like hours before unconsciousness finally claimed him.

He swum out of sleep to the sounds of barrels knocked over and distant thunder. The sound repeated, and again. There must be a lot of barrels. And a storm. He tried to plunge back into sleep again, but something kept pulling him back. The sense of something being out of place grew into irritation, then a realization. Hadn't he only just got to sleep? There was something important to do early tomorrow. But then having done so, could not sleep for hours. And now this.

Not barrels. Not thunder. Someone was banging on the door. He started. Valognes was not so very long ago.

"What is it?" he growled, trying not to sound thick with stupor.

"My Lord," Bourdas called softly from outside the chamber. "It's Grimoult. He wants to speak to you."

"Now? Why?" Why could it possibly not wait until morning? "Didn't he say everything he had to in the trial?"

"I'm sorry, Lord, but he insists. He says he wants to make further confessions and give further names."

William buried his head in the already-cooling sheets for a moment. "I'll speak to him in the morning."

Bourdas paused, looked awkward. "There may not be the chance in the morning, Sire."

William sat up, now fully awake. "What do you mean?"

"He may not last the night. A physician has been attending to him, on my authority, my Lord, but he is declining quickly."

"Oh. All right, bring him to me."

"I fear he is not capable of coming here, Lord."

William dressed hurriedly and they rushed over to the knights' quarters, where Grimoult had been placed for the night. All feared the baron was dying. From what William could tell from Bourdas and the guards' garbled explanations on the way over, he had taken ill about an hour after nightfall, seemingly unable to stand and complaining of stomach cramps. Initially, no-one had done anything. They thought he was trying to get out of the trial by combat the next day, or perhaps play for time. Then he'd started coughing up blood. They'd called a physician from the abbey, who had been unable to do anything. He had weakened quickly, and then insisted on seeing William, claiming to have further names, but would only confess them to the Duke himself.

William was led into the chamber. "Careful, Lord," said a robed figure by the bed. The physician, a hospitaler from the abbey. "It could be a pestilence. I wouldn't come too close if I were you." At that moment, an astringent scent hit the back of William's throat. He felt the bile rising and choked it down again. Having made itself known, the aroma seemed to fill the room like smoke.

It was clear from where William stood by the door that Grimoult was dead. His chin, neck and chest were soaked in something almost black. His eyes were open and staring at the ceiling. His face was contorted into a form that resembled a carved stone grotesque. The muscles stood out so much, and the skin seemed so hard upon them, that the baron might have been petrified. William suppressed an involuntary shudder. It was then that he noticed that du Plessis was still chained, despite his orders.

"There was nothing I could do," the hospitaler said. "Soon after I arrived he began coughing up blood. Whatever I gave him, he just threw up again, then started vomiting blood. He called for you. And then he appeared to be calling for the Archbishop."

"What did he say?"

"Just 'Mauger, Mauger'."

"Hmm. Is anyone else sick?"

"No, my Lord."

"And what, in your opinion, killed him?"

"Well, there are sicknesses that might kill a man in such a fashion. I've seen them in the Holy Land, Sire. But never so quickly. I suppose he was weakened from his imprisonment..."

"...But you do not think this is what killed him?"

His lips pursed, and he hesitated. "My suspicion, Sire, is poison."

"Poison?" William heard an edge of hysteria in his voice that he had not intended. "He was poisoned in my castle? How?"

"We could ask Hugo of Reviers," Bourdas said.

"Who?"

"A knight, my lord?"

"Not one of my acquaintance," William frowned. He knew the Calvados district reasonably well after making a study of it, following Grimoult's treachery. He hadn't come across a Hugo of Reviers at all. "Why ask him, anyway?"

Bourdas hesitated, perhaps sensing that more was wrong than he had realized. "Well, according to the guards he came to see Grimoult earlier this evening. Around the time he was brought his food."

"On whose authority?"

"Er, on yours, my Lord. He had a warrant apparently signed by you."

William uttered an involuntary noise in his throat. "I signed no such warrant. When was he here? How long was he with Grimoult? Did anyone hear the matter they discussed?"

No-one seemed quite sure, although it seemed that Hugo had not been with Grimoult for long. There had been a brief conversation, but no-one had heard the detail – Hugo had insisted that the guards withdraw, and no-one had thought to question it.

William quickly issued orders to have the castle sealed, no-one to leave without his direct permission, and the grounds to be searched for the mysterious 'Hugo'. It was too late, of course. The assassin—as it was now clear the 'knight' actually was—had had over an hour to get out, and William had no reason whatsoever to suppose that he would have lingered after secretly administering the poison to Grimoult. Earlier in the evening, orders to replace Grimoult's irons had been received, again, supposedly bearing William's own mark. And now, no-one could find the keys to remove them. Grimoult, by all indications the instigator of the attempt on his life and the subsequent insurrection, was dead. And yet William could feel no satisfaction whatsoever. He had been cheated of justice. The baron had presented a pathetic figure at the end. Faintly ridiculous in his irons that he could not be released from. It was a poor end, and after everything, he did not wish that on his former enemy.

But there was more. There was a traitor in his castle. Possibly even another conspiracy. Someone who had the ability to trick his guards and present orders as though he had dictated them himself. Someone who had wanted Grimoult dead before the trial by combat could take place. Before he could name further parties. After everything he had been through, the conspiracy was not defeated yet.

Once again, he was a mote, tumbling through empty space, in darkness, at constant risk of simply being blown into eternal nothingness. The walls began to topple, and he had to put a hand out to steady himself. He would have to find his way, and quickly, or everything he had fought for might be lost in the blink of an eye. The fight was not over.

CHAPTER 18

ÆLFGIFA had gradually become less of an oddity at Deorham. She had seen her father but once since he had left her in her brother's care, but over time she had carved out a place for herself in Harold's household. A strange position perhaps but one that made use of her unique talents. There had been no mention of a possible husband for her and Ælfgifa had not brought it up. She had heard one of the ceorls, a seamstress, saying to her friend that their lord's daughter was no more improved in appearance at thirteen than she had been at ten. The comment had stung and Ælfgifa had been at great pains to hide it. She knew that if Edith were to hear such talk, her sister-in-law, would, with that cold fury she was capable of, order the women to undertake several years' worth of mending. It touched Ælfgifa that Edith's offer of friendship had proved genuine. All the same, the gossips had only said what was true and Ælfgifa did not need enemies. Enemies paid attention to you. Ælfgifa had become even more accomplished at coming and going unseen. Better still, people often assumed at first glance that she was simple as well as deformed, uttering things in her hearing that they would not dream of saying otherwise.

For all her affection, Ælfgifa knew that Edith in particular valued this skill. The household had quickly fallen in line under Edith's management and the rumor, muttered amongst the serfs and ceorls and even amongst some of the thagns, was that their countess had been blessed with the Sight. There was no event so small that the Lady Edith did not know of it, no action taken that she was not aware of. And none of those who muttered such rumors ever suspected that intelligence came to Edith by mundane means. Ælfgifa had stifled a smile as she reported that particular tidbit to Edith. They had been sitting privately, embroidering an altar cloth, and Edith had fallen into gales of laughter as Ælfgifa watched her, ruefully amused. Wiping her eyes, Edith had smiled and said that she would not disabuse her people of the notion, since of course they knew her for a good Christian woman. Ælfgifa hardly needed to be told why. A woman with good intelligence and the right information could, by clever guesswork and a knowledge of others' natures, make it seem as if she did indeed have some supernatural gift. Since Edith used any intelligence Ælfgifa gathered to ensure the smooth running of the household and estate, to break up disputes before they started and to further her and Harold's interests, Ælfgifa saw no reason not to keep her informed.

There were times now when Harold asked her to sit unobtrusively in a corner while he and Edith spoke with a thagn or gave some other audience. Several times now, she had been present at *Things*—those meetings held at every turning of the moon, where any person, serf, ceorl, thagn, might approach their lord with a problem or a complaint. Such meetings were also where Harold meted out judgment to those who needed disputes settled or to those individuals who had transgressed. Afterwards, Harold always asked for her impressions. While he did not always share her viewpoint, Ælfgifa felt sure that it was not merely to flatter her vanity that she was asked. Edith had often said that Ælfgifa had a way at seeing all angles of a problem and often came to the most just or logical conclusion, even if that solution could not be applied due to certain other factors.

This day's *Thing* had a more serious bent. Harold was adjudicating a case where one of his wealthier thagns, Ulfric, stood accused of raping Nessa, a fifteen-year-old Pretani ceorl, one of Edith's own handmaids. There was no doubting the evidence arraigned against the man. Nessa had been badly beaten at the time and now the household midwife had confirmed that the girl was pregnant. The question was what to do with Ulfric.

In her corner, Ælfgifa plied her needle, seemingly oblivious to the proceedings. All the while, she watched the trial out of the corner of her eye. Even if Ulfric had not been a bully and a rapist, she would have disliked him. He was a bluff, lazy man, perpetually red-faced and sweating, smelling strongly of leeks. She had brought reports of his cruelty towards his serfs to Edith several times. Ælfgifa glanced at Edith now. Her sister-in-law was white with fury, her lips pressed so tightly together that they were nearly invisible. One of her graceful hands rested on the swell of her belly showing through her gown. Ælfgifa would be an aunt soon.

"Didn't do nothing the girl didn't ask for," Ulfric was saying, loud and belligerent. "She speaks out now because there's a bastard in her belly-"

"Enough," Edith said, her voice devoid of all its customary warmth. "You have spoken your piece, Ulfric. The council has found you guilty. We have moved on to the verdict. Do you be silent, or must you be muzzled like a dog?"

Harold glanced at his wife but did not raise any objections to her words. Ælfgifa watched as he gave a short nod and turned to the men charged with guarding Ulfric. "See that he does not leave. I will take a moment to review the case in private."

Ælfgifa slipped out of the room before Harold finished speaking. She knew she would be required and it was less noticeable if she went now. She poured wine into five goblets set on a table in the lesser audience chamber and looked up as Edith came in, resting a hand on Harold's arm. Brother Ashwine followed him and behind the tall, gray-haired clergyman, came Harold and Ælfgifa's cousin, Beorn. A small handful of those truly in the Jarl's confidence for such a large household.

Beorn eyed Ælfgifa as if he did not know what to make of her, just as he always did. *I might be a great hound that walked upright and spoke a human tongue, the way he looks*, she thought, keeping her expression bland.

Harold lifted a goblet. "Well I'm of a mind to thrash the man no matter what the outcome. I will hear your thoughts first."

Ashwine drank from his own goblet. "He has too much land and too many ceorls under his command. His lands are at the reaches of your rule, my Lord. It is difficult to watch what he does on his own land."

"Land he holds in trust from me," Harold growled.

"Surely he must pay the standard fine?" Beorn said. "What else can be done?"

"I am sure he assumed that would be his sole punishment when he agreed to come with my husband's men," Edith said, tone unreadable. "And when you announce his punishment doubtless he will say 'pay it and be damned, I'll hear no more of the chit!' A fine piece of respect from a thagn who owes you fealty."

"What would you have me do?" Harold demanded. "Had he raped a serf we might have raised the fine to a level where even Ulfric would feel the pinch. As it is, the girl's father is dead. So is her mother. There is no older brother to speak for her and now she has a bastard on the way. The girl belongs to no one under the law."

"She belongs to herself," Edith said sharply and then smiled. "I would hear Gifa's thoughts."

Ælfgifa looked up, deep set hazel eyes level. Harold nodded. "Well then, Gifa? Speak your mind."

Ælfgifa had been thinking about this since the matter was first broached. With her knack for piercing the murk and predicting the logical outcomes, she had come up with a solution. She might have tried to find a way to make the suggestion to Edith if Harold had not invited her to speak— one did not advise the Jarl unasked, brother or no. But Harold *had* asked her. She drew a deep breath.

"There are several levels here I think," she began.

Beorn snorted. "Naturally, you never know where her fey little mind will go next..."

Ælfgifa ignored him. "First you must think of the health of your estate as a whole. If part of the body sickens then the body will likely follow. Ulfric and the land he holds in trust is a canker in East Anglia. At least while he is thagn. This is not his first indiscretion, but his carelessness and cruelty have now given you a ripe opportunity to remove him from his lands and replace him with a better master. Or mistress. It would be a shame to miss such a chance..."

"Remove him? Supplant a man because he couldn't keep his prick in his trews? Are you mad?" Beorn looked around at the others. "At that reasoning we would all be losing our lands."

Edith looked at him scornfully. "My sister assures us that this is not his first crime, merely the one he was caught over. She has my full confidence. If Ælfgifa says such a thing is so, then it is so. And for shame, Beorn, that you are too stupid to distinguish a willing dalliance from a serious crime."

Beorn flushed red with anger but Harold silenced him with a look. "Go on, Gifa, how is such a thing to be accomplished."

"We must consider his crimes as separate items, to be punished individually," Ælfgifa went on, smiling internally. "First there is the matter of his assault on a free woman, a servant to the Countess, which left the girl unable to perform her duties for over a week. Second there is the rape itself, for which he might be expected to pay a fine to the girl. Third there is the matter of a fatherless child, who must be provided for." She paused. She had their attention now. "For the first crime, Ulfric must recompense Lady Edith for loss of the girl's labor. My suggestion is that Lady Edith demands this recompense in land rather than coin, requiring immediate payment."

Edith had started to smile and Harold had a gleam in his eyes. Grimly amused, Ælfgifa went on.

"For the rape, the girl is owed payment in silver. At present it is a small sum that will not impact Ulfric greatly."

She took a deep breath. Now she would find out exactly how much Harold valued her judgment. "I recommend that you adopt the girl, Nessa, into your household, Lord. Make her a member of your family."

"What?" Beorn yelped. "Raise a ceorl to nobility?"

Harold looked thunderstruck and even Edith seemed discomfited. Ælfgifa wondered if she had made a mistake but then the monk chuckled. "That would be well done, Lord."

"How so?" Harold asked, eyes not leaving Ælfgifa.

"Why for then you would be in the stead of the girl's father. Within reason, with the girl being part of a noble household, you might ask for ten times the normal fine. Ulfric will have to sell his land back to you to make such coin so soon." Ashwine laughed again. "He might only narrowly avoid selling himself into indenture to pay. It would certainly send a message to the other thagns and their ceorls."

"That I protect my own but none are beyond retribution," Harold mused. "It cannot become a habit however."

"It would not," Beorn said grudgingly. "Ruin one thagn and all the others will be fighting each other for a chance to prove their uprightness of character. The ceorls will work even harder for you. The only problem I see is that of Ulfric's family."

"Allow his wife the opportunity to divorce Ulfric before he settles the debts," Edith said coldly. "The children are all young and will go with their mother. The land that was her dower will go with her, further reducing Ulfric's income and property. If she proves to be a clever manager, let her keep the land. I am sure you can make it clear that her husband would no longer be welcome there if she wants to remain a landowner, without saying so explicitly."

"Keep me in mind not to make an enemy of you, Lady," Harold chuckled. Edith smiled at him, sweet and deadly, dark as nightshade. "I suppose for the third matter, that of the unborn child, you would impose a further fine, Gifa?"

"Not a 'fine' exactly, more a payment in advance. An amount to be held in trust for the child. A dowry for a daughter if it is a girl or a good start in a trade if the child is a boy." Ælfgifa shrugged.

"Very well, say that I implement this plan," Harold said. "What then is to stop him attacking another woman in the future? And how is he to live? I cannot declare him *nīthing* for this, nor can I exile him from my lands—he might repeat his offenses in another Jarl's estate."

"My Lady Edith has lands in Grantaceastr, does she not?" Ælfgifa said coolly. "Perhaps it is time a further attempt to drain some fen land was made. Doubtless Ulfric would make an excellent addition to the party."

All four of the adults turned to stare at the thirteen-year-old girl who had just calmly proposed putting a man in harm's way and letting the fates decide the outcome. "You might make it clear that further crimes of this nature will bear the harshest punishment though," Ælfgifa mused. In her opinion being declared *nīthing* was exactly what Ulfric deserved. A man who was *nīthing* was an un-person; a man without honor deserving none of the considerations even the lowest serf might expect. Anyone might murder a man under such a ban without fear of the slightest repercussion or even notice. Ælfgifa felt she had offered the next best option. Clearly the rest of Harold's inner circle thought so too.

"God keep me in good standing with you also, sister." Harold shook his head. "I would not have you for an enemy either!"

Ælfgifa smiled, lips pressed together over her malformed mouth, and set down her goblet. With a gesture of respect she left the others to work out the fine details. Best if she was seen back in the hall now, before the official members of Harold's council returned. She had replied with cool self-assurance to all of her brother's questions, yet, while she thought that he would on this occasion take most of her suggestions—Ulfric after all had been a thorn in Harold's side for some time—she was never fully easy speaking out in such a way. Ashwine had surprised her too, she had felt sure the monk disliked her. He would not be the first holy man she had met who believed that God had marked her externally to show displeasure at her twisted soul. Yet he had been the first to support her. Perhaps he had been watching and assessing her all along, and the judgment she felt emanating from the huge, old man was merely her own private fear.

She took her seat and picked up her embroidery again. Ulfric had been allowed a cup of water but the guards had kept him standing. She set a stitch more forcefully than necessary. It would be far safer if he was dead. Dead men did not go on to rape other women. But then justice must be done. Or at least it must appear so under the law, even if it was not enough justice for Nessa. She would have an adopted family of high birth and a good sum of silver as well as an assurance of a livelihood for her child. But there was nothing that could undo the damage Ulfric had wrought, not the bruises and cuts, but the damage that didn't show. Ælfgifa eyed Ulfric with loathing from beneath her lashes. Nothing could be done, save to send a message to any other would-be Ulfrics that *this* was what they could expect for transgressing the law set down by Ælfred decades ago.

Harold and Edith came back into the hall and took their seats. As her brother laid out how it would be to Ulfric—who swore and protested, and at one point idiotically insulted Lady Edith with such filthy language that Harold ordered him whipped publically—Ælfgifa felt cold and clear as a morning star, far removed from everyone in the hall. She could not find it in herself to feel any remorse for ruining a man's life.

***

It was a mild day and Ælfgifa was tearing the palms of her hands trying to cut enough fibrous stalks of woodruff and lady's bedstraw to make a new batch of dye. She paused to wipe the back of one hand over her sweaty forehead and found herself the subject of Brother Ashwine's intense scrutiny. She swallowed her immediate irritation at being watched and forced herself to call cheerfully, "A fine day, Brother."

"It is," the monk replied continuing his scrutiny.

"Can I do something for you, Brother?"

He smiled faintly. It hardly softened his hard, square features. His iron gray hair was tonsured in the more common style, not like that of Brother Caedmon. It lay flat and close to his scalp. "I think not at present." He said nothing more but continued to watch.

201

Well, I'm not going to fill the silence, Ælfgifa though in annoyance, *let him watch me pick weeds as if it were a matter of political importance.* She went on in silence for some moments, acutely aware of the weight of his gaze. It was an itch between her shoulder blades. The older she became, the more she disliked being stared at. She was certain Ashwine knew that. Finally, she tied the last bundle of plants and tossed them into her basket with her small knife. She stood and found Ashwine standing much closer than she had expected. It was easy to forget what a giant he was. Mostly the monk's habit and his mannerisms diverted attention from that fact that he was a hale and muscular man in his late fifties. Ælfgifa did not stand even so high as his collar bone.

"You are done then? I thought to ask you to take a turn about the herb beds." Ashwine's voice was rich and resonant.

He'd been waiting for her to finish her task? Ælfgifa frowned slightly and then nodded. The monk reached out and took the basket from her hand with a small tug.

"How old are you, Ælfgifa?"

"Thirteen. I think you know that already."

"You speak as no girl of your age I have ever met," Ashwine replied.

Ælfgifa rolled her eyes. "I suppose your acquaintance with girls my age must be vast, Brother. Really for all you know, we all speak as I do and the few you've met who speak of husbands and hair ribbons are the exceptions." It was hardly polite but in the name of God, *this again.* How strange she was. How odd. How unnatural her mind must be. Ælfgifa sighed. To her surprise Ashwine laughed.

"You may have the right of it," he conceded. "I doubt it but as you say such acquaintance as I have had with girls your age has been limited."

Emboldened by his words, Ælfgifa found herself expressing thoughts she would not have otherwise given voice to. "I had thought you disliked me, Brother. That you scarce approved of my standing with my brother, Harold."

"Ah, well I can say with honesty that dislike never came into it. I did however suspect you of being one of the most dangerous people I had ever met." His gray eyes twinkled but his mouth was a flat, serious line.

Ælfgifa was startled into a laugh and hastily covered her mouth. "You have rectified that suspicion now, I trust?"

"On the contrary, you confirmed it this sennight past with your advice at the *Thing*." He stopped walking and looked down at her. It was as if she was being assessed by a great pillar of stone. Something implacable that had stood for hundreds of years. "Tell me, Ælfgifa, are you a good Christian?"

"That is no easy question to answer. Is the Church not like a great oak with many spreading branches? Were I to say yes to your question, surely I should only satisfy one branch? Let us say instead that I attempt to be a good person, and, having not the wisdom of one of God's chosen, leave the decision on whether I am a good Christian to Him." Despite the firmness of her tone, heat crept into her cheeks.

Ashwine somehow managed to wince and smile at the same time. "And thus you prove my initial point." He rested a hand lightly on her shoulder, and Ælfgifa started a little— few people touched her willingly, let alone so casually. "I have known many clever women, Ælfgifa. Yet none have combined your precise set of skills in one parcel. I never thought I would endeavor to teach cynicism to one so young but I think you need such a dose. You are sharp, quick-witted, logical, observant and yet you are compassionate. Your loyalty, once earned, is not easily lost. I fear affection has too great a hold on you."

"What if it does?" Ælfgifa snapped. She had not sought advice from this man.

"It is very well, child. But do not let it blind you or ever make you act outside your conscience. You are an unlikely weapon but there are clever enough people to see you for what you are. They will not hesitate to use you for their ends." Ashwine looked into the far distance at a past Ælfgifa could not see.

"I think I've wit enough to know when I am being manipulated," she said tartly.

"No doubt. Does that wit serve you equally well when it is someone you love who seeks to use you? Someone who loves you? Make no mistake, they will love you, have affection for you, but use you just the same."

Ælfgifa didn't know what to say to that. It had planted a nasty seed in her mind however and she found herself resenting the old man.

"There now. Perhaps what I fear will never come to pass. You are no fool, no matter what the common herd believes." He passed a hand over his eyes. "Forgive me, I meant only to put you on your guard."

"I understand," Ælfgifa said and anything else she might have said was lost as one of Edith's servants ran up.

"Lady Ælfgifa, your sister-in-law requires that you wait upon her in her private chamber as soon as you may," the maid panted.

"Of course," Ælfgifa turned to the monk. "Excuse me, Brother Ashwine. Thank you for your counsel." The monk raised a hand in benediction and it seemed to Ælfgifa that there was something ironic in his gesture, but the maid was already hurrying her away.

***

Edith was well into her pregnancy now and could not sit long without becoming uncomfortable. Still Ælfgifa had not expected to find her sister-in-law holding on to the back of a chair with white knuckles, nor to find Harold pacing the floor in furious, long legged strides.

"Whatever has happened?" Ælfgifa said, shutting the door.

"A messenger came," Harold said shortly. Ælfgifa looked to Edith, hoping for further clarification. Were Godwin and Gytha well? Was it Ealdgyth? Surely not Wulfnoth?

Edith must have seen the anxiety in her face and took pity on her. "It is your brother, Sweyn," she cast a side long glance at her husband who continued to pace. "He... has done something foolish, I fear..."

"Foolish?" Harold exploded. "The festering hothead has gone beyond merely foolish!"

"What has he done?" Ælfgifa barely remembered Sweyn. *He must be near thirty now*, she thought.

"He has abducted the abbess of Leominster. From her own convent," Edith said in a low voice.

Harold stopped pacing long enough to swear.

Ælfgifa stared at Edith in shock. "What?"

"It is true. He took Eadgiva, daughter of Hakon the Grave. She inherited the Leominster estate." Edith said.

"And Sweyn wanted the land?" Ælfgifa cast a wary glance at Harold. She knew he and Sweyn had been close as children but it was a friendship that had cooled as they had grown older. "Why did he not petition the king for her hand? Assuming the lady was willing..." She trailed off.

"There, you have hit upon the problem. King Edward forbade the union when Sweyn approached him, and Abbess Eadgiva was not in the least willing," Edith said.

"It seems my elder brother, that paragon and favorite of our mother, has taken to heart the adage that what a bold man may take and hold is his by right." Harold glowered.

"You mean... he forced himself on her? To make her agree to a marriage?" Ælfgifa saw the disgust she felt mirrored on Edith's face.

"At any rate she still refuses to consent to a union and the king has expressed extreme disapprobation of the plan. Our sister Ealdgyth writes that her husband had the wrath of God upon him. I am not surprised. Edward was most likely fit to be tied when one of his vassal Jarls disobeyed a direct order and compounded it with so many divers crimes." Harold's voice was full of fury and sarcasm.

"What now?" Ælfgifa asked.

"Now?" Harold raised his brows mockingly. "Why now, sister, we wait. Sweyn is on the run. Eadgiva is even now returning to her convent and Ealdgyth writes that the king has demanded Sweyn's exile on pain of death. Such a brother do we have!" He shook his head. "Sweyn will either limp to our father with his tail between his legs, or he will try here."

"He will try here," Edith said coolly, resting a hand in the small of her back and wincing as the babe turned within her. "He will still count you his greatest friend and expect you to take his part. Godwin will put your anger in the shade for weeks to come and is as like to thrash Sweyn himself, and put him on a boat too."

Ælfgifa thought Edith had the right of it. "What will you do, Harold?"

Harold made a gesture of helplessness. "Hear him out, feed him and send him to the nearest port. Sweyn has gone too far this time. I cannot help him."

As if Ashwine's words earlier had left a stamp upon her, Ælfgifa found herself thinking, *no, brother, you will not help Sweyn. You would never risk your own estate to help anyone less than our father himself. Certainly not Sweyn. And,* she concluded, *if it has not already occurred to you that someone must take charge of Sweyn's lost inheritance, it soon will.* Ælfgifa fixed Harold with a long look. It *had* occurred to her brother, she was sure of it. That was what made Harold truly dangerous of course. He might be in the heat of fury but he never stopped thinking, assessing, searching for advantage or weakness. For the first time, Ælfgifa made a conscious decision that Harold would have her support, on this matter at least. It sounded as if Sweyn was little better than Ulfric, an unknown older brother who had no claim upon her. *But,* she decided, *I will be well sure of where my allegiance lies and why in future. I disliked Ashwine's advice, but he was right. I have let affection for Harold and Edith lead me. I must be sure my choices are the best I can make or if not I must not go blindly into alliance but know why I act.*

***

Sweyn did not arrive as soon as expected. It appeared that he had not gone to their father either. Ælfgifa put the matter from her mind for more immediate events took precedence, and there was no time to think of dishonored family members. Edith went into labor a month too soon and sent for Ælfgifa, which greatly vexed the midwife.

Privately, Ælfgifa wondered herself why she had been sent for. There was little she could do, she had never delivered a child nor so much as helped a cow in calf. It was an area of medicine in which she was somewhat ignorant, despite her impressive knowledge of herbs and their uses. At first she thought the midwife objected to a young girl who had never given birth herself being present. Maidens were usually kept from a birth. *For good reason*, thought Ælfgifa, as she helped support Edith, gritting her teeth at her sister-in-law's cries. *Any woman doing this would have to be mad and yet thus does our race continue.* They were walking Edith, Ælfgifa on one side, a ceorl on the other, up and down, up and down.

It was when the midwife thought her distracted that Ælfgifa's sharp ears caught her comment to her helper. "Not right to have such a deformed thing in a birthing chamber."

Ælfgifa ducked her head, feeling her face go hot. Edith wanted her here, that would have to be good enough for the cantankerous old woman.

"I can't... I can't walk anymore," Edith groaned, slumping between them. Ælfgifa strained under the taller woman's weight.

"A little more, my Lady, not so long now. It will help the babe come safely." The midwife's voice was warm and reassuring but the look she shot at Ælfgifa was venomous.

Ælfgifa shuddered. She had no doubt who would be blamed if anything went wrong with this birth. She bore up under Edith's weight and urged her on. It was not long before Edith slumped again and this time she could not be persuaded to walk more. She was allowed to sink, panting into the clean straw that had been laid on the floor for her. Her hair was loose and plastered to her head with sweat. Ælfgifa watched in fascinated horror as her sister-in-law's distended belly moved and squeezed seemingly of its own volition. Between contractions Edith chatted to Ælfgifa but soon she was too far along to do even that. She could only grip the girl's hands crushingly and scream between her clenched teeth. Ælfgifa didn't need to be an experienced midwife to know that this labor had already gone on far too long. Edith was tiring and the child would be as well. Why wasn't the midwife giving her anything to help?

"Would not sundown be a good time for this child to be born?" she hissed in an aside to the midwife as Edith screamed again. "There are things that will bring the child more speedily now, are there not?"

The midwife gave her a glare so full of malice that Ælfgifa felt as if she had been physically struck. "You'll not tell me my business, you little bitch," she snarled back. "And I'll not aid the child in coming any sooner while your hands are on her ladyship. If that child is born deformed it will because you touched the mother, mark me!"

Edith heard none of this vicious exchange, she was almost delirious with exhaustion and pain. The world disappeared in a white hot sheet of fury. Ælfgifa stood in a forge fire and was hammered by the bigoted old woman's words. With more strength than she knew she possessed, Ælfgifa said calmly, "have you such a mixture as will help Lady Edith, or no?" *Sweet Christ, the woman would lose both the child and the mother to her superstitions!*

The midwife pressed her lips together and Ælfgifa took that to mean the answer was no. How did this woman come to be serving in a noble household? "Did you intend to collect your fee?" she snapped and then berated herself. None of that mattered just now. She turned back to the struggling woman, trying to release her hands. "Edith? Edith, I must fetch something. I need to let go for a moment."

"No... Sister don't leave me..." Edith said thickly and then groaned.

"Amma?" Ælfgifa called the ceorl who had been cowering in the corner. "Come take Lady Edith's hands for me. I will be back soon, sister."

She headed for the door. The midwife grasped her upper arm in one huge, hard hand and jerked her back. "Don't think to meddle, devil's brat. I know your tricks! I'll not be responsible for your mischief."

"Then leave!" Ælfgifa snapped.

"I have seen the births of every member of this household for the past twenty years!" the midwife was outraged.

"Then I am astounded that so many have lived! So far all I've seen you do is bring in a female cat, cuff your assistant and curse a lot!" Ælfgifa wrenched her arm free and elbowed the midwife in the stomach. She snapped her fingers at the grinning assistant. "Get a pot on the fire and boil water. Now!" The chamber door shut behind her. She took a longer route to the still room when she saw Harold and one of his men pacing the hall. She didn't see Beorn as she backed hastily away before they could see her, but she heard his voice.

"Hold fast, Harold. It won't be long now and there'll be a fine son at the end of it. Women have been giving birth since the first days. They know what they're about." Ælfgifa couldn't help rolling her eyes at the pompous speech. What did her cousin know about it? And she wished she shared his confidence that all would be well, but then Beorn and Harold did not know that the midwife had actively been hindering the delivery.

In the still room, Ælfgifa fumbled and dropped things in her haste. Something to make Edith relax, she thought, and something for pain but nothing that will make her drowsy... and something to help her gather strength for one final push. Mechanically, she mixed and measured. Despite never being allowed in a birthing chamber, she had seen Beddwen make just such a mixture. Praying she had not made a mistake, she hurried back and this time Harold did stop her.

"Sister! How goes it with my wife?" Harold demanded.

"As well as can be expected," she replied unwilling to lie or to bring up the matter of the midwife just then. She hoped the assumed cheerfulness of her tone would reassure him as her words could not.

Ælfgifa glanced up and found Beorn and the man-at-arms, Abrecon, watching her. She forced a close-lipped smile. "All will be well, brother. For all your son is arriving early, he is not in a hurry. First children are like that." She spoke with as much authority as she could muster and Harold and Beorn at least looked reassured. Abrecon was older and doubtless had several children already. From the look in his eyes he knew better than her brother or cousin the dangers of too protracted a labor. *Say nothing*, she ordered him with her eyes. He gave a half-nod and Ælfgifa excused herself.

"Gifa!" Edith screamed as she entered the chamber.

"I'm here," Ælfgifa called. "I'll have something truly foul tasting for you to drink in a moment."

Despite her pain, Edith managed a weary chuckle. *Not as beyond reason as I thought*, Ælfgifa mused. She dumped her mixture into the pot of boiling water and gave the assistant an approving nod. The midwife had not left but retired to a corner with the cat, both in high dudgeon. *I must find out why they thought bringing a cat in was so festering important*, Ælfgifa thought distractedly, scooping some of the brew into a small horn cup.

She coaxed Edith into drinking it all and then everything seemed to go very fast. The child was born feet first in a gush of bloody fluid and clumps of mucus. The midwife stirred herself enough to help when she saw it was a perfectly healthy boy, tiny but squalling in red-faced outrage. There were many hands then to help with washing and wrapping. Ælfgifa wiped sweat off her forehead with the back of one bloody hand and knew that she had been lucky. She needed to know more practical midwifery. Anything could have gone wrong. As it was, the child was a breech birth and she hadn't known until he was born. She eyed the midwife, who glowered at her, clearly still resenting her presence. Why had she not tried to turn the child? Ælfgifa shook her head and scrubbed blood and mucus from her hands.

Edith smiled at her sleepily. "I think Harold will be impatient to see his son," she murmured. *Amazing*, thought Ælfgifa, *can she have forgotten her agony so soon?*

She squeezed Edith's hand. "I will fetch him."

The midwife caught her at the door once more. "No need to come back," she hissed. "He's well enough now but you might still mark him with your deformity. I shall tell the Jarl that."

Ælfgifa strove for patience and lost, hurrying from the room. There was nothing to say to the old fool and striking her or causing a scene would not help Edith. *I'll just make sure that Harold knows that it really it is time the woman is pensioned off,* she thought. Though when she gave Harold the news, he nearly knocked her over in his haste to get to Edith.

Bone weary, she gratefully accepted a goblet of wine from Abrecon who complimented her in his stilted, taciturn way. Beorn was nowhere to be seen. What she most wanted now was quiet. To sit and let her mind stop for a moment. Ironically the great hall seemed to be the only deserted place in the entire house. Abrecon followed her but showed no sign of interrupting, merely taking up a position near one of the doors. He had a knack of fading into the background and Ælfgifa found herself able to be alone and quiet with him there.

She had drifted into a surreal, half-dream state, staring at nothing when the huge doors at the other end of the hall burst open and a dark haired man strode in. Abrecon moved forward but the man barely favored him with a glance. "Tell Harold that his brother is here," the newcomer said, and dismissed Abrecon from his notice. Ælfgifa felt the guard bristle and held up a hand to stay him. The dark-haired man was going on. He snapped his fingers at Ælfgifa. "You there, bring me wine." He sat down at the partially laid board, still set with food that few people had had appetite for. He speared an entire roast fowl and tore a loaf in half, stuffing food into his mouth as if he had not eaten in days. He had a look of her brother, Tostig, Ælfgifa thought, and then she knew who this must be.

She raised an eyebrow and whispered to Abrecaon, "Please tell my brother that Sweyn has called upon him but given the circumstances, there is no need to hurry." She smiled thinly.

Abrecon was less than happy. "I should not leave you alone," he protested.

Ælfgifa rested a hand lightly on the long knife hanging from her girdle. "I will be fine. He is my brother too after all. And I am not such a temptation as all that in any case." Abrecon left, muttering to himself and Ælfgifa lifted a jug of wine, walking towards Sweyn. Whatever she did, she must not spook him into flight before Harold spoke to him.

"Christ alive, but Harold keeps ugly servants," Sweyn said, taking the jug from her hands and drinking straight from the neck. Ælfgifa watched, faintly disgusted, as he crammed more food into his mouth before he had even swallowed the wine. "Could they do no better that you? I wonder you are allowed to wait in the hall. Are they drowning in pock marked swineherds then?"

Ælfgifa smiled in a chilly way and seated herself opposite Sweyn. "I am no servant."

"Well you're not likely to be Edith the Fair unless someone has a bloody good sense of humor." Sweyn continued to gorge himself, giving Ælfgifa time to study him. His hair was as dark as her own but muted from the dust and dirt it had collected. His eyes were like Godwin's and there would have been a fineness of feature that could be traced to Gytha had he not clearly had his nose broken several times. It seemed she was not the only one who found Sweyn objectionable. He was not near so tall as Harold and his face seemed closed in and fierce, lacking the openness and waggish charm her other brothers had. He lacked the cruel twist to his mouth that was Tostig's. *A thoughtless, rutting brute rather than actively savage*, she concluded. *And what a prize fool he is. Harold is right, such a brother we have!*

"Must you stare? You're putting me off my food!" Sweyn snapped thickly.

Ælfgifa raised her eyebrows scornfully as a piece of fowl fell from his stuffed mouth. "Why, brother, that is a most uncordial greeting after so long a parting," she said with scathing sweetness.

Sweyn choked on his wine. "Brother?"

"Aye, do you not recognize me? I am told I have a face few would forget. Though since I was scarce more than a babe when you saw me last, I will extend you some latitude." She took a wry pleasure in needling him.

"God's bollocks, you're the third girl. The deformed one. What is Harold at to be keeping you here?" Sweyn had stopped chewing and searched her face as if looking for any family resemblance. He seemed reassured when he found none. "Our mother should have smothered you at birth."

The fact that he said this conversationally with no intention of wounding, hit Ælfgifa harder than if he'd attempted a deliberate insult.

"Doubtless after raising so fine a son as you have proved to be, our mother was more open to pity," Ælfgifa replied acerbically. The faint stress on the word 'fine' was too subtle for Sweyn to pick up on. She was also sure that Gytha probably had considered smothering her. Good Christian principles had no doubt stayed her hand. She reminded herself that Sweyn's was not a good opinion she cared for and swallowed back her irritation.

Sweyn might have been too stupid to pick up on subtleties but he knew when a barb was being aimed at him. "Got a mouth on you," he grinned, bits of food stuck in his teeth. "In more senses than one." He guffawed at his own joke. For the second time in half an hour Ælfgifa decided against striking someone.

"So brother," Harold's voice came from behind her, "you grace my hall at last." His tone was wintry.

"Harold!" Sweyn lumbered to his feet. "Harold, there's been a misunderstanding. A bit of high spirits. I need your help, brother."

Ælfgifa sipped her wine and settled back to watch. This might prove to be interesting.

"What misunderstanding would that be, Sweyn? When you abducted a holy woman? Or when you tried to force her to marry you? Or the fact that you ignored the King's express orders against any union? I confess that I am confused as to which part of the matter was unclear."

"Harold, you know what these women are like. Say they don't want a man when they do. Eadgiva needed a husband. Just needed a man to show her what she was wanting." Sweyn's tone was oily.

"I suppose her inheritance had no bearing on your benevolent endeavors in enlightening the lady?" Ælfgifa couldn't help commenting. Out of the corner of her eye she saw Harold's mouth quirk slightly.

"Gifa!" He admonished.

"My apologies," she said in a dulcet tone.

"Leominster needs a man to manage it..." Sweyn began.

"Spare me," Harold snapped, his anxiety and helplessness of earlier finding a good channel here. "You are no stripling of eighteen but a man of thirty. This was not a lark. The lady did not want you, her estates were being well cared for and more importantly you disobeyed your king!"

"That pious old fool," Sweyn sneered.

"Your opinion means nothing. You have committed an act of treason. And now you've brought your treachery here. Did you expect to find welcome?" Harold stormed.

"I expected to be treated like your brother!"

"You are not my brother! I have no brother so much a fool as this!" Harold ran a hand through his hair. "You are banished from England, Sweyn."

"What?" Sweyn looked almost comical in his shock.

"What did you expect? If you stay your life is forfeit." Harold's voice softened, a sure sign that he was at his most dangerous. "More importantly, if you try to stay on my lands I will hand you to Edward myself."

Sweyn's mouth gaped. *He does not realize,* Ælfgifa thought. *He cannot understand that Harold is no longer the younger brother who adored him and looked up to him, but a Jarl in his own right. A powerful man of political influence.* Her disgust for Sweyn grew. He was not only intemperate, hasty and of poor judgment. He was also stupid, coarse, ignorant and weak. Those last crimes were things Ælfgifa could forgive even less readily than his rape of a rich Abbess.

"I have men waiting who will take you to the nearest port tonight. They have saddled a horse for you. There is also a small sack of provisions and purse of coin. That much I will do for my mother's child. But you are not welcome here, brother, and I will not suffer you to stay," Harold said.

And here, thought Ælfgifa, *is the crux. No matter how despicable Sweyn is, it is the fact that he might taint Harold's standing that causes him to act harshly. Harold's kindness will not stretch past his ambition. I must be mindful of that, though on this occasion I am glad of it.*

With no need to see any more, she slipped away to the quiet of her own chamber and then finally, sleep.

CHAPTER 19

WILLIAM had reached the point that he felt his frustration would burst Falaise's curtain wall open, so he resolved to spend a morning riding around the country outside the town with Bourdas, Gallet and fitzOsbern. Ostensibly this was to see the villages nearby, to show his face, which he had done little enough of lately. In reality though, he needed time to think, and he could not do that at the castle with near constant demands on his time, and the further distraction of events weighing heavy. In addition to all that, there was no little sense that he felt safer outside the castle walls than within it. It was not that he feared the smiling friend with a knife beneath his cloak, or poison in his food, so much as an oppressive feeling, a claustrophobia whenever he was within the solid stone of the castle. The place seemed to be withering, somehow, without Ralph. Only that morning he had wandered into a walled herb garden that no longer seemed to be tended. Perhaps a gardener or herbalist had died or fallen ill and not been replaced. His guardian would have known, and seen that someone new was appointed.

He needed the kind of advice he had always had on hand when Ralph was around—even if he could no longer look to Ralph to take the decisions that he felt sure his guardian had always steered him into until the last year. The Conseil de Duc was worse than useless. Far too many people, half of them at odds with the other half, and committed to using their place to further their own ends rather than to give him the advice and information he needed to make decisions in the best interests of the Duchy as a whole. If anything, it was even worse since the rebellion had been defeated and the nobles who had quietly backed the traitors or kept themselves out of it altogether returned. The first council after Grimoult's trial and death had been little more than an unseemly squabble over his estates, and William had had to call a halt before anything of any significance had been decided. It was infuriating. As Ralph had said to him not too long ago, what was good for the Duchy was surely good for its nobles and common folk. Why was it so hard for the rest of them to see that?

No, he needed a way of discussing matters with people he trusted that didn't mean calling upon them at a moment's notice and expecting them to drop everything.

He called fitzOsbern over to ride beside him. "How would you feel about being Ducal Steward?" William asked. "Not just because your father was, I mean. In your own right. I need a right hand man. Someone to try out ideas. Tell me when I'm being an idiot. And as you can read..."

FitzOsbern smiled, guardedly. "All right, Lord. It would be an honor. I don't have Ralph's intellect, of course. I can't promise to be the fount of all knowledge."

"Don't denigrate yourself. You grew up in the house of a steward, after all." FitzOsbern was right though. He did not have the many years' experience of lordship that Ralph could call upon. "Well what do you think of the idea of an inner council?" he added. "Just a few fellows I can trust to put the Duchy before their own interests. And to tell me how things are without dressing it up."

FitzOsbern thought for a moment. William knew that look. He'd spent a chunk of his childhood running around after FitzOsbern, who was a couple of years older, as his father had been one of Duke Robert's stewards. Osbern had also been William's guardian for a short while until he'd had his throat cut. Two boys whose fathers had departed the mortal realm while they were still children.

"If it would help you, yes, of course. It would be bound to annoy the wider council though, don't you think?"

"I suppose so."

"It would, trust me. They'd think they were being cut out of decisions and sidelined."

"That's exactly what I mean to do."

"Well, obviously. But you don't want them knowing that, do you?"

William thought about it. Not too long ago he wouldn't have cared in the slightest what his nobles thought. But that was before a gang of them had turned on him and tried to kill him. Either way, it wasn't good for harmony.

FitzOsbern laughed. "Imagine Archbishop Mauger left out of any important body! You'd never hear the end of it."

"Good God, no." The combination of Mauger's name and the word 'body' made him shudder. There was still something disconcertingly unresolved about the

221

Archbishop's role in Grimoult's murder. In truth, this was one reason he wanted to address the issue of a closed council. He wanted to be able to talk to someone about his suspicions. But this couldn't wait until he'd had the chance to establish a circle of advisers. "There's something odd going on with Mauger, and I don't like it."

"I know what you mean. I understand he spent most of the time we were away working on people. Grimoult, which was odd enough, but there were others."

"I think he might have had something to do with that business with Grimoult and that young fellow, Salle."

FitzOsbern nodded enthusiastically. "Yes, I think you're right. I just can't think what though."

"And Grimoult apparently said he wanted to name more conspirators."

"Before he was conveniently poisoned."

"By someone with access to the castle at Rouen."

"Like its Archbishop, perhaps?"

"But why?" William sighed expansively. "At least when people were trying to kill me I knew what was going on in my own Duchy. I can't stand all this maneuvering, plans within plans, secret alliances, feuds and all that nonsense."

"Congratulations Lord, yours is the lot of a Duke."

"Isn't it just?" They reached a crossroads and turned left towards Damblainville. The fields were deserted. Above, the twitter of a skylark reached them. William looked for it, but the sun was too bright and glaring, leaving colored spots in front of him wherever he looked.

"This Salle. If he wasn't with the rebels, why wasn't he with us?"

"Still a squire. Hasn't won his spurs yet. And his father Huon is sick. Has been for a year and more, but from what I hear he won't see out the winter. I don't think there was anyone to look after the estate but Salle, he's de Gornai's only son."

"Hmm."

Out here among the fields and hedgerows, the intrigues of men of power seemed very unlikely things.

"What about Huon de Gornai's lands. Are they rich? Might they be the kind of territory someone of influence in the Duchy might covet?"

"I don't know, my Lord, I'll find out."

Perhaps the bishop was trying to engineer the lands to become intestate, and use Grimoult to do it. He'd spoken up for the traitor quite obsequiously. It wasn't like Mauger to put his own standing at risk just to give a good character to someone so obviously out of favor. And there was that arrangement he'd cooked up with Grimoult to get land and new churches. Perhaps Grimoult thought Mauger had more influence with William than he actually did. It would be easy enough to convince a man of it. In fact, Mauger's power was growing. He was already one of the premier men of Normandy. Might he have been trying to kill two birds with one stone? Secure a chunk of Grimoult's wealth and get de Gornai's heir out of the way?

...But then William had agreed to trial by combat. The strongest likelihood was that Salle would walk away with his reputation untarnished, free to inherit, while Grimoult was subject to further loss of reputation and honor, unlikely to regain his estates so as to transfer some of them to Mauger...

"FitzOsbern, do you remember where Mauger was in the hall when we were trying Grimoult?"

"Yes, Lord, he was on the bench behind you, with the grands and other bigwigs."

"I know, but where, which side?"

FitzOsbern pursed his lips. "I'm not entirely sure."

"He was to the left," Gallet called from behind them. "I don't go into a room with a rat in it without keeping my eyes on the vermin."

FitzOsbern's eyes widened. "Gallet, that's the Archbishop of Rouen and your Lord's Uncle you're talking about!"

"Yes. And he's a shit."

William chuckled. "I agree. Just try not to be quite so open with your views in the company of others, Gallet."

"Very well, Lord. Anyway, why do you ask?"

"When Grimoult was accusing Salle he kept looking to my left. I thought at the time that he was just avoiding looking at me. But now I think he might have been looking at Mauger. Not deliberately, perhaps. I think the Archbishop might have put him up to naming Salle."

"Quite possibly. My God, do you think it was him that had Grimoult poisoned when he looked as though he might be making further confessions?"

"It could just have been someone with a personal grudge and the timing was a coincidence. But..."

"If I had a grudge against Grimoult," FitzOsbern said, "I'd have been only too happy to see him humiliated by Salle."

"That's true. God curse it. There isn't much we can do now. Just keep an eye on Mauger and try to stay one step ahead." And that was the problem. Everything pointed to Mauger. He could be certain Mauger was troublesome, dangerous even. But with no firm idea of what he might be up to, never mind proof that it was illegal or against his Duke, William could take no action. It made the idea of a council of trusted advisers even more important though. "So what if we kept this inner council secret? Or at least private."

FitzOsbern frowned. "It would probably still arouse suspicions."

Gallet moved his horse closer. "You could meet in a whorehouse."

They laughed. "I fear we'd have even more chance of bumping into Mauger if we did that," FitzOsbern said.

"Not if I were with you," Gallet replied. "He runs a mile whenever he sees me."

"I can't imagine why that might be," William said.

"There's your answer then." fitzOsbern nodded at Gallet. "Put Gallet on the council and none of the 'grands' will want to be there."

He had a point. It was probably closer to the mark to say that if Gallet was involved, Mauger and his ilk would not guess that the council had any importance. They could say they were planning next season's hunts perhaps, or just drinking. "All right then. Gallet? You're in my inner circle now."

"What if I don't want to be?"

"Will no-one do their duty by their Duke?" William sighed expansively.

"Oh all right." He smiled. "Helisande will be delighted. She's always saying I could make more of myself."

"Oh good. Well, give her my regards, won't you?"

"Not this side of Domesday," Gallet snarled. "Lord."

Still a bit touchy about the girl then? Noted. William knitted his brows. He doubted Gallet had much to worry about, but he could understand the man's sensitivity given the circumstances of their meeting. "All right, I meant no offense."

"Sorry Sire."

"Quite all right. Well then, who else should attend our little gatherings?"

FitzOsbern snorted. "I was thinking we could ask Gallet's wife, actually. Thought you could do with some feminine insight."

William nearly fell off his horse, so hard did he laugh at the idea of a woman giving counsel to a Lord. "What about that bishop?" he wheezed when he had recovered his breath enough to speak.

"Which one?"

"The fellow from Bec."

"Oh, him. Smartarse. Lambswool?"

"Lanfranc."

"That's him. He seemed to have a bit of sense."

"I don't like him," said Gallet. "Too clever for his own good."

"As long as he isn't too clever for ours," fitzOsbern answered. "Montgomerie and Beardy Beaumont, presumably?"

"Well, I trust them but I'm not sure they have the sense they were born with."

"No." They rode on in silence for a while. "I don't suppose Ralph would be available?" fitzOsbern added.

"I doubt it. Not yet, anyway. I think he wants me not to rely on him."

"Hmm. Shame. I feel we need someone who's had a bit of experience of these things."

"I agree. But who is there?" William knew more soldiers than you cared to name, but statesmen? They seemed in short supply. If only he had listened more closely to Ralph's lessons on statecraft. "What about Hubert de Ryes?"

"He's only just been made a Baron."

It was true. He'd elevated the old knight after he had given William protection when he was on the run from Grimoult and his cohorts. "Well yes, but he's been around a while. Seen several lords and kings come and go. He knew my father fairly well, I believe."

"So I understand. It seems lordly experience is in short supply."

Yes, the more established barons had all tried to overthrow him and were either dead or scattered. "An ear to the ground from someone with an estate in Upper Normandy will be worth its weight in gold. And his eldest, Raoul, has done well since he was knighted. Well we'll ask Hubert and throw him a bone or two in the way of roles for his sons. I hear my mother's husband is looking for a steward for my half-brother since I made him Count of Mortaigne. How do you suppose Raoul would do for that?" It felt good to reward loyalty.

"Very well, I'd say. Robert will be a handful, but no doubt he'll manage."

"Then we'll see how things are with the fellows we've named. Other names may present themselves in time. If we achieve nothing that the Conseil doesn't, then at least we've lost nothing."

"Some good drinking time, perhaps," Gallet muttered, but his tone was good-natured.

They rode on in silence for a few minutes. The road passed out of open fields of winter crops into a small copse, and began to sink between high banks. In less than a minute the trees were beginning to thin, the light more visible up ahead, when William sensed a slight movement deep in the wood to his left. He had not fully turned his head toward it when something struck the saddle just behind his thigh. His horse reared and he threw himself forward on it, gripping hard with his knees. The horse dropped forward again and began to gallop. He let it. A quick glance back revealed an arrow sticking out of the leather, buried right into the wood of the saddle tree. Mercifully it had not gone through into the horse's flank, or he might have been thrown. Shouts from his companions revealed they were just behind, and after a few moments, his horse answered the reins, dropping back to allow them to catch up.

Gallet and fitzOsbern caught sight of the arrow at the same moment. The former looked furious, the latter horrified. Bourdas caught up a moment later. "I heard the arrow," he said, "but I could not see who shot it. Apologies, Lord, I didn't feel like tarrying to find out."

"It's probably just an accident," William said. "Someone hunting. The arrow went astray." As he spoke the words he knew they were nonsense. That the arrow happened to strike the saddle of the Duke rather than any of his companions itself spoke of a deliberate attempt.

"I'll come back with a detachment of knights," Gallet growled, "and kill everything that moves."

"No, no." William said. "Whoever was responsible will be long gone. We'll just have to be more careful when we're going round the Duchy in future." If he was at risk even on an informal ride out arranged at short notice, then surely there would be few places he was truly safe. His jaw tightened. If the rebellion was over, opposition to him clearly was not. And if he did not want to spend the rest of his life dodging arrows and quelling uprisings, then he was going to need help.

CHAPTER 20

KING Edward divided Sweyn's lands between Harold and Beorn. Ælfgifa was grimly amused at how precisely circumstances had fallen out as she had predicted. She was never quite so easy about Harold's motivations after that. Many times she wondered if a piece of intelligence she communicated to Edith wouldn't fall into Harold's hands and be used for a purpose she had not foreseen or intended. Then she would chide herself for foolishness, finding work for herself in the still room or brewery or dyesheds, heavy activity to quiet her mind. If there was no other task to be had, she would take a long walk around Deorham. The physical exertion stilled her mind, for a while at least. After all, Ælfgifa would tell herself, those matters she reported to Edith were generally small affairs, not great matters of state. Sometimes she resented Brother Ashwine for sending her thoughts down such a suspicious track but she was forced to concede that she would have reached the same conclusions eventually. Ælfgifa was not in the least naive in general. Ashwine had simply made her examine matters a little earlier. But it hurt, as if the last part of her that had any pretensions to being an innocent child was being squeezed out.

Winter came and Harold's household weathered it well. One of Edith's women gave birth to a girl who was the living image of Harold, and Ælfgifa attended that birth as well. Gradually she was becoming more skilled. There was no need to pension off the old midwife in the end. The woman caught an ague just after midwinter and died quietly in her sleep, part of that year's midwinter harvest. For a while there was no replacement and Ælfgifa worked with the old midwife's apprentice, Glenna, doing the best they could. A strange sort of friendship sparked between them and Ælfgifa learned much of the practical technique from Glenna. There was always something lacking though. Glenna was a sunny natured, uncomplicated girl. Ruefully, Ælfgifa admitted to herself that she craved intrigue.

More and more often she would slip into a hearing or *Thing,* or even on occasion a strategic meeting on troops and placements, which even Edith rarely attended. Ælfgifa found these discussions fascinating although she never took part and always took care to have some handiwork—sewing or embroidery—by her. The men barely noticed her—it always amazed Ælfgifa that men in particular seemed to believe that when women sewed or embroidered they were blind and deaf to all else, but there it was—and she was free to drink from this fresh font of knowledge. She thought Harold probably knew she was interested in more than just company while she sewed. She was certain Brother Ashwine did. It was in these councils that Ælfgifa learned about the lands and wealth of other Jarls. But she also heard tales of other rulers and nobles across the sea.

Harold muttered darkly about Baldwin, Count of Flanders, on more than one occasion. It seemed that Sweyn had sought refuge there, which was all too close for her brother's liking. There was Henry, the Holy Roman Emperor from Germany. But she found herself most curious about Willelm, who was the current Duke of Normandy—and having a difficult time of it from what she could gather. Not that she had the least sympathy for his predicament as such. She did not know the man and was hardly likely to meet him. Nor did she think his deeds were especially noteworthy to date. No what interested her was that Willelm was the bastard son of Duke Robert. While it wasn't unheard of for illegitimate sons to become heirs, it was unusual. And then as a fine piece of folly, Willelm's father had died on a pilgrimage to Jerusalem, leaving his son—then about ten years old—as child Duke.

That caught Ælfgifa's imagination. Had the young Duke had loyal supporters? Had the boy merely been launched into a snake pit of noble intrigue? When she imagined Tostig in Willelm's place at the same age, she could only conceive a picture of a spoilt, savage brat with too much power and no idea how to use it. Yet when she thought of Gyrth or Wulfnoth in the same situation, she saw a frightened, lonely child with the makings of a superior intellect. She would amuse herself with such imaginings during the darkest days of winter, wondering which scenario was like to be closest to the truth. Perhaps neither. Perhaps in his way, Willelm was as other and strange as Ælfgifa herself. So she occasionally thought to pity him in the abstract but she did not care over much for his wellbeing in general.

Sometimes, listening to Harold and his thagns strategizing, it would seem to Ælfgifa that England, Europe, the world perhaps was naught but a great tapestry. A vast piece of cloth on which their lives stitched the events others would call history. If she were to create such a scene, she wondered who would figure largest. Harold must have some place in it. Surely Edward was already stitched into the fabric, so long had he been king. But what of the others? These men she would never meet who squabbled and scrambled for power? What of the kings of Cymru? What of the women? Would anyone bother to embroider them in at all? And then such thoughts would spiral as her mind tried to leap from point to point, finding the most likely path of connection. Searching for the pattern which would ultimately be set down and it would seem to Ælfgifa that something cold and dark passed over her. She would need to go out of doors and let the wind gust through her because the surest path always meant that the cloth of England would be stained crimson with blood.

Spring arrived and rolled into summer which gave way once more to winter. Harold and Edith's son, Godwine, had grown and toddled after his aunt whenever he was able. His shouts for his aunt "Gifa!" made Harold and Edith laugh and though they pleased Ælfgifa, they tore at her too for they reminded her too sharply of her brother, Wulfnoth. It had been almost four years since she had seen him. She wondered if he remembered her at all.

Edith was pregnant again and gave birth to another son just as spring took hold properly. They called the boy Edmund, and Ælfgifa judged it wouldn't be long before he was trotting after her just as Godwine did. Now that Edith had a babe in arms again, Godwine was left more and more to the care of a ceorl, the one who had given birth to a girl that Ælfgifa was privately certain was Harold's bastard daughter, and the care of Ælfgifa herself. It was well enough for the present, Ælfgifa thought. Her daily round of working at dyeing, brewing, weaving, speaking with Edith, caring for her nephews and a girl who was probably her niece. There were debates to be had with Ashwine who, while not exactly a friend, felt like an equal, a colleague. There were herbs to prepare and medicines to make. There were her studies in Latin and Frankish to pursue. And there was always more she could learn about calligraphy, although the household scribe glared at her so fiercely as much for her skill as for her face.

So for now Ælfgifa was content. She felt sure that a change was coming though she could not say exactly how she knew. It was more intuition than fact but there were times when she felt Harold's gaze on her, speculative and assessing, as if he were wondering to what other uses she might be put. She might have thought she was being presumptuous and perhaps a little hysterical, but for the fact that Ashwine mentioned in passing that he had noticed the same thing. It would be a very difficult feat to turn Harold down, Ælfgifa realized. Not only would she be contending with his natural charisma, which often felt like a palpable force when it was fully directed at her, but there was the issue of personal debt. Perhaps Harold and Edith considered it a light matter to have given her a home at Deorham, but Ælfgifa remembered that she had not been wanted. That she had been an outcast of sorts and her brother had taken her in. She had little personal wealth of her own and no immediate way of acquiring any, just as she had said to the Abbess of Wintanceastre so long ago. Add to that the fact that she loved Harold and Edith, and well... no. Disobliging either of them would not be easy. Then again, who was to say that her wishes and conscience were not in concert with theirs? Until the matter came up, it was useless to worry about it. So Ælfgifa tried to keep busy and put such thoughts from her mind.

***

Ælfgifa was sitting in her favorite concealed window nook, when she saw the horseman riding into the yard. The horse was very fine, a peach-roan gelding with a reddish mask and stockings. From the way it pranced after what was likely a long journey, Ælfgifa guessed that it was a fast, spirited animal. Certainly not a war horse of any kind. Far too light and leggy. *A messenger*, she decided, watching the man who had rode in, swing down from the saddle. As if to confirm her words, the messenger collected a package in waxed cloth from the saddle bags. A glance at the man's clothing and boots told her this was no ordinary messenger. Someone sent by the King? Ælfgifa folded her work and went to find Edith, guessing that Harold would either join his wife or send for both of them.

Edith looked up as Ælfgifa let herself into the chamber but did not question her sister-in-law's presence. Doubtless she already knew there was a messenger just arrived. It was but a few moments before Harold arrived.

"I have had summons from the King, my Lady," he said without preamble.

Edith nodded but Ælfgifa noticed that her knuckles whitened on the shirt she was sewing.

"Does he intend to go to the Emperor's aid? Henry did ask for assistance did he not?" Ælfgifa asked.

"You have the right of it. Baldwin of Flanders has been like a hungry dog, snatching a bite here and there. Now however, the Count may have trapped himself. Our king sends word that I am to command a fleet and beset Flanders' men from the sea, while Henry of Bavaria and the king of Norway will attack him from the land." Only someone who knew Harold very well would be able to tell that more than a vassal lord's duty drove him. Ælfgifa could see that a quiet life would never suit her brother. Edith was well in mind of a wife's duties, whatever her fears as a mother might be.

"Then do you strike him well and be sure he is beaten this time, husband," she said with a smile that was almost savage. "Be sure and I am certain Edward will favor you."

"Henry's regard is no trifle either," Ælfgifa commented. "When shall you depart?"

"In a day or so. I must gather the *Fyrd* along the way," he paused and for a moment he looked almost uneasy. "I feel I must warn you. Sweyn, our brother, is no longer with Flanders. He set off for Denmark, from where he was soon exiled for crimes unknown."

"Think you he played at gaining status through another ill-conceived attempt at marriage?" said Edith. "But why would he be such a fool? He must know his deeds go before him."

"I fear my eldest brother has not the art of learning from past mistakes," Ælfgifa said drily. "I suppose having exhausted all other options and with Baldwin at war with Henry, he will attempt to contact what kin he has."

"That is my reasoning too," Harold said. "And my absence would be just such a chance as he would look for. He knows he does not have my countenance and that he is forbidden to enter my lands. You are neither of you foolish. You know what he is."

Ælfgifa exchanged a look with Edith. *Men*, it said, *such a fuss! And they say women are ill in control of themselves.*

"He will receive no succor here, husband," Edith smiled. "Should he try he will find a deal of comfort in your lordship's lock-up until you or Edward have leisure to attend him."

"He will not come himself," Ælfgifa mused. "He will send a message, perhaps request a meeting. Somewhere neutral. He will require us to go to him."

"You are on no account to answer such a summons," Harold said severely. Both women rolled their eyes.

"Brother, we can certainly assure you of that. Writing to Sweyn is a waste of good vellum. Speaking to him a waste of good air," Ælfgifa said glibly.

Edith laughed and Harold grudgingly joined in.

***

Ælfgifa paced the length of the unused hall, what she'd come to think of as the tapestry room because of the embroidered curtains that hung over the recessed windows. It was unseasonably hot and humid for May. Small black flies had hatched early and were making the warm weather even more of a misery. That was not what plagued Ælfgifa however. She could not shake the feeling of disconnection from events. *How can Edith bear it?* she wondered. Weeks with no word and this disturbing... peace. There had been nothing of note at the last three *Things* even. East Anglia was disturbingly prosperous and quiet. Ælfgifa wondered what it was that made her thrive on a crisis. Was it perverse somehow to relish knowing things that no one else knew unless she told them? Was that where her own susceptibility to power and corruption lay?

The skirts of her dark green gown swished angrily about her ankles as she walked. Her own embroidery lay forgotten on a window bench. She wished she knew what was happening, dwelling on her restlessness to the extent that she did not see her sister-in-law enter the chamber.

"Gifa, do you mean to give us a new root cellar before Sunday?" Edith said tartly.

"What?" Ælfgifa stopped and looked at Edith, uncomprehending.

"You are wearing the floor out, sister," she relented a little. "Why do you not call upon Gunhild at Cnobheresbugh? Surely she would like a visit?"

"Perhaps," Ælfgifa considered Edith's suggestion. "I will have no new tidings for her since the last time I saw her, though."

Edith smiled. "Is not your presence reason enough? Must you always carry intelligence?"

I do not know, Ælfgifa thought sardonically. *Am I valuable to you otherwise, sister-in-law?* She said none of this aloud but Edith must have caught some of her thoughts from her expression. Her mouth teased into a mocking smile. "Gifa, you are always most welcome to me and not least for the knowledge you are so adroit at collecting." Edith's smile became more genuine. "But do not ever think that you are not sufficient in and of yourself."

The words warmed Ælfgifa. "I am sorry, Edith. I just feel so restless and I do not understand why."

"Our household is not big enough for you any longer, I fear," Edith commented. Seeing Ælfgifa's enquiring expression she explained. "We are not at the heart of matters. Close but not close enough to divert you for long in a quiet spell. You feel the waste of your talents. All women do at some point – we spend a great deal of our time waiting— for a child to be born, for a husband to return. You do not serve best by waiting, sister. You never have."

Ælfgifa felt the rightness in this statement. "What of you?"

Edith linked arms with her and paced the hall with a slower stride than Ælfgifa's earlier, impatient patter. "I am a wife, lady of a large estate. In my husband's absence I rule and pass judgment. I ensure enough is sown and planted and reared and culled to see us through the winter. I negotiate trade. I am raising the Jarl's heirs." Edith paused and laughed. "For the time being sister, I have enough to occupy me. Other ambitions may wait!"

Ælfgifa gave her a wry expression. "Have I been very annoying?"

"Nay, mildly irritating only. Now be off! Send my good wishes to Gunhild."

Ælfgifa smiled and nodded, leaving Edith in the sultry air of the hall.

Gunhild was happy enough to see her. She even persuaded one of the older nuns to allow them to sit in a cool part of the herb garden. Since the nun in question was Sister

Æfweh, who was head of the kitchens, it may have had more to do with Ælfgifa's gift of a stone jar of honey as much as fondness for Gunhild herself. Convent life suited her sister, Ælfgifa decided. There were strictures and routines, but the forms and rigors of religious practice gave Gunhild a pattern to which she could adhere. A sense of security. It was not a drear and desolate convent either, but one where the nuns worked in the community, healing, teaching, aiding where they could. Gunhild gave Ælfgifa a tour of the still rooms before she left and Ælfgifa was impressed. She headed back to Deorham with several ideas for improvements in their own household.

All thoughts of herbs and contentment vanished when she arrived home. The moment Spyrryd was spied carrying his mistress into the stable yard, one of Edith's women came running towards her, breathlessly explaining that Edith had asked Ælfgifa to wait upon her as soon as she returned.

"Whatever is the matter?" Ælfgifa asked. "There is no news of the Jarl, is there?"

"Nay, my Lady. But your cousin Beorn has sent word that he will call upon you soon. And, Lady," the ceorl lowered her voice, "there is a messenger here as well."

Have a care what you wish for, thought Ælfgifa recalling something Beddwen had said to her long ago. She hastily washed and changed into the first clean gown that came to hand and then went to Edith's chamber.

"Gifa!" Edith rose and took her hands. "No, be not alarmed. I have no reason to think ill has befallen Harold. It is your brother Sweyn. He has sent word that he is back in England."

"What?" Ælfgifa gasped. "Does he love life so little?"

"He hopes to be able to extract a pardon from the king and he requires Harold and Beorn's help to do it," Edith said, her expression grave.

"Then he is indeed a fool. Harold will not help him."

"No, I think not," Edith replied. "And there is that matter of his recent expulsion from Denmark, which is troubling."

Ælfgifa examined Edith's expression carefully. "What else has Sweyn asked for?"

Edith laughed mirthlessly, fingers working on the sleeve of her gown. "How well you know me, Gifa. Sweyn has demanded the return of his estates. I doubt not that is why Beorn is on his way here."

Well, Ælfgifa thought, *I did want news to arrive. God has a sense of humor beyond creating me, it seems.*

Beorn arrived the following day. He had ridden hard and his horse was lathered with foam, its muzzle drooping. Ælfgifa went so far as to walk out to the yard to meet her cousin and noted the state of the animal with disapproval. She was fond of horses and it was wasteful to run a good animal into the ground like that.

"Well cousin, you have grown apace these past two years, though not so very tall after all." He scanned her up and down while Ælfgifa fought to keep her tongue behind her clenched teeth. "Has Harold not found you a husband? You're of an age for it and your figure at least is good. Small as you are, you'd foal well enough." All this was delivered in Beorn's customary hearty tones while he rumpled his dark, sweat soaked hair.

"I am not inclined to marriage at present, Cousin," she returned, striving for an even tone. "You surely do not mean to suggest that my brother is remiss in his duties as a guardian?"

"I suppose it's none of my business," Beorn shrugged indifferently. "Harold must know what he's about. Although," he went on, as if he had sought hard for the most offensive thing he could say, "what he is thinking of to encourage all this reading and calligraphy and language nonsense, I can't imagine. Your chances of a good match were already slender. Few husbands want a wife who is more learned than he is. I'd nip that in the bud now, if I were you."

If you were me, Ælfgifa thought, *your temper at such insolence would have resulted in your jabbing your seax through the offender's throat.* Instead she said sweetly, "I will take your words under advisement, Cousin. I find it most curious that you believe you would make a more ladylike woman than I do, but perhaps you have access to sources of womanly wisdom I do not? Tell me cousin, do you actually practice the arts of a lady? How is your deportment in a fine gown? I should be grateful for advice, even though I imagine your beard must be a disadvantage, for I am aware that for all my diminutive build, I have not a delicate carriage. Perhaps you could instruct me better?"

Beorn's expression soured like milk. "Are you saying I am less than a man?" he barked.

Ælfgifa feigned innocence. "Not at all cousin. Only that you should make a better lady." As Beorn tried to work out exactly where the insult in that sentence lay, Ælfgifa suppressed a smile and took a moment to relish turning the knife. "I think it is only that your hands are so white and fine. And of course you are a perfectly respectable height for a man. We cannot all be hulking giants like Harold, after all."

"God in heaven," Beorn snapped." You will work an issue threadbare with your twisted logic!"

Having worked him up into a fine state of ill-temper where he was inarticulate with annoyance—as well as getting a little of her own back for his looking her over as if she were a defective brood mare—Ælfgifa dropped her arch tone, took both of his hands and said, "I am to bid you welcome, Cousin. Lady Edith will see you as soon as she is able. In the meantime will you let me show you to your chamber? There will be water for bathing as well as refreshments."

Beorn followed her, grumbling. She heard him say under his breath. "No wonder you're not married. A man would have to sleep in armor lest your tongue cut him from cock to craw."

Ælfgifa laughed to herself.

***

Edith glanced across at her sister-in-law. Ælfgifa knew that look. Unfortunately there was little she could say to shut Beorn up. He must storm until he had blown himself out, like all squalls. Edith had a mask of politeness in place as always. It would be far too easy to believe Edith meek and docile until you heard her talk, looking as lovely and fair as she did. *How strange, Ælfgifa thought, that Edith is underestimated because of her beauty and I am underestimated in the same way because of my ugliness. I must find a plain woman of the same intelligence and see if this is universal to our sex, or if it is only extremes of attractiveness that lead others to such false conclusions.*

She realized that Beorn, whose words she had allowed to drift past her for some moments, had paused ready to launch himself into a repetition of his arguments, and swiftly headed him off by passing him a goblet full of wine.

"Cousin, I see your reasoning. Do you try to see mine and Lady Edith's," Ælfgifa tried again. "To agree to a meeting with my brother, Sweyn, is folly. He has nothing to lose and everything to gain. He is also an unthinking brute with little regard for-"

"I do not expect you to understand, Ælfgifa," Beorn snarled. "What do women know of honor anyway?"

"If that is your opinion I wonder you graced us with your presence," Edith said tartly. "T'would seem folly to seek the advice of those whose judgment you hold in no regard."

From his place in the corner, Ashwine made a choked coughing noise that Ælfgifa suspected was a muffled laugh.

"I came not for your advice but for your compliance! Harold is right, we should not simply hand land back to the Sweyn. But to leave a kinsman in exile when he is seeking to make amends? Harold is wrong, in that. He and I should meet with Sweyn," Beorn argued passionately.

"We have no indication that Sweyn does seek to make amends," Ælfgifa replied, exasperation leaking into her voice. "In fact if his sudden expulsion from Denmark is any matter to choose by, we would be as well to be on our guard."

"Were Harold here, he would see reason!"

"But my husband is not here. And I fancy I know the measure of his judgment better than you, Beorn." Edith's tone was crisp but Beorn was not to be dissuaded.

"Then let me meet with him. I know you cannot leave your sons my Lady but send Ælfgifa in your stead. We shall reason with him and I doubt not we might present a case to the king." Beorn said.

"Your confidence is exceeded only by your folly!" Ælfgifa exclaimed.

Edith's beautiful violet eyes were wintry. "You suggest I send my young kinswoman into a situation where she is like to be taken as a hostage? Tell me Beorn, do you consider her life cheap because she is a woman or because you have no great affection for her?"

Beorn looked as though Edith had slapped him. While Ælfgifa appreciated Edith's words, she was also keenly aware that they must not let Beorn go either.

"Cousin, you may be right that Harold would consider supporting our brother, were Sweyn truly repentant. But he would not go about it this way, meeting Sweyn at a place of Sweyn's choosing, known to few, with only a small contingent of men." She threw up her hands. "If I thought I would be in any way a deterrent, I would go with you. But I will not throw my life away to no good purpose and neither should you. Please, heed our counsel. Await Harold's return and plan a way to meet on neutral ground then."

Beorn looked at her for a moment and then shook his head. "What are we if not the land we work and guard and command? Sweyn is without purpose and has been so for two years. I would bring him home."

"Then you are a fool," Edith said. "As well cut your own throat as meet him in this manner."

"You have what he wants, Beorn. He will take it by foul means since he cannot get it by fair," Ælfgifa pleaded. She didn't like Beorn over much but neither did she want him to come to harm.

Beorn swung round sharply and hurled his half full goblet across the room. The wine splashed across the wall and the sheepskin slung over a low chair. "Cowardly, womanish thinking! I'll hear no more of it! If you will not do as you are bid then at least refrain from preaching your *vaunted wisdom* at me," he raged, storming from the chamber.

Ashwine uncurled and stood, a gray stone giant coming to life. "I will go after him," he said. "He may see reason when he has calmed down."

"I pray you are right," Edith replied, pale and troubled.

Ælfgifa shook her head. She couldn't tear her eyes from the flung goblet or the red stain seeping into the white sheepskin. For a moment it did not seem like wine. It looked —it smelled—like blood.

CHAPTER 21

THE ceorl sent to wait upon Beorn in the morning reported that he was gone. Edith exchanged a grim look with Ælfgifa and by tacit agreement they did not speak of it further.

When news came, it came with Harold's return. The Jarl had been successful in battle and the Holy Roman Emperor had sent him back laden with gifts. Some which must be sent on to Edward but enough remained that Harold acquired a fine store of cloth, jewelry, silver and serfs of his own. There was no time at first for him to adorn his wife in new finery however.

With him, Harold brought the sad, shrunken bundle that was his cousin Beorn's corpse. He warned everyone away from it but when no one was paying attention, Ælfgifa snuck into the room where her cousin's body was laid and pulled back the cloth covering him. She could not say what compelled her, save that she would always rather know the worst than speculate. Beorn was barely recognizable. There were fingers missing and the marks of burns on his body and face. One side of his face was so burnt that half of it was gone. Cold with certainty, she thought what an idiotic way to torture someone that was. No doubt by that point Beorn would have been willing to swear to whatever Sweyn asked, anything to make his cousin kill him and put him out of agony. With so much damage done however, Beorn would not have been able to give voice to any sound except the most bone freezing screams of pain. She let the cloth fall back over her cousin's remains. Sweyn was as she had thought. A brute and a fool. Poor Beorn. The punishment for folly was so often harsher than the punishment for wickedness.

Harold gathered his household together, as well as all the ceorls, thagns and serfs of his lands that could be summoned.

"My brother is no longer my brother. Sweyn is a kinslayer. He deserves the kinslayer's curse." Harold paused and Ælfgifa was struck by how different his rage was from another man's. A hard focused thing, driven, sharpened like a blade to cut with. Harold was dangerous in rage because he did not forget himself. Was not prone to making mistakes. "King Edward has declared Sweyn's crimes abhorrent and against the sight of God. But Sweyn is craven and has fled. He will not return to atone for this latest piece of villainy. From henceforth let it be known that Sweyn is *nīthing*. He is a dead man and the lowest amongst you may aid him to his final rest without reproach." He paused again, holding his audience as if bound by a spell. He had a knack for capturing and holding the attention of a great number of people. Ælfgifa watched as Sweyn's doom was ensured. "I have no elder brother. If Sweyn enters my lands, you may bring me his head. There is no further word to be had with him. *Nīthing*. Remember this well."

Ælfgifa's mind skipped ahead. With Sweyn as good as dead, Harold had just become one of the most powerful men in England. She did not doubt for a moment that Godwin would officially name Harold as heir to the Jarldom of Wessex. Ælfgifa met Harold's gaze and under the charismatic leader, under the kind brother, she saw another man. Lean and hungry, one whose eyes glittered fiercely with the knowledge of the taste of power. She nodded to herself and slipped away.

Harold found her later. "I have a gift for you also, Gifa." He held out a fine gold necklace. Ælfgifa barely looked up from her needlework.

"Such adornments ill-become me, Brother, though I thank you for the thought."

"Gifa," Harold said, voice warm and humorous, calling to mind years gone past when she still lived in Wessex. "Will you not at least look at it?"

Smiling wryly, Ælfgifa took the necklace in her hand. She did not care for baubles in general and owned few jewels but this was exquisite. A short chain of links shaped like rowan leaves, interspersed with amber beads like rowan berries, and here and there a crystal blossom like the pale flowers of the same tree. The three great seasons caught in a single necklace. Even she had to appreciate the craftsmanship. "It is too fine, brother," she said. "you ought to give it to Edith."

"And here Edith helped me choose it for you. Come, I will not allow a refusal. You need not wear it," he smiled and Ælfgifa shook her head and accepted the present.

"My thanks," she said tucking it away in a pouch. "Now brother I am happy to see you returned and well. I sorrow for Beorn. But most of all I am curious what you would ask of me?"

"I did not hide it well then?" Harold said ruefully. "Dearest sister is it not wearisome to always be so sharp?"

"Only for the dull fools who cut themselves on me," she retorted but she closed her lips in a smile to show that she was teasing.

"It is as well," Harold said. "I want you sharp. You are to go to court to wait on our sister, Ealdgyth. You will be happy to see her, I think?"

"Why yes, but…" Ælfgifa fumbled. "I am not of a fashion for the Royal Court." She felt a stirring of something low and hot in her belly, whether excitement or panic she wasn't sure.

Harold grinned as if he knew what she was thinking. "Our sister shall help you. And of course Edith will depend upon hearing from you very often. So shall I." His grin hardened into something more calculating and Ælfgifa felt herself respond with a sardonic smile of her own as he went on. "It is a mercy you write so well and so fluently in several languages. Without that I do not think my lady wife and I could spare you at all."

Ælfgifa nodded. So that was Harold's plan. This was the moment she had dreaded. When she would have to choose whether to be his creature or not. But then reporting to Harold did not mean being disloyal to her family or her king. Here was an end to her restlessness. Catching Harold's intent blue gaze, she nodded again. There would be other moments of choice like this. On this occasion there was no need to say no.

CHAPTER 22

WILLIAM'S 'inner council' had helped matters but had not solved every problem. With the others' help, the council had taken a weight off his mind in respect of the day-to-day management of the Duchy. Certain roles—the organization of messengers, records of men fit for military service in each district, the maintenance of ships and so on—had been possible to hand over to competent senior servants recommended from within the council's experience. This had in turn led to their promotion, which further bolstered their loyalty. Hubert had been particularly useful in that regard. Beneath his graying hairs sat a sharp mind, if one that was sometimes over-apt to believe the best of people.

It was a start, but only that—William felt as though he was beginning from scratch. But as things continued, and the year progressed, he felt less and less willing to seek Ralph's assistance. It was partly that he was more confident of running things on his own account, but he recognized that his reluctance was also partly down to a greater desire to show that he could manage without his guardian.

The small council was certainly of more use than the unwieldy Conseil de Duc, which had if anything become even more difficult to manage than ever. He had, if it were possible to do so, made even more of an enemy of Mauger over the business of Grimoult's estates. Grimoult had been quite plain about the lands and other wealth he wished to transfer to the church, and although the gift was dependent on the baron regaining his lands and titles, William felt it should be honored, even with all the estates passing to the Duchy as they now did. Many witnesses had heard Grimoult agree to the plans. However, it was equally clear that the gift was to be made to 'the church', and nothing more specific had been promised. So it was that William made the gift to the bishopric of Bayeux rather than Rouen. Mauger could say nothing, but William could see the fury on his fat, red face.

He could not resist putting the toe of his boot once more into Mauger's ample gut. When the cleric pointed out that the bishopric of Bayeux was vacant, William announced his intention to appoint his half-brother, Odo. It was a stupid thing to do, but the lad was eighteen and his guardian had suggested that a bit of responsibility might do him some good—though William doubted that he had a bishopric in mind, less still such an important one as Bayeux.

William could not help feeling that Ralph would have appeased Mauger, or at least refrained from openly frustrating his maneuvers, just to keep the peace. But there was method to his seeming recklessness. The others had been able to find little that would lead them to the identity of the man who had shot at William while they were out riding. Or, more importantly, who might have sent him. Provoking Mauger might spur him to an act so rash he would make his treachery plain. *Or it might,* he reflected, *lead to an assassin slipping quietly into my chambers and slitting my throat.* As long as he didn't go after Odo. *Curse your impetuousness,*

William chided himself. But there was nothing to be done. The arrangements had been made.

"Don't we have any intelligence at all?" he grumbled, thumping his wine goblet down a little heavily.

No-one came forward with an answer made up of actual words. Just a few grunts and snorts, and no-one met his gaze.

"How hard can it be to find out if someone is plotting? Surely you can't plan a revolt or a coup d'état without making arrangements of some sort?"

Eventually, fitzOsbern took up the challenge. "No, Lord, but after the failed attempt at Valognes, anyone opposing you is most definitely on their guard now. They will not act unless it is with the greatest caution. We are vigilant, but such foes as you may have are taking care not to reveal themselves."

"But someone knew exactly when I rode out with a light escort and where I was going, in enough detail to station a bowman in our path. It means we have spies in the camp, doesn't it? And they must be sending messages to others?"

"Yes, Lord." FitzOsbern bowed his head. "We suspect there are a number of spies in each of your castles. We've intercepted a few messages here and there, enough to get an idea of how widespread they are."

"Widespread?" He did not mean to shout, but the very suggestion that his estates were riven with conspirators..!

"There are probably spies reporting to lots of people, Sire," Hubert said. "Certainly the King. Most probably the great houses of Maine and Burgundy. Anjou. Flanders. Your uncles, I imagine. Possibly Guy himself, although I would say that it is unlikely many reports reach him, given his castle at

Brionne is surrounded. Even the King of England, I dare say."

"Edward? But he's my cousin? Don't tell me he's plotting against me too?!" At this rate two of every three people in the Norman court must be a spy for someone else!

"It is just part of the normal business of lordship, Sire," Hubert said, reaching out with his palms down as if patting a huge and unpredictable dog. "Great men need to know what is happening with their neighbors and rivals."

William's eyes widened. He had no idea there would be so many.

"Well where are they all?"

"If we knew that, Lord, we could remove them, or have them watched. But they could be servants, members of the household, even knights and noblemen if they were paid enough. Anyone, really."

"And are we spying on the King? Burgundy? Maine?"

"I... think we might still have a few people in one or two courts. Unfortunately a number were discovered around the time of the rebellion and have not been replaced yet."

"Good Lord." William's head fell and he pulled at his hair for a moment. Not for the first time did he wonder if being Duke was worth all the trouble. Quickly replaced by even greater respect for his former guardian who had clearly looked after much more than William ever realized. *If only I'd listened to a tenth of what he tried to teach me...* "Do we have a master of spies or something like that?"

"No, Lord... I think it's usually looked after by the Seneschal," Hubert said.

FitzOsbern sank even farther into his seat.

"It sounds as though we need to take more control," William sighed. "Fitz, are you in a position to take this on? Or would you rather someone else?"

FitzOsbern's mouth flapped a few times but no coherent sounds came out. He was already buckling under his responsibilities. He looked at Roger de Montgomerie, who happened to start studying the carpentry of the table at that moment.

"Why don't I have a crack?" Gallet said. "I'm closer to the servants than you lot. I bet I can soon sniff out who's passing information elsewhere."

"And you blend in more." William pondered it for a moment. Few of the barons took Gallet seriously. There were even rumors that he was William's fool, that William had 'given him of his clothes', meaning he'd taken him into his household as his personal jester. Though why they thought William would have given him such stained old attire, he could not say. It irritated him that no-one wanted to see how capable the knight was, but he could use that to his advantage. "What about getting a few eyes and ears in other people's courts?"

"I'll see what I can do. Might need a bit of silver just to grease a palm or two?"

"All right then, it's settled. Talk to Montgomerie for the money. Roger, you have authority to dispense Gallet the funds, but keep an eye on things. I'd like to know who we already have in other courts and what they've been communicating to us."

"Yes, Lord." Gallet bowed, perfunctorily. "I'll get a report together."

"All right." If only he had someone with a sharp mind who could read people the way you would read a book. Perhaps there was something in those stories of Mauger's demon. He shuddered at the thought that some imp or devil might be watching him even now... More likely Mauger was just more expert at plotting and scheming than the rest of them, and had the coin to bribe the right people.

"In any case," Hubert said. "We needn't just be on the defensive. We are here to strengthen the Duchy, and the position of the Duke."

William leant back and looked down his nose at the old knight. "And how do you propose to do that?"

"Military alliances. And Sire should strongly consider marriages. The right marriage could greatly increase the Duchy's strength and act as both a bulwark against attack from outside, and deter trouble within. Your sister is of marriageable age. You should be considering a match for her as soon as possible."

"Adelaide? I suppose so. That sounds reasonable. Who is there that we might make an alliance with? The other Duchies?"

Montgomerie leant forward. "We should probably avoid Burgundy. That would anger the King."

"Aquitaine then?"

"The Duke has no sons."

"Any brothers?" William felt he should know, but keeping track of the other great families of France was no easy matter given that it seemed every five minutes one of them died, got married or was overthrown.

"Odo and William the Fat are dead, what about Guy?"

"Guy's already married," fitzOsbern said.

"Oh. Who else that that leave?"

"In France, the Counts of Meaux and Troyes, and Flanders. In Flanders Baldwin has two sons, Baldwin the Younger and Robert. Odo of Troyes and Meaux is not yet of age, and has no brothers, or sisters for that matter."

The scrapings of the nobility then. Not a rich field, in any respect. "What about the Capets, anyway? Henri's looking for a new queen is he not?" Adelaide wouldn't be too happy with marrying that old bore, no doubt, but needs must... and she'd certainly be comfortable.

There was another bout of shuffling and looking at shoes. "Lord, I find it highly unlikely that the French king will look favorably on an alliance with you."

"Why not? We're allies now, aren't we? He's already approached us for help with another military campaign."

"True," Montgomerie said, "but the fact remains that he views you with suspicion. The domains of the French king are smaller than they have ever been since Charlemagne split the kingdom between his sons. If ever he has half a chance to take Normandy back, in whole or in part, he will take it."

"But a marriage could see France and Normandy united, could it not?"

"Perhaps. But it could also see a Norman king of France."

William sighed. "So France is out. What about England?" Edward. William's cousin. A strange, dry fellow he remembered from childhood as a weakling who a strong breeze might have dispatched, but who, according to Ralph, had become the model of a successful lord and king. Odd to consider Edward leading the Saxons, whom everyone knew were quarrelsome and impious yet effete—even though half of them were of Danish stock. Edward was only half a Saxon

257

himself, of course, but he seemed the antithesis of everything William knew about that race. "We sent de Taisson to pay our respects didn't we?"

"And try to secure a loan and some troops for an assault on Guy."

"If conditions were favorable." As if he could forget. It rankled that he was reduced to begging for help, and from his dried up old cousin, of all people. "Have we heard back from them?"

"Nothing of any substance, my Lord. De Taisson is already returning. He says his estates need his attentions."

"Hmm." Before the attempt on his life, Ralph said he'd wanted the two to meet again, for William to learn at Edward's feet. Well it was too late for that now, but perhaps they could help each other in other ways. "We'd better send another envoy."

"Your cousin Eustace has ties in England," Montgomerie said. "And is also a relative of Edward's. He would not so easily be fobbed off. I will entreat him to travel there at his next convenience and pass your greetings to Edward."

Eustace? That mustachioed peacock? "Very well. See to it, would you? Where were we? Edward's family?"

"Edward has no sons," fitzOsbern continued, "so no-one to pair Adelaide with. And no daughters. No children at all, in fact. Nor, if the reports from his court are accurate, is he likely to have any."

"Oh? Is his queen barren?"

"Perhaps. Or he is. But there are rumors that he does not consort with his queen at all."

Somehow that didn't surprise him. During Edward's time in Normandy William had only seen him take an interest in prayer and hunting. But not 'consorting' with a woman who was to hand? "Is that true? She must be ugly as an ox or a great shrew."

"On the contrary, she's twenty years younger than him and something of a beauty, in a Saxon sort of way. Everything I've heard suggests she is pleasant and graceful company."

"Does he have any children by anyone else?"

"No."

William raised his eyebrows. "What, none at all? He's never fathered a single child in all that time?"

"Apparently not, Sire."

"Interesting." *And impossible to believe. We really need better spies. A halfwit stable boy ought to be able to find out who the king's natural children are.* "Who's his heir then?"

"I don't think he's named one yet,"

"But in any case, my Lord," Hubert added, "the Saxons have their *Witenagemots* to decide who the new King will be on the death of the old."

"What's that?"

"A gathering of the nobles and great men of the land," fitzOsbern cut in, apparently desperate to show off his knowledge of Saxon politics. "They cast votes for the next King."

William stared at his steward. "The King does not have the right to pass on his Kingdom?" What madness was this?

"He may nominate a successor, Lord, and in the majority of cases that choice will become the next King. I would not say that the *witenagemot* is a merely a formality, but the word of the old King carries the greatest weight."

"Does anyone know who Edward is likely to nominate, if he should have no sons?"

"There aren't many obvious candidates. Edward Atheling, his father's brother's son, probably has the closest familial connection, but he's in exile and likely to stay that way. Otherwise, the house of Wessex is by far the most powerful, but they're not related to Edward."

It seemed remiss of Edward not to provide an heir, even if the Saxons did have the ridiculous performance of a vote of the barons to decide. It was no wonder the succession of England had been an unholy mess for most of William's lifetime and the decades beforehand.

"What about this great family then? Any candidates for a marriage there? Would that secure us Edward's support?"

There was another ripple of uneasy shuffling around the table. "Unlikely, Sire, at the moment in any case. The family is led by Jarl Godwin, who is a false and treasonous lord. The rumor is that it was he who had the King's brother's eyes put out, and later killed him. Edward was lately on good terms with Godwin—the Queen, Ea... Eald... Eald-gyth, is Godwin's daughter—but it seems Godwin's sons are cut from the same block as he is, and the family may not always be in favor."

"What makes you say that?"

"Godwin's eldest son, Sweyn..."

"He has incurred the displeasure of both church and king," said Lanfranc, in that quiet, even voice of his. These were the first words the churchman had uttered in the council, and everyone looked at him as if they had forgotten he was there—William certainly had.

"He kidnapped and despoiled an Abbess in an attempt to force her into marriage and gain control of her estates. He fled to Denmark, but earlier this year returned to England to seek forgiveness for his many sins. Instead of acting with penitence and humility, however, he turned on his own cousin, a young man who had supported his return, and murdered him, causing him to be exiled once again and declared a man of no honor. I believe he is also to be excommunicated."

William's first thought was that the church seemed to have better access to information than his own people did, and wondered whether priests could be prevailed upon to gather and return reports from other courts. Naturally the network of churchmen could be an ideal conduit for intelligence. His second thought was that the Saxons seemed even more unpredictable than he had thought. Perhaps it would be better to have nothing to do with England.

"What else do we know?"

"There are several other sons, Lord," Lanfranc continued, "two of them 'Jarls' in the Anglo-Saxon style, the equivalent of a Duke or a powerful Count. Harold is the second son, and it now seems likely he will inherit. He is already the Jarl of East Anglia. According to reports from Flanders, Harold recently led a force of English warships in support of the Holy Roman Emperor against Baldwin. It seems he is a capable soldier, at sea and on land."

"Hmm. Any daughters? Other than the queen?"

"Gunhild, who has taken holy orders. And another, Elf-gifa, of whom little is known. She is but rarely seen at court."

Montgomerie laughed. "According to de Taisson, she is an unholy creature with deformed features who is said by some to be a changeling or a demon child. She has the mark of the devil on her and some say she has second sight."

That sent a shiver around the room, and a moment's quiet.

"There is, Lord," fitzOsbern said uncertainly, "the matter of your own marriage?"

William was taking a sip of wine as fitzOsbern spoke, and choked on it. The next minute of the council was taken up with him hacking and coughing until it felt as if his lungs had been scraped out from the inside.

Marriage! The very idea. But he was not a youth any more, and in full control of his Duchy. Well, ostensibly. But his father had never married. Surely it was not essential? At least, not yet?

"You should be thinking of producing an heir, Lord... preferably a legitimate one. And at least one more son in case of... the unforeseen."

William narrowly avoided choking himself to death a second time before he had arranged an heir. "Um. Did you have anyone in mind?"

"How about the Saxon changeling?" Gallet laughed.

A shudder ran through William and he shifted in his chair to shake it off. "I think we can rule that out," he said, trying to laugh, though it came out as a nervous bark.

"If she does have second sight it would save a lot of effort with spies," Gallet smiled.

"Maybe you should marry her then."

"Sorry, Lord, but my heart belongs to another." Despite all the laughter which greeted that comment, Gallet could clearly he heard to add "and I'm not setting aside my Helisande for any man." William looked away briefly. *No, have to stay in control...* Gallet would have to get over his insecurities.

"There are no obvious candidates from the most powerful houses, I'm afraid to say," fitzOsbern shook his head sadly when the hilarity died down.

Thank the Lord!

"The Duke of Aquitaine has no daughters. He has two sisters, but neither is suitable for marriage I fear. Agnes is married to Henry, the Holy Roman Emperor. His half sister Adelais is the widow of the old Count of Armagnac and rather old, I'm afraid. Certainly beyond childbearing age."

"I think we can leave out Aquitaine then. Anyone closer to home?"

"Baldwin of Flanders has a daughter, Matilda, who is of a suitable age," fitzOsbern said. "It is probable that the Count will look favorably on a match between you and she, Sire."

"All right, what's she like?"

"I... um... that is... I hear she is fair."

"You don't know. Never mind. You can find out, I presume? We can make some enquiries at any rate. If Baldwin will stop barking and snapping at the Emperor like a terrier, that is. It sounds as though she's the only real option at the moment."

Just then, Lanfranc cleared his throat and everyone turned to look at him. He seemed deep in thought.

"Did you have anything to add, Bishop?"

Lanfranc looked up, apparently surprised to find himself the object of everyone's attention. "Oh, no Lord, just trying to disentangle the great families of Europe."

"Aren't we all." William was about to conclude the council when Lanfranc cleared his throat again.

"There is... one potential objection to the Flanders match, Lord."

William sighed. *Nothing's ever straightforward, is it?* "Yes?"

"I believe she is related to you. Distantly. Going back to Richard the First. But that would place you within seven degrees of consanguinity, which is prohibited by the Church."

William was about to laugh but saw that Lanfranc was deadly serious. "But people get married who are more closely related than that all the time don't they? Most of the great houses in France are intermingled to one degree or another? Eustace is betrothed to a closer cousin, is he not?"

"I cannot speak for the Count of Boulogne, Lord. But the Church is clear. Without a Papal dispensation, Rome could not give its blessing to such a union. It is partly your blood relationship-"

"Our *distant* blood relationship."

"...Yes, and furthermore I believe the current Count's father married Eleanor of Normandy, Richard's daughter and your great aunt."

"But they had no children, as I recall?"

"No, Lord, but the Church considered relations of marriage to be the same in the Lord's eyes as relations of blood. When it comes to who is permitted to marry, that is."

William felt his hands tensing as the churchman spoke, but struggled to master his annoyance. He had asked for a council that would be honest and straightforward with him. But what was all this nonsense about the Church prohibiting distant cousins from marrying? And Baldwin's stepmother being his great aunt? He did not see how that was any impediment. "Oh. Well, it's only a suggestion at the moment," he said, hoping to shut off Lanfranc's wittering.

The bishop made no further points but looked as annoyed as William had ever seen him. He made a note to indulge the bishop's great fondness for lecturing on obscure points in the future.

"Very well then," he said, hoping to sound conclusive. "We look into the details if Count Baldwin is amenable, in the first instance. Then we might need to give some thought to getting a piece of paper from the Pope. I think Fitz has enough to keep him busy at the moment, so Montgomerie, you shall be charged with exploring the various options for marriage, for both me and Adelaide." He'd have to speak to his sister about it. He realized it had been nearly a year since he'd done more than exchange a few pleasantries with her. "Gallet, as we discussed, you'll deal with the spies and root out any further conspiracies."

The knight rolled his eyes. "A simple matter, Sire."

"Quite. And bishop Lanfranc, if I may beg a moment of your time to enquire about the news the church may receive from travelling priests..."

After the business of the council was concluded, and a conversation with a strangely monosyllabic Lanfranc, William retired to his chambers. Suddenly they felt very empty. Perhaps it was all the talk of marriage but he felt a desire for the company of a woman, a surge of visceral and heated physical need. He sat on his bed. He had not had a woman in months. It wasn't for lack of time or opportunity. It was just that since that night in Valognes, he had avoided bedding any woman who wasn't obviously willing. Especially since Gallet had married the very girl... he could not help remembering the way she had submitted to him, attempting to play the dutiful but vivacious consort, but beneath that, an anxiety. Even fear, perhaps. Oh, he had no doubt there had been physical attraction – the long gaze they had shared in the courtyard was testament to that. And women existed to be the property of men, of course, and they must understand that... but did men and women think so very differently? Perhaps it was the associations of Valognes, but at that moment he remembered the hart as it stood, cornered, waiting for the arrow. Not fearful, not even resigned... but knowing that although it accepted the order of things, it could still harbor a wish that its lot was different.

The question kept returning. What was Matilda like? What were any of these women like? He would have to find someone to share this life with. In amongst all the politics, would there be room for someone warm? Pleasant? Someone, perhaps he could talk to about these anxieties?

No. He was the Duke. The Duchy was his to bear.

The mote spun on through the universe. But this time the mote was fixed and the vastness of creation moved past it, inexorable, unshakeable, bearing prince and serf alike to their fate.

There was a precise bang-bang-bang at the door. A messenger. William called for the man to enter.

"My Lord," the man said breathlessly. He'd run up the stairs, it seemed. "There has been an attack on Château-du-Loir. Geoffrey of Anjou has seized it and imprisoned the Bishop of Le Mans. King Henri calls for your assistance."

"What? Good Lord!"

"There is more, Lord. Bellême has been deposed by his son. He has fled."

William Talvas, Lord of Bellême, William's vassal. He was supposed to be holding the castle of Alençon against Angevin

266

aggression. With the Bellême clan in disarray, there was nothing to stop Geoffrey taking a bite out of Normandy if he was of a mind.

Once again, it seemed William had common cause with the King.

CHAPTER 23

ÆLFGIFA could not complain of too stifled or quiet an existence now. She had been resident at court a month and while generally sequestered with her sister's ladies, the flow of gossip and intelligence to be had by those means alone was almost intoxicating.

Initially Ælfgifa had found her reception a little cool and discouraging. The king was much as she remembered him, though he was now past fifty, and had become more fixed in his ideas and practices. She had been left with the strongest impression that he did not like her although Ælfgifa could not recall on what occasion she might have given offense. She supposed it must be the reason she gave offense to so many without trying—her face displeased them. Certainly, next to Ealdgyth, no one would have supposed them both to be children of Godwin, Jarl of Wessex.

Her relationship with Ealdgyth was strained to start with. After her sister's obvious delight at seeing her after so long, it seemed that conversation between them was stilted and silences were painful. Ealdgyth was as beautiful as she had ever been but in the last five years that beauty seemed to have achieved the fixity of marble. She was yet childless and while Ælfgifa did not think that was entirely the reason for her sister's distance, she could not help but remember Gytha's comments to Godwin when the matter of Ealdgyth's marriage had been discussed. She wondered if there was something there which might be at the root of it.

Ælfgifa almost wished she had not come. She could not remember feeling so small and unimportant since she had lived in her mother's house. The king's household at Lundenwic was undoubtedly the finest building she had ever visited, so much so that she felt like an insect in the belly of a great beast. Perhaps the only thing that stopped her turning tail and fleeing back to Deorham in those first few weeks was her curiosity. And Ælfgifa *was* curious, about everything. From the way in which the King's great house was built to the many subtle and layered tides in the rivers of power that flowed through Lundenwic and its court. So Ælfgifa weathered a lonely existence, cut off from the confidences she was used to, in the hopes that as the household grew used to her, she would be admitted to closer trust. She did think that perhaps Harold had overestimated her ability as a potential spy. It was one thing to invisibly gather information from those who were used to her and barely saw her. Quite another to act effectively and without causing suspicion in the King's own household where everyone, even Queen Ealdgyth, was watched to some degree.

The first chink in Ealdgyth's armor appeared a month after Ælfgifa arrived. She had joined her sister and her ladies in waiting in a chamber set aside for that purpose. It was a pleasant solar with wide windows that looked out onto the sunlit garden. Stocks and rue and Sweet Williams grew in profusion. Honeysuckle sent tender creepers over the dry stone wall and filled the air with scent. Ealdgyth's solar was part of the house which was, most unusually, built in stone. The cold walls were offset by rich tapestries, several of which Ælfgifa recognized as her sister's work. The benches were finely crafted of polished oak and scattered with needlepoint cushions. Ælfgifa wished she could have warmed to Ealdgyth's ladies as she had to the room but it was hard to warm to people who universally snubbed one. There was Suela of course. The dark-skinned ceorl held a much higher position than any she might have hoped for elsewhere. That the exact nature of that position was unclear did not seem to matter. She was obviously Ealdgyth's first confidant and close companion as well as her maid.

Ælfgifa cast an eye over the rest of the room. Two of the ladies were the wives of Edward's favorite thagns, decent matrons in their thirties. Maud was rather stout but friendly. Deora was as thin as a twig and nearly as brown and wrinkled. It wasn't kind to think so but there it was. Years of child-bearing and living virtuously on gruel and apples appeared to have sucked all the juice out of her. There were two girls of Ælfgifa's age who giggled together over their spinning. Berenice was the only really old woman there. Ælfgifa reckoned her to be ten years older than Gytha would be now. She had apparently served the king's mother, Emma of Normandy, and with very little provocation could be nudged into telling tales of the old queen.

And then there was Aofra. Ælfgifa didn't think she would warm to Aofra even if the older girl did not mock her whenever she thought Ælfgifa's back was turned. She was about twenty years old. Pretty, with shining chestnut hair and deep blue eyes. Her father had been a great friend of King Edward's when he lived in Normandy and the King had been happy to accept her as his ward after he had become king. Aofra thought a great deal of herself as a consequence of this connection with the king and was sufficiently lacking in intelligence to needle Ealdgyth whenever the mood pleased her. She was also well into her first pregnancy—perhaps six months if Ælfgifa was any judge—having married a favored thagn just under a year ago. Aofra was blooming with health and not at all subtle in her jibes at Ealdgyth for not having produced an heir for her husband yet.

On that morning Aofra was making a fuss at the midwife's insistence that she try to walk a little in the gardens each day.

"Aofra, we have one of the best midwives here," Ealdgyth said a little sharply. "I think you ought to do as she recommends. I have noted that many young mothers-in-waiting have benefited from some activity. I doubt shutting yourself inside and sending the ceorls here, there and everywhere fetching things at your whim is benefitting your child at all."

Aofra gave her queen a patronizing smile. "I am sure you mean well, my Lady. But you are not yet a mother and have not yet a mother's instincts. Doubtless that is something you have to look forward to when God wills it."

Ælfgifa watched as two spots of flaming color rose in her sister's cheeks and spoke up. "Her majesty is quite correct, as is the midwife. From my own experience I have seen that women who remain active as long as possible whilst breeding, have easier labors, healthier babes and recover more readily."

Aofra looked at Ælfgifa in astonishment, as if one of the myriad lap dogs scattered about the room had suddenly sat up and offered advice. Ælfgifa felt her sister's eyes on her as well, but was too busy bracing herself for Aofra's retort. The girl's lips had twisted spitefully, despite her low intelligence she was adept at placing a barb.

"What would you know?" Aofra demanded. "You are not even wed. Nor are you like to be. What sort of lady concerns herself with learning a trade in midwifery? No decent woman I'm sure. You must be spinning a tale to impress your audience!"

Ælfgifa found this statement so extraordinarily ignorant that she could not for a moment think where to start in order to pick it apart. *I suppose she thinks that a bible placed in a crib will ward off rickets as well,* Ælfgifa thought, *instead of feeding her child herself or ensuring the wet nurse is not ill fed. God help the babe.*

"No I am not wed and as you point out it is unlikely I shall be. However I have assisted at many births now. Certainly enough to have formed an opinion," Ælfgifa replied. "Lady Aofra, I do not speak of a matter unless I am aware of the facts, nor do I formulate opinions based on popular misconception. You may take my advice or ignore it as you choose, but allow me the courtesy of being known for truthfulness."

"I cannot think what woman would allow you to touch her when she is breeding," Aofra said, apparently furious at not have silenced the deformed girl, even if she was the queen's sister. Ælfgifa felt the blood leaving her face. She pressed her lips together tightly and kept stitching, slow and even, breathing in and out. She would not show that she was wounded.

"I must have misheard you, Aofra," Ealdgyth said sweetly. "For a moment it seemed that you suggested my sister, Lady Ælfgifa, was in some way defective." She laughed a little. It was a sharp sound, glittering like a blade's edge. "Of course I know you to be too well bred to ever offer such an insult. Perhaps you would care to explain what you meant?"

Aofra flushed the color of beets. "My lady... I did not mean... that is... It is not common for an unwed woman with no children to attend a birth..."

"Not common, no. But not so very unusual after all." Ealdgyth looked at the girl coldly. "I think that was not your first meaning at all."

"It was, Lady Ealdgyth, I swear!" Aofra looked genuinely alarmed now. Ælfgifa watched, unmoved either way by the girl's discomfort but pleased that Ealdgyth was now putting her in her place.

"I would not swear, were I you. It is always folly to swear to a truth that you do not hold to be true. Although I am inclined to believe you foolish rather than malicious. Only a fool would insult one who might make a difference to whether you live or die in a scant few months' time. Are you a fool, Aofra?" Ealdgyth said silkily.

Aofra stared down at her hands, stilled on their work. She was red-faced and muttered something unintelligible.

Ealdgyth tapped her forefinger against her lower lip as if thinking. "I believe that the midwife is correct about you, my dear. A little walking will do you good. Currently Brid, one of the kitchen ceorls takes flowers to the ladychapel every morning. I think it would do you good to accompany her. In fact I am minded to send you to her now."

"If it please, your majesty," Aofra muttered, humiliated and clearly not wishing to lose any more status.

"Good. You need not return here for the remainder of the afternoon," Ealdgyth turned back to her own needlework. Ælfgifa noticed the tiny hook of a smile at the corner of her sister's mouth and was glad of it, even as she weighed up the possibilities over Aofra now being an enemy. Shrugging, she decided the girl could do very little to her. More importantly, Ealdgyth who had welcomed her but held her at arm's length for several weeks, had just shown that her sister enjoyed her favor. She was sure that the other women would soon make overtures of friendship toward her, whatever their personal feelings on the queen's deformed sister. This would both help her blend in better but also hamper her in gathering more specific intelligence. *Well I'll deal with that when it comes,* Ælfgifa thought. *I must speak to Ealdgyth in private soon however. She must know that she can hardly have done me any favors.*

Later, Ælfgifa slipped away from the chamber she shared with Berenice and made her way to the ladychapel where she was sure her sister had retreated for compline. The chapel was a small, square stone building with a thatched roof. It was set some distance from the house and the main chapel therein, and was used only for women's prayer. Occasionally a priest would give a service there but that was not its true purpose. Ælfgifa thought the dressed gray stone, softened by the evening light, rather lovely. The lancet windows, though glassless, cast long strips of shadow and gold. There were even a few fine oak benches and woven mats for kneeling upon arranged in front of a carved altar. It might have been a tiny building but it was cared for. The candles were of beeswax not tallow. Weavings showing scenes from the lives of the saints hung on the walls and fresh flowers were arranged around the altar. It was a peaceful place.

Ælfgifa found Suela inside waiting while her mistress was at prayer. Otherwise the chapel was empty. Suela eyed her warily but did not try to prevent her entry. Ælfgifa knelt beside Ealdgyth and waited. At length her sister was finished and looked up. Her eyes searched Ælfgifa's face and she seemed to come to some decision. "Suela, would you wait outside? Close the door and tell anyone who tries to enter that the queen is at prayer."

Suela's eyes flashed again to Ælfgifa, in warning it seemed, but she did as she was asked. "The door will not stop her overhearing if we are not quiet," Ælfgifa said.

"Even if she did hear anything, I trust Suela. She will not repeat it."

Ælfgifa supposed not. In some ways Suela was as much an outcast as she was. With her black skin she was frequently taken for a Moor. It was far more likely though, that Suela's grandparents or her mother or father had not been a freedman but a serf, perhaps brought over from Norway, where they still captured slaves from far across the sea. Suela was a ceorl, a free woman and presumably her parents had earned their freedom if they were serfs once, but she was still regarded with suspicion despite being as Saxon as anyone else.

"Besides," Ealdgyth broke into Ælfgifa's musings, "you would know all about listening I imagine."

Ælfgifa gave her a wry smile. Here was the sister she remembered. Intermittently sharp and kind. Ealdgyth, the autumn day. "I would," she said honestly. "It does pain me

275

sister, that we are not so easy in our friendship as we once were. Is there no way back to such a state?"

"Gifa, how can I admit you to my confidence as I long to do, when I know perfectly well you are here at Harold's behest?" Ealdgyth sighed. "You are his creature, are you not?"

"I am not," Ælfgifa replied honestly. "I had my own reasons for wishing to attend court, and seeing you again was not the least of them. Though I did come at his request."

"Then how am I to trust you?" Ealdgyth exclaimed.

"I am not quite the spy you imagine, though you might look to at least one of your ladies, a groom and two of Edward's men at arms."

Ealdgyth stared at her. Ælfgifa raised a thick dark brow. "Do not tell me sister that you have been queen these five years and not been aware of spies in your household. I will not believe it."

Ealdgyth's expression darkened. "We knew of the groom and one other. We left the groom as he could not gain much information. The other we sent away."

Ælfgifa shook her head. "The wrong way round, I fear sister. The groom will know whenever a messenger is sent out since he will ready the horses. Who was the other?"

"One of the King's body servants," Ealdgyth sighed. "We will have to round up all of these spies and send them away or else..."

"Or else arrange accidents for them?" Ælfgifa asked innocently. "If I might tender some advice, choose the least of the spies and make an example of them. Of the others, act as if you have no notion of their existence."

"Why do you say this?" Ealdgyth frowned at her.

"Firstly you must appear to be watchful. Removing the least important spies shows that you are. It will make anyone who seeks intelligence on the court believe that you are now confident you have caught all those planted or turned allegiances in your household. Your vigilance will not be so relaxed, of course, but it will cause those who spy on you to relax theirs." Ælfgifa said.

"Go on," Ealdgyth replied. It was so much like their last conversation before Ealdgyth was wed, that Ælfgifa almost smiled.

"The spy you are aware of who believes he has not been caught is a valuable creature. Where your vigilance should be increased, unobtrusively, is those channels that convey the information. There are messengers of course—all of which should be tested and of proven loyalty to you and the king. Tell me, does Westminster yet have a pigeon loft?" Ælfgifa asked.

"This past year," Ealdgyth nodded.

"Then you need a tame monk who has your interests at heart intercepting the messages and reading them before sending them on."

"Sending them on?" Ealdgyth exclaimed.

"Aye, if you stop all messages of a contentious content then your enemies will become suspicious. You must stop only those messages that cannot be allowed to go further and those should be very few and far between." Ælfgifa studied her sister's expression and went on. "After a while you can start to feed false information to the spies you have identified. This is why you do not replace them. Were you to get rid of all of them, then their masters would merely replace them with spies you had not identified."

"And we should be starting all over again." Ealdgyth gave a wry half-smile. "How do you come to know so much of this, sister?"

"How come?" Ælfgifa said in puzzlement. "Is it not logical?"

Ealdgyth sighed again. "Which leaves me with the question of what to do with you."

"I hope you will keep me," Ælfgifa said. "Have I not proven my usefulness? Besides, all thoughts of spies aside, I have missed you. You are my kin."

"Yet I know you will pass on information to Harold..." Ealdgyth began.

"Only such information as he would hear in the fullness of time anyway," Ælfgifa said. "Make no mistake, I am not Harold's spy. I serve God, my king and my family."

"And what order do those allegiances come in?" Ealdgyth said sharply.

Ælfgifa smiled. "They jostle next to one another under the demands of my own conscience."

Ealdgyth gave her a long look. "Stay then. For now. As a sister you do have my confidence, Gifa. But as a creature of our brother? I am not so sure."

"Time will tell then," Ælfgifa replied. "I will not try to convince you. Let my actions speak for my good intentions."

"Very well, tell me the names of Harold's other spies," Ealdgyth said her voice suddenly stony.

"There is no need, your majesty. I arranged for them to be sent away during the first week of my stay." Smiling faintly, she preceded the queen of England from the ladychapel.

Ealdgyth was watchful of her sister for another week, but Ælfgifa noticed a softening in her sister's attitude toward her. She was aware that the queen took her suggestions regarding spies in the royal household, and acted upon them. Ælfgifa supposed that the children of Godwin and Gytha were unusual in a degree. They had been raised as a close family. From what she could gather about Edward, he had not been brought up to *like* his brothers. Ælfgifa had no difficulty in gleaning drops of information that painted a rather grim picture of the king's early life. Berenice was an avid gossip and often talked until she fell into a heavy sleep, leaving Ælfgifa to sift through what she had said for nuggets of interest. There was nothing so far which she would risk Eadgyth's displeasure by putting in a message to Harold. Still it drew an interesting portrait of Edward. He was the seventh son of Æthelred—called, by some long dead wit, the unræd. Ælfgifa had laughed privately when she heard that, for in the Anglish tongue Æthelred meant 'noble counsel'. It seemed Edward's father, who had come to the throne at only ten years of age, had grown into a king who compounded foolish mistake with foolish mistake. Well might he have become known as '*noble-counsel the ill-advised*'!

Then Edward's mother, Emma of Normandy, seemed to have been an especially cold and calculating woman. She was Æthelred's second wife and Edward was her first born son of that union. She had thrown her support behind Edward when his father died in an attempt to have him recognized as king over his elder half-brother, Edmund the Irensīde, then married Cnut when he conquered England, sending her sons by Æthelred into exile in Normandy. After which Emma preferred the son of her second marriage, Harthacnut, over Edward and his brother Alfred. But Harthacnut had died.

Ælfgifa had heard that Edward held some bitterness toward his mother and she could see now why this was so. It appeared that Emma of Normandy had ruthlessly used her sons to advance her own political influence. Oddly, despite her treatment at her own mother's hands, Ælfgifa could not disapprove of the woman. She felt little sympathy toward Edward on that score, since he had risen high in the world and surely ought to have overcome any sense of ill use. All this was pieced together over several nights from the elderly Berenice's chatterings. The unpolished gem of information that Berenice had unwittingly dropped into her lap that night was that Edward had received his greatest support from the now-dead Robert, Duke of Normandy. The father of the young illegitimate Duke, whom she had wondered about. Ælfgifa could not tell why but she felt a ripple of disquiet at learning this. It was a disquiet that crystallized, still unrecognizable in form, when she heard that the same bastard Duke, Willelm, had recently sent to Edward, on more than one occasion, for assistance in putting down dissenters in his Dukedom.

In the cold, clear way that was becoming so common to her, Ælfgifa was leaping between points of connection and influence, looking forward at the most likely outcome and she did not like what she saw. Norman influence was already considered too great in England with Edward on the throne —despite his being king for many years. She had heard the mutterings of discontent. The people would not accept another king from Normandy, she felt sure, yet Edward showed favor in that quarter. Had connections in that country. It was only standing back and looking at the whole of the tapestry in her mind's eye, that Ælfgifa realized how fortunate a time she had been born in. England was unified under Edward, and whether she liked him personally was immaterial. England at the time of Edward's childhood was unstable, subject to frequent raids by the Norse men and the Danes. And Edward had no issue. In fact Ælfgifa did not think he had any illegitimate issue either which made her wonder about her brother-in-law. She could hardly ask Ealdgyth but five years was a long time for a young and healthy woman not to have become pregnant. And it seemed to her now that Edward *must* have an heir.

Of one thing she was certain—although she was following a trail that led so far forward into an unknown future that she sometimes wondered if she was mad—if Willelm ever did succeed in subduing his Ducal fief, then she was certain he was not a man to be treated lightly.

CHAPTER 24

THIS was, William reflected, an unusual kind of war. He had prepared for battle, calling his sworn men to him and assembling the serving-knights, setting the swordsmiths and fletchers to work, arming and re-arming his forces. But instead of going into the field, he and his retinue had been summoned to court, at Senlis, to celebrate Whitsun.

He put Montgomerie in temporary charge of the Duchy, barking a hasty "talk to Arnulf and try to make sure everything is secure at the border," as he mounted his horse. "Send word the moment there's even the slightest sign Geoffrey might be moving on it."

"What should I do if Talvas comes to Falaise, my Lord? He is your man, after all." *Trust Montgomerie to think of that.*

"Give him protection, of course," William said, after thinking about it for a moment. "But offer him no further support, nothing against Arnulf. We can't go antagonizing the younger Bellême. Not now he holds Alençon."

"Very well, my Lord. Is there anything we might ask for in return?"

William smiled. Montgomerie could be relied upon to find an advantage in any situation. "All right. We might insist he give up his family's claim to any part of Maine to us."

Montgomerie raised his eyebrows then grinned. "He won't like that! I'll have the scribe draw up terms. If Talvas comes to us, of course."

"Of course." No doubt as soon as Montgomerie returned to Falaise he would send out parties scouring the country for the exiled Lord. At least there was an army waiting and kicking its heels at Falaise if one was needed to march South. It would be good to give the men something to do.

It had been the worst possible time to leave, and strip the Duchy of some of its most powerful men while Geoffrey strengthened his grip. He hated leaving with his Southern borders in a mess, the man charged with their defense seemingly wandering the countryside – no-one had been able to tell him where Talvas was by the time they had left, although there were lurid tales starting to spring up suggesting Talvas had provided the pretext for Geoffrey's action. The cursed idiot had kidnapped a vassal of Geoffrey's, having lured him to Bellême on the pretext of a reconciliation, then tortured and mutilated the prisoner in ways that made William wince to hear about, before killing him and seizing his lands.

William found himself thinking he should have dealt with it before. It was well known the two had been at each other's throats for years. Perhaps Talvas' son Arnulf had done William a favor by casting his brutal father out. William would have been forced to make some sort of example of Talvas anyway, if it did not turn out he had been provoked. Yet he also had a duty to stand up for his vassal and give him every reasonable support. It would not look good amongst all the grands here if word got around that the former baron had been trudging round the countryside with nothing but the shirt on his back while his liege lord enjoyed all the luxury and pomp of a royal court.

Not that there weren't moments when he would consider that changing places with Talvas would give him the better part of the bargain.

After they arrived at Senlis, William heard through snatches of conversation that on top of everything, Hugh, Count of Maine, was gravely ill. He was an old man and it might well be his final decline. It seemed very likely that Martel had seized the opportunity while Normandy's attention was distracted with Talvas' exile, and the Count was too weak to respond.

It wasn't that Senlis wasn't impressive. Far from it. According to Lanfranc, the walls dated back to the Roman occupation, and the great hall where they now stood, a large, high-roofed structure hung with tapestries, and if the carving of the stonework around the pillars and arches was beginning to look plain by modern tastes, the floor had been laid with glazed colored tiles forming the Capet house symbols at regular points. The surroundings were put in the shade by the throng filling the hall. Everyone with a perche of land to their name must be here. The King's retinue, his relatives, every shade of nobleman, and emissaries from other kingdoms had attended on Henri's summons. He could make out several bearded Saxons and even a Dane or two. The representative of the Holy Roman Emperor. Churchmen of every color robe. The demesne of the French Kings may have been reduced over recent generations, but it still commanded great influence.

And as far as William was concerned, it was all to absolutely no good whatsoever. They needed to be marching on Anjou, forcing Martel to release the bishop. Not holding court, however spectacularly, leagues and leagues away.

"The King's flaunting his royal power and majesty without actually doing anything," fitzOsbern said through the side of his mouth as they waited at the edge of the room, while others were called to pay court before the throne. "I can't see that it will impress Geoffrey, somehow."

William hmmed his agreement. They didn't call Geoffrey 'Martel' - 'The Hammer' – for nothing. From what they had been able to glean from the other nobles called to the court, Martel had been casting his gaze at Maine for years. He wasn't the only one. William remembered his father's hopes that one day Maine would be part of Normandy... Another part of his legacy that William had thrown away. By the Saints' bowels it was intolerable!

"Whoever rules Le Mans has already achieved most of the control of Maine," a Baron from that country told him, as they waited. "Financially, ecclesiastically and administratively. Whoever controls the bishop controls Le Mans." As with many cities in France, the bishopric controlled a great deal of temporal power – in some cases, the bishops were effectively the lords as well, and such had it been in Le Mans. Not without numerous nobles trying to wrest it for themselves.

Eventually he was called forward. The King blathered something in that bizarre third-person, God-and-I way, that William vaguely caught the gist of, as he prostrated himself on the impressive but rather cold floor. Something about the overweening ambition of Anjou, the great insult to the Holy Church, and speeding to put the wrong to rights. After an appropriate period of mass and feasting, of course.

Oddly, Henri seemed well disposed towards William. Perhaps he had been more impressed with his young vassal's performance on the field at Val es Dunes than he had let on. Or less inclined to make an enemy of William.

After the session of court, everyone crammed into the castle's chapel for mass, again. He was introduced to Count Baldwin of Flanders, and as he bowed, blushed slightly at the thought that not two days before he had been discussing marrying the Count's daughter.

"And how is your daughter?" he blurted out before he could stop himself.

The Count looked at him as though he had realized he was talking to a different person than the one he thought he had been. "Well, thankyou, your Grace." His eyes narrowed, and he seemed to be considering what to say next for some time. Deciding whether or not to be open about a possible suit, perhaps?

"I had... thought to have an envoy attend you in Bruges, Your Grace, perhaps to touch upon how our two great houses might... become closer."

Baldwin smiled at that, a little frostily, but a smile nonetheless. "He shall be most welcome." The Count broke into a broader grin. "Ha! The thought of you and my little Matilda. She's only so high, you know, and slender as a willow-wand! Great big fellow like you? You could pick her up with one hand!"

William's expression froze, as indeed had all thoughts.

286

"Don't worry my boy," Baldwin laughed. "Send your envoy. When things have quietened down a bit, we'll see." He leaned forward. "Heard about your charge at Val es Dunes! Marvelous. The minstrels will be singing about that for a few years to come. And tell me, is it true that you once ran down a stag, wrestled it to the ground and broke off its antler with your bare hands?"

William muttered an explanation, trying to refute the exaggerated version that seemed to have gained currency while not downplaying the real kill.

"You know Matilda is here, don't you?" Baldwin said when he'd finished plying William with questions about both the battle and the hunt.

William shook his head, a sudden wave of nerves rippling through his stomach.

"Let's see if we can arrange a meeting then. You can tell her how you broke Burgundy's line, I'm sure she'll enjoy that."

It turned out that a fair number of people had heard of his part in the battle and were eager to meet him as a result of it. If he hadn't been so desperate to be away and fighting another, he might well have enjoyed it. He also found himself wondering about Matilda again. Was she as tiny and delicate as all that? It made him feel hulking and clumsy just thinking about it.

He sent a messenger to Montgomerie as soon as he was able, asking for news on Talvas and Alençon. A message from Falaise arrived just as William and fitzOsbern were finally about to meet the King to talk about their next move. William handed the missive to fitzOsbern, who broke the seal with shaking hands, read the few short lines... and burst out laughing.

"What is it?" William asked, frowning.

"Roger Montgomerie found Talvas on the road to Caen with his daughter, Mabel, and took them into his household. It seems not everyone is finding it difficult to find the right wife. Mabel and Roger are now married."

William frowned. That meant Montgomerie would be heir to the Bellême lands... He had been given instructions to give Talvas shelter at Falaise in return for passing the claim over to William. Although those instructions were only in the event that Talvas arrived at Falaise. It was no less irritating. His chest tightened. He did not like being outmaneuvered by someone he counted a friend...

Fitz turned over the page. "Oh, and the Pope is coming to Reims. He's going to hold a council there. That'll set a flutter in the dovecotes."

When Henri heard about the Pope's council, all talk of plans to tackle Anjou evaporated. The King's face turned even redder and the spit flying from his lips reached half a dozen pieds seemingly in every direction. "No Pope may hold a council within the Kingdom of France without the permission of the King! It has been thus since the days of Charlemagne! Who does this Leo think he is, that he may breeze into our kingdom and hold court." A bevy of courtiers fluttered round Henri, vainly trying to placate him. William and fitzOsbern waited before the throne, mute, waiting for the storm to subside. William did not envy Odo of Meaux, sprawled before the King and taking the brunt of it, as if he had any control over what the bishops did.

It turned out that the Pope had been invited by the bishop of Reims to bless the new church of Abbey of Saint-Remi, and had decided to hold a council while he was there. The bishop of Reims had neglected to inform Henri. Leo probably knew it would infuriate Henri. If the great men of the world spent less time maneuvering and more time governing, they might all be able to get more done.

Abruptly, Henri calmed himself. William had never spent long in his company, and did not know if he was a man of sudden rages that passed like spring squalls. Somehow, though, he doubted it. Everything he'd heard of the King spoke of long-nursed grudges and resentments that went to his very bones. William doubted Henri was about to let this go.

"We shall send emissaries to Pope Leo begging our Holy brother to explain himself." Henri's voice was beginning to turn stony. "And we shall call upon those men of the Church whose fealty is sworn to us requiring them to do their duty."

"What do you suppose he meant about men of the church's duty?" fitzOsbern asked, cutting across his thoughts as they fled from the audience chamber.

"What? Oh, no idea. He'll probably make them reaffirm their oaths of homage. If it makes him feel better, why not?"

"If I didn't know better, I'd say the King and the Pope were going out of their way to provoke each other."

"Ralph always used to say that the Roman Church was like the Roman Empire of old—it had to keep expanding its power or it would wither on the vine."

"And it's expanding into France?"

"Expanding everywhere, by the look of things."

"Must be good to have God on your side."

289

...Though what they've done to deserve His favor is anyone's guess. The thought of Mauger as favored by the Almighty!

And yet there was an obvious solution to the problem. God favored the strongest. Whoever won on earth got to carry the message, the Holy Cross itself. And it was said that the army that marched with the Cross at its head could never be defeated. What it must be to go into battle with the Papal Banner and all the funds and support that entailed...

When they reached their quarters, a messenger was waiting there.

"My Lord," he said, bowing to William. "His Grace the Count of Flanders wishes you to know of the very great regard he holds you in, and desires that you do him the honor of attending him and his daughter in their chambers upon the instant. If you would be so good as to follow me, Lord?"

William was hardly ready for a meeting with his prospective bride but had little choice in the matter. He hoped his tunic was not too obviously spattered with the King's saliva.

The messenger led him at a rapid clip to the chambers given over to Baldwin. William tried not to let his lip curl into a sneer. They were somewhat grander than his own, despite him being a Duke and Baldwin only being a Count. A very wealthy Count, with extensive territories and great influence, but a Count nonetheless. He had recently been at war with the Holy Roman Emperor himself. How the Emperor must have taken that! Having his ankles well and truly bitten by a mere Count!

How on earth were you supposed to address a prospective bride, anyway? His lessons with Ralph had never covered that. Or at least if they had, he must not have paid sufficient attention. The messenger showed him into a well-appointed room, in which sat Baldwin and a women so tiny William's first thought was that someone had made a mistake over how old the girl was, and she was nowhere near being of age. Then she looked up at him, and the intelligence and experience in the glance that flashed up at him revealed she was no adolescent. Matilda—he presumed it was she—must be easily less than five pieds in height, and he nearly six. She was, it seemed, in complete proportion for a woman of such small stature—he had mistaken her slender form for girlishness. It was not her size that struck him, however, but her gaze. Superior but not haughty, somehow. All expressed from a single look from eyes of a striking shade of green, set in a perfectly oval face, capped by braided, dark gold hair. There was something unreal about her, as if she were a statue pretending to be an earthly woman. Then she smiled momentarily and the gaze was human, the eyes no longer flashed but sparkled.

"Ah, there you are Normandy. Was beginning to wonder where you'd got to," Baldwin said, standing and giving him a curt bow.

William tore his eyes away from Matilda. "An audience with the King," he stammered, bowing in return. "Though little of the military campaign against Anjou was touched upon. An unfortunate matter with the Pope deciding to invade his sovereign territory."

Baldwin laughed, a little thinly. "You mock us, Normandy."

"I wish it were not true. The Pope has declared his intention to hold a council in Reims. Unfortunately he omitted to ask the King's permission."

Baldwin laughed more heartily this time. "Oh he has, has he? And Henri doesn't like that one little bit, I'll be bound. Well, I'm glad it's one of Odo's bishops and not one of mine. Anyway, I wanted to introduce you to my daughter, Matilda."

William turned and bowed, feeling so lumpen and clumsy in her presence. "My Lady," he said, hearing his voice making almost a growl in the small space.

"I understand you would like to marry me," Matilda said.

His cheeks immediately flushed. How on earth to answer that? He mumbled something about their great houses, strengthened in union, and greatness, and... good God, what on earth was he talking about?

"I'm afraid it's impossible," she said, after he had ground to a humiliating halt. "I am nobly born, and you are a bastard. I'm afraid it cannot be."

He had thought all his blood must be in his face, with his previous nervousness. Now it seemed he had been wrong, as a crimson flood roared and pounded in his head, burst into his chest and surged into his arms. She had called him a... That word that only varlets and criminals dared hurl at him. For a moment he wanted to lunge out, grab her braids and swing her round with them, smashing her against the floor when he'd tired of the sport. William turned his enraged stare on Baldwin who was simply beaming beatifically at his daughter. Was this why they'd dragged him here? Humiliation?

He fought the blood. This was a battle he would always have to fight, and he could bring no lance, no sword to help defeat it. It would have to be subdued whenever it rose up with his will and nothing else.

He attempted the sweetest smile he could manage, sensing that it manifested itself as a vicious leer, and bowed again. The room was silent. When would they dismiss him and end this torment?

Waiting for dismissal. By the Saints' bowels, had he no pride left? The thought of Flanders and the other nobles, laughing at the base-born Normandy, thinking he had a chance at a marriage with the daughter of a great house. What kind of fool was he?

Matilda smiled, and met his furious stare with a level gaze. Those eyes... He felt as though she could look through his flesh as if it were a light sea mist, and understand everything about him that even he struggled to make sense of.

"My Lady," he said, haltingly. "I was not born in wedlock, it is true. But my father, the Duke, named me as his heir ahead of men who were nobly born, at a young age. Perhaps he saw in me a man who could be his successor. I only know, however, that it is God's will, not man's, that decides who shall be a lord. Better born men have tried to take Normandy from me. I am still the Duke. You may make of that what you will."

William was shaking now, and took a step towards Matilda. It was a moment before he realized his fist was clenched. He hurriedly put it by his side, but out of the corner of his eye saw Baldwin stiffen, his hand move to the weapon he no doubt had concealed in his clothing. "I think we've all taken enough of each other's time," he hissed. "Lord. My Lady. May you make a match worthy of your station." He bowed comically low, turned on his heel and stormed out of the chambers, shoving a Flemish guard out of the way as he did so.

The air seemed to hit him as he left the hall. What had he just done? Destroyed his best chance at an alliance that could have saved his Duchy from its enemies at a stroke. Just for the sake of pride. Fool! Ralph had been right. He was not worthy of the title. He had only himself to blame.

William sloped back to the Norman quarters and demanded privacy. Fitz acquiesced without a word. It must have been fairly obvious that things had not gone according to plan. He shut himself in the cabinet chamber and stomped around trying to resist the temptation to break everything not fixed down, hoping for and dreading a messenger from Baldwin. None came. He swung between stomping around, kicking and shoving at the furniture with long periods sitting and staring into space, going over what he could have done, should have done.

Before he knew it, night had come. He had no idea how long it had been since he had returned from his humiliation. It had been a busy day, full of nothing good. All the threads he had to keep hold of as Duke... Just as he thought he had a grip on them all, began to unravel. And now he was the Duke, in his own right, they were his to hold alone. If he could solve more problems with a sword or a lance!

There was one problem that was entirely in his own gift to resolve though. The way he had spoken to Matilda. A lady. Turned around and walked away without being dismissed. It was unforgivably brutish, and not becoming of a lord. The story would spread through the court. Just as he had scraped together a little respect, he had crushed it through his own pride and impatience. Unforgivable.

He may have ruined his chances at the best marriage and alliance that had been on offer, but he could at least go part of the way to repairing his reputation as a gentleman before too much more damage was done. He must go back and apologize. Beg forgiveness. He might have shamed Ralph with his rashness earlier, but he could at least make the Baron a little proud with the way he resolved things.

William stormed back out into the vestibule. Fitz was there. Still there. Seated on a sentry's stool, head resting on his arm, eyes closed. Had he been here ever since? "Fitz?" William said, softly.

Fitz's head snapped up, and he leapt to his feet. "My Lord, is everything all right?"

"Yes, fine. I'm going back to see Matilda again."

Fitz rubbed his eyes. "You're what? But it's late. They'll be abed."

He was right of course. But this wouldn't wait until tomorrow. "I won't be long," William said, and strode out before Fitz could say anything else. He kept up a marching pace, fearing that if he stopped and thought about what he was doing, he would not be able to go on.

To return, to find Matilda, to make a gracious apology for his earlier conduct, to wipe out the insult, to return the two great houses to their former relationship, if never to build on it. Before he had quite realized, he was back at Flanders' apartments. A bored looking guard challenged him, once it was clear he meant to be there and was not a drunk guest who'd got lost. William announced his objective, mustering all the hauteur he could.

The sentry did not appear to recognize him, though he clearly saw he was of high station. "I can't admit you, Lord," said the guard. "It's far too late. His Grace has retired. Please come back on the morrow."

"It's the Lady Matilda I mean to see," William said, impatience giving an edge to his voice. "I only require a moment."

The guard's eyes widened slightly. "I'm sorry, Lord, you'll have to speak to His Grace in the morning."

He should have known it would come to this. Tomorrow everything might be different. It had to be now! "Let me in," William hissed.

The man's hands tightened on his pike. He had just begun to move it across his chest, symbolically barring the way and readying himself for a fight, when William struck. He swung his fist, hitting the guard full in the face, wrenched the pike out of his hands and smacked the shaft into the side of the fellow's half-helm. The sentry was already going down after the first blow, but the second shocked him into silence. He lay on the floor, gasping. William knelt and grabbed him by the throat.

"Where is Matilda's boudoir?" He growled, trying to be quiet, struggling to hear himself over the roaring of blood in his ears. *Why did he have to go and raise his weapon?* William thought. *Now he'd only made everything twelve times worse.* The guard's eyes bulged, and William relaxed his grip a touch, but dug the point of the pike gently into its former owner's chin. "Tell me where her chamber is, and don't even think about crying out or I'll skewer you with your own weapon."

The guard appeared to think about it for a moment, then stammered out where the lady was to be found. William made haste. There was no doubt the guard would raise the alarm. A patrolling guard was making his way along the darkened corridor, and William had to duck into an alcove as the man passed, no more than a pied away. Somehow, William remained undiscovered, and slipped out behind the sentry, making his way quickly to the door he had been directed to. He tried the handle. There was no lock on it, and the door swung noiselessly open.

The room was lit by a single candle. Matilda was sitting on the bed. She looked up at William and surprise, shock, fear and then anger flashed in her eyes. He opened his mouth to speak and no sound came out.

"So this is how it shall be?" Matilda said, voice level, only a slight reediness betraying what she must be feeling. "You come and take me in the night so I will be ruined for others, is that it? Do you mean to win an alliance as you would win more territory—by rape and pillage? You Northmen haven't changed."

It felt as though every one of William's muscles turned to hot metal rods and began contracting. He had come to apologize, and simply had more insults thrown at him!

"My ladies are just through that door," she went on. "And guards. Lots of guards. I will call out and they will come in and kill you if you don't go."

She took a breath as if to scream, and William stepped forward and pressed his hand over her mouth. Now the anger in her eyes turned back to fear and she started to struggle. He pushed her back onto the bed, tightening his grip to muffle the staccato squeaks that were all she could utter. He could feel her wriggling beneath him. It would be so easy to... Oh God, how easy it would be.

He pulled back, keeping his hand over her mouth. "My Lady," he said, fighting for breath. "I came here to apologize for my conduct earlier. I did not want any ill feeling between our families. I did not mean to... I swear, I meant you no harm."

Matilda stopped struggling, and the fear in her eyes turned to disbelief. Then something else. Amusement.

William took his hand away. Matilda took a couple of breaths, and shuddered a little.

"Do you mean to say that you broke into my apartments at night, came to my boudoir... manhandled me... to apologize?"

William breathed in, and with the air, a rush of epiphany. Barbarian! It was as she said, exactly! What a cursed idiot. Maybe he should be a tanner, for he was clearly no Duke.

Matilda uttered a sort of yelp, swallowed it back, and then began to chuckle. She threw her head back and laughed. William smiled, wanly. The anger evaporated at the sound. He knew she was not laughing at him, not exactly, and he could have laughed himself, had he not been concealed alone with the daughter of a powerful noble whose guards were no doubt looking for him at that very moment.

A shuffling sound issued from behind the door to the adjoining room. William stiffened, but it was a woman's voice, thick with sleep, that called out. "My Lady, is everything well?"

"Yes, yes," Matilda answered. "I was merely thinking of something the Duke of Normandy said earlier. His Grace is very amusing."

"Oh," said Matilda's lady. "That's as well, for he is not very handsome. Goodnight, Lady."

"Good night," said Matilda, turning back to William, lowering her voice. "And good night to you, sir."

"Good evening, Lady. Please accept my apologies, for my earlier brutishness, and tonight's... intrusion."

To his surprise, she smiled. "The foolishness of it is that I thought my judgment was premature. You spoke well, Lord. All you said was true." She leaned forward. "Most of all I see how hard it was for you to hear my judgment of you, and yet you restrained your temper, more or less. I see that your actions were taken in preference to actions you might regret more. Tonight as well as earlier. A man who can maintain his composure, his calm... somewhat... in the face of such provocation is not one to be underestimated, I think."

He laughed, a bitter snort. "Calm? I could have ripped your throat out and disemboweled your boor of a father."

"But you didn't." She exhaled. "As a matter of fact, I was about to withdraw my objection when you left."

"Oh." He felt himself deflate. He had defeated himself once again.

Matilda's mouth twisted into a wry smile. "There's no need to sigh, I haven't changed my mind. If anything, your... intriguing behavior tonight has reinforced my opinion that you might be a man worthy of notice." She drew herself up in formality, or a parody of it. "Very well, William of Normandy. I shall consider your suit favorably. I shall talk to Father. He won't be hard to persuade. He rather likes the idea of his heirs inheriting a Duchy."

Could it be true? He realized his mouth was hanging open, and snapped it shut. "Really? Oh. Thankyou, my Lady."

His heart fluttered and then, at the sound of boots tramping on the floor outside, fell. William prepared himself for armed men bursting through the door, but only a polite tap-tap sounded, then a cough. "Lady Matilda, is all well?" said a voice from outside. "It seems there was an intruder in the apartments."

"All is well, thankyou Captain," Matilda answered. "I have seen or heard nothing."

"Very well, Lady. We'll leave a guard outside"

"No, Captain, please don't. I couldn't sleep with an armed man shuffling and clanking outside my door." She looked at William, arching an eyebrow. William didn't know how the men outside could have failed to hear his pounding heart.

"Oh, all right, Lady. Sorry to disturb you," the captain of the guard answered after a brief pause. An exchange of whispering outside followed, and William heard the captain say "probably just drunk and hit his head, then made up a story to cover up for it. All right, let's go."

The boots moved on up the corridor. William took his leave of Matilda and managed to sneak out without being seen. As he staggered back to his own quarters, he could not decide whether or not he had in fact dreamed the entire encounter.

FitzOsbern was in the Norman quarters when he returned. William found him pacing the floor, giving every appearance of having been in that state for some time. "Where on Earth have you been, Lord?" he cried when he saw William in the door. "I thought you might have been kidnapped."

William paused before speaking. "I think I might be betrothed."

FitzOsbern goggled. The look in his eyes suggested he thought William had lost his sanity.

"Honestly, Fitz, I haven't lost my reason. I have just been conferring with Matilda. I am serious."

"My congratulations, Lord," fitzOsbern laughed, stepping over to William and grasping him by the shoulders. "What do you mean – you *think* you might be betrothed?"

"Well. Earlier she rejected me. Then she insulted me. I stormed out and thought that was an end to it. But it turns out she'd changed her mind, so when I went back to apologize just now she said she'd agree to marry me."

"But that's wonderful!"

"Yes. I suppose it is." Although being married to a woman who'd managed to put him through such torment in such a short meeting might prove to be a challenge greater than any he'd yet faced. "She's got to persuade her father, of course. I'd better send a very flattering proposal and see what happens."

CHAPTER 25

AFTER a time, Ealdgyth thawed still further towards Ælfgifa. She was unsure if it was due to the queen being lonely or whether their natural bond as sisters began to reassert itself. Ealdgyth seemed to have decided to trust Ælfgifa to an extent, at any rate, enough to put her to the test. The day was fair and crisp, with just a hint of autumn in the air. The leaves on the great oaks and beeches were just starting to turn. Ælfgifa paused and raised her face to the morning sun, taking a deep breath and enjoying the simple pleasure of being outside. Ealdgyth had requested that she ride to Westminster with a small escort to speak to the monks who kept the pigeon lofts. Ælfgifa had not needed Ealdgyth to spell out her task for her: find a monk who is trustworthy and entirely devoted to the Crown. One who will read and intercept any messages at her behest. As she made her way to the stables, Ælfgifa thought it extremely unlikely that Ealdgyth would not have seen to this matter already. She imagined her sister wanted to know two things; whether Ælfgifa's choice would match her own and whether Ælfgifa could chose as wisely as she spoke. She supposed that if she made a poor choice, one who would be careless in his duties or was in some other way untrustworthy, then it would be an indicator to Eadgyth that her sister could not be relied upon. There was once again the need to balance personal feeling against political expectation. Ælfgifa decided that it would never be a comfortable experience.

The stables were well kept and smelt of clean hay and contented horse. It was dim inside as she made her way to Spyrryd's stall. No doubt as a gently reared lady she was expected to await her horse and her escort outside, or even to wait inside until someone should be sent to tell her they were ready for her, but Ælfgifa had missed Spyrryd. He was the one friend of her childhood she had kept who neither demanded anything of her nor took her for anything than what she was – the bringer of treats. She slipped the gray pony an apple and ran her hands over his legs and flanks while he crunched happily. He had been well cared for, she thought. His coat gleamed like molten silver and there wasn't a burr or knot anywhere in his mane or tail.

She nudged the horse's belly with a knee and he blew at her. "You are getting fat, my lad," she murmured. "Not that the rest hasn't done you good."

"He's a sound boy, that 'un," a cheerful voice said. "Getting along a bit in years but a good, steady mount. Not much dash and fire mind." The voice was unmistakably male. Reluctantly, Ælfgifa turned toward the speaker. He was a young man, perhaps only a few years older than herself. She felt herself flushing hot and told herself that it was because she felt self-conscious being caught here in a pony's stall, with muck on her boots and bits of straw on her gown and in her hair. Her embarrassment certainly had nothing to do with the fact that this was the first young man she'd met who wasn't close kin to her. Nor did it matter that he was uncommonly well-favored, being tall and broad with reddish hair and a wide, smiling mouth.

"I do not need much dash and fire," Ælfgifa replied, embarrassment making her tone crackle. "I am not like to be riding him in to battle!"

The young man peered at her and Ælfgifa realized that it was dim enough that he couldn't see her features clearly. *But he will in a moment and then he will be less cordial*, she thought going hot with humiliation all over again.

"You're not a ceorl at all!" He cried and then shut his mouth abruptly as if he had caught some of her embarrassment.

"I should hope not," Ælfgifa said tartly. *Any moment now and I shall have to move into the light. I wish he would go away.* "What is your name?" God in heaven, why was she asking that?

"Garyn... my Lady?" He replied uncertainly as if uncertain that she *was* a lady. Which confirmed Ælfgifa's assumption that the queen's ladies didn't go into the stables themselves.

"Well, Garyn, perhaps you might pass me a bridle? If I do not stop lolling around here the morning will be half done."

"I'm sorry, Lady, but I can't let you take him. He's Lady Ælfgifa's mount and she's to have him this morning for an errand. We're just waiting for her now, me and a few others. I came to get this fellow ready for her." Garyn grabbed a halter and entered the stall. Spyrryd raised his head and snorted. "Easy there, lad," Garyn murmured and made the soothing whistling through his teeth that so many grooms and stable lads used. "Best come out of there my Lady," Garyn said holding out a hand. *No help for it*, Ælfgifa thought. She reached out a small hand which was swallowed by his huge, callused palm. "I am Ælfgifa," she said. *He will have heard about me and will drop my hand as soon as he can...*

Garyn twisted his head to look at her so quickly that Spyrryd started. "My Lady? I... I'm sorry... I thought... But what are you doing in here?"

Ælfgifa smiled wryly. She supposed he had had a shock so his tone was not meant to be impertinent. Also he had not let go of her hand. She had expected to be dropped like hot iron. *He hasn't seen your face yet...* "I was seeing to my horse," she said waspishly, bracing herself against the moment when she would move sufficiently into the light for Garyn to recoil. Hating herself for caring. Despising herself for the sharp thrill of a handsome young man's hand on hers. Then she caught sight of Garyn's expression. He looked so thoroughly miserable at not realizing who she was from the start that she relented. It was hardly his fault that she had a face that would make him shudder in disgust. His reaction would only be natural, only to be expected. It was not as if she were not used to it. The shock of finding the queen's sister in the stables and mistaking her for a ceorl was surely more of an occasion for dismay. After all Garyn did not know her at all. He might be expecting a whipping for how he had spoken to her. There were ladies—and Ælfgifa thought they were hardly worthy of the title—who would take pleasure in exercising even so much power as that, over a young man who was helpless but to obey them, free man or not.

"Well," Ælfgifa said briskly, shaking off her own discomfort, "I suppose I'm the first 'Lady' you've ever seen down in the stables. No harm done, Garyn, if you can perhaps keep quiet about my liking to tend my own horse?" She doubted Ealdgyth would care a straw that she was feeding apples to her pony but making Garyn a co-conspirator of the most innocent kind should relieve the lad's embarrassment. Why she cared, Ælfgifa chose not to dwell on. She stepped into the light and resisted the urge to cast her gaze down or otherwise hide her face, meeting Garyn's eyes squarely with her own. Garyn did not back away. At her words the tension in his shoulders relaxed. Instead he smiled at her. "You are too gracious, my Lady," he said and Ælfgifa felt as if she was standing in a hot wind as Garyn turned his not inconsiderable charm upon her. Then instead of releasing her hand, he turned it and gently kissed her knuckles. It was a gesture of homage but it went through her like fire. She felt her face heating as if the simple contact had set her alight. Flustered, she watched as Garyn let go of her hand and went back into the stall to collect Spyrryd.

Master yourself, she thought fiercely, *no good will come of misinterpreting an innocent gesture. You are not a silly young milkmaid to have your head turned in such a way. If he meant well it was gratitude. If he did not, then you hardly want to be caught in such games.* But she wished for a moment to be less analytical. To enjoy the illusion of drawing a man's attention, even if only for an hour or two. It was the greatest folly. She was quite sure she would never cross paths with Garyn again. In that she was to be proved wrong.

***

Brother Dubhne was actually in the pigeon loft when they arrived at Westminster but by then Ælfgifa was only too glad to escape into the hot, thick darkness of the loft. There was a smell of straw and droppings, competing with the yeasty warm scent of contented poultry. It was very dim and the inhabitants of the roosts cooed and churred. Occasionally there was a scuffle and slap of wings. Ælfgifa barely noticed her surroundings. Garyn had been the groom assigned to accompany her escort to Westminster, charged with caring for their mounts along the way—quite unnecessary for such a short and easy distance, Ælfgifa thought. While the four men-at-arms had been distant and respectful, Garyn was incorrigible. If she had not known better she would have suspected him of flirting with her. It had left Ælfgifa feeling hot and confused, distracted from the task in hand. She had seen girls lose their heads over a likely young man and always laughed into her sleeve at them. She wasn't laughing now. Blush had piled on blush as she rode to the abbey until she half hoped, half feared one of her escort would put the groom in his place. Ælfgifa supposed it was her own fault for not acting the haughty lady with Garyn and putting him down from the start. Too late now.

She wondered if he was laughing at her. It was clear that Garyn thought a lot of himself and was by no means unaware of the admiring glances other girls cast his way—even in the short distance they had travelled. Occasionally he had answered a particularly saucy look from a girl along the way with a wink or a low whistle. Ælfgifa had found that she wanted to rein Spyrryd in, jump off her pony's back and scratch the offending girl's eyes out.

She had left her escort below and much to her relief one of her guards had aimed a kick at Garyn's backside, bellowing for him to tend the horses and rest them for the return journey. Ælfgifa had almost forgotten why she had come on this errand and was miserably wondering whether she could stay in the pigeon loft for good, when she heard a different sound from the other end. A noise that was definitely not made by a bird. The labored, stertorous sound of an old human breathing through phlegmy lungs. Ælfgifa jumped, brushing straw nervously from her gown for the second time that day.

"Good day?" she called, trying to make her voice strong and unflinching. Something hunched and hesitant moved in the deeper shadows at the end of the loft.

"No need to shout, girl. I'm not deaf," a crusty voice said testily. The faint light limned the outline of a bent old man in a monk's habit. He spoke with the unmistakable lilt of Erin.

"I am sorry. Are you Brother Dubhne?" Ælfgifa asked politely.

"You were not expecting Saint Cuthbert, I trust?" the old monk replied.

Ælfgifa suppressed a smile. "Not amongst pigeons, no, Brother. Perhaps if Westminster kept messenger ducks or gulls I should have been set up for such a disappointment."

"Ha! You're a sharp one. What would you do if I were Saint Cuthbert after all?" the monk demanded but something in his voice made Ælfgifa think she had pleased him.

"I should commiserate with you on what is proving to be a most unrestful *eternal rest*. I believe your bones have toured half of England now."

Brother Dubhne laughed, long and creaky. "You will be the Queen's sister then. Elf-gift, is it?"

"You were expecting me?" Ælfgifa said, puzzled.

"Oh yes. Queen Ealdgyth said that if a girl with a sharp tongue and a fey mind came asking for me, I would know her kinswoman." The monk came closer and even in the dim light, Ælfgifa could see that there was a milky caul over his eyes. He was blind. Under her breath she cursed Ealdgyth. This, apparently, was more of a test than she had imagined. She was certain, though, that she had the right man. This was the skilled scholar who would catch and intercept all messages. She had not made the wrong choice when she had asked to speak to the brethren who looked after the lofts. So Dubhne, blind or not, was the best choice. Ælfgifa decided to tackle the issue head on.

"May I ask how you know who to pass an incoming message on to?" Ælfgifa braced herself. There was no delicate way of asking and if Dubhne was proud then he'd hardly thank her for a question that drew attention to his lack of vision.

Dubhne sliced a thin smile at her. "I hear a pigeon landing now. Take you the message and if you can tell me how I know who it is for, I'll explain."

Ælfgifa frowned just as there was a flurry of slapping wings and a pigeon landed on the tiny window sill. Whatever else, Dubhne was right, there was nothing wrong with his hearing. She managed to catch the bird after it had eyed her with its small, yellow, half-mad eyes and bobbed around awkwardly for a turn or two. Dubhne laughed as if he could see the entire enterprise. Feeling rather cross, she pinned the bird's wings and ignored its redundant pecks as she freed the tiny cylinder tied to its leg.

"Read it then," Dubhne said. Ælfgifa let go of the pigeon and received a slapping wing in the eye for her pains. Eyes watering, she glared at the monk. "It's too dark to read up here," she said.

"Is it?" the monk smiled again.

Still feeling off balance and not kindly disposed toward pigeons in general, she unrolled the scrap of parchment. There were wiggling lines of writing but it was too dim to even make out what language it was. Ælfgifa paused. Somehow Dubhne knew which messages needed checking and which needed to be sent on without interference. *Stop using your eyes*, she thought, *the monk doesn't*. Instead she stared ahead and felt along the parchment with the sensitive pads of her fingertips. There. In one corner an indentation. Tiny as if made by a needle but with a very definite shape. Three pointed, like a flower. In a flash of intuition, Ælfgifa understood. "Anything coming from a trusted source ready to be sent on, has a mark you can feel," she said. "I suppose you can tell where it must go and with what urgency based on the shape of the mark. Or where it is placed in the message."

"Very good, little Gift," Dubhne smiled a real smile now.

"I would guess that as this was a trial of my skills, my sister sent that bird." Ælfgifa swallowed her annoyance. She had made less of an impression on Ealdgyth and her manner of dealing with intelligence than she thought. *That entire conversation in the ladychapel was a test, to see if I would mislead her*. She felt a stab of pique at having underestimated Ealdgyth.

Dubhne seemed very pleased however. "The queen said you were sharp. She was right. And now you will help me develop this method further."

"I suppose I will," Ælfgifa replied. "Is this message for me, then?"

Dubhne nodded. "Take it and read it when you go."

ÇHAPTER 26

ÆLFGIFA found herself less distracted by Garyn's presence on the return journey, thanks to her irritation. She was not entirely insensible however, especially when he casually reached up, placed his hands on her waist and lifted her out of the saddle when they had arrived back at court. She could not stop herself reddening. It seemed to her that Garyn enjoyed her discomfort, even if there was no malicious intent behind it. This did nothing to improve her general mood. She stormed off in the direction of the ladychapel and was not at all surprised to find Suela waiting for her outside. As the ceorl shut the heavy oak door behind her, Ealdgyth twisted on one of the otherwise empty benches and smiled wryly at her sister.

"Are you very cross, Gifa?"

"Yes, although mostly with myself in truth." Ælfgifa hesitated and then sank with a small sigh on to the bench next to Ealdgyth. "You might have stopped me the last time we spoke in here, you know. Of course I realize why you didn't but it does seem hard being tricked by one's own sister."

Ealdgyth gave her a sly look. "You are but newly come here. Were you like every other gently reared maiden I should have hesitated to take you into my confidence without a test of some kind. As it is, you are more cunning than a fox and sharper than a blade. Any test needed to be proportionately knotty." The queen paused and her expression softened a little. "I am sorry that you are caught up in such things, sister. It is all too late to extricate you now. I believe it would have been too late five years ago. And you would never have been happy to be kept out. Others might use you but you forged yourself into the weapon."

"If such words are meant to be a comfort, I beg you not to trouble yourself further on my behalf," Ælfgifa said sourly.

Ealdgyth startled her by laughing. "Come now, sister. We have found a fitting occupation for your unique talents."

"And you are now satisfied that such talents are in place and at your disposal," Ælfgifa said flatly. "What then of my missives to our brother?"

"Send them if you care to. I'll take no steps to prevent you and I doubt I could if I wished to. You are quite creative when thwarted." Ealdgyth paused as Ælfgifa repressed a smile. "Besides Harold, for all his ambition is no traitor. It is as you say, it will be nothing he could not discover for himself given time."

"You sound as though you mean to make it a challenge to find out such things as would not be common knowledge, my Queen," Ælfgifa suggested archly.

Ealdgyth gave her a cynical smile. "I doubt I could prevent that either. However I do believe you can be trusted with such intelligence. You would not pass on anything that might lead to trouble for your monarch, that I do know."

"Such faith, sister," Ælfgifa murmured.

"Besides," the queen continued, "your counsel has proven invaluable to Edith and our brother. I desire the same level of... consideration."

"Did you not think to simply ask? Rather than to play such games."

"Oh, Gifa, when you have been here a little longer you will understand. This is not Harold's household. Royal court is a nest of vipers all bent on furthering their own ends and sinking fangs in where necessary. The true currency of England is power. Who you might call friend, supporter, ally, enemy or foe—that is what matters. Wealth buys you such things in one way or another. You know this. As you are my sister I do love you, but never would I trust you without proof." Ealdgyth sounded resolute and a little sad. "Nor anyone else."

"What would you have of me then?" Ælfgifa said, trying for a lighter tone.

"Your advice for one. It has served me well so far. You bade me once to attend the king and ensure he believed our aims were the same. Wise counsel from a child. There will come a time soon when I shall need such wisdom again and I cannot trust anyone else to deliver it."

"What do you mean?" Ælfgifa said in alarm.

"You will see, sister. I doubt not you will see before I need tell you." She leaned in and kissed Ælfgifa's cheek. "I am glad you are come here, Gifa." The queen rose and left the chapel, the smell of lavender lingering in the cool air behind her.

***

Between Ealdgyth fully embracing her into her confidence, working out a system of tiny, different shaped indentations and a code on their placement with Brother Dubhne, coupled with the duties that all well born ladies were expected to perform, Ælfgifa was kept so busy it felt as if her feet rarely touched the ground. She made no great progress with Edward. His attitude to her did not soften, though she thought her sister might have put a word or two in his ear, since he was now more cordial, or seemed so. Ælfgifa surmised that his dislike of her was down to her disfigured face and shrugged. Since coming to Lundenwic she had seen far more ghastly faces than her own. Whether they were the product of disease, punishment or an accident of birth was immaterial. The old Abbess of Wintanceastre had been right all those years ago during the strange meeting in the herb garden. As it was, Ælfgifa could still not fathom her sister's affection for the king. If he had seemed old when she was ten, he seemed to have aged fifteen years in the last five or six. His hair was now completely white. Soft and pretty as snow fall but not very kingly. Ælfgifa suspected that the rosiness of Edward's thin cheeks owed more to some chronic ailment than to robust health.

Not that her opinion would ever be sought. Edward had a physician with whom he frequently consulted. A scrawny nothing of a man, middling in height whose hair, skin and eyes were all the same dull shade of pale beige. The thought of the man, Camus, made Ælfgifa shudder with disgust. It was partly the way that the physician's hands were always caked with filth, the nail beds black. His clothes were rarely better tended although he dressed richly for a physician. Her disgust also had root in his methods. Curious, Ælfgifa had found an occasion to sneak into the physician's workroom when it was deserted and poke around. She had been horrified at some of the remedies on his shelves – *hippus fimus* had proven on olfactory examination to be exactly what the label suggested. Ælfgifa's already uncertain confidence in the physician's ability had waned further when she discovered that he treated his patients with worse than dried horse shit. She had been sorely tempted to throw out the most dangerous medicines as well as what was unmistakably a withered hand taken from a dead man. At least, Ælfgifa hoped he had been dead when it had been taken, especially if the physician had been the one to amputate it.

The bulk of her disgust however, came from the way Camus examined her face whenever they met. He made her feel like a strange, new presentation of an old disease that had long lost its fascination for the medic. An unexpected find, an eccentric symptom. A freak. That his interest was in no way malicious but genuinely, coldly fascinated made it worse. She avoided Camus as much as possible as a consequence. Ælfgifa did wonder if she ought to suggest to Ealdgyth that Edward consult another physician but since she could not be certain Edward was ill let alone what was wrong with him, she was hesitant to mention it.

The king is still weak of digestion, she thought at board, watching surreptitiously as Ealdgyth sliced an apple for him and spooned a fine-grained gruel into a bowl. *Is it all part of the same complaint? Is it why Ealdgyth has no child?* Ælfgifa swallowed hard. A king with no heir was a tricky proposition. A sick king incapable of getting an heir was a very dangerous thought. Ealdgyth was right. Ælfgifa knew she would never share such a suspicion with Harold, or indeed anyone. The slightest whisper in the wrong place could cause untold harm. *Besides,* she thought, glancing around, *I cannot be the only person to have such a suspicion. Likely they blame my sister for the lack of a child. Men always seem to cling to barrenness being a special prerogative of women. Heaven forbid that anything should be amiss with the sacred sacs.* She realized that she was scowling and smoothed her expression out. *Ealdgyth knows what she is doing,* she told herself. *Likely she has even drawn the blame to avoid any suspicion of Edward appearing weak.* Ælfgifa pitied her sister, though. She felt that Ealdgyth must want a child and was likely sensitive about the subject. And yet Ealdgyth spent a great deal of time building her husband's legend as a Godly man, a saintly man who ate little not from illness but from piety. Who had no child because he would not put away a barren wife rather than because he himself could not father one.

Ælfgifa had been grimly amused that Ealdgyth had commissioned texts and books on her husband's goodness. Now she could see how clever her sister had been. She had all but made herself indispensable to Edward despite a lack of issue. If her suspicions were correct and it *was* Edward who was barren, then surely her sister's actions would make the king think twice about supplanting her. And yet Edward was a cold, querulous man who showed little warmth to anyone save Ealdgyth. He did not relish life – a state of affairs Ælfgifa found puzzling when she compared him to Harold or her father, or indeed any of the small collection of men she knew at all well. A wrong word could send the king flying into a fit of shrieking passion in which he would throw bowls and goblets. He was a puzzle. The pieces of his character did not fit together to make a whole that Ælfgifa could warm to. Equally puzzling was just what Ealdgyth *did* see in him, because her sister's affection was genuine.

CHAPTER 27

"YOU are not paying attention, girl!" Dubhne barked. Ælfgifa jumped, startled and then felt annoyed with herself. Exactly how *did* the old monk do that? She knew he couldn't see her and yet if she was distracted for a moment, he always knew. She might have thought that the stilling of her quill gave her away but for the fact that she wasn't writing at all at that moment. Dubhne had barely said a word to her since she'd arrived, other than to indicate that she should be seated and stay absolutely still. *So how does he know?* She wondered resentfully.

She forced herself not to glare at the old man, certain he would be able to tell if she did. As if Dubhne could read her thoughts, he chuckled under his breath and went back to writing. Dubhne writing was one of the strangest and most awe inspiring things Ælfgifa had ever seen. He did not look down at the page but sat upright, milky eyes fixed ahead while his quill—Ælfgifa noted that he favored a goose feather with a broad nib—moved unerringly on the page. His calligraphy was superior to any other example she had seen. It never wavered from the straight even lines. The letters stayed the same height and were even in style. He made no mistakes. Between that and his unerring way of knowing

319

exactly what she was doing, Ælfgifa would have thought his blindness a ruse if she had not examined his eyes herself.

Dubhne reached the end of a line and finished with a slight flourish. Carefully he lifted the quill away and wiped the end. He didn't have so much as an ink stain on his fingers.

"In my youth," Dubhne said, "I would have given this a fine border of some kind. Hounds and harts perhaps. Such things are beyond me now, I fear." He smiled ruefully.

"How are you able to do so much?" Ælfgifa asked before she could stop herself. "I mean I know you can feel the pricked lines where the text must go but..." She trailed off.

Dubhne turned his blind eyes towards her and gave her a wide grin. "I wasn't always blind, Girl. I know what the letters are supposed to look like."

Ælfgifa shook her head and the monk went on, "the point is for the words to be uniform. You don't need eyes for that. Just a place to set them down. Now the pictures, they're not uniform and we have not so much pigment and gold leaf that we can waste it on me making a holy mess. Not enough good vellum come to that." Ælfgifa still didn't really understand but she suspected that in order to do so, she would have to attempt to write blindfolded, an experiment she was not keen to try, even for curiosity's state.

"So, Girl, are you going to tell me why you are so distracted when you've been allowed the rarest of privileges —that of being female and allowed to enter the scriptorium?" Dubhne creaked.

Ælfgifa forced herself not to pull a face. The fact was that since Ealdgyth had been sending her here—to all intents and purposes to improve her Latin and Greek, although Ælfgifa

320

needed no such help—Garyn had often formed part of her escort. A fact that was both deeply distressing and secretly wonderful. He continued to flirt with her and she could not seem to make herself put him in his place once and for all. She was almost ashamed of how much she enjoyed his attention. While she cautioned herself against paying him any notice, she could not help vague, nebulous daydreams rising bright in her mind's eye. There was no power on earth that would see her confess such secret fantasies to this crusty old monk however. While she debated what excuse she might give him that was not entirely untruthful, Dubhne sighed and leaned back. "What lad is it that you moon after then, Girl?"

Ælfgifa flushed as hot as if she had been dipped in boiling water. "Why would you say that?"

"Curious thing about being a monk and blind to boot, you see a great deal more of human nature than people expect." His shaggy gray eyebrows pulled together. "Well it's no business of mine, though I will say you'd be wasted in a marriage, Girl, whatever your fine relatives might plan for you."

Recovering from her embarrassment Ælfgifa smiled, feeling a rush of warmth for the old man. "I think you need hardly worry on that score, Brother. I am under no illusions about my suitability for a match, political or otherwise. You are not so ready to lose your pupil I hope?"

"Certainly not," Brother Dubhne scoffed. "You're the only one in the entire festering Abbey who trims the quills the right length."

"My teacher, Brother Caedmon, had me do it when I was bored as a child," she replied feeling nostalgic. She had not seen or heard from Caedmon in many years, although often

Brother Ashwine would write in reply to her missives to Edith—she would know that crabbed script anywhere.

"Caedmon? I knew a Brother Caedmon. He left his Abbey in the end."

"It may be the same man, Brother Dubhne. I think he had a disagreement with a new Abbott on Celtic or Latin rite—though as a child it sounded to me as if they were arguing over how a monk should shave his head." She smiled at the memory.

Dubhne laughed like a creaking gate. "That disagreement goes on, Little Gift. And it makes as much sense as if it were merely about how one cuts ones hair. As if God cares." He looked sad for a moment and then heaved himself up, reaching unerringly for the ash staff he used to get around.

"The lofts?" Ælfgifa asked, casting a last look over the carefully piled scrolls on the shelves, the desks, the jars of pigment and ink and precious gold leaf.

"Aye, Girl. I've a flutter in my bones," Dubhne said and held out his arm.

Ælfgifa took it though it was offered as a courtesy rather than to guide the blind man. He certainly didn't need her to lean on. "How goes your study of Frankish?" He asked as they made their way across the courtyard.

"It comes on apace, Brother. Easier than Latin I think, though they turn a phase most oddly on occasion." Ælfgifa replied. "I practice with Ealdgyth... I mean the Queen, when we sit with our needlework."

"Good," Dubhne replied absently. "I fear you'll need that skill before long." He was scanning the sky as if he knew a pigeon was incoming, even though he would not see it if there was. Ælfgifa had laughed at his colorful way of saying that he thought news would arrive until he'd been proven right not a moment later. She turned her own gaze from the sky and frowned at the old man. "What do you mean?"

"Now that," Dubhne replied, "the good lord has not made known to me."

Ælfgifa looked at him doubtfully but somewhere near the base of her spine a shiver of foreboding began.

**

When she arrived back at court, Ælfgifa headed straight for the chamber where Ealdgyth and her ladies were sure to be gathered, trying to conceal her nervous energy. Dubhne had been correct. No sooner had they entered the pigeon loft than a smoky pink-colored bird had alighted on the sill. The message was from an Abbey in Boulogne. Their liege lord, Eustace the Count of Boulogne, was making a visit to King Edward and hoped to be received at his court. The Latin script was beautifully rendered in swift precise strokes using what Ælfgifa guessed to have been a crow's quill. What interested her, however, was the note of ambiguity in the second line. She had long known monks to have a sense of humor but the writer of this missive bordered on sarcastic, or so it seemed to her.

His Lordship hopes that his presence will cause no discomfort to His Royal Majesty, to which end he regrets that his wife, Ida of Lorraine, will not be accompanying him.

She had sat down next to Dubhne on the steps outside the pigeon loft. Dubhne had scarce seemed to have heard her when she read the message.

"Brother," Ælfgifa had said at length, "is there some reason that Lady Ida would have caused discomfort?"

"Your brother-in-law is a godly man, Little Gift. The count of Boulogne is... *eccentric*, I have heard. I know no ill of his wife other than that the union was forbidden by the Pope." Dubhne's mouth had twisted into a grim line.

"But the Count married her anyway? Could he not have got dispensation? I assume it was a matter of kinship?" Ælfgifa could not think of any other reason which would preclude such an eminently suitable match.

"It is known that they were within the degrees of consanguinity prohibited by the Latin church. It may not have been a problem if so many of their forebears had not already claimed such dispensation." Brother Dubhne had snorted derisively, "Of course the rumors that Ida is in fact the count's half-sister may have had more to do with it, though not so much as the unification of two large estates, which was greatly against the Holy Roman Emperor's design. It is said he has the Pope's ear."

More politics, Ælfgifa had thought. "Count Eustace was excommunicated?"

"He was, not that I think it troubles him greatly." Dubhne had turned toward her then. "Be careful, Girl. He is known to be a proud, vain man who is used to doing as he pleases. The people will not be happy to have him as a guest in Lundenwic. You'll see why."

"I had better take this news back to the Queen." Ælfgifa had stood and shaken out her skirts.

"'Ere you do so, send any messages you have need to. I do not think I shall see you here again for a time." Dubhne had paused and then seemed to come to a decision. "Alert your father. The Count will arrive in Doubvres, part of Jarl Wessex's lands. Any other messages... well, be guided by your own conscience and good sense."

In the end, Ælfgifa had sent a concise, hasty note to Godwin, although she had never written to her father before. She knew that Dubhne would not have advised it without good reason. She also penned a slightly more detailed missive for Edith. Dubhne stood by and said nothing as she released the birds. She wished she knew why his brow was clouded with such trouble.

Now, as she entered the Queen's solar, she wondered how she would give Ealdgyth the news. She managed to catch her sister's eye on entering the chamber but Aofra intercepted her before she could slip into the seat that Suela had hastily vacated.

"Good. You're finally here. You can hold the skein while I wind," the young woman snapped.

Ælfgifa repressed a sigh, catching Ealdgyth's eye. The Queen made a slight motion of blessing which Ælfgifa knew to mean 'when I am at prayers.' The ladychapel later then. Trying hard not to roll her eyes, Ælfgifa sat down beside Aofra. She accepted the skein of newly spun thread on her outstretched hands as Aofra began to wind it into a ball. Motherhood had been a rude awakening for Aofra. She had given birth at midwinter – an easy delivery as such things went although she had screamed and cursed Ælfgifa with such foul language that anyone would have been forgiven for thinking Ælfgifa *was* responsible for the girl's predicament.

She eyed Aofra covertly. She was still pretty but blurred somehow. Her body had not yet regained its youthful slenderness and sagged where it had not sagged before, despite Aofra demanding a wet nurse as soon as the child was born. Aofra was now perpetually grumpy and dissatisfied. Sharp with the husband of whom she had been so pleased to boast before. Ælfgifa thought that perhaps now Aofra regretted marrying a much older man, despite his wealth and the fact he obviously doted on his young wife and infant son. She felt heartily sorry for the man. His pretty butterfly had transformed into a shrill, contentious shrew. The only good that Ælfgifa could see was that Aofra was now too ill-tempered to be creative in trying to torment her.

Still, a sense of professional pride had made Ælfgifa stay for the birth, concocting a pretext that would take Camus the physician as far away as possible. The thought of those filthy hands delivering a child had made Ælfgifa's stomach churn. Gritting her teeth, she tried to look serene as she bore the brunt of Aofra's bad temper.

Ealdgyth chuckled at her, when Ælfgifa finally made her way into the ladychapel, feeling frayed and on edge.

"I do not know why you keep her, sister!" Ælfgifa cried, annoyed past endurance. "She would try the patience of a saint and I have no pretensions to that kind of goodness, I assure you!"

Ealdgyth took her hand and drew her to sit down beside her. "You did very well, Gifa. I should have stabbed her with a needle in half such time."

"You are the Queen. You could probably have her nose cut off." Ælfgifa grumbled.

Ealdgyth tapped a finger against her lower lip as if considering the suggestion. "I think not. Her husband is too important a thagn to offend, unfortunately."

"Her tongue then," Ælfgifa snapped. "I doubt not but that he would find that to be an improvement."

Ealdgyth laughed. "Come, deliver your tidings."

Ælfgifa sighed and passed on the contents of the message and her own impressions. Ealdgyth grew grave and thoughtful. "Does anyone else know?"

"I sent a message to our father. It seemed politic as Count Eustace will land on the coast of Wessex."

"You are right." A small frown puckered Ealdgyth's forehead. "Let us hope Godwin has not lost his edge." At Ælfgifa's enquiring look she said, "In Wessex, more than any other part of England, the people are proud to be Saxon."

"They will not like a Norman lord passing through," Ælfgifa said.

"Nor will any in England, but most especially not there." She sighed. "I could wish it had been any of Edward's other relations. Eustace is volatile. I shall not breathe easy until he has gone." She smiled. "You have done well, Gifa. I thank you. I must inform the king." She left her sister alone in the lengthening gloom of the chapel, the shiver of foreboding growing stronger.

CHAPTER 28

AFTER the best part of two months hanging around at Senlis, military discussions regarding what to do about Geoffrey Martel had barely progressed. At least, though, Matilda was as good as her word. A surprised Baldwin announced to William that Matilda had declared to him that she wished to marry the Norman Duke after all, and while Baldwin admitted he had felt like thrashing William for his impudence, he was prepared to let the couple wed.

As if that wasn't enough, the Pope was now on his way to Reims. William sent for Lanfranc to try and find out what on Earth was going on and work out how they might deal with it.

"Do you know which route Leo will come by? I wouldn't want him coming too close to Anjou. It would be just like Martel to kidnap him, too. Then Lord knows where we'd be. He'll have a proper guard, won't he?"

"I will speak to the Archbishop and ask, my Lord," the bishop answered.

"And we can send troops to protect him if he decides to pass through Normandy, assuming we can spare any. Well with any luck we'll be able to call upon Flanders for support by that time."

"Flanders, my Lord?" Lanfranc's polite mask of an expression did not change. Only something in his voice served to alert William to the question being more than straightforward. Of course, the bishop would know nothing of the speed with which events had moved.

"Ah, yes. I have spoken with Count Baldwin and his daughter Matilda, and it has been agreed that we shall be married."

Lanfranc's brow gave a slight ripple, perhaps what passed for a frown. "But the degree of consanguinity, my Lord-"

"Yes, well I don't see it being such a great barrier. I'll appeal to the Pope."

"My Lord-"

"We'll deal with it, I'm sure. Now, the matter of this Papal Council."

Fitz frowned, pushed some sheets of parchment around the table. "It could be messy. I hear the King is considering holding court at the same time as the Pope."

"That won't affect us, will it?" William tried to think through the implications.

"Not directly, but the King will expect everyone who owes him homage to attend and confirm their oaths. Including the bishops."

William cast another glance at Lanfranc, but the clergyman seemed to be deep in his own thoughts. "And the Pope will see that as a slight."

"He will have no choice but to," Fitz went on. "I wouldn't be surprised to see him excommunicate all bishops who don't come to Reims."

"What will the position of our bishops be?" William addressed the question to Lanfranc, but once again the bishop seemed to fail to notice.

"Er, they won't be bound by fealty to Henri," Fitz said, "and he won't have any grounds to punish them. He might make his displeasure known and ask you to punish them, but that would be unlikely. The Pope could protest that, and he'd have the backing of the great houses from here to Rome."

"All right. It's still a bloody annoyance." He felt the irritation rising thick in his ribcage again. "And it's Henri in a foul temper after all the work we'd done to cajole him into acting." So much for Ralph's ordered world... "Bishop Lanfranc, we'll need as much information about the Pope's court and progress as possible, so I expect your priests to... Lanfranc? Lanfranc!"

The bishop jumped an inch in his chair and stared at William, blinking as if he had just awoken. "Sorry, my Lord, did you have a question?"

William tried to refrain from gritting his teeth. Blasted cleric was in his own world half the time! "Information about the Pope's visit. We'll need it."

"Yes, my Lord. I will see to it."

"Was there something you wanted to add?"

"Yes." Lanfranc's expression returned to that peculiar half-smile that William was learning hid the thoughts behind so well. "The marriage to Matilda of Flanders. It will undoubtedly be discussed at the Papal Court."

"Then we'll need to be ready to ask for the dispensation. Will you see to that too please?"

"No, Lord."

330

For a second, William thought he had misheard. Then, that he had somehow misunderstood. "No? What do you mean, no?"

There was a soft fluttering sound as Fitz dropped the pile of parchments.

"I cannot support the marriage," Lanfranc said. "As I have said on numerous occasions, the degree of consanguinity is too close. The marriage would be unlawful and immoral."

"I am your liege Lord." William sounded each word carefully. Forced his voice to remain low. He could feel the quivering in his flesh start, the same as when he'd realized the full extent of the Barons' plotting, and when the rush of the flight had worn off after he was almost struck by an arrow.

"I am sworn to the Holy Church as well as to you, Lord. I must place Holy above earthly matters. My Lord, no true priest will conduct this marriage."

What nonsense! Someone could be prevailed upon. Mauger would do it for a fistful of gold. If Odo had been bishop for a little longer, he could do it. Curse the timing! That damned half-smile still stuck on Lanfranc's face. It was all William could do not to wipe it off with the pommel of his sword. What was so Holy about one degree of separation more than another? "Then you will not support your Lord?"

"It is my duty to speak against this marriage, your Grace. I have done so here, to no avail. I must do so before the Pope instead."

This was too much! William thumped the table. "So not only will you not help me, you seek to thwart me?"

"I seek to maintain God's law, Lord, nothing more."

Everything in the room became oddly blurred. William climbed slowly to his feet and turned to fitzOsbern. "Get him out of here. Out of my sight. From this moment he is no longer my man. He is no longer the Bishop of Bec."

Lanfranc remained silent. William was thankful for that at least. He would not have been able to stop himself from killing the cleric had so much as a squeak passed his lips.

"My Lord." Fitz bowed stiffly. "Bishop, please come with me."

So he was going. It was as simple as that. It was not enough. Not for the insult, nor the rage. FitzOsbern and Lanfranc had taken only a step towards the door when William's fury surged up again. "The Abbey at Bec is to be dissolved." He heard the words as a hiss. It did not sound like his own voice. "Give orders for its destruction. All buildings will be torn down. Burn the crops. Drive all the people away. Kill any who resist."

They both looked at him. William could not read the expression in fitzOsbern's eyes. In Lanfranc's... something like pity. He gripped the edge of the table. "Leave nothing. Wipe it off the earth. And for God's sake go before I kill him."

William stumbled out into the inner courtyard and wandered until he happened upon the stables. He demanded a horse be saddled and galloped out into the May air. It was late afternoon and pleasantly mild, but he barely took that in as he clattered through the narrow streets. Before he knew it he was on the outskirts of the town and careering down a lane that delved into thick woodland. The horse rushed on, and he let it gallop until it tired and slowed. It was dark in the forest and he realized how vulnerable he was, out on his own with no guards and only his sword for protection.

He'd given orders for Bec to be razed to the ground. Good God. Even as his fury over Lanfranc's betrayal redoubled, he felt the excess of his actions. A word from him and how many lives might be wrecked? The back of his neck prickled and he whipped around, half expecting to see Ralph standing there, disapproval in his eyes. But there was no-one there. He turned the horse and made his way back to the castle.

CHAPTER 29

THE Count of Boulogne was also known as Eustace *aux Gernons*, Ælfgifa discovered. She saw why he had earned the title the moment he walked into the King's hall. As a general rule, Ælfgifa was not given to mocking another's appearance. She was hardly in a position to, for one thing, and for another, she knew how deep such barbs could cut. When she saw the Count, however she found herself struggling against a desperate urge to laugh. She saw that Ealdgyth had fixed a look of cordial serenity on her face and suspected the queen was maintaining it with difficulty. Several of the queen's ladies had lowered their veils over their faces and from the shaking of their shoulders were finding it even harder to suppress their mirth.

Eustace was a fine figure of a man, or at least, it was apparent that *he* thought so. He was rather short and boyishly slender despite being around two and thirty by Ælfgifa's reckoning. She had seen dancers in the marketplace with similar figures and Eustace played his up with a close-fitting tunic dyed a deep mulberry over hose some three or four shades darker. From the way he held himself, Ælfgifa suspected he was inordinately proud of his legs. The bands of embroidery at his sleeves, collar and the hem of his tunic were very fine work and a semi-circular cape of wine colored velvet swirled around his form, clasped with a golden boar's head at his left shoulder. All of the finery was entirely eclipsed by the man's mustaches. Two, great reddish-brown whiskers ran from either side of his upper lip, sweeping up his cheekbones until the tips—which had been twisted to points and fixed with some kind of unguent—almost touched the top of his ears. The Count kept the rest of his face clean shaven and his hair, rather unfortunately, was beginning a long slow descent down the back of his scalp from his mid crown, having ceased to grow on the upper reaches of his head entirely.

Ælfgifa bit her lower lip so hard that she could taste blood. Eustace *the mustaches* looked as if he had trained a squirrel to lie motionless in the shade of his prow-like nose. His habit of tossing his head back and attempting to look down said nose, only added to the impression that he was trying to aid the small furry creature's balance.

Count Eustace bowed low before the seated Edward. "Your Majesty, brother-in-law, it is so good to behold your noble countenance once more," he said in Frankish. "As always your goodness shines from your face like light from a lamp."

Good angels, is that the way all the nobles at Norman court carry on? Ælfgifa wondered, her eyes widening. Not that Edward didn't have a few sycophants. It was the occupational hazard of being king. Still Saxon flattery was far less... oily. As a whole, the Saxons venerated strength, vigor, cunning. Goodness and nobility were all very well but no one thought they were especially desirable qualities in a king.

Ælfgifa could not stop her eyes cutting sideways to Ealdgyth but her sister was looking ahead with fixed politeness. Edward stood and embraced his kinsman while Ealdgyth stood demurely by until it was time to offer her own greeting. The pomp and ceremony reminded Ælfgifa horribly of how bored she had been at Ealdgyth's wedding. True, she was now sixteen rather than ten, but she still hoped this audience would be brief. Standing around attempting the impossible—for her—task of appearing graceful and decorative while noble men fawned all over each other was not her idea of an afternoon well spent. Eustace made several more bows. One in particular to Ealdgyth's ladies. "Flowers and jewels," he said, "that would grace the brightest of courts. Surely only their virtue outshines their luminous beauty."

A very pretty speech about nothing, Ælfgifa thought acidly, noting how Eustace's eyes lit on her, slid away and then returned as if drawn against his will. The Count choked a little on the word beauty. *Nothing amiss with his eyesight, for all he garbs himself like a pheasant cock*, she mused sardonically. Eustace was close enough that she caught a throatful of the strong flower and musk perfume he had doused himself and probably his clothing in. A few more commonplaces. A few more compliments and crawling flatteries. Edward seemed in better spirits that he had in some considerable time. Ælfgifa tried to shift her weight from one foot to the other without giving away her impatience. Catching her eye, Ealdgyth announced, "Perhaps you would excuse us now, Lord? Husband? We have seen to a feast and it wants but the finishing touches."

Thank the almighty father, Ælfgifa thought, filing from the room with the other ladies.

***

The feast was something of a trial. As the Queen's sister, and therefore kin to King Edward himself, Ælfgifa was expected to sit at the high table. She felt horribly exposed and would much rather have crept down to a lower place beyond the salt or missed the feast entirely. Despite the enticing scent of roast boar, stuffed with spiced grains and glazed with honey, she found she could eat very little. The only person who ate less was Edward himself, a fact that did not go unnoticed by Eustace.

"You are too good, brother-in-law. To resist and eat so frugally at such a feast as this... why, we mere mortals cannot begin to keep up."

Edward seemed pleased but Ælfgifa thought she detected a hint of mockery in the Count's words. Was Eustace being sarcastic? Somehow she doubted that Ealdgyth's propaganda was quite so successful. Ælfgifa had been seated next to Eustace, who had the King on his left, and was constantly tormented by wafts of that cloying perfume, under which the unlovely stench of stale sweat reigned supreme. At this range his moustaches did not seem comical so much as positively terrifying. They had had a fresh twist and a coat of what she now believed to be bear fat infused with juniper. Combined with the perfume and the smell of so many people pressed together as well as the scent of the food, it made Ælfgifa's stomach churn with nausea.

Edward turned to address a few words to his queen who was seated on his other side, leaving Eustace free to turn and stare haughtily at Ælfgifa. And stare he did. She felt her cheeks heat with annoyance under his gaze but refused to look down. She was the queen's sister and had nothing to be ashamed of. Certainly nothing that this effete and rather stupid man could complain of.

"You have the most unfortunate combination of features I ever saw," Eustace said in Frankish, more to himself than to her. Ælfgifa kept her expression straight, allowing nothing to betray that she understood him perfectly. "I have never seen a hare's foot so bad as that—and my cousin had one. Why it's quite twisted your face. Cloven like a goat's hoof and I see that not all of your teeth grew as a consequence." He shook his head murmuring on in a low voice. "Then to have been afflicted with that ugly crimson mark and pocked like a pauper's child. No one would bed you, I fancy. Why are you here, I wonder? And what devil worked upon your features?"

Ælfgifa decided that the moment had come to abandon subterfuge. Surely the only thing worse than having to engage Eustace in conversation was to sit here in silence while he heaped insults upon her.

"My face was made according to God's will, *my Lord*," she said in his own language. "If you find it such a grievous insult then I can but refer you to my maker for an explanation." She was furious and determined not to show it. *Ignorant fop! Cloven like a goat's hoof indeed! At least I do not secrete rodents under my nose or smell like a sennight dead civet.*

"You speak Frankish!" Eustace said, insultingly surprised.

"Your Lordship is keen in his observations." Ælfgifa gritted her teeth and refused to allow her expression to change.

"Very good Frankish. You barely have an accent. But this is impossible!" He was now looking at her in that way she especially hated. As if she were a two-headed dog or a counting ass.

"Vis me Latine loqui? Linguam vestram meo ore informi nolo commaculare." Ælfgifa asked this with a thick crust of irony to her words.

Eustace stared blankly at her. She decided that to ask him the same thing in Greek would be showing off to no good purpose. She switched back to Frankish.

"Do you have any Anglish, Lord? If you would prefer we did not speak Frankish."

"Frankish is well enough," Eustace replied. She noticed he did not answer her question and thought it unlikely he spoke Anglish well, if at all.

"From whom did you learn my language?" Eustace continued, looking at her with a mixture of disgust and interest. It wasn't hard to guess the direction of his thoughts. *You were gently reared and no one supposed you would ever make a match of strategic importance for it is beyond unlikely that any lord worth his salt would have you, even if your father is one of the most powerful men in England. Therefore they have educated you far beyond your needs and fitted you for a convent life. An Abbess might wield power enough to be of benefit to her family and no one expects her to be fair of face.* Ælfgifa could see this train of thought on the Count's face as if it were an illuminated manuscript. She felt the corners of her mouth tightening in a moue of disdain.

"I am a pupil of the Abbey at Westminster," she replied, "but much of my Frankish has been learned from my sister, the Queen." Well, in the beginning it had been so. Now she was faster and more fluent than Ealdgyth.

Eustace shook his head. "It amazes me how you Anglish throw away money on educating women. Do you not have enough to do without undertaking learning best left to men?"

Ælfgifa bit back her first reply. "I find it strange how you seem to have studied the art of the compliment. The way you turn words is a privilege I have not been treated to before. Excuse my impertinence but is this something taught to all noblemen of Normandy or is your Lordship a special case?"

Eustace grinned, making his mustaches bristle like a dog that had spotted an intruder. "I have always made it my study to know what to say that will best please my audience in any situation. Although it is true, Norman court is much more refined. We have the art of manner and comportment. Our ladies are chic and demure."

Holy mother of God. The man was impervious. Ælfgifa wanted to roll her eyes and resisted by sheer effort of will. If he had been of sufficient intellect to warm an empty chair, Ælfgifa would have suspected him of playing games. As it was, it seemed that he really did not understand that he had just revealed himself as a liar and an opportunist, and then insulted the coarseness of his hosts. And it was especially annoying when she had deviously implanted a barb in her words and he no more noticed it than if a flea had bitten him. Less in fact.

What is the point, Ælfgifa thought, *of being clever enough to insult someone in public without it appearing offensive to any but the recipient, if your target has less in the way of brains than poleaxed ox. Really, I'm wasting myself on him. I wish this feast would end.* She almost scowled when she saw a bevy of ceorls bringing in another course. No escape yet.

Meanwhile Eustace quaffed his wine and gnawed on a rib bone, tossing the bone over his shoulder without looking when he was done. There was a snap and snarl from two of the canine occupants of the hall as to who should have the Count's leavings. The Count wiped his mouth on an expensive sleeve and grinned at her again. Ælfgifa was revolted to see flecks of food and shreds of meat caught in his moustache which now glistened with grease and tiny droplets of wine. It came to her that the Count thought she should be flattered by his attentions. Noticing Edward casting a frosty scowl in her direction, she hastily pasted on as pleasant an expression as she could manage. The conversation required little of her. The count expanded on his prowess in battle, his cleverness in strategy, his daring, first in the hunt and then in defying the Pope for the most beautiful of brides (*and she is most welcome to you,* Ælfgifa thought). And then the Count said something that caught her full attention.

"Tell me, have you heard who the King intends to name as heir?" Eustace asked this casually but there was an avaricious gleam in his eye that made her think that he intended to demonstrate his vaunted cunning.

Ælfgifa forced a little laugh. "You cannot suppose that His Majesty would confide such plans to me, Lord."

"No, all the same, you are not such a fool as most women. You may have heard something." Eustace raised an eyebrow at her, his ridiculous moustache twitching with a suppressed smile.

Ælfgifa was suddenly livid with rage. *And if I had been a man would you be trying such a tactic?* She wanted to say. *Do you not suppose that as you have flattered me with having more wit than most women I might also have wit enough not to talk? How dare you practice upon me as if I were an ignorant child or a trained animal.* "I have heard little, Lord. The King is known for his justice and wisdom. Doubtless such things will weigh greatly with him." She cast her gaze down as if embarrassed to be speaking of so masculine a matter. Eustace however would not let it go.

"Come, come. You know more than that I wager. Give me your best guess." He smiled in a way that was clearly meant to be charming.

Ælfgifa was un-charmed. *You want to use me*, she thought, *just like everyone else. Unlike everyone else, I do not even like you and such a liberty is not permissible.* "I imagine when the King does cast his vote, it will be for his own son, Lord, unless there is a better candidate. Even so, by our laws the English throne is not in the King's gift. The Wintenagemot will convene and elect the successor upon the death of the current king—may that day be many years hence." She didn't like Edward but she couldn't dispute so many years of relatively untroubled rule.

"The king has no son," Eustace said abruptly, scowling with an intensity that she found bewildering. Surely Eustace did not think *he* might be considered?

"Not yet, Lord, but as you see he is hale, in the prime of his life and has a young and fertile queen. Surely it is only a matter of time?"

"*If* the queen *is* fertile, which is in dispute. Six years of marriage ought to have settled that matter."

Ælfgifa's face burned. To be discussing such a thing at a feast in this repugnant man's honor with the queen not a half dozen paces away... how far into his cups was Eustace? She opened her mouth to give him a sharp reply, all thought of propriety temporarily forgotten. Such a thing bandied about in her father's hall or in Harold's would have been met by a challenge of arms—and that considered fine entertainment too!

However Eustace leaned even closer and murmured in a low voice that nevertheless carried, "Unless it is as rumored and the King does not even touch his beautiful bride?" Over the count's shoulder, Ælfgifa could see the King's expression attaining the rigidity of stone. Behind him, Ealdgyth had paled. There was the briefest of lulls in conversation, the beginning of an expectant hush as if those at the board held their collective breaths. Few had understood the Count's words but everyone watching the emotional weather on the King's face could read a storm warning. Surely the King would fly into one of his famous rages? In that moment, caught between terror and the thrill of danger, Ælfgifa discovered a liking in herself for walking along the crumbling clifftop of human nature. She knew she could nudge this situation in either direction—mirth or ruin—and there was a heady sense of power in that which was ambrosial. Pay for it afterwards as she might.

She gave the Count—possibly the only person present oblivious to the oncoming storm of Edward's rage—a faint frown, allowing her mouth to pout as much as its misshape would allow. "I think you mean to tease me because I am an ignorant young girl who has no husband of her own," she accused sorrowfully. "It may be that I shall never wed, as your lordship astutely observed earlier, but I am not so ignorant as to believe that a man in his prime with so beautiful and gracious a wife as my sister, should not be wed to her in all the forms of matrimony." She pulled a face as if she were an angry child. "You mock me, my Lord. It is most ungallant." She lowered her gaze and gave a hitching breath as if she would cry, hoping desperately that she was convincing. Glancing up under her lashes, she said wistfully, "I suppose you have had many beautiful ladies fall in love with you, my Lord?" She had never heard herself sound so girlish and meek. The Count swallowed the bait whole.

"There, there. Perhaps there will be for you a husband in time, for all that you are so very ugly. Looks are not everything." He chuckled. "There is breeding and acreage too." Ælfgifa chanced a look at the King and Ealdgyth, who were now continuing as if there had been no disruption. Sighing internally, Ælfgifa turned back to Eustace, who treated her to a long sermon on all the many conquests he had made—such details as were risqué but not inappropriate for a maiden's ears.

She sincerely hoped the Queen appreciated this.

***

Ælfgifa leaned her forehead against the hard, muscular neck of her pony. Spyrryd champed contentedly on the apple she had brought him. She could feel the vibrations of his powerful equine jaws through her skull. A peculiar comfort, that. One that mixed with the warm, earth-musk smell of horse and fresh hay, easing her aching head. She should, of course, be in bed. It was long after midnight and gently reared maidens did not wander around in the dark. Ælfgifa doubted that Berenice would report her absence or that Ealdgyth would mind greatly if she did—unless she were caught of course.

There had been nowhere to go. Or at least, nowhere she could bear to go. The flush of power and triumph at averting disaster with Eustace had faded into weary boredom long before the Count had tired of talking to her. Indeed, despite his innate disgust at her appearance—something which he took no pains to hide—Ælfgifa thought he might have become a little fond of her. The stupid man little realized how dull, self-indulgent and ridiculous Ælfgifa found him. As the feast wore on, Ælfgifa had found herself biting back more and more caustic comments. Her head throbbed as if someone were tightening a leather band around it. She had been unable to face the gossip of the Queen's ladies or the rambling narrative of Berenice as they readied themselves for bed.

I wonder that Ealdgyth never feels like this, she thought. *One evening of simpering and making a foolish man believe he is cleverer than I, and I am exhausted. I have gone from jousting in politics to being a little girl who only wants her pony. A sad state of affairs.* But she stayed, leaning against Spyrryd's broad back and drinking in the quiet of the night.

Except it wasn't quiet. What was that noise?

A muffled *thud thud* like something rhythmically pounding wood.

And a sharp, high repetitive noise somewhere between a sigh and a sob. Was... was there someone here in the stables with her? Someone hurt, perhaps? They weren't quite cries of pain...

Later Ælfgifa would curse her own stupidity. In that moment it seemed that someone might be injured or hurt, and have taken refuge in the stables just as she had. She did not put the sounds together to make a picture, not even when she caught the heavy, half-swallowed grunting that added a third layer.

She rounded a corner to an empty stall. The sight that greeted her stopped her in her tracks, her body reacting before her mind caught up. Two people, pressed against the stable wall. The picture came in fractured shards, like broken ice on a thawing river.

Aofra, head thrown back, gown unlaced in front and rucked up to her waist baring long pale thighs. A red-haired head, undoubtedly male bent hungrily over her breasts, large hands holding the thagn's wife up by her buttocks as he rammed himself home between her legs, his hose in a tangle at mid-calf. And still Ælfgifa could not make sense of what she was seeing, not until some crisis point was reached between the pair, the thrusts becoming more frantic. The man lifting his head to yell as Aofra writhed and cried out his name.

Not that Ælfgifa needed that to identify him.

Garyn.

Of course. Of course.

He even had that cocky hint of a smile when he... when...

Ælfgifa turned sharply away, hands flying to her mouth to smother her cry of horror. She had to leave. She mustn't be seen. What if they... if they... oh God! Garyn? But... Her veins were full of plummeting ice water. A torrent of jealousy and despair that she had never known she was capable of feeling. Sanity was a distant light she could not reach. To rage. To scream. Yes and to weep like other women did. To finally feel like other women...

No.

It was abrupt and hard. That part of her that side-stepped away and viewed the world through cold eyes. *No. You will not make a scene. You will leave and be silent, for now.*

Ælfgifa might have done so had Aofra's next coherent words not caught her attention, making her turn back towards them as if pulled on a hook and line.

"Will that satisfy you? Or will you be making eyes at the Queen's ugly sister in the morning?" Aofra's voice was heavy but even breathless there was no mistaking the hatred in her tone. She wriggled in Garyn's grip like an eel but he seemed in no mind to set her down. Still wedged firmly between her legs he grinned down at Aofra.

"Jealous, my Lady?"

"Of *her*?" Aofra's face twisted into a sneer. "Of course not! But I've seen how she looks at you. Unkind to encourage her. Unless you really do mean to bed her? That would be quite the addition to your collection, would it not? A royal sibling."

Garyn chuckled low in his throat. "Nay, I'd as soon poke a hole in the ground, or one of the goats."

"The goats are certainly more attractive." Aofra smiled and from the way Garyn gasped, Ælfgifa imagined the thagn's wife had tightened some very strategic muscles.

"Ahh... My...La-dy..."

"You can remember that when you're flirting with other women," Aofra said, escaping Garyn's distracted grasp with a lithe twist. She shook her skirts out and pulled the laces of her gown tightly closed over her breasts.

"Done are you? Sure of that?" Garyn seized her waist and pulled her in close, still naked from hip to calf.

"Let go! If I do not return soon my husband will miss me."

"Very well," Garyn said, suddenly indifferent. "I expect I'll be wanted for my stud services again soon enough." He untangled his hose and pulled them up, oblivious to the livid expression of hurt and fury that crossed Aofra's face. Ælfgifa saw it though and drew silently further back into the shadows. *Dismissed by the stable boy*, she thought, *not so fine a lady as you thought, are you?* Her heart was hammering against the anvil of her ribs but there was no fear. *Leave, go now. What more can they say that you would desire to hear?* But cold habit kept Ælfgifa rooted to the spot. There was a perverse wish to see if they would malign her further. To hear the worst of herself spoken almost as if she were looking for confirmation of her own suspicions.

"You may hold your breath on that score," Aofra said in a frosty voice. "But take heart horse-boy. I've seen the way Ælfgifa looks at you. I doubt your bed of straw and horse blankets will remain cold for long. It might be the making of her, creeping, po-faced little rat that she is."

Ælfgifa felt her mouth drop open in shock. What had she *ever* done to Aofra to earn such spite?

Garyn merely grinned at Aofra. "You are jealous," he said. "Jealous of a girl who is so ugly even the devil wouldn't ride her."

"I am not. I'm... I'm *not*..."

"Yes you are. Must be most disagreeable. You being the King's ward and an important, pretty, lady-"

"Pretty!"

"And her with her face that is like to have been smashed in by a horse's hoof, but still so high in royal favor." He smiled at Aofra. Not his usual soft, beguiling smile. Ælfgifa had never seen him look so malicious. Aofra stood tight-lipped and rigid under Garyn's scorn. "I'd not tup her. No man would. But there are plenty of pretty girls, of beautiful women who find my company agreeable and not all of them have husbands to worry about, neither."

"You may bed down with horses but you're a pig, Garyn!" Aofra hissed at him like a cat then whirled and ran lightly out into the night.

"As you say, Lady," Garyn called before adding to himself. "She'll be back. That old man won't keep her happy for long."

Ælfgifa shifted and her foot caught against a broom, knocking it to the floor.

"Who's there?" Garyn cried, peering into the darkness.

It was moment of choosing. Ælfgifa recalled a Greek tale of a jealous goddess who had exacted a terrible vengeance on the insult of her priestess and her lover desecrating her temple with their rutting. She would have liked such power for herself now. But she locked away the part of her that was consumed with shame for her small, loathsome body and malformed face. The part that felt Garyn's words like hot knives – only slightly less painful than the humiliation of seeing him for what he really was, and with such a rival as Aofra. She pushed that nausea aside. Cool logic reigned. Composed, she lifted her head and stepped from the shadows.

Garyn's annoyed, faintly anxious expression collapsed into bulging-eyed, whey-faced shock so quickly it was almost comical. Ælfgifa could find no pleasure in her old wry sense of humor nor in the utter ridiculousness of the situation. She warred within herself. *Why her? Why not me?* While the cool, sensible part of herself pointed out that it was folly to feel a sense of betrayal over a man for whom she'd had only a passing fancy and who she had always known would never really look at her, even if she had been willing to flatten some hay with him.

"My Lady, I... You are out very late..." Horror dawned on Garyn's face as it occurred to him to wonder just how long she had been hidden. How much had she seen or heard.

Ælfgifa felt a perverse thrill. She did have power. She might ruin both Garyn and Aofra if she wished. All she would need to do was bring her concerns before Ealdgyth. She might even do it before Edward, playing the shy, simple younger sister who did not fully understand the implications of what she had seen. Ealdgyth would never believe such a performance but Edward would. If Ælfgifa chose a time when the King's gut was especially paining him, punishment would not necessarily be restricted to divorce and loss of status for Aofra and a public whipping for Garyn. Ealdgyth had no love for Aofra and would likely be content to see the flighty girl gone from court...

That dizzying sense of walking along the edge of influence again. One tilt either way and she could change the course of events.

Ælfgifa sighed to herself, cutting straight to the core of the matter.

"Garyn what do you suppose the punishment is for seducing the wife of a thagn?"

"I... My Lady... please!"

"Of course I doubt Lady Aofra was blameless but as a ceorl you are without powerful friends to speak your part and I fancy it will go very ill for you when this comes out." Ælfgifa watched him carefully. She needed him frightened but not so frightened that he became dangerous.

"My Lady you can't... I beg you!" Garyn's face was blanched but Ælfgifa thought she detected some resentment in it also. *Not good enough.*

"Fornication out of wedlock? Not looked on particularly favorably by this household, though doubtless people turn blind eyes if no harm is being done. However adultery is another matter." Ælfgifa gave Garyn a grave look. "I may not have the King's ear but I assure you my sister does and he would be most distressed to discover such a matter concerning his ward, wife of one of his most trusted vassals."

Garyn looked truly fearful now, a fear that was hardening into anger. "I can be gone by daybreak," he snarled.

"I can have guards sent after you long before then."

"And what will they think of your ladyship being here in the dark to see such improper sights in the first place? Or is that why you came? Fancy a roll in the hay yourself, do you? I can scrape up a cockstand for you if you'll turn your face away! Maybe I should show you what the fuss is about—

you'll not be so high and proud then. Doubt you'll say a word." He took a step towards her.

"I cannot imagine anything more foolish than to attempt to insult and threaten me now," Ælfgifa said coldly holding her ground and gazing steadily up at him. "But try it." She smiled mockingly. "I'll have the devils that attended my birth shrivel your member like a leper's finger. I wager that will solve the problem."

Garyn gazed at her uncertainly, then swore and backed away, all fight gone. "What do you want, Lady?" he said in defeated tones that did not fool Ælfgifa for a moment.

"Have nothing further to do with Aofra. In fact restrict your charm and your... services, to women who are available and interested." Ælfgifa gave him one last, hard look. "I will know if you play me false on this, Garyn. Believe me, I will know. Now swear it on the holy cross."

He did.

***

Ælfgifa did not sleep that night. The ladychapel was open and empty, and the remainder of her night was spent pacing the cold, stone flags while turmoil rolled through her like a flash flood. Every cruel word Aofra and Garyn had spoken seared her mind. Over and over she could hear their laughing voices. Could see as if it was etched into her thoughts with acid that first sight of them joined against the stable wall. She flashed hot and cold by turns. Secret half-formed fantasies dropped into cold ashes and she cursed herself. Vanity was the beginning and end of Garyn's character. There was no intended kindness in his flirting. And Aofra's behavior should not have surprised her at all. Yet it had. Ælfgifa had thought Aofra's spite and selfishness did not extend to her husband. *I must talk to her,* Ælfgifa thought. And then she was awash with shame and humiliation at what she had overheard once more. She was aware of an inclination to entirely blame Aofra and knew that it came from a previously half-unacknowledged physical desire for Garyn. How could she despise him so much? Know now exactly what manner of man he was, yet still want him so badly? It seemed for a time that her loathing for herself was a sea without end.

Towards dawn Ælfgifa's mind grew quieter and she settled on one of the oak benches. It did not signify. None of it signified. Garyn was beneath her. Better to forget him now. She would speak to Aofra and then the pair could do as they pleased. If they went on despite her warnings, well they would be caught. It did not matter to Ælfgifa anymore.

I am not made for the normal destinies of womanhood, she mused. *I was a child to not think of it before. I know better now. And what I have – my wits, my learning, the ability to shift the tides of power, to know how someone will act before they do themselves – such things are worth far more than the temporary joys of marriage and children or the fleshly pleasures other women enjoy. I must be ice and stone against such temptations in future.*

CHAPTER 30

WHEN William reached Senlis again the courtyard was a bustle of activity. He returned the horse to the stable, and, as he strode back into the courtyard, almost collided with fitzOsbern.

"What's going on?" He took in carts being loaded, horses having saddles fitted, servants, squires and armed men storming in every conceivable direction.

"Henri's decided he ought to move against Martel. He's taking the army to Angers. He wants you to join him there."

"What, now?"

"A Royal whim, apparently." FitzOsbern leant closer. "Where have you been? We've been looking for you everywhere."

Just perfect. Bishop Gervais had been seized months ago, and in that time rather than prepare for war William had presented himself at court, attended more mass than seemed reasonable for two lifetimes, become betrothed and heaven knew what else. Anything but going to war. And the moment the decision to fight was finally made, he was away. "I went for a ride."

Fitz turned white. "My Lord! After what happened at Falaise?"

"I'm all right aren't I? Anyway." He rubbed his face. "Those orders I gave regarding Bec. I think I went a little too far. I want Lanfranc gone, but the rest of it..."

Fitz's mouth fell open. "My Lord! I've already sent messages."

"Damn!" Why did Fitz have to be so efficient? "Well then, send new ones. No-one is to be harmed. No damage is to be done to person or property. That includes crops."

"I will, my Lord, right away. But if we are too late? It will be hard to find a messenger free with the King gearing up for war."

It was like a stone in the pit of his stomach. *This is what comes of rash actions.* Well, he was the Duke and he would have to put it right.

"Find someone. Send one of our own people if you have to. Damn it, go yourself if there's no-one to be spared. If we can't get word there in time then I'll make good any damage from my own pocket." *And just hope to God that no-one has been killed or injured.* These were his own people, after all. "We'll appoint a new bishop quickly, and perhaps we could arrange some grants for new chapels or something."

"Yes, my Lord."

"And in future, if I give out commands in a rage, perhaps you should wait a little while before carrying out my orders."

"Yes, Lord."

"Well, what are you waiting for? Quickly!"

"Yes, Lord."

After a hurried discussion with Valois, the commander of Henri's armies, they made preparations to leave, while Edward de Ryes rode on ahead to instruct the Norman host to meet them at Rouen.

Without Mauger to slow them down, they made good progress and within a few days were back in the bounds of the Duchy. William began to relax somewhat. The weather was still fine, and if he hadn't had so much to think about, it would have been a pleasant jaunt.

They passed the occasional peasant or tradesman on the way, all of whom moved off the road as soon as the status of the party was apparent. In the early afternoon on the day they passed into Normandy though, scouts reported a lone monk ahead. Unlike the others, he did not move off the road, but he was going so slowly, on foot and leading a pony, that they soon overhauled him.

Guilt over Bec still knotting his stomach, William rode a little ahead and shouted to the priest, "Can we offer you any assistance, Father?"

The hooded figure's head turned, and immediately William's mouth fell open. It was Lanfranc, travelling alone, dressed as humbly as any penniless friar. William did not know which looked in a sorrier state, the bishop or his pony.

"I ordered you to leave Normandy, didn't I?" He had intended to say the words harshly, to play the angered lord. In his own ears they sounded like the words of a petulant boy.

"My Lord," Lanfranc bowed creakily, and on straightening, gestured at the poor animal beside him. "I am fulfilling your orders as fast as a lame horse will allow."

William sighed, and decided to dismount. "I am sure we can provide you with a fresh horse. Rest for a moment. I shan't drive you away at sword-point."

"Thankyou, Lord."

William called for some wine to quench Lanfranc's obvious thirst, and to see if there was a suitably docile horse they could replace the bishop's with.

"Might I ask where you are going?" William asked.

"Rome."

"That seems a long way. Is there no abbey or cathedral in France that will give you sanctuary?"

He smiled. "I hardly need that, Lord. No, I have been invited to Rome to debate with a priest there who is accused of heresy against the holy church. The cardinal had invited me some little while ago, but I had declined on the basis of my responsibilities to you, Sire."

A stab of guilt, as physical as any blade, lanced into William's chest. He seemed to catch a whiff of smoke on the air—surely his imagination, it was gone in a second. But for that instant it had seemed that he smelled the burning crops at Bec, the burning thatch of the roofs. Or perhaps it was the fires of hell he had caught scent of.

The wine arrived, and William handed the skin to Lanfranc. The bishop took several long draughts, then handed it back. William took a swig himself. It was warm, but he hadn't realized how thirsty he was until the liquid trickled down his dry throat. He took a long pull, and passed it back to Lanfranc. The bishop would need it more than he did. "Keep it. What is the matter you go to debate in Rome, Bishop Lanfranc?"

"The matter of the body and blood of Christ, Lord."

Oh, is that all? These priests and their matters of life and death, all fought over with talk and parchment. "That is no small matter!"

"No, Lord."

"But what specifically?"

"The matter of whether the bread and wine consecrated for the holy Mass are the body and blood of Christ."

William had never really thought about this. The familiar words often repeated suddenly seemed strange in his mind. "And are they?"

"Yes, my Lord. Or rather, I go to Rome to argue that they are. The priest Berengarius says they are not. The argument is held to be heresy. It may turn out to be true."

A strange way to put it, William thought. "And the arguing of priests makes something so or not so?"

Lanfranc chuckled a little at that. "I can see it must be strange to one who is not of the church."

"So do you believe that the bread and wine are the body and blood?"

"My concern is with what is true, My Lord, not what is believed, by me or anyone else. The cardinals in the Vatican wish me to argue against Berengarius. I will do so to the best of my ability. There is much to recommend the argument, after all. The Lord Jesus Christ said 'This is my body, this is my blood,' and the Lord Jesus Christ was not given to using metaphors in that way. But that is not the important thing. The important thing is that God will make his truth known."

"But the bread stays bread, and the wine stays wine. I've partaken of the mass, I'm sure that what passes my lips tastes like bread and wine, not flesh and blood."

"All things are possible to God. It is possible for a thing to change its nature without changing its substance. You became the Duke. You were not always the Duke. But you were always William."

358

He laughed. "I believe you could discuss the hind leg off a donkey."

"If God willed it."

"And does God will you to win the argument?"

Lanfranc smiled. "I would not presume to say what God wants. But if I win the argument, it will be obvious – that that was what God wanted."

William narrowed his eyes. "Do you actually believe what you're arguing? The truth of it? Or are you arguing one way rather than the other because you've been asked to?"

Lanfranc smiled gently again. "What I believe is not important. What is true will be decided by God through my debate with Berengarius. The truth is the truth, it has simply not been established for man, yet."

William rubbed his chin for a few moments. And the priest had given him so much trouble over Matilda. Just one degree of separation! And only barely one. And yet here he was prepared to argue black was white because he'd been asked. To test the truth.

Because he'd been asked...

"So what if God wants me to marry Matilda?"

Lanfranc looked a little shocked at that. As well he might. "My Lord, the church's laws on consanguinity..."

"Yes, but the Church has a law on the bread and the wine, doesn't it?"

"In a manner of speaking, Lord..."

"But perhaps this is something that God has not established for man, yet. What would happen if I, as your liege lord, ordered you to Rome to argue for me to be allowed to marry Matilda?"

Lanfranc furrowed his brows.

"I'm not asking you to believe it's right. Just find the arguments. God will pick the right one, will he not?"

"If my liege lord ordered me... then that would suggest the matter should be put to the test. And if my Lord were to submit to the Pope's ruling, when the matter was heard?"

"Of course!" Well, he'd cross that bridge when he came to it. For now, he might get his clever priest back and have the Pope reconsider his views. He looked at Lanfranc. The man seemed deep in thought already, the kind of look that suggested someone trying to find their way backwards through a labyrinth in the dark. "And I'll have churches built, create new prebends—anything you like!"

Lanfranc smiled at that. This was the kind of bargaining of lords he was used to. "Sire is most generous."

"But you will make an argument in Rome?" Was it fair of him to ask Lanfranc to do this? After everything he had put the man through. "This is not a matter of conscience for you?"

"It is a matter for God's will. My conscience is as nothing. Very well, my Lord. We will put the argument to the test."

Not for the first time, William parted from Lanfranc thinking him a very odd kind of churchman indeed. A fresh horse was found, and the prelate left, showing every sign of being in a hurry. What an odd fellow he was.

Now that the company had stopped, this seemed as good a time and place as any to rest. They moved off the road, sent pickets out, stretched sore muscles and swigged warm wine from skins. William reclined on the ground, feeling the sun on his face and for a moment experiencing the life of a man instead of that of a Duke.

A muttered word from Fitz attracted his attention. Further along the road, the way they were heading, a streak of movement, and when everyone had been shushed, a distant drum of hoofbeats. Just one man though, not a raiding party. A messenger then?

A little way off, the pickets intercepted the horseman and he was led to William. His horse was covered in froth and he'd clearly been riding for some way at speed.

"Lord William," the messenger said when he'd recovered his breath and presented his credentials. "Geoffrey has moved before us. He has invaded Maine, seized Le Mans and is said to be moving on Laval."

William and Fitz stared at each other. Oh, by Saint Experius' scrotum. This was worse than he could have imagined. While they had tarried, Martel had prepared. And now he was sweeping through Maine. There was one thing William could be sure of. Normandy would be next.

CHAPTER 31

ÆLFGIFA drew Aofra aside as the ladies gathered in the queen's solar. The older girl curled her lip on seeing who had caught her arm and Ælfgifa felt less angry than thoroughly weary and exasperated. She was about to do Aofra a favor after all.

"What do you want?" Aofra hissed.

"Merely to advise you not to make any more trips to the stables," Ælfgifa said low and even. "Your conduct has not gone unremarked."

Aofra paled and a look of spiteful hatred settled on her pretty face. She looked for a moment as she would look as an old woman, when youth and beauty no longer concealed her nature. "You... I do not know what you mean."

"Very well, since I cannot be plainer in my meaning, perhaps your husband can explain things to you in a way I cannot."

Aofra's fingers bit into Ælfgifa's arm in a desperate clutch. "What do you know? Who have you spread your lies to?" She bent until she was almost nose to nose with Ælfgifa. "You spiteful bitch. You want him for yourself, that's why you're doing this!"

"With such keenly intelligent insight, Lady Aofra, you must be aware that I admire your taste in clandestine lovers at least as much as I admire your other accomplishments," Ælfgifa said drily. "Keep the stable boy if that is your preference but divorce your husband first. 'Tis sense if you hope to keep your dowry and child, after all, not to be found out as an adulteress."

Aofra's grip tightened further. Ælfgifa thought she would find finger marks later. "You know nothing of passion... nothing of having a man's touch. How could you? Who would want you?"

Ælfgifa rolled her eyes. *Enough*, she thought grabbing Aofra's little finger and slowly bending it back, so that the older girl let go with a gasp of pain. "I have chosen to believe that you are merely a foolish girl who made a mistake. Were I you, I would not give me cause to think you planned calculated assignations." She watched scornfully as easy tears rose in Aofra's eyes. "I truly think that without someone to pet and admire you, you would cease to be. I would not be you for worlds!" Ælfgifa turned away, tossing over her shoulder, "and you may find someone else to fetch and carry for you." *After all, I ought to get something out of my silence.*

***

Eustace aux Gernons stayed a full fortnight. It was a kind of torture for Ælfgifa as he seemed to take especial delight in singling her out for his attentions. It seemed particularly hard since when they were at board, Ælfgifa was always seated with Eustace. She suspected Ealdgyth's hand in the matter, trusting her to keep Eustace in check. He was always patronizingly amused by her, just as if she were a trained monkey. It was exhausting, striking the balance between being clever enough to keep him entertained and foolish enough to appear to be a sheltered, naive girl. Then too, was the biting back of her natural inclination towards waspish replies at his folly and bragging. Ælfgifa swallowed it as well as she could and privately prayed for him to leave or contract a sudden, swiftly killing illness.

Leave Eustace did, to collective muffled sighs of relief, Ælfgifa's and Ealdgyth's amongst them. He took his leave very prettily, charming and flattering the King in a way that made Ælfgifa queasy to watch. *A fortnight ago, I stopped this man being expelled from Lundenwic with fire under his tail for speaking unguardedly of King Edward's lack of potency and the barrenness of his wife, Ælfgifa mused. I ought to have let the fool speak himself into the king's disfavor, we should have been rid of the foolish cock pheasant the sooner!*

Yet he had offered a kindness as he made a special point of saying farewell to Ælfgifa, saying he would be happy to convey news south to her father, if she had any messages she would like to send, since he would be passing through Wessex on his way to the coast. Ælfgifa concealed her surprise at this strange sign of fondness in the Count, and handed him a package of sealed letters for her family. She had little fear of the letters being intercepted and read. If a spy could get valuable intelligence from accounts of needlework, brewing and herbalism then perhaps he deserved to succeed. The only missive with anything at all compromising was the one addressed to her father. It was couched in such terms that she felt certain were entirely ambiguous and misleading unless the reader knew her well enough to know what she likely meant. Eustace looked surprised at the package of vellum and cast a sharp look at Ælfgifa, which she returned innocently. She would have loved to be there when Godwin received this man and read *'Be assured, Father, that the Count of Boulogne is exactly the picture of manhood that one would take him to be. Naturally he stands high in the King's graces with such talents at his command. The good Count has been most attentive to the young, simple sister at court. I would beg your favor and ask that you treat him with all the attentions men of his stature must surely command..."*

Godwin had as wry a sense of humor as Ælfgifa herself. He would know exactly what she meant.

With Eustace gone, Ælfgifa had thought she would be quite herself again. No longer feeling oppressed or marked. In truth, though, after the Count of Boulogne's departure, Ælfgifa's spirits sank further. There was no maddening distraction from the blow to her spirit that Garyn and Aofra had dealt. She went about her daily tasks, her observations, her reports to Ealdgyth but it was all gray and lackluster now. Outwardly she appeared calm, she knew, but inside she was nervous in a way she had never been before. She fought constantly with the urge to hide her face or cast her gaze down when anyone addressed her. *A stupid reaction*, she told herself but she couldn't shake that low, creeping sense of exposure. As if she had never really understood how deformed she was until she had heard Garyn's words. The fact that he was now utterly terrified of her was no balm at all. Nor was Aofra's determination to stay as far away from her as possible.

"Gifa," Ealdgyth said one evening, as Ælfgifa was about to leave the Ladychapel. "The strangest rumor has come to my ears." She hesitated as if unsure how to go on and Ælfgifa found her interest caught despite herself.

"Stranger still that you should hear it before I, sister," Ælfgifa replied. "What is this rumor?" She wondered if Aofra had ignored her warning and been caught out after all. But no, that would have had the entire household buzzing. She would have certainly heard that.

"It... well I do not know how to say this but it concerns you, Gifa." Ealdgyth bit her lower lip, frowning.

"Me?" Ælfgifa returned the puzzled look. There *were* rumors about her, she knew that, and she had thought she had heard all of them. How one look from the Queen's sister could sour milk or make a child turn in the womb so it would be born feet first. How she had been marked so the devil might know his own. How her skill with healing and midwifery proved that she served the forces of evil—she was fairly certain Camus had started that one himself. Ealdgyth would never bother her with such nonsense though. So what had the Queen heard?

"It... it was noted by many how the Count of Boulogne singled you out for special treatment while he was a guest here. I would never suggest that anything improper occurred but he is known to be a... a connoisseur of... of female charm and..." Ealdgyth cleared her throat and went on delicately. "I would pay no heed to such tales if it were not for the fact that since Eustace left you have not been yourself, Gifa. You seem distracted, low spirited. I... I often wanted to speak to you as

366

one woman to another, so I must ask, are you grieving over his lordship's absence?"

"You are asking me if I formed an attachment to the Count of Boulogne?" Ælfgifa wondered if she had somehow fallen asleep. This was too strange to be anything but a dream.

"I know he is married and frankly, rather peculiar, but he made such a pet of you and you are still so young. We forget because you are so sharp but you are yet a girl and might... might..."

"Fall in love with a married man old enough to be my father, who dresses like a peacock and is excessively vain, not least of the squirrel's tail he has wrapped around his face? Is that what you are asking? If so, sister, I first wonder at your wits and secondly that you trust my judgment at all!" Ælfgifa flushed with fury—then surprised herself by doubling over with genuine, unexpected laughter. "Oh, Ealdgyth! Surely you didn't believe such a thing?" She gasped between giggles. "You will ruin your reputation as a clever woman if anyone finds out you gave it a moment's credence!" Tears ran down Ælfgifa's cheeks and the laughter seemed to have undone some knot that had worked tight inside her. There was a slightly hysterical edge to it but she could feel the laughter lifting the gloom she had been under.

Ealdgyth looked both embarrassed and relieved. "No. Of course I did not truly think that. But you have given me some concern, drifting about a pale shadow of yourself these last few days."

"I have been a little ill, Sister, but I am better now. Truly." Ælfgifa smiled her close-lipped smile and Ealdgyth nodded.

And Ælfgifa did feel better. There was nothing to disturb her peace. No annoying Count to entertain. If Garyn's words sometimes came back to haunt her, well, they grew dimmer with use and she had no reason to care for his opinion after all. Life came back in full color and she was herself again. She wondered how Godwin fared having received her letter, laughing to herself at the idea of the Count at Godwin's hall.

Then news came and she lost any inclination to laugh.

***

Ælfgifa didn't even look up at the sound of hoof-beats coming from outside. She was setting stitches in the hand of a young kitchen ceorl who had been careless with a knife. The boy was pale and sweating but he hadn't fought her. Ælfgifa was pleased with him. "There," she said, cutting the end of the fine, silk thread with a small knife. "I'm going to put a poultice on it now to draw out any ill humors and then I want you to sip that tea."

"It smells fearsome bad, Lady," the boy protested trying to subtly test the movement in his hand. "Like rotten hay. Bet it tastes of horse piss." His face fell as he realized how unguarded he'd been in his speech.

Ælfgifa pinned his hand so he would stop moving it. "And when would you have had horse piss to drink for comparison?" she asked, concealing a smile. He ducked his head, grinning, his ears turning red.

Ælfgifa smeared a mixture of honey and herbs on the neatly stitched gash and wrapped it in strips of clean linen before handing him a cup of liquid which did indeed smell like rotten hay.

"You're to keep that hand clean and not use it for a few days. I won't be pleased if I have to sew you up again," she said, trying to sound severe. "And you're to bring that back to me mind. No one else."

"No fear, Lady. My cousin went to Camus to have a boil lanced and lost two fingers."

Ælfgifa opened her mouth and then shut it again, deciding not to ask. If people began to come to her over Camus then at least no more fingers would go missing. Unless they needed to. The boy's trust was important. Of course, if Camus noticed he was losing patients then he was likely to change from coldly courteous to looking for a way to be rid of her. Ælfgifa decided that was a problem for the future.

"Lady? Lady Ælfgifa? Are you there?" The tone was distraught and choked but Ælfgifa recognized Suela's voice all the same.

"Stay here. Drink it all mind," she told the boy. He grinned at her impishly.

Shaking her head, Ælfgifa stepped out into the herb garden.

"Lady Ælfgifa!" Suela was ashen, her tightly curled hair springing from its usual coils.

"What is it? Is it the Queen?" Ælfgifa asked in alarm.

Suela shook her head helplessly. "Please. Just... just go to the lesser audience chamber. The Queen... the King... You need to go."

"I will. But you can't go anywhere like that. Sit in the still room. Take some ale." She tried to usher Suela through the door but the older woman resisted.

"Now. Do not worry about me. But please, go now."

Despite the thick oak doors, Ælfgifa could hear Edward bellowing from down the corridor. A guard shifted uneasily from foot to foot, clearly embarrassed by what he could hear. He caught sight of Ælfgifa hurrying towards the doors and his expression collapsed into relief. He opened one door for her without a word.

Ælfgifa had a moment to wonder why she seemed to be inspiring such confidence in people today and then the full impact of the scene struck her eyes. A trestle table had been upended. Goblets lay here and there, leaking their red contents into the rushes. Edward was on his feet, the rosiness of his cheeks flaring into an enraged red that subsumed his normal pallor. Everyone save Ealdgyth seemed to be edging away from him. Even the dogs had taken fright and were bunched up in the corners of the room. No one had noticed Ælfgifa's arrival at all.

"...disobedient. Means to make a mockery of me. Me! His liege lord and king and master!" Edward raged.

"My Lord, I am certain there is some mistake. Jarl Godwin would never intentionally flout your commands, nor would he be impudent," Ealdgyth said, trying for a level voice.

"Do you call me a liar, Madam? Read this if you will and tell me then that your father is not a traitor and a scoundrel!" He thrust a sheet of parchment at Ealdgyth, who took it with a hand that shook a little. "There. You see! He will not comply!"

Ælfgifa watched as Ealdgyth grew paler. She looked up at the King once more. "All I see my Lord, is Jarl Godwin pleading the case for his people, as a good master ought. He feels that there is at least some blame on both sides and that in his opinion the burden of it lies with the Count of Boulogne's men not his own-"

"You see! He calls Our cousin a troublemaker and refuses the order of his king! Your father is a traitor, Madam." Flecks of spittle shone in the King's silvery beard like sea foam.

There will be no reasoning with him, Ælfgifa realized. *He is working himself up to some plan of action based on a hatred he has nurtured in private since his brother's death. This is not a normal rage. This is a test to see where Ealdgyth's loyalties truly lie. If only I could warn her!*

Ealdgyth seemed to be holding on to her own temper by her fingertips. "My Lord King, I beg you. Reconsider...there may be another explanation-"

"God's blood, Lady! I would call loyalty to your family a virtue save that you are so blinded by that den of foxes that spawned you, that you cannot see that you are merely an ignorant pawn! Godwin has disobeyed his last order. If he will not punish the men of Doubvres then he is not fit to be their lord!" Edward snarled.

"You speak ill of my wits, my Lord?" Ealdgyth said tightly, an angry flush rising into her cheeks.

Oh no, Ælfgifa thought. She cast about for anything she might do but this was not a situation where her sudden interference was likely to help. It was more likely to cast oil on the flames.

"Your wits!" stormed Edward. "I did not marry you for your wits, woman. You persist in failing at your true duty – that of providing me with a son!"

The hall went utterly silent as if a thick cloud had descended and muffled all sound. Edward never spoke so to his queen, least of all in front of other members of the court.

Ealdgyth went as white as if she had been hit low in the belly. Her eyes glittered dangerously. Ælfgifa held her breath, waiting for the answering storm of her sister's rage, but Ealdgyth did not speak. She merely met the king's gaze with a hard and telling one of her own. *You know and I know, that I am not the obstacle in getting a child,* that gaze said. Ælfgifa had heard from ceorls' gossip that the King visited his lady's chamber seldom. She now wondered exactly how effective he was on such conjugal visits as he did make. Eustace, it seemed, had been right. And Ealdgyth had managed to declare it to the entire hall without saying a word.

The King paused in his fury. Edward knew he had gone too far but a public apology would undermine his authority, doing untold damage. As King he must appear to be, if not faultless, at least beyond reprimand for those faults.

And then there is his pride, Ælfgifa thought. *He will never lower himself to apologize to a woman, not in public. Not even his wife. And nothing less will do for Ealdgyth now. Lord save us all.*

At length Ealdgyth spoke. Her voice a taut harp string that might snap any moment. "An heir is desirable my Lord, but as God has not bestowed such a gift upon us we must bow to His judgment. Much as I sorrow not to have a child, I content myself that the Witenagemot will choose the next king of England wisely, in the event of your lordship's death —may it be *many* years hence!" The last words came out in a half hiss, half snarl that suggested Ealdgyth hoped entirely the opposite. Fewer words than that might have ignited the fire of Edward's fury.

"The Witenagemot will decide nothing! It is an archaic practice that ignores God's will. The throne is in my gift, Lady! Mine! And I will give it to the bastard Duke of Normandy before I ever name one of the tainted blood of Wessex heir! Nay, not even if you should bear a son, Lady! The entire line is poison and I welcomed a viper into my bed."

"And just what do you intend to do my Lord King?" Ealdgyth said, her tone deeply sarcastic. "The house of Wessex and its lands are the richest in England. We rely on their farms, their men, my own father and brothers for generals to defend against the Nords and Danes and Irish. We have a better understanding with the *Wealas* thanks to my brother, Harold. You too may claim a tie of kinship with Wessex since you married the daughter of the house. Wessex has ties with Mercia, Northumbria and East Anglia. You cannot fracture your kingdom over so small a matter-"

"Enough," roared Edward. He took a deep, stertorous breath and limped back to his throne. He tried to hide how it pained him but even if he convinced the other silent courtiers, Ælfgifa's experienced eye could see that he was unable to stand longer. Edward half-lowered himself, half-fell into the high backed chair with a thud.

Ealdgyth has lost her reason, Ælfgifa thought. *To bait the King with our family's power and influence? Now, when he is beyond reason himself and thinks through the veil of his own pain? Madness.* She was moving before she could stop herself. Throwing herself to her knees before Edward's feet she cried, "Please, Sire, I pray you. Please treat with my father. He is a reasonable man. He will want no quarrel with you, I am sure. He has ever held you in high esteem. Please!"

Edward's hard gray gaze fell on Ælfgifa so heavily that she felt he had clapped his large, folded hands down on her shoulders. There was nothing in that gaze except revulsion and dislike. Her words were in vain.

"Exile," Edward intoned. "Godwin must leave England. Any sons or other male sprigs of that foul tree who will not swear an oath to me shall share his fate."

Ælfgifa felt as if she were falling, even as Ealdgyth helped her to her feet.

"My Lord King, reconsider-" Ealdgyth tried to say.

Edward smiled. For the first time Ælfgifa was genuinely frightened of him. Here was a man who walked along the edge of sanity because all who rule must tread that road. Unlike others, however, all that prevented his fall was a tenacious grip on his own narrow view and the neutered version of Christianity that was taking greater root in the kingdom. Edward's stock was in being holy and learned and wise, like Solomon. *There is nothing more dangerous than a man of power who believes his own propaganda*, Ælfgifa thought.

The King's words dropped like pebbles, almost softly, pleasantly, as if this were a game and he had waited long to make this move. The ripples were deadly.

"We shall reconsider Our edict when Godwin returns Our brother, Alfred, alive and well." The smile both widened and closed, like a trap. "Meanwhile, Lady Queen, you shall be housed in a nunnery where you shall have ample leisure to contemplate your allegiances."

Ealdgyth gave Edward one last burning look, then curtsied in a perfunctory manner. Sarcasm for the old fool.

"As it please you my Lord King. I shall do as your widely vaunted wisdom demands."

Ælfgifa felt her arm grabbed by her sister, who towed her along as she swept from the room. Neither waiting to be dismissed nor staying to hear any further words from Edward.

CHAPTER 32

ÆLFGIFA drooped over Spyrryd's damp gray neck as the pony plodded gamely on. They had been on the road since before sunrise, after little sleep and a long ride the day before. Ælfgifa had had the entire story from Ealdgyth as they rode to the nunnery outside Lundenwic, to which Edward had banished his queen. As a further insult he had confiscated all of Ealdgyth's lands, leaving her virtually penniless. Ælfgifa thought that such an act might be challenged were a court held to discuss it, even if it was the King's decree, for Edward had no reason at all to punish his bride. But then it was hard to argue one's side if one was shut safely behind nunnery walls, which was doubtless part of Edward's intent.

"It was Eustace," Ealdgyth had explained, filling in the gaps in Ælfgifa's knowledge. "He and his men were to stay in Doubvres until they could take ship for France. There was some carousing and a few of Eustace's men seem to have started a fight. The man they attacked killed one of the Normans, which in turn led to his own death and that of his family and some others. Who knows how tangled these things may be." Ealdgyth had paused. "I do know that were it not for the very great ill-feeling against Norman influence

376

coupled with Eustace's high-handed ways..." The Queen shook her head. "He thinks we Saxons little better than barbarians."

"I know it," Ælfgifa replied colorlessly. She could not help remembering that she had pulled Eustace's chestnuts out of the fire. That sense of walking along the edge of power and influence. By God's blood, she was stupid for one reputed to be so clever. She had seen but two moves ahead on the game board. Had she looked a little further, she would have seen the potential for disturbance the Count of Boulogne really represented. She would have left him to the King's untender mercies as Eustace insulted Edward. Ælfgifa had badly underestimated Eustace—or rather his capacity for damage— seeing only the foolish popinjay. *If I had not interfered, if I had not needed to prove myself so clever, then Eustace would have been packed off sooner with his tail between his legs and any trouble-making he indulged in on the way back would not have fallen on sympathetic ears, whether the King has a private preference for Norman ways or not.*

The rest of the account was easy enough to piece together. Eustace had complained to Edward. The King had demanded that Godwin punish his men—all those involved in killing Eustace's men in Doubvres. Godwin had refused. Ælfgifa was not surprised. Her father was known to be staunchly anti-Norman. He had become somewhat of a rallying point for those with like sympathies these last years.

"I am undone, Gifa." Ealdgyth's hands had tightened on the reins and her jaw had clenched. Another woman speaking those words might have sounded desperate but the Queen sounded furious. "Edward will try to divorce me or annul the marriage. The Bishop of Jumièges will see to that. Edward will go to all lengths to sever ties with our family."

Ælfgifa frowned. "I think the king will stop short of divorcing you, Ealdgyth, for all his rage. Our father has not left England yet and is not to be easily forced away."

"Edward has the support of Siward of Northumbria."

"And I suppose he is not the only Jarl nervous of our family's reach and wealth," Ælfgifa said grimly.

"You have the right of it. So dearest sister, how is this to be remedied?" Ealdgyth sounded so acerbic that Ælfgifa flinched. It had been a long time since the Queen's temper and sharpness had been directed at her.

"Ealdgyth, do you want this remedied? If the worst were to happen and Edward were to divorce you, surely you can be reproached with nothing but barrenness? He would be forced to return your dower lands—when I am certain he cannot do without the income from them. You might then marry another and have many children—quietly proving that the King was at fault..." Ælfgifa trailed off. Her talk was dangerously close to treasonous. To her surprise Ealdgyth let out a hard mocking laugh.

"Gifa for one so wise you can be too simple. I do not wish to be free of Edward. I have put far too much time and work into him. He garners respect and love now, where once there was only grudging acquiescence. Without me, Edward will cease to be such a King as he is."

"And you will no longer be Queen," Ælfgifa observed shrewdly.

"No, I should not. But, Gifa, that is not all. I still prefer Edward and he, for all his words, prefers me." Ealdgyth sighed. "You do not understand, I fear."

"If you talk of matters of the heart, I own I do not understand," Ælfgifa said in exasperation. "The King humiliated you in front of the entire court. He insulted our family. Yet you want to return?"

"I want to return to him," Ealdgyth agreed, a small unpleasant smile on her lips. "Who else loves him dearly enough to make him miserable for the rest of his life in recompense?"

Ælfgifa shook her head, having no reply to this piece of insanity.

In an attack of spite, Edward had not even sent Ealdgyth to a nunnery where she had connections. St Arilda's Abbey was an enclosed and retiring nunnery. The daily routine of the inmates was strict and regimented. They were not a sect that went out into the community to teach or heal, and they had no contact with their brothers in a partner monastery. Their effort seemed committed entirely to prayer and purity of living – such small amount of needle work as they were allowed to do was plain sewing. There was no fine embroidery, no illuminated manuscripts. Only the Abbess had any learning at all and that was of the most rudimentary kind. Ælfgifa could barely conceal her scorn. Did none of them have any idea what they chanted in Latin? Had they all walled up their minds and spirits as well as their bodies? She thought of Gunhild and how her sister was active and useful, turning her learning and talents to God's work. This was wasteful. No, worse than that. This was a kind of hell where eventually even the spirit would stop raging towards light and liberty, turning itself towards death, the only escape left.

"Gifa, you cannot stay here," Ealdgyth had said.

AN ARGUMENT OF BLOOD

***

Shifting in Spyrryd's saddle, Ælfgifa thought back and wondered if her scorn and disgust had been more apparent than she'd intended. Surely St. Arilda's was a sanctuary for some. *But I should go mad. I do not see how Ealdgyth can bear it,* Ælfgifa thought with a shudder. It had been agreed that Ælfgifa should return to Wintancaestre and meet with Godwin and Harold there. Before she left Lundenwic, Ælfgifa had sent a hasty message to Brother Dubhne, telling him what had happened and begging him to send word to her father. With luck Godwin would be expecting her. Unless he assumed she had stayed with the queen.

Ælfgifa twisted in the saddle, trying to ease sore muscles, Spyrryd grumbled and fidgeted beneath her. It was a much smaller escort than they had left with from court. Most of Edward's men had returned to him leaving only two, who had drawn the short straws, to accompany Ælfgifa. Added to that was Suela, who was put out at being sent as a chaperone when she should be with the Queen, and, irony of ironies, Garyn, brought from Lundenwic to tend the horses. Ælfgifa found it all too easy to ignore the groom. She wished she could say the same regarding Suela, who had kept up a steady stream of complaint for the last ten miles.

It's no good, Ælfgifa thought, *we shall not reach a town or village before nightfall. We shall have to camp overnight.* The light was failing and the thought of huddling in the chill drizzle at the edge of a forest until morning depressed her. They pressed further on but it was even worse inside the forest. The leaves dripped with fallen rain. Faint cracks and crunches told of other creatures in the woods and it was darker than ever. A chill of disquiet rippled across Ælfgifa's back. She realized that Spyrryd was tense and twitchy. *The noise,* she thought. *There's no sound. No animals or birds at all now.*

No sound meant predators.

"Stop," Ælfgifa called in a low carrying voice.

She turned to ask something of the men just as Suela said, "What is it, Lady?"

Ælfgifa opened her mouth but her reply was lost forever.

The taller of the two guards had been riding his gelding close to his fellow guard. He yanked hard on the reins forcing the poor beast to spin on its haunches straight into the path of the other guard's horse, putting him momentarily off balance. This gave the tall guard time to plunge a dagger into his throat, ripping it free with a lush, wet spatter of blood that Ælfgifa heard despite the muted drizzle.

The bushes erupted with movement. Suela screamed, kicking out frantic and blind at the dark-hooded assailants that exploded on to the path. Three men. Four if the false guard were to be counted. Against herself, Suela and Garyn. Ælfgifa's heart was trying to escape through her throat. Suela flailed again and booted one attacker in the face, only to be dragged from her frantic, shying horse by the two other hooded men. Ælfgifa saw the ceorl disappear in a tangle of limbs that ended in a single choked scream, abruptly cut short. A flash of movement and the false guard's horse was bearing down upon Ælfgifa as she struggled to keep Spyrydd from bolting. Still reeling in shock, she froze, unable to do anything but watch as her death raced towards her. Sheer luck sent Suela's panicked, riderless horse blundering into the oncoming charge, sending both horses crashing into the mud. Suela's dun mare scrambled up and bolted in the next second. The huge blood bay, belonging to the guard, whinnied high, sounding disturbingly human as it thrashed to its feet, taking off after the other horse. The false guard lay helpless and twitching.

Ælfgifa's vision narrowed to a blade point, her mind grinding out of shock and into action. She yanked cruelly on Syprydd's reins, forcing her poor pony to turn. She was in time to see one attacker fall away from Suela's limp form, clutching at the long knife buried in his chest. He staggered and fell to his knees. *That leaves two.*

The cold, clear part of Ælfgifa had taken over. One man made a grab for her leg but Ælfgifa had swung her foot free of the stirrup, and sheared it up under the man's chin, knocking his teeth together so hard they nearly severed his tongue. He swore and dove away from the lunging pony, as Ælfgifa cast around frantically for the last attacker. She felt Spyrryd sink abruptly onto his haunches, a hideous, agonized scream coming from his throat. Sheer instinct made Ælfgifa throw herself from the saddle before her hamstrung pony could roll on her. She landed hard on her front in the mast and debris of the forest floor. Winded, she forced herself to focus. Her seax was trapped under her body but her small boot knife was somehow in her hand, though she did not recall drawing it. Lying face down in the mud, just raising her head enough to see the attacker who'd slashed Spyrryd's legs coming for her, she waited.

She knew she stood no chance in a physical brawl. Her way must be trickery, cunning. The sly strike to buy time and then perhaps survival. The man neared. As he kicked her onto her back, Ælfgifa switched her knife from one hand to the other, slashing out at the tendons in the back of his ankle. The bruising pain of the kick winded her anew but her knife had done its work. As her attacker rested his weight on that foot, it gave way beneath him, sending him to one knee. Ælfgifa let the momentum of his kick help her to her knees, jabbing up with the small knife into the man's groin. Something popped on the point of her knife, sending a warm flood over her wrist. The man howled and curled around his pierced bollocks. Ælfgifa forced herself to her feet, half-doubled over, and kicked the man in the face. She caught the side of his jaw—mercifully, his eyes rolled up in his head and he collapsed, senseless. *One left.* There was a wave of exhausted despair. She could not hope to beat a skilled man armed with a sword. The last man didn't spare a glance for his fallen comrades. He held out his darkly dripping sword, then threw back his hood and grinned.

Ælfgifa drew her seax with numb and trembling fingers, all the while her mind was racing. Trying to work out why she knew the man before her. *He was bigger once,* came the unbidden thought. *Still tall but not so brawny. He has seen hunger and hard times. I think his hair would be yellow under all that dirt and grease... He looks even more dangerous now than... than he did that day Harold and Edith sentenced him in Harold's hall. At the Thing.*

"Ulfric." Ælfgifa was surprised to hear how steady and remote her voice was.

"You remember me. How touching." Ulfric grinned, showing new gaps in his teeth.

"So you didn't drown in the fens. A pity. Fertiliser is about all you were ever good for." Ælfgifa backed up a step as

Ulfric paced towards her. Circling her like a wolf, as if he were enjoying this moment, drawing it out.

"Not such a simple little thing after all are you?" Another step forward. Another step away from him.

Stop, the cold, clear voice in her mind said. *Give way before him and he will take it as weakness. Hold your ground or you are as dead as the others...* "It's a mistake that is often made in my case," Ælfgifa said, raising an eyebrow. "What brings you to this part of the kingdom? Thagn to footpad. Quite a step down in the world, is it not?" *Keep him talking.*

Ulfric scowled at her words. "Little bitch! Ruined everything, you devil's whore." His anger settled into cruel amusement. "Still, this has earned me a good bit of silver. Played your tricks one time too many. Made an enemy of the wrong person. Maybe I'll send your head to that self-righteous quim, Edith the Fair. Nice present."

Someone had actually paid this man to kill her? Ulfric was an assassin not a vagabond? No doubt it was meant to look as though robbers had set upon the party at random. But who? And where in God's name was Garyn?

"Send her your balls for a necklace," Ælfgifa suggested. "I know Lady Edith's tastes and that would please her better." A tentative plan had formed. Ulfric was big and strong and better armed. But he wasn't quick. Or desperate. And he could never imagine how ruthless Ælfgifa was prepared to be. "Hold, no it won't do. Your bollocks are scarcely large enough for a fitting ornament. How can they be when you need a frightened, weeping girl to make your spear spring into action in the first place?"

Ulfric's expression twisted and he snarled. For a moment she wondered if she had made a mistake and was about to die for it. Then he raised his sword and took the last three paces in a rush.

There was all the time in the world. Time to watch the slashing descent of Ulfric's blade. Time to calculate the angle. Time to take a shallow, steady breath and change the incline of her seax...

A determined rush from a large, armed opponent is terrifying. The natural response—the desire to run away—is nearly always an error if you do not have a sword of your own. It puts the object of the attack in the path of the blade's downstroke. Ulfric was no swordsman and he wore no armor. Ælfgifa knew that had he stabbed rather than swung with the sword, had he been wearing anything tougher than ill-tanned leather, she would have died. As it was Ælfgifa took a step forward and to the left, ducking under the elbow of the descending sword arm. She held her right arm out as she moved, and Ulfric's own momentum sent him running up the blade of her seax to the hilt. *The utter fool,* Ælfgifa thought in contempt. Then, *stabbing a man feels like sticking a knife into an uncooked pig carcass...*

Ælfgifa stumbled away, the seax ripped from her nerveless hand. Ulfric made a strange, bubbling gulp of sound and fell forward onto his face. *Got you, you bastard.* And then she was doubled over, spewing the contents of her stomach endlessly into last year's fall of leaves, retching until her whole body shook.

It was the pitiful whimpers coming from her pony that brought Ælfgifa back to the moment. Spyrydd was trying to rise but the tendons in his hind legs had been sliced and all he could do was flail in the mud. *I can't leave him like that,* she thought numbly. She looked down at the boot knife clenched in her left hand. *Not big enough. I need my seax.*

Without letting herself think too hard, she rolled Ulfric over. His eyes had already filmed over. The trickle of blood at the corner of his mouth was drying even as the dark stain spread out around the handle of the long knife buried in his gut. Ælfgifa gripped the hilt of the seax and yanked but the blade caught against Ulfric's sternum and wouldn't shift. *At least I got the angle right,* she thought humorlessly. She'd been aiming to go in just under where his ribs met so the blade would have no resistance as it entered the heart. Of course she hadn't calculated on Ulfric's weight wedging the blade through bone as he fell. Gripping the hilt in both hands, she set one boot on his chest and heaved. The blade grated free with a final, wet sucking noise. The forest swung around her head and she thought she might be sick again.

She wiped the blade clean on Ulfric's clothes and then turned to her whimpering horse.

"I am so sorry, Spyrryd," she said, stroking the gray muzzle as she sliced the blade through the big blood vessels in the pony's neck.

What to do next, that was the question. It was almost fully dark. A weak, watery-yellow moon peered through the branches at the carnage. Suela was dead. A knife slash that opened a red grin in her throat had ended her struggles, but not before she had stabbed one of her attackers. Ælfgifa laid her out straight, closed the ceorl's eyes and folded her hands over her breast. It was all she could do. She tried to say a prayer over Suela's corpse but it was poisoned with rage and seemed pointless. Surely God would let her sister's loyal maid rest.

Ælfgifa checked on the false guard. If he hadn't died when his horse rolled on him, he had died soon after. She rifled through his pouches and doublet, finding a pouch of coin which she took for herself. There was also a flask of mead which she was grateful for. A swig cleared the taste of vomit from her mouth and made her head stop ringing. Warmth spread through her, and the aches and pains of her fall eased. She laid both guards out just as she had with Suela. She even did the same for the man Suela had stabbed. There was nothing Ælfgifa could do for Spyrryd now. She had done the only thing she could. She blinked hot, stinging eyes and swallowed thickly. That left Ulfric and the man who had hurt her horse. She couldn't bring herself to touch Ulfric. *God can decide just as well without the presentation,* Ælfgifa thought grimly. As for the other man, he was alive but still unconscious.

The stench of blood hung heavy on the air. In the distance, she heard the lone howl of a wolf quickly picked up by its pack mates. Ælfgifa didn't want to think too hard about what that might mean. But it was time to leave. She bypassed the unconscious man, coming to the conclusion that if God wanted him to live then God would intervene.

I need a horse, Ælfgifa mused. She had found a saddle bag with some food, a water skin and a cloak in it. She had also lifted all the coin she could find—who knew how far she may have to walk or who she might have to bribe? But she would see that Suela's and the real guard's families received back whatever she had to spend, along with a few small items of Suela's jewelry. *I know where two horses went at least, unless they fell and broke their legs in their flight.* Heaving a sigh, she threw the saddle bag over her shoulder and set off through the broken undergrowth in the hopes of catching at least one of the horses.

She had not gone far when she heard a low whimpering noise. Her heart hit her ribs and without thought her boot knife was in her left hand—she couldn't make the fingers of her right hand close properly around the hilt of her seax. There. It came again. A low noise of fear and pain.

Silently, Ælfgifa slid the saddle bag from her shoulder to rest at the base of an oak. She pulled her hood forward over her face, the dark folds hiding her features and masking the stiff, blood stained skirts. She stepped forward, knife at the ready.

A figure lay half-propped against a fallen tree. Skin pale in the faint glimmer of moonlight. Eyes wide and glittering. *Feverish,* Ælfgifa realized. *Oh God, Garyn!* She didn't need to see to know what was wrong with him. Experienced healer that she was, she could smell it from here. Belly-cut. A sideways swipe of the knife that had slit him open like a rabbit for the pot. He was holding himself together. Literally. Obscene, frilled white tubes like empty sausages, spooled between his spread fingers. There was some blood but not much. A man could live in agony for hours like this. Sometimes even days. Death came only when the foul stuff that leaked from split intestines poisoned him with ill humors. It was that almost sweet, thick, acrid scent she had caught.

Garyn was already dead. Nothing could be done for him. Except perhaps one thing.

Ælfgifa hesitated. It was one thing to spare a dying horse hours of suffering. But to kill a man in cold blood? One who did not threaten her? *I want no part of this. Let some other deal the final blow.* But there was no other. Could she truly walk away and leave him?

"Is it you?" Garyn's words were clotted and weak but she turned toward him all the same. "Have you come for me finally? I'm... please take me now... the pain..."

Oh God have mercy. Ælfgifa slipped to his side, realizing at the last moment that Garyn had no idea who she was. The hood concealed her face. It was too dark and Garyn was in too much agony to recognize her.

"Wait... before I... I want to confess..."

No! Absolutely not. But Ælfgifa inclined her head so the hood bobbed, saying nothing.

"I haven't... I should have warned the lady. Lady Ælfgifa. I thought... I never thought Aofra would..." he paused, clenching his teeth against a new wave of pain. "And then... I ran... crawled away... They're all dead and I did nothing..." Tears glinted as they rolled down Garyn's cheeks. Ælfgifa laid one hand softly on his brow and he quietened. She made the sign of the cross and gestured 'go in peace'. She could think of nothing to say and in the end no words were needed. Garyn relaxed, reaching toward death. "Thank you'.

A dip of the hood again and judging that he would have little feeling below his waist, she used the boot knife to open the big artery in his thigh, sending Garyn's spirit rushing out and to God on a hot, red flood in the strangely peaceful night.

CHAPTER 33

ÆLFGIFA arrived in Wintancaestre almost two days later. The food had lasted her a frugal day's worth of meals, though she had little appetite. She had slept little, starting and waking many times, certain she heard the approach of interlopers. Logically, she knew it was her mind tricking her, nerves strained to snapping point in the aftermath of the attack. But there was something else too. For someone who eschewed much human contact and preferred her own company, Ælfgifa realized that physically at least, she had never been alone like this, without even one other person in shouting distance.

She had caught up with the horses, both miraculously unhurt although the dun mare's reins were tangled in a hawthorn. The blood-bay gelding had raised his head and nickered to her. So at least she had not had to make the entire journey on foot. Both horses were much too big for her and after a while she would grow uncomfortable, switching to walking and resting both horses before changing again to the more rested horse. They went steadily, avoiding large towns and settlements. Only once as Ælfgifa skirted a village, was she spotted by two boys of about twelve throwing stones at a scolding squirrel as it darted around the tree trunk.

Ælfgifa opened her mouth to scold the boys herself and found that she couldn't find her words. There was no need. Both boys yelled in fright and ran back to the village, shrieks of 'Demon!' trailing behind them on the breeze. Ælfgifa thought it best to disappear from the area quickly and had swung up onto the gelding's back.

It was only later when she was forced to stop and rest the horses by a stream that she had finally looked down at herself. Her hands were filthy, caked with flaking rust-brown stains. The blood of at least two men. As if waking up, Ælfgifa felt the tight skin on her face and realized there was unwashed, dried blood there too. Her skirts were stiff with it. The red tide that had poured first from her poor Spyrryd and later from Garyn. Her scalp crawled and she wanted to peel her skin off. Settling for flinging the ruined gown over her head, she waded into the stream in her shift and small clothes, scrubbing at skin and cloth alike with handfuls of sand from the bank until the water ran clear, carrying the last pinkish tinge of blood away.

Shivering, Ælfgifa wrapped her cloak around herself and sat near the grazing horses. *I'm a scarce few hours away from home,* she thought. *In fact I may be in Godwin's lands now.* Still she had had no news since the attack. She couldn't bring herself to trust any of the towns or villages she had passed. *Their allegiance might be anyone's—for all they know they will have a new lord soon.* It was unfair but logic said to make her way alone. Logic also said to aim for the nearest house of prayer and ask for sanctuary but Ælfgifa stubbornly refused that. While she would not make it easy for anyone to kill or capture her, or turn her into a hostage, neither would she hide in a nunnery, starved for intelligence where she might be forgotten and left to languish. *Eat*, she told herself, feeling nauseated at the thought, *and press on.*

***

By the time Ælfgifa finally rode through the gates to her father's hall, the sun was westering and she could barely keep her seat on the dun mare's back. Both horses were fresher than she was. She reined the mare in outside the stables and then found she couldn't dismount because her legs had cramped into one position and now felt numb. Furious with herself she tried in vain to get down from the too-tall horse, only to slither gracelessly off one side while the mare turned her head inquiringly as if to say *that's not how it is done.*

Fortunately a stable hand was nearby to take both horses, leaving Ælfgifa to limp over to the dry stone wall and sink against it. Now that she was safe—as safe as she was likely to be—she felt strangely reluctant to go inside. The last two days had been silent except for the sound of the horses and the natural sounds of outdoors. She had not needed to speak. Ælfgifa knew that now she would be required to and she felt as if she had not yet returned from wherever she had gone. That dark night when she had played the angel of death to so many...

"Mwyalchen!" The familiar voice took Ælfgifa straight back to her childhood and before she knew it she was pushing her numb legs into a broken trot to reach the bustling Cymri nurse. She flew in to Beddwen's broad arms and felt as if tiny pieces of her might be coming back finally. As if she might have come home.

"Beddwen," she croaked, laying her head on the old woman's shoulder just as she had when she was still a fractious child. "Oh Beddwen."

***

The sense of homecoming did not last. Godwin welcomed her affectionately enough, calling her 'Blackbird' and kissing her forehead, but he was distracted and distant all the same. Ælfgifa thought there was the look of a winter wolf about her father now. He had grown thinner and more sinewy in the years she had been from home. His beard and hair were liberally touched with frost and there was some almost frightening bright hunger in his eyes now. A man on the verge of accomplishing his desires who stood on the precipice of losing all he had worked for. Godwin was all nervous energy and had little time for a younger daughter with no political value. Familial love and duty must take a place behind the needs of his Jarldom and its affairs.

Ælfgifa had not expected much of a greeting from her mother and so was not disappointed when Gytha was unable to receive her for a day or so after she arrived. It gave Ælfgifa time to reflect, to clean off the blood and dirt of the road and gather herself once more. But she could not seem to rally.

Despite now being excluded from the *Things*—Godwin was far less apt to use Ælfgifa's abilities than her brother and sister it would seem—she had heard that Robert Champart, Bishop of Jumièges, had accused Godwin of plotting to kill King Edward, just as he had killed the king's brother Alfred. There were other accusations: Wessex had appropriated lands rightly belonging to the church; Godwin's daughter, the Queen, had made a compact not to bear children so the king should die childless without an heir; that Ealdgyth was barren.

That it was all senseless rumor, and much of it contradicted itself, did not matter. The poison seed fell on ripe and fertile ground. Edward was of a mind to hear any ill against Jarl Godwin and if it came from one of his Norman supporters, so much the better.

The King is advised by entirely too many bishops, Ælfgifa thought, staring listlessly out of a window, her embroidery forgotten in her lap. She wondered how she had managed to underestimate Robert Champart and then realized that she had not. He was what he had appeared to be. A dull-witted, ignorant man with little political skill and an ambition that outstripped his meagre talents. He was simply an opportunist and this was a better opportunity than he could have dreamt of. Ælfgifa knew he had befriended Edward before he became king, while he was still in exile in Normandy. She suspected he had ties to the Duchy of Normandy as well and wondered just how idle Edward's raging threat to put Willelm the Bastard on the throne had really been.

Footsteps from further down the long gallery jerked Ælfgifa back to the present. The figure was in shadow but there was something in the way he held himself...

"Come, sister, have you no greeting for me?"

"Harold!" Ælfgifa scrambled up and flung herself at him like a child, dropping her needlework on the floor in her haste.

Harold laughed and hugged her then held her at arm's length. "What's this? You do not look well, Gifa."

She snorted. "I never look 'well' brother. I am... I am merely tired from my journey. It... it seems to be taking me a while to come back." She shrugged. "Besides, with all that has happened..."

"Ah yes. Our wise king and his tantrums. Did Ealdgyth try to cosset him with sweetmeats before she left? T'would have saved some weary hours of counsel here." Harold grinned. There were fine lines at the corners of his eyes but otherwise he was much as Ælfgifa remembered. Handsome, vigorous, charming and careless of his own health and strength.

Ælfgifa managed a small wan smile but could not share her brother's mirth. "This is no mere tantrum, I think, Brother. The king has at last all the excuse he needs to move against Wessex. I do not doubt he will do so in some form."

"Have heart, Gifa. Giving him Ealdgyth was only going to quell his resentment for a time. We knew that." Harold said, resting one hand on her shoulder and steering her back towards the window seat. "Neither the king nor the house of Wessex wishes for a civil war. It would leave the country open to foreign invaders, which is a price we will not pay. If Edward agrees with us on one thing it is that."

"What then?" Ælfgifa said. "Are we to be driven from our lands into exile? Where is the remedy?" She sighed. "I turned out to be a poor source of intelligence for you, Harold."

"Nay. Not so. On your information we have had plenty of time to prepare for such an eventuality as this. Were it only another twelve moons from now and we should not have to move at all. But it cannot be helped." Harold paused and while the hint of a smile never left his face, he was grave in a way that made Ælfgifa wary. "Gifa, I have a task for you."

Her heart, which had seemed to be still in her chest since she had ended Garyn's life and suffering, now plummeted into her stomach. "Brother... you cannot... I failed at the last task. How can you set me another? And besides..." *Besides I'm weary and heartsick at the games people in power play with each other. I am tired to my bones of controlling every word, every gesture, every glance. And I am small... so much smaller than I realized. Some part of me died that night on the road and now I do not know myself.*

She did not speak her thoughts aloud but Harold nodded. "I heard somewhat of your misadventure on the way here, sister. Is it true you were the target?"

"I have no reason to think my attacker lied. It was supported later by something the dying groom said."

"Why so meek? You did well against a greater force—you were outnumbered, ambushed, unprotected and they were men with some knowledge of the blade." Harold looked genuinely puzzled. Ælfgifa supposed this was one of the great differences between them. Harold might pass off such an attack as a lark. She could never be so sanguine herself.

"I do not like to kill," Ælfgifa said and yet she felt a traitorous warmth at her brother's praise. *He means to use you again...*

"I trust it will not be a regular occurrence! What of the author of this assassination attempt?" Harold asked but he was distracted, already thinking of the favor he wanted to wheedle from her.

"I doubt she will have means or opportunity to make another attempt." Ælfgifa had had time to give this some thought and while she would not lower her guard, she felt sure she was right. There was no way of knowing how Aofra had raised the tidy sum of silver now in Ælfgifa's purse, but she imagined the stupid girl would have some fast explaining to do to her husband. She had also lost her lover in the ham-fisted attempt. With Wessex in disgrace, it was unlikely another attempt would be forthcoming. "It was a quarrel over an imagined slight and an... an infidelity on the lady's part."

"Really?" Harold was suddenly unreasonably interested. "Which lady?"

"The king's ward. Edward will scarce believe you if you accuse her, Harold. I have only one man's word to implicate her and inconveniently for me, he died."

Harold smiled in a way that was new and sly. Ælfgifa found herself not liking this side of her brother.

"What favor do you crave, brother?" Ælfgifa said, trying to bring Harold to the point.

"Edward is demanding political hostages as a gesture of goodwill from Godwin when he and I go into exile. The hostages are to be given into the care of Robert of Jumièges and conveyed to Normandy, where they will be guests of Willelm the Bastard." Harold watched her face intently and Ælfgifa felt like a small creature in the gaze of a bird of prey.

"You wish me to be a hostage?" She took a deep breath. "No, you wish me to be *your spy*. What then, brother? Am I to attempt to gain the Duke's confidence? If you wish for someone to play Salome surely you could choose a more tempting woman!" For the first time since she'd sloughed the blood of two dead men from her hands, Ælfgifa was angry.

Harold watched her flash of temper impassively. "Whatever information you can gain will be welcome, Gifa. I do not expect my sister to play the harlot—though as a daughter of Wessex you should consider your importance where a marriage alliance might be made. All I ask for is what you have been doing already."

"With a deal more care since as a hostage, if I am caught sending secrets, I doubt I will have the fair treatment I might expect here!" Ælfgifa snapped. Harold asked too much.

"You are clever enough not to be caught. To weigh risk against reward. Willelm is becoming a player in the great game, Gifa. After Edward's words, be they spoken in wrath or not, we must all look to our coasts with a clear eye." Harold was not teasing at all now.

"Think you the danger is that great?" Ælfgifa said, feeling already the weight of duty settle upon her.

"Would you care for a Norman liege lord upon the throne of England?" Harold shook his head. "Besides you will be able to keep an eye on Wulfnoth."

Whatever argument Ælfgifa had been about to make disappeared in a rush of horror. Wulfnoth, her twelve-year-old brother, a hostage!

Feeling bitter but darkly resolute, she nodded her acquiescence. There was nothing more to say.

CHAPTER 34

WHEN William received news that Martel had seized Le Mans, he had been set on gathering all available forces and marching there with haste as they joined up with the King's army at Dreux. Henri, it seemed, had other ideas, bizarrely demanding to move West through Normandy before swinging South to head for Angers.

Gallet said what everyone was thinking. "Ludicrous. Bloody stupid if you ask me. He's an idiot. Just been marching East for days and he wants us to go West again. The pox must have spread from his cock all the way to his brain."

Odo yelped with laughter. After being in almost the sole company of priests for a month William's half-brother was apparently not used to such talk. It was past time for him to go on campaign in any case, so William had called the young man away from Bayeux. He was not yet sure whether it had been a good idea.

"That's your king," fitzOsbern hissed, throwing a disapproving glance at the new Bishop of Bayeux. "Mind how you talk about him."

"Sorry, Lord. The pox must have spread from his Royal cock to his brain."

The impromptu council of William's captains all laughed this time, and even Fitz smiled, a little ruefully.

"Come on Fitz," Gallet said. "You know as well as we do. If we go for Le Mans Geoffrey will have to face us, but if we go to Angers they'll just lock the gates and Martel won't need to lift a finger. What does Henri think Martel will do? Hotfoot it back and face him in the field to protect his capital when he could just wait? The King doesn't like sieges, it seems to me. Just wants to ride round with his cavalry and show off."

William couldn't blame Henri for that, anyway. Beaumont and a few score useful men were still pinned down at Brionne, hoping to starve Guy out or force him to come to terms. Odd to think that the swift glory of Val es Dunes and the long drag of waiting at Brionne could both be called warfare. He still had not found time to challenge Montgomerie for circumventing his instructions about Talvas and essentially making a grab for the Bellême lands himself. Perhaps he needed to look closer to home for threats than Anjou.

"Well there's nothing we can do about it now," William sighed. "Maybe force the pace of the march a bit. Sack any small towns or villages on the way. If we ravage enough of his country, perhaps he'll be persuaded to leave Maine." He realized he was almost shaking with the need to fight. While he'd been trying to play the good and patient Lord, Martel had taken what he believed was his. It didn't matter to Martel that he'd gone against his liege lord. Damn them all. May the Devil stop their arses up.

As if to further frustrate him, the next day it began to rain. For two days, a deluge of fat water drops hammered onto the trudging army, and on the third, a gusty wind rose from the West and drove the rain into their faces. The roads became soft, then turned to slop. Every few leagues a cart got stuck, and they began to go through horses at too fast a rate to replenish from the stables they encountered on the way. The rain got into everything. No man had a single piece of dry clothing. Food turned to mush. Swords began to rust in their scabbards and mail in its wrapping despite the oil everything had been treated with. Progress slowed to a crawl, and they were still not one toise inside Maine itself. Odo's mood had shifted gradually from delight at his freedom from religious duties, and now looked as though he missed the comfort of the bishop's mansion at Bayeux like a drowning man misses the shittiest patch of dirt. Which was quite possibly what they were marching through now. Every man grew utterly sick of the stink of ox dung.

It seemed Henri was concerned that Martel would garrison every small fort and they'd find their way barred. So the army continued marching through Southern Normandy, living off Norman food and livestock, trampling Norman fields to mud, and occasionally killing or raping Norman serfs who dared to resist calls to give up what little they had for the sake of the army. He thought of the corpses of his vassals strewn across the road on the march to Val es Dunes. Now he was doing it to his own people. Madness.

At the point Henri decided they must have outflanked the Angevins, despite the scouts coming back with very little useful information, they turned South. The army became horribly strung out along the tiny lanes cutting through thick woodlands. It was perfect territory for an ambush, so scouts and pickets had to check virtually every tree before the main force moved through it. A week's march was turning into a month.

There was only one fortified position on the road to Angers—a small wooden motte and bailey at the former site of a mill, and consequently known as Mouliherne. It commanded the road, but should have been easy enough to deal with.

Yet again though, Geoffrey had got there before them. As the bedraggled army finally came within site of the fort, William realized with horror what they were facing. He called up Odo to ride beside him.

"Well, Brother. How are you finding your first campaign?"

Odo sighed and wiped a wet strand of hair from his eyes. "I didn't think anything could be duller than being a bishop, but I may have been too quick to that judgment. It's not all like your last great success then?"

"No, I'm sorry to say. Pitched battles are rare. Most of war consists of sieges and raids."

"How very boring. I don't understand why anyone would lock themselves up in a castle when they could come out and fight."

Good Lord. What have they been teaching him? William made a mental note to take a look at Odo's tutors and, if need be, replace them with someone a bit more knowledgeable. Ralph would know someone. In fact, maybe if Ralph came back...? He realized with a jolt that perhaps the teachers weren't the problem. Taking a sidelong look at his half-brother, he wondered if this was what he'd been like before the attempt on his life? "Half of victory is knowing when to fight," he said. "And most of the rest is being able to pick the place."

Odo raised his eyebrows skeptically. "It doesn't sound very glorious. Anyway, Charlemagne didn't always choose where to fight. Neither did Roland."

"No, and look what happened to him."

"He was a hero!" Odo huffed. "He was assumed bodily into heaven."

Oh, so the priests are getting some of the message through then? "He still died. As did all his men."

"They defeated the paynims, didn't they?"

William sighed. This was getting them nowhere. "It's fellow Christians we fight today. Can you see why they've put us in the shit?" He gestured at the scene below them in the shallow valley.

Odo shrugged and grinned stupidly. "It looks like a tiny little wooden castle. I don't know why we haven't battered it down and killed everyone inside already."

It may have looked that way, at first glance, to those ignorant in the ways of battle. William pointed out how the castle itself—a classic bailey atop a conical motte – had been surrounded by an outer palisade atop an earth bank, itself surrounded by a ditch. He did not doubt that the place had been heavily garrisoned after all the effort to fortify it. The works here spoke heavily of manpower.

The fort itself was not all. Further ditches and earthworks had been dug across the valley, funneling any force into the road where it passed below the walls. The low ground was clearly flooded, probably from dams in the river. Woods to either side meant that if they wanted to get around the place they would have to leave the road and go leagues out of their way, over uncertain ground, and leave themselves open to attack by an army that could choose the place and time of combat.

He called his captains, Montgomerie and Fitz, to join them and asked what they thought of the situation. Both looked glum.

"It's a bad place for a battle, if you ask me," Montgomerie said. "Very bad. We've no room to maneuver. An army coming from just about any direction could wheel round and bottle us up."

"Not that there's likely to be a battle. In Angers they'll know we're here," Fitz added. "They'll have sent scouts as soon as they knew we were coming. By the time we got there they'd have the place shut up and packed with stores."

"No fighting?" asked Odo. "None at all?"

"I dare say they'll send a raiding party or two when we're particularly vulnerable," Fitz said brightly.

"God curse it!" William spat in the mud. "We should never have come here. We should be at Le Mans!"

"Henri doesn't care about freeing Maine from the Angevins just so you can take it," Fitz said softly. "His priority is curbing Martel."

Damn it. Fitz was right. Why did he have to be so reasonable all the time? "All right. We'd better go and see what the King wants us to do. I'd like to have suggestions ready to offer. I favor leaving a small force to besiege Mouliherne and taking the rest of the army round. We should only lose a few days before we're back on the road. What do you think?"

Both agreed, though it was clear to William that neither was keen on any of their options. Soon it was clear that the situation was more difficult still. They found Henri by his retinue, who were busy erecting a pavilion.

"Ah, Normandy," Henri said after William had done the necessary groveling. "We cannot proceed until the threat of the castle is neutralized. Therefore we will dig in and invest it."

"Very well Sire. What size of force do you intend to commit to the siege."

"Why, the whole army of course. All of it." Henri looked at William as though he were simple. "We've brought them all here, after all."

"An entire army, Sire? To reduce a small fort?" William struggled to keep the disbelief out of his voice.

"Exactly. It won't take long."

"A small fort it may be, but well defended. And given the evident recent reinforcement of its defenses, we must assume it is well garrisoned and provisioned. My army is not equipped for a siege."

Henri nodded, vacantly. "Exactly. It won't take long. A few days and we'll be on our way. A mere trifle to the victors of Val es Dunes, eh? Speak to Valois and sort out a plan of attack, if you'd be so good."

William was not so much dismissed as ignored. He wandered from the King's sight to find the commander of the King's armies, the Count of Valois. "I'm to establish a plan of attack with you," he said.

When Valois had finished laughing, he threw up his arms, turned to the fort and shook his head. "It won't be today. The men are exhausted, the ground is churned up as under the plough, and everything is soaking wet. Including the ramparts, which means our only option, to burn them out, isn't possible. We're just going to have to wait."

"But where are the belfries? The pirrières? How are we supposed to break through the walls without machines?"

"They say Henri isn't very fond of siege engines, my Lord. Apparently his grandfather managed to set fire to the whole French camp with Greek Fire while trying to invest Laon once. The Capets haven't trusted them ever since."

"When was this?"

"Oh, seventy, eighty years ago."

It was all William could do to avoid language not becoming of a Duke. "So what do we do?"

"I'd recommend offering terms."

"And if that doesn't work?" Not that Henri would countenance it anyway.

"Wait until it dries up. *Then* burn them out."

It rained every few days for the next three months. A few tentative assaults on the castle achieved nothing, and things kept getting worse. Whole companies started to get sick with the bloody flux. And when William attempted to spar with Odo, his half-brother proved to have such little skill with a sword that it was unclear which side he would pose more danger to.

"Perhaps, brother, you could consider carrying a club into battle," William suggested after one particularly ludicrous bout of flailing and ducking. Odo looked offended at the suggestion but William was saved by the appearance of a messenger, escorted by a guard and Fitz, who looked even gloomier than he had for most of the last three months.

"My Lord," the newcomer said. "I bring grave news. Martel has taken Alençon and Domfront."

What? William uttered a stream of invective so blasphemous that the messenger blushed and Odo almost choked with laughter. "And we sit here buried in this dunghill! Saint Clement's holy piss! Alençon... I can perhaps understand if he threw his whole army at it, but Domfront? It has stone walls, it's well situated... How in God's name did Martel overcome both towns in a few months? How much damage is there to the walls? Could we retake them while the defenses are vulnerable?"

"Sire..." The messenger bowed his head. "There is no damage. There was no fighting. Both towns opened their gates to the Angevins."

The sky turned black. The earth screamed. For a moment, the world spun on its axis and William thought he would be thrown off his feet. This was the beginning of the end. Bas-Norman border towns willingly handing themselves over to the hated Martel... It was only three years since Haut Normandy had almost gone over to Guy of Burgundy in its entirety. Was any of his Dukedom loyal? He had realized too late how easily it might be taken from him. Now Normandy would fall. His lands laid waste. His forefathers disgraced...

William looked up. Fitz and Odo were staring at him. Gallet and Montgomerie storming over from the siege lines to see what the fuss was about. He would not lose it all without a fight. If it was all lost he would give Martel a bloody nose at the least, and show the rabble who called themselves subjects that there would be consequences for presuming to choose their liege Lord. "All right," he growled. "Let's finish off this shithole, leave the King a detachment and get to the border towns. We'll take them back or fall trying. We attack tonight. If we can get Valois to join in with

Henri's men, then all well and good, but if not we'll just have to carry the place ourselves. Any ideas?"

They discussed the assault. It was simple enough. At nightfall, the entire Norman force would attack the gate. Archers would keep the defenders' heads down while they took a battering ram to the gate.

It cost a lot of men. Even with the best archers keeping up a steady rate, the hail of arrows, spears and rocks from the ramparts was punishing. The Angevins didn't even try too hard to defend the outer wall. They didn't need to. The motte was small but steep and slippery. More than a few Normans injured themselves just by falling. Some fell to an arrow or javelin when they slipped and dropped their shields for a moment. Maneuvering the battering ram to the gate would have been awkward even without the barrage of wood, iron and rock from above. They had to endure that without answer for few minutes, until they'd gouged steps into the slope, enough to properly drive the heavy log with enough force.

It seemed like hours, in which the men huddled under their shields against rocks and spears. William tried to organize protection for those at the ram, with shields held above them, but it wasn't easy and many men fell in the mud, dead or wounded before, finally, the gates gave way. William was third or fourth man through the breach, despite Bourdas' attempts to get through ahead of him, and he swung his sword at anything that moved. A big fellow loomed at him to the side with an axe, and he brought the top of his shield up under the man's jaw, feeling cartilage mash. He tried to follow up with a stab with his sword, but could not get the large blade round quickly enough, and the

Angevin easily blocked it. For a moment they were shield to shield, face to face, and William felt sour, hot breath on his face. A brief panic fluttered, and he shoved it back. The sword's blade was down and he could hardly move it, so he shoved it into the man's foot. His adversary issued an angry yelp and stepped back. William grabbed the moment's freedom and heaved the sword at the Angevin's unprotected side. The metal thudded into leather and flesh, which elicited barely a grunt, but the soldier must have lost his balance, and went down. William kicked the man in the head to make sure he stayed down, and swung his shield round to meet the next attacker.

Almost before William realized it, they had carried the fort. A few of the defenders were wounded, unconscious or whimpering in pain and fear as the sky began to lighten. The Normans moved round the interior of the stockade, finishing them off with sword, knife and axe. The Duke knew you were supposed to leave a few alive and set them running so they spread tales of cruelty and ruthlessness to strike fear into the hearts of those who might be next. But today there seemed something cleaner about leaving every man dead.

"You were right about the club!" Odo called, waving a stout wooden cudgel over his head and showering drops of blood from his last victim over himself. "I wouldn't have killed half as many with a sword!"

"Make sure you clean your mail," William puffed. "Blood turns to rust in no time."

"Ha! With all the taxes Bayeux brings in I could buy a new set of mail every week. How many did you kill anyway? I got five."

"Twelve," Gallet said, wiping his sword on a corpse's houqueton. "Not a bad night."

The stench of blood and shit hit William's nostrils for the first time and he almost gagged. He looked round to see if his squire had survived. Bourdas looked bloodied but unhurt. "Let's clear out. The wolves can have this lot. The sooner we can be on the move, the better." They'd been fighting through the night. Need to find out how many men had been killed or wounded. A fifth part? Please God not a fourth... He should want to sleep but he was full of energy. Bury the dead, send carts bearing the wounded back to Falaise. They could be on their way by the afternoon. Send word to his uncle at Arques to bring every armed man he commanded. *Need to get a short sword. A long blade is no good for this sort of close-in fight. Maybe a club wouldn't be such a bad idea...*

He stumbled back down the slope, and almost bumped into Montgomerie. "My Lord. Another messenger," he said, the expression on his face unreadable. "From Falaise. It's urgent."

By the Saints' grotty toenails. Not more bad news. Normandy in revolt? Was his time as Duke already over? "What is it?"

"Best see him in your tent, I think. Not really for everyone's ears."

They hurried to the tent, Bourdas fussing round him as William started to feel soreness bloom through his arms and legs. The man was waiting, on his feet, and refused refreshments. William tried hard to tear his mind away from the next stage in the campaign. Next time they would have siege engines, damn it.

"My Lord," he said. "I bring compliments from his Grace the Bishop of Jumièges, and important news from England."

William glanced at Montgomerie. Jumièges? What on earth did he want? And what could be possibly have to say that was so important? About England! He gestured the man to continue.

"His Grace the bishop brings an embassy from his Grace King Edward, who commends himself to his cousin with affection and respect, and requests that your Grace host certain hostages that he has demanded of the Jarl of Wessex to ensure the Jarl's good behavior."

It took William a few seconds to disentangle who required what of whom. "Edward wants me to hold hostages of him? Who are they? When are they coming?" *God*! They would have to be sent to Falaise. But to have some Saxons wandering about his castle, living off his hospitality while Anjou tore chunks from his Dukedom. The timing couldn't be worse.

"They are already on their way, my Lord: Wulfnoth, the Earl's youngest son, Håkon, his nephew and Ælfgifa, his youngest daughter."

Playing host to some minor Saxon nobility? How irritating. But hardly worthy of all the drama. William sighed. "Is that all? Pray convey my compliments to Jumièges and ensure that the hostages are comfortably accommodated, but I regret I cannot attend them in person. The campaign against Anjou is at a dangerous stage. It is not possible."

"My Lord," the messenger continued, looking extremely awkward. "I am commanded to convey to you that there is a matter of great importance that his Grace must discuss with you in person."

William frowned. Was he not to be allowed to fight for his territory now? "What does it concern?" He snarled.

"The throne of England," said the messenger.

CHAPTER 35

THE envoy had insisted there was nothing further he was permitted to say. William briefly considered threatening to kill him, but decided that he probably didn't know any more himself. Jumièges would not have wanted valuable information to fall into Anjou's hands, or Henri's for that matter.

They hurried back to Falaise, leaving Montgomerie in charge of the army, with orders to march on Domfront, give battle if success was likely. William apologized for keeping him away from his wife for a little longer, while it tore at his heart that someone else might get to fight the battle for his Dukedom. Montgomerie shrugged. "She'll keep," he said seeming perfectly content with the situation. Men could be odd in their differences, William reflected. Montgomerie, who'd seemingly fallen in love at first sight (or so the story had it) content to exchange his bride for mud and violence, while gruff Gallet still took every excuse to slip away to Helisande even after three years. They had two children already and Gallet had confided in a puzzled William that he hoped there was a third on the way. It sounded horrific. At least he could understand Montgomerie marrying Mabel for her lands...

But as they rode back down the same treacherous and sodden roads they had marched up previously, William's thoughts were never far from the business the herald had raised. What on earth was the matter with England's throne? And what did it have to do with Normandy? Was Edward in danger of losing his Kingdom?

And if he was? What did he expect William to do about it? Normandy was under invasion already. True, not a full invasion – just the nibbling away of a couple of border towns. But William felt in his guts that Geoffrey would not stop there. Fivescore years ago, Normandy had been French land. Now it was Norman. It could just as easily be Angevin.

And this had been the painful lesson. No man was entitled to something he was not prepared to fight for. No Dukedom, Barony, County, or Kingdom belonged to anyone who could not take or hold it by arms. And yet shouldn't there be more than that? Had they come all this way from the frozen North, as the stories said, paynim barbarians, burning and robbing, dragging themselves into civilization just to find themselves doing the same thing from castles instead of longboats? What now of Ralph's ideas of the good lord sitting at the top of an ordered society? It seemed an impossible dream. An illusion. Something you could fool yourself was real until the next strongman came to seize everything.

Falaise again. Home. Security. The last place on Earth he wanted to be. Hubert de Ryes was waiting for him as the small party rode through the gates and told him of the latest developments as he dismounted.

"Jumiéges is most insistent, I'm afraid," the knight said. "He's waiting for you in your audience chambers. I would have had him dragged out and thrown in the vault but didn't see any sense in causing a disturbance before I'd spoken to you."

"Did he say what was so cursed important?"

"Sadly, no. He is adamant he'll only speak to you. Which is a bit rich, given that King Edward supposedly trusted this vital intelligence to a second-rate cleric."

Indeed. William vaguely remembered some recent scandal about Edward wanting to install Champart in some important post against the wishes of the church there. He hadn't really been paying much attention to Anglo-Norman ecclesiastical politics. They left their horses in the charge of the stable hands and began trudging to the castle.

"...So will you see him or shall I have him flogged for an insolent knave?" de Ryes went on.

"No, no, I'll see him. The sooner I can get this over with, the sooner I can turn round and start defending my Dukedom again. The envoy said something about hostages. Have you found accommodation for them all?"

"Yes, Sire."

Something in de Ryes' tone made William look back at the knight. "They aren't causing any trouble are they?" Because if they were, he would have them sent straight back to Edward.

"No, they aren't. But some of our people..." De Ryes leaned closer. "It's the girl... Woman. Elf-gifa. None of the ladies of the court will go near her. They refuse to have her quartered with them. I think... Montgomerie's not here is he?"

"No, he's with the army."

"Oh. Well, I think, to tell you the truth, that it's Mabel de Bellême who's been stirring things up. She says the Saxon is a demon, a witch... She's got the others convinced that the girl's putting the evil eye on them."

Christ's wounds. This was the last thing he needed. He remembered what cousin Eustace had told him about the Earl's youngest daughter. In his letters he'd made her sound like more of an amusing performing animal than an evil creature. William even had the impression that the Saxon girl might have got the better of Eustace in a contest of wits, so hard had his cousin tried to emphasize how amusing their exchanges had been.

"So no-one will be companion to her while she is here? What does that say for our hospitality, Hubert?"

The old knight shrugged.

Damn. "Gallet!" He gestured to the soldier, who'd been following with Odo and Fitz. Gallet hurried forward.

"What is it, my Lord?"

"How would your lady like to come to court?" William saw Gallet narrow his eyes a little. "No, you fool, I wouldn't risk you murdering me in my sleep. It seems all the women here are foolish and superstitious and won't attend to one of our hostages, who's the daughter of a Count or something like that. I'd like Helisande to do that. If she and you don't mind, that is. Then, if my marriage ever happens, she can have a place in the Duchess' household, above all the others."

Gallet frowned. "I'll ask her. I dare say she'll be pleased."

"Good. That's settled then."

"Yes. Oh, and my Lord, if I ever murder you, you'll be awake and have a sword in your hand."

"That's reassuring Gallet."

"I do my best, Sire."

***

William went to his audience chamber without even having the dirt of the road brushed from his clothes and hair. If what Champart had to say was so important, he wouldn't mind seeing William in such a state. However much he wanted to keep the insolent bishop waiting and show him exactly where he sat in the order of things, he wasn't prepared to cost himself the time, so appearing before the bishop disheveled and dirty would be insult enough. They could be on their way by sunrise, anyway. He burst into the room without ceremony. Jumièges, a thin-faced fellow rose to greet him as if this was his castle. He had been deep in conversation with two pale functionaries – scribes or some such—who bowed deeply before Champart dismissed them and they scurried from the room. He bowed ridiculously deeply.

"Duke William. I trust you are well?"

Good Lord, all this and now he expected pleasantries? He sighed. "I am beset by traitors and invaders. Every day the threats to Normandy grow. I have ridden long from a battle where I lost a fifth of my men to little purpose. What brings you to Normandy, Bishop? What could be so important that it could prevent me from defending my lands?"

Champart's eyes widened and his mouth twitched. Behind his face, some kind of calculation seemed to be going on. Perhaps deciding whether to respond to the insult. Instead, he bowed again. "My Lord. Excuse your humble servant. I am merely an instrument doing the bidding of a

417

King. I have no influence over the great events that move peasant and Lord alike, but am swept along as required by-”

“You were going to tell me why you dragged me here?”

That look again. Champart puffed himself up, and raised his voice as though addressing a sermon. “Yes, my Lord. My King, Edward of England, declares his great affection and love for his cousin, and in his Royal munificence-”

“Yes?”

The bishop sighed, and all the air seemed to go out of him. “Edward wishes to name you his heir.”

What? “His what? Why?” William sat on the nearest chair. He considered bidding the bishop sit for a moment, before deciding to leave him standing. Was Edward serious? He collected himself. “Why would Edward wish to name me his heir? He’s married isn’t he? And his queen is yet young? And if she won’t bear him any children, he can get another queen can’t he?”

The bishop’s face turned slightly pink. “Unfortunately, to his profound regret, the King has found it necessary to punish his queen and her family for disobedience. He has ordered the Lady Ealdgyth to a nunnery.”

A nunnery? How will she notice the difference from living with Edward?

“He has exiled Jarl Godwin and his adult sons, and required that certain hostages be held of him—hence, I bring the Jarl’s youngest son, his nephew and his youngest daughter. Along with the King’s offer.”

Not much of an insurance, William thought. *The sweepings of the family. This Jarl probably wouldn’t miss them.* Good heavens! To be offered the throne of a whole country. A rich one too, if somewhat rough around the edges.

418

And at the very time he might lose Normandy. Was God mocking him? Punishing him for his old ways?

He couldn't see any way he would one day be king in England. Good God, there was enough to do in Normandy. No. Impossible. And in any case, what if there were conditions attached? "Does Edward ask anything in return for his most generous offer?"

"No, not at all," the bishop said, steepling his fingers. "The King requires that you pay him homage and become his man, of course, but makes no demands."

William tired of the man swaying from one foot to the other and gestured to him to sit.

"But why me?" William asked. "Why now? There are others with a greater claim than I, surely?"

Champart looked distinctly uncomfortable for a moment, and William wondered if the chair had given him a splinter in the arse. "His Grace... That is to say..." He cleared his throat. "The family of Wessex has become overmighty and arrogant. There is no doubt that Jarl Godwin wishes to take the throne for himself, or one of his. The marriage with Ealdgyth was forced on his Grace to that end. And now he finds himself entering the autumn of his years, with no queen, no issue nor any immediate prospect of such. And so naturally he looks to Normandy, the country of his mother, the place he spent his childhood, and his mother's family. To you, my Lord."

William stood and took a couple of paces across the room. It was impossible. Ridiculous. No doubt Edward was amassing allies to counterbalance Wessex should there be fighting, and there was no chance that Normandy could spare a single man at arms. And yet if it did not require anything yet but an act of homage which need not sit too heavily on him... Perhaps he could call on Edward for arms, gold, men now. Edward could hardly refuse if he expected the same from William when the time came. He'd just have to deal with that when it happened.

"All right," he said. "Tell my cousin I accept."

That was just the beginning of course. They needed parchment and scribes and seals and Lord knew what else, but William was quite happy to leave all that in Fitz's hands. It took some time though for the servants to track him down, and when he finally appeared he appeared red-faced and unsettled. William asked him what the matter was.

"Lady Montgomerie," he said, rolling his eyes. "She's been chewing my ear off about the hostages. Apparently they have better quarters than she thinks they should have. And she wants the Saxon girl confined to those quarters as she's roaming about, scaring the other ladies, apparently."

"Roaming about? Where?" William could not blame her for that, if all the other ladies had shunned her. Good God, if he could knock their heads together and not offend his friends he would.

"In the courtyard, apparently. Would you like me to deal with her?"

"No, there's some business here with the bishop of Jumièges I'd like you to see to. I'm to be the King of England, apparently."

He left Fitz goggling and went to find the troublesome Saxon. It seemed easier than to try and get anyone else to do it. Besides, after being in Champart's company he felt a powerful need for fresh air.

***

William found the hostage before too long. She was easy to spot, with dress that seemed of fine quality, but plain, and noticeably different in style to that worn by the Norman ladies. Moreover, she was standing still, in a space where most people were hurrying from one place to another and rarely stopped to take in the sights. In fact, she appeared to be studying the gatehouse rather intently. As he approached, she turned to face him and he almost took a step back. Her face... The stories did not exaggerate. The first thing he saw was the birthmark, like a huge bruise. Then the haresfoot and then the blotches and craters. God, here was someone who'd attracted more than one curse.

His mouth was open. He'd better say something, quickly. William introduced himself, haltingly. "Lady... er, Ælfgifa is it?" he tried to keep the edge from his voice, and not succeeding. "I did not expect to find you outside." He attempted to soften his tone, adding, "is it customary for Saxon noblewomen to examine castle walls?" which only made it worse.

"My Lord." She curtseyed, and there seemed something almost sarcastic in the way she did it. Her Frankish was all but accentless. "I would imagine it customary for anyone to examine a barrier when it separates one from one's perceived freedom. Especially such a barrier." She turned back to the wall. "You must have fine quarries? Forgive me. I do not chatter idly often. Your Norman ladies seem content to be mewed up like so many hawks. I am used to rather more activity." She gazed at him, seemingly coldly, but there was something twinkling in her eye, perhaps. "There. I have confirmed your Lordship's opinion that Saxons are indeed unmannerly."

William almost choked and felt the heat rising in his face. Never had he been spoken to by a woman that way! Well, not since Matilda. "Activity? I'm afraid I don't understand." It took an effort of will not to let his mouth flap open again. "You are a hostage. What do you expect?" He realized he had no idea himself how one was supposed to treat noble hostages. If only Ralph were here. He grasped at the one thing she had said he could answer with authority. If only it didn't sound so petulant as it came out of his mouth. "And we have very fine quarries, as it happens! Caen stone is the best there is."

Ælfgifa inclined her head briefly, in acknowledgement. The stone clearly met with her approval. But the other matter was not to be abandoned. "I am accustomed to being useful, my Lord. I am certain so robust a mind as your Lordship's will comprehend the need for an occupation of some kind. As to my being a hostage, I had no expectations other than the fair treatment one noble personage might expect of another. You asked me about custom and I merely answered. I can see now that it was not in a manner you expected. I do not blush or simper prettily, Lord. In fact you may have my assurance that I do nothing prettily."

William laughed a little, almost despite himself. "I see my cousin Eustace was not exaggerating," he said. "You're not related to the Bishop of Bec are you? He speaks just as confusingly as you do."

For the briefest of moments a look of discomfort crossed her odd face. "My reputation has preceded me? How interesting. Might I perhaps inquire as to what intelligence the Count of Boulogne has not exaggerated?" William was about to answer when she collected herself and continued. "I am always fascinated by the tastes and opinions of a man who shows such excellent judgment in his own attire and... facial adornments. God was most generous there, I think. And I can claim no kinship with the good Bishop, although speaking in a manner calculated to confuse the listener seems to be a trait of the clergy, I have found."

He laughed properly this time. She'd clearly seen right through Eustace. And churchmen. And although she had the same effortless cleverness Lanfranc displayed, there was none of his infuriating abstraction in her speech. He could not point to many times in his life when he'd encountered someone so obviously very much cleverer than himself, nor any time a woman had – and there was no point jousting with an opponent who could hold a lance twice as long as your own. "Good heavens but you are exhausting company. Eustace... well, he's given to tall tales, shall we say. The way he spoke about you was as if... you would not want to hear such things, I am sure."

From her expression, not quite perfectly masked, she had evidently not been spared the opinions of others. Well, if he had a sou for every time he'd heard the word 'bastard'... This was not a fit subject for idle chat.

"...But if I may put your mind at rest as regards our walls," he stammered, "I can assure you that you wouldn't be happy to be 'mewed up' in a wooden hall. Not if you'd seen how poorly they stand up to siege engines. You may have heard I have some... unruly neighbors. A good stone wall can be a comfort." He patted the smooth, yellow stone as if it was a favorite hound.

The amusement was back in her eyes. "Siege engines, Lord? I have heard a little of such devices but much of it is contradictory. Perhaps you might relieve my ignorance?" Again, he was about to answer when he sensed she was toying with him. No wonder folk thought her a demon. "Is the Count of Anjou amongst these unruly neighbors you mention?" she added.

"Anjou? You've heard of him then." Who hadn't? In time he might be lord of all this, and king to boot. "He and his ilk have been grabbing all the land and wealth they can for generations now. Now he's having a crack at Normandy. And why wouldn't he? If you have the strength, why not make use of it? It's up to me, and our good Caen stone here to stop him. Don't you fear, my Lady, you shan't come to harm." As he said it, the ridiculousness of the notion was obvious. This creature seemed scared of nothing. But then his aunt had seemed scared of nothing too. Emma of Normandy, mother of the King of England. The apple had fallen far from that tree. "Only you're not worried about that, are you?" he went on. "Most women I've met swoon at the mention of battle or being besieged. It must be very peaceful where you come from."

She covered her mouth and what issued from beneath might have been a laugh. It was not a charming sound. "Forgive me, Lord. The idea that I come from a place of peace caught me off guard. While it is true that King Edward had kept a united England for several decades, we are an island kingdom and subject to the threats that such a position must pose to us. My brother, Jarl Harold, has led many campaigns by sea and by land already. It is not unusual for one Jarl to attempt to annex more land or power for himself either. We have raiders along our coast line betimes, who have no affiliations. And the *Wealas* dwell to the West of our lands—uneasy bed-fellows even in times of peace."

Things were not so very different in England then. Perhaps he should invite Ralph to Falaise for a while and let Ælfgifa set him straight about Edward's perfect realm... William felt a sudden sense of the strangeness of standing in his own courtyard among the horseshit and servants talking to a hostage. "Perhaps you would care to take a walk around the curtain wall? If you are not tiring of the outside air, that is?"

"I do not find the air tiring," she said, and submitted to walk with him. They ascended a set of wooden steps up to the rampart, while guards stepped aside with even greater promptness than usual. William was sure more than one crossed himself as they passed. The tiled canopy over the curtain wall provided welcome shade, while the view across the Norman countryside, its fields and orchards was as welcome as ever.

"Do your ladies really swoon?" Ælfgifa said, breaking into the silence after they had traversed half the circumference of the courtyard. "That seems an inefficient way to defend oneself or one's land and kin."

William let himself laugh again at that, and it felt good. "Better they swoon than run about shouting and get in the way." He looked at her, sidelong. "Do you really mean your ladies might play some part in a fight? Good Lord. I hardly know what to make of you Saxons. But all is not a paradise of amity in England then? My former guardian, Ralph, used to speak of England under Edward as such a place. He thinks too well of men, perhaps."

"I doubt there is a place on earth that is a 'paradise of amity' unless no men or women dwell there. We are a quarrelsome breed."

William nodded. It took no great scryer of human nature to tell that. Beyond the horizon to the South lay Domfront and Alençon, places that sooner or later would play host to violence.

"I did not mean to imply that women went to war," Ælfgifa went on, "although there are certainly a few who do. But when men are away who do you suppose guards the lands of their husbands? Or their own lands? Who else would mete out judgment on miscreants and offenders of the law? War may drag for long periods of time. Shall a wife or sister say 'we will put off this dispute or this trial until a more convenient season, when our lord shall be present?' That would be folly! Besides a wife should be a partner and helpmeet to her husband. A sister might become an advisor or advocate – a link with the Jarl's people."

He raised his eyebrows. He had no wife, and his sister was... How had Ælfgifa put it? 'Mewed up' until a husband could be found. William felt a pulse of guilt. Perhaps he should see Adelaide more often.

As if breaking into his thoughts, Ælfgifa said "I find myself wondering exactly how much your lordship has enjoyed the society of women."

He almost choked again at that. "Enjoyed the... well. Not in..." Damn her, but she was enjoying this. He had kept himself under control when talking to Matilda, he could bloody well do so now. "That is to say, I am not yet married,

426

though I have been betrothed for some time. The details have been a little complicated, it turns out. But you mean to say in England, a lord expects his lady to run his household when he is not present? Do you not have seneschals? And what do you mean by an advocate to a lord's people? That a lady would actually go out into the country and talk to the common folk?"

"A lady would hold a *Thing* in her husband's absence. When a Jarl is home, he and his lady often sit in arbitration together. No one is excluded from a *Thing*. Anyone might bring a complaint or a problem they cannot solve by normal means, be they noble, thagn, ceorl or even serf. One submits to the judgment of the Jarl and his counsel by doing so. And a wife's opinion weighs heavily with her lord, in most cases. As I have said, the lady performs this task herself when her husband is away. As for going amongst the people, do you not do such a thing yourself? How are you to tell if they are content or planning a revolt otherwise? It is as well to send a lady in any case. The small folk will speak to a lady, just as other women will speak to a lady, where they might not to a man and their lord."

"Going amongst my people? Last time I did that, I got an arrow in my saddle. Planning a revolt? Surely lords and knights plan revolts and the common folk go along with them. Like the sheep that they are." But did she have a point? It wasn't so very long ago that going out into his country with a small guard had almost led to his assassination—no-one would fire an arrow at a lady, would they? But how could anyone be sure? "No wonder you are fearless, Lady."

"As much as I should like to own to being fearless," Ælfgifa continued, "I find I must correct you. I do have fears although doubtless they are not of the common sort."

No, William thought. *I doubt much about you is common.* They carried on walking, now heading back towards the Keep, at the North-Western corner.

"More and more I find myself wondering what use you *do* put your women to," Ælfgifa said, almost to herself. She turned to William. "I suppose it is impertinent to ask. But still you seem to credit them with such low capabilities, such a narrow catalogue of talents. How do Normans get anything done when half the population is not permitted to do the vast body of tasks?"

"Use?" *What an odd thing to say.* "You speak so strangely of women. A lady may provide companionship for a lord, and, if it please God, children. I must say I have not given much thought to what they might get up to the rest of the time. Music, I suppose. And some sort of work with threads and fabrics? Of course the common women may do other things. Cook, I dare say, and clean. You talk to me of all these fantastic things—of ladies acting as advisors and castellans and Lord knows what. You would not be mocking me in my own castle, my Lady? I understand that you are a captive, but neither I nor any of my people have shown you any ill will, have they?"

As he said it, William recalled the mention of Mabel, and the other ladies refusing to attend her, and regretted the remark. He doubted such things had gone unnoticed. And he should not have risen to the bait.

"No more ill will than I am used to, Lord and no doubt that is God's plan for giving me such a visage." There was a tiredness in her voice at that, but with an edge of steel. This strange Saxon princess was determined to control her fate as much as she could despite the lot life had granted her. Were they all that different? "I assure you that I do not mock you— at least not in speaking of the ways of my people." She smiled, a little triumphantly. "I have perhaps said too much. I can see your ways are very different here. Still I cannot believe that people are so very different depending on which side of the sea they happen to dwell. Surely you must have canny and intelligent women and small folk, just as we do? Here I hold an opinion that is not universal in England, I fear. It was a chance of birth that allowed or denied access to better lives and opportunity, not a lack of innate ability. It is unfair to term the common folk as sheep, my Lord. Many of them have no option but to follow their masters and are only free in their own minds, simple and uneducated as those minds might be..."

She tailed off, perhaps in reaction to the look on his face. It was hard not to sneer. Yet as Ralph had been fond of saying, the peasantry had its place in life.

"I will stop," she said, though there was clearly more in her mind. For a moment, William thought she would keep the thought private, but she turned to him again as they descended the steps back to the courtyard. "Though I will mention one other concern. Treat with it as you wish although since you are to be a husband it may set your lordship's marriage off on the right footing – an unhappy wife can be... creative. I would advise you to find out exactly what women of sense and reason actually do. I fancy the answer might surprise you."

What on Earth did she mean? He thought of Mabel, stirring up trouble. He had assumed she just needed a firm hand, not to be indulged. But what if Matilda acted in that way too? God knew she had a strong mind. It was a depressing thought. Yet Gallet and Helisande seemed happy, didn't they?

"I can see you have had time to think about these things, Lady," he sighed. "I apologize, I didn't mean to suggest you weren't being truthful. God's wounds, I might be a fortnight thinking about the things you have said, which would be all very well if I didn't have so much to do. My own castles turning against me, Martel at my gate, and Heaven knows what the King will do next. I have people to think for me—a clever priest and... well, fitzOsbern does his best. Women of sense and reason? What a terrifying prospect."

She curtseyed again, a little more respectfully this time, and turned to go, but he gestured her to stop.

"There's no need to leave, Lady. I would not wish you to be 'mewed up'. Carry on your inspection and return to your quarters when you wish. I have work to do in any case." *So much work, and so little of it here.* And now his mind was tumbling like a rock from a pirrière. "Creative, you say? Great God. My father never married, you know. I begin to see why."

Ælfgifa merely smiled at that. But as he turned to go, he recalled she had mentioned a brother, Harold. The name was familiar, and with all this thought of sieges, he realized why. "It was your brother Harold who gave my future father-in-law a hard time at Liège, wasn't it?"

"I believe it was, although I doubt Harold would describe it as a 'hard time'. I bid you good evening, Lord and... I thank you for your hospitality."

CHAPTER 36

ÆLFGIFA was reluctant to return to the women's quarters. She had thought that after so many years of stares and mutterings, that she could no longer be disquieted by idle gossip or that frosty breed of hostility practiced by women of the nobility. The summary banishment from Edward's court, the attempt on her life and her family's disgrace had left her feeling as if her skin was as fragile as a dragonfly's wing and might tear at the least word or blow. Ælfgifa knew that this increased sense of vulnerability was a reaction to taking the lives of two men. More importantly, she knew it would pass. There were no regrets over things that had to be done in a heated moment in order to survive, and helping Garyn on his way had been an act of mercy. Still it weighed heavily with her. Aofra was still at court and still an unaddressed, though incompetent danger. Then too, she was sure Harold was playing a long and perilous game.

Ælfgifa turned away from the battlements and looked down towards a small yard where boys played at fighting with swords made of wood. Her ribs clenched around her heart when she recognized Wulfnoth. She took a deep breath and forced herself to relax. It was natural that he should want to join in the sport with boys his own age, and here were noblemen's sons aplenty. They laughed, squabbling and teasing, and Wulfnoth's voice could be heard raised in merriment, a polyglot mixture of Anglish, Latin and broken Frankish. So easily was her youngest brother accepted. She supposed it was his youth or bold, careless manner, or perhaps he had a little of the charisma that Harold used to bend people to his will.

On the journey and the voyage here, Ælfgifa had found the restraint and formality imposed by years apart crumbling to nothing in a matter of hours until she may well have still been the child who played with her brother in the snow so many years ago. Wulfnoth was easily four inches taller than her already but his mind was still a child's and had not caught up with his body. He had a curious way of standing so that when he spoke to his sister he both stooped and looked up at her, just as if she were still the taller of two. Ælfgifa had been painfully amused when she realized what he was unconsciously doing—the only thing to spark a smile from her since her dreary homecoming. Wulfnoth was a jumble of elbows and knees, overlarge hands and comically sized feet. He had the pinched, slightly unhealthy look boys who have grown suddenly acquired, when the rest of them had not yet caught up. Still, her brother had not been left unmarked by the fever that had nearly killed him.

Wulfnoth would not let Ælfgifa examine him when she had tentatively suggested it, but she thought he was too thin, too pale. Too much activity left him gasping for breath. She thought that either the fever or the mandrake had permanently weakened his heart but she had no access to the strong herbs she would need to help him here. Nor did Wulfnoth have any patience with his sister's coddling.

Ælfgifa supposed that if he were truly afflicted with anything, he would let her help then and resolved not to embarrass him on what he saw as a grand adventure. No need for her twelve-year-old brother to understand the very real danger of their predicament, Ælfgifa had decided, forgetting that at Wulfnoth's age, she had already been sitting in on *Things* with Harold and Edith.

As her gaze lit once more on the vast forest beyond the battlements, she found herself turning over her meeting with William. In many ways the Duke was just such a man as she had expected. Not boorish perhaps but certainly rough and unrefined. Hardly surprising since he had spent so much of his time with soldiers. From what she had heard he had more or less been constantly at war with his neighbors since he became Duke. No great mystery then, that while he was far from being a fool, he was ignorant in many ways, and had clearly not had the time or taken the trouble to challenge his perceptions regarding things not immediately needed to secure his ducal fief.

And yet he had surprised her, she would own that. William had been as disturbed as any man on first beholding her. She had seen with resignation the flash of disgust in his eyes but he had recovered himself quickly. Far more so than many Saxon lords she could name if she chose. There were grown men and women who flicked their forefingers in tiny gestures meant to ward off witchcraft, or spat between the spread V of their fingers against the evil eye when Ælfgifa was near. This Duke Willelm had mastered himself and spoken with courtesy. Not that that had stopped her needling him, pushing him to see just how close to the surface his reported temper lay. Again he had controlled himself—with a visible effort of will, it was true, but still it bore consideration.

Ælfgifa had rather enjoyed wrong-footing and teasing him. For a moment she had almost been able to forget her homesickness for England, her frustration at being unable to hold an intelligent conversation amongst the Frankish ladies. But for all his blunt features, imposing height and clumsy manner, William had the rudiments of a native kindness and curiosity about him. Qualities that wanted rather more husbandry than they'd been getting but there nonetheless. Ælfgifa gnawed her lower lip. She had not expected to like the Duke but she suspected that she might well have begun to. Blast Harold for putting her in this situation! Beholden to a man she had expected to find a brute, but was instead treating her with somewhat more cordiality than she was accustomed to expect. And this was the man Harold had set her to gather intelligence on, whilst acting as a place holder for her father and brother's good behavior. *Perhaps*, Ælfgifa thought, *I am not permitted the luxury of honor.* But it sat ill with her and she brooded over her turbulent feelings as the twilight fell.

***

Mabel de Bellême was a full blown and handsome woman, if rather stout. A decent matron who had lately borne a child for her Lord and already looked to have another one on the way, though Ælfgifa supposed she could not help that. These Frankish ladies lived quite inactive lives, all natural energy pent up and if it could not be subdued, funneled into women's crafts; weaving, embroidery and for some, spinning. Ælfgifa had been set to spinning now and she did not doubt that it was an insult. Only the very youngest, most inexperienced ladies spun. Those with no education who had not yet been taught the finer arts of needle work. She was not surprised that Mabel had taken exception to her presence.

In fact Mabel had far more cause to do so than some of the ladies of Ealdgyth's court or the women of Edith's household. Ælfgifa was a Saxon amongst Normans; an owl shut up amongst the hens. Still, she reflected grimly, more courtesy was a reasonable expectation. She felt quite certain that if she had been docile and frightened and soft-voiced with flaxen hair and an open, innocent, dewy face, that that old besom would have made a pet of her. Instead, staggeringly ugly and deformed, dark-haired, bold and outspoken, Ælfgifa had put Mabel's nose quite out of joint. She had not bothered to demonstrate her perfect grasp of Frankish yet, and Mabel's strident derisions over the 'ignorant, uncultured barbarian' rang in her ears.

Worst of all, Ælfgifa was bored out of her wits. One single day in the ladies' solar and she was ready to stab Mabel with the rod of her drop spindle. Abruptly she stood, sketched a half curtsey to Mabel and her more important friends, and passed a hand over her belly as if to indicate an upset stomach. She tried a rueful smile and one of the ladies gagged involuntarily. That was quite enough as far as Ælfgifa was concerned and she almost ran from the solar. At least her hasty retreat would add credence to her deception.

If you just spoke to them in Frankish then by degrees you might win their respect, she told herself severely. She could not be sure what had caused this burst of stubbornness. She only knew that as childish as it was, she would reveal the extent of her learning only when it would cause the most distress to Mabel.

Once outside, Ælfgifa took what felt like the first full breath she had managed all morning. A glance across the yard told her that Wulfnoth was playing with the Norman lords' sons once again. Their young nephew, Håkon, darted in and out of the larger boys, trying hard to keep up. Ælfgifa smiled wryly. Clearly Sweyn's son had a serious case of hero worship for Wulfnoth. Her smile faded as she drifted unremarked across the courtyard. She recalled her own idolization of both Ealdgyth and Harold, something of which lingered to this day, pondering over how it had led her here. This alien country with fields and forests that looked deceptively like those of England but which her bones and gut recognized as imposters. These low people who did not know how to value intelligence if it came in an unconventional package but instead set women to endless stitching and gossiping and backbiting, yet called *her* a barbarian.

It was the scent that drew her. Clean, astringent, faintly floral and sweet. Ælfgifa rounded the base of one tower and found a small, tucked-away garden with walls of its own. The gate was unlocked and gentle tug on the latch saw her out of the way of prying eyes and almost knee deep on a path overgrown with lavender. There was rosemary here too, fennel and cinquefoil, speedwell and mint. By the wall grew some of the herbs used in cooking – sorrel and parsley and thyme. But there were also herbs that would never make their way into a cooking pot, showing that once this had been a medicinal garden. A long time ago judging from the neglect. Ælfgifa bent automatically to pluck weeds away from a clump of heart's-ease and then froze. Once again she had wandered into a private herb garden without realizing there was already someone here. She knew the duke at once – there was no mistaking his height or the set of his shoulders, nor that slightly unkempt mane of dark hair. William was part concealed by a clump of witch hazel and did not seem to have seen her.

Ælfgifa considered leaving – really, what more could she and he have to say to one another at present? – instead, unsure of what prompted her, she moved towards him.

"A fine evening, my Lord," she said, dropping a small curtsey.

William started. "God's blood! Lady Ælfgifa! What do you mean by creeping about like a cat?"

Ælfgifa raised an eyebrow at him. "I sincerely hope you have good watchmen, Lord, both at home and in the field. Or walls or no, I shall fret when I lay down to sleep of a night."

William's piercing eyes focused on her and Ælfgifa fought a smile. Color had risen in his cheeks. *Chagrin*, she thought. She changed tack. "It is good news upon which you meditate so fiercely, that you do not hear me macerate several pounds of lavender underfoot, I hope?"

William eyed her soberly. "Just what are you doing here, Lady?" There was a touch of pique in his tone. Ælfgifa was untroubled. Harold never cared for being startled either.

"I have found a day sampling the delights of Norman femininity has quite overwhelmed my appreciation for such things. Possessing a rough and jaded palate, I sought out homelier fare. I thought I might put this garden in order since I find it rather overgrown. I am, I assure you, merely a competent spinner at best." William looked so thoroughly confused that she wanted to laugh. "The good Lord forgive me," she went on in a darkly amused tone. "I am being much too forward once again, am I not?"

"Lady, did I hear you aright? You wish to perform menial work in this garden?" William seemed to be grasping for the one part of her outburst that made sense.

"If you have no objection, Lord. I would offer my services in the dairy but you seem to have many people who can make butter and cheese or collect eggs. And I doubt I would be a success as a warrener." Ælfgifa smiled her close-lipped smile. "However I can certainly tell a foxglove from an onion so this little patch of earth would be in good hands."

"I've never heard the like. A lady wanting to grub in the dirt like a common kitchen slattern... ahem, begging your pardon, Lady." William shifted his weight uneasily.

"It is of no matter. I am well aware that my sudden appearance is a shock whether I give voice to an odd request or no," Ælfgifa said, with a touch of irony.

"Are you tired of the society of the women so soon? Surely there are those your own age... of similar interests..." William trailed off.

"Were I not so remiss in my interests as to broaden them beyond embroidered altar cloths, catching a husband and waiting for him to put a bairn in my belly, then doubtless you would be right, Lord," Ælfgifa said with some asperity. "As it is I have been in a bad school for friendship and have ruined my prospects with such trivialities as Latin grammar and herbalism." She pulled herself up short, irritated at having given herself away so much. With an attempt at playfulness, she said, "I seem to be developing something of your lordship's distaste for my sex." *And if this is a fair sampling of the women you have had any conversation with, I no longer blame you at all for that distaste.*

There was a small frown between William's brows. "In truth, Lady, I find it hard to tell if you are in jest or in earnest but since you desire an occupation you may certainly tend the garden—I will have a chamber cleared for use as a still room for you as well, since you are so keen to be useful. God knows we may need all the healing skill we can get before long." His eyes snapped to hers again and there was perhaps a glint of humor in the depths. "It may give my household a better chance to grow accustomed to you."

Ælfgifa smiled ruefully, curtseying deeper this time. "Then I thank you, Lord."

"Is there anything else you desire? Since you seem determined both to disturb the peace and to frighten away my ill-humor?" He was laughing at her but there was no malice in it. Ælfgifa felt instinctively that he liked her boldness and found her sphinx-like way of talking diverting. *It can change*, she cautioned herself, *with great lords, it can change so fast...* Still, he had asked.

"I should like to send a message to my sister, Ealdgyth, to say I am well and that my kinsmen and I have been treated with great consideration," she said. "I realize this will present difficulties-"

"Difficulties! Impossibilities, more like!" William cried. "Lady, there is no messenger who can be spared at present. Even if there were, the castle scribe died some weeks ago. Soon, I must lead my army on campaign and I am afraid any able lawmen and priests—in short anyone who could write your missive for you—will be wanted elsewhere. Surely your sister will know you are well enough?"

Ælfgifa felt heat flood into her face but forced her voice to remain level. "That need not be a cause for difficulty. If you could spare me a little parchment and ink, I will write my own message. As for delivering the message, why I could not help but notice that the Abbey church of La Trinité keeps pigeons. I saw it as we rode here. I cannot be certain but even if they have no pigeons from my sister's current abode, they will likely have some from Westminster. I know the monks there well and they would be happy to pass such a message on to the Queen."

The line between William's brows deepened. "You can read?"

"Yes, Lord." Ælfgifa strove to keep the irritation from her voice.

"And write?" William's expression grew blacker by the minute.

"Yes, Lord."

"And how, pray, am I to know what message you might be sending to England?" William's voice ground like churned stones. "I doubt the monks speak Anglish and if they do they almost certainly don't read it."

"Do you think me to be a spy, my Lord?" Ælfgifa asked, innocent and wicked, prompted by God knew what familiar to needle the Duke as he struggled with his temper.

"I have no idea what to make of you! *Elves'-gift*? That is your name, is it not? I put no credence in such peasant tales until I met you, Lady! I can only assume the elves would not take you back!"

441

Ælfgifa bit down on a hasty retort. A sharp reply would hardly aid her cause even if he had wounded her unwittingly. "Forgive me, Lord. I have an unfortunate, careless way of speech on occasion. I am happy to write my message in a language the monks will understand—Latin perhaps? Or I might write it in Frankish and you shall read it yourself."

Instead of clearing, William's expression clouded further. *He cannot read, Ælfgifa realized, or at least not well enough to be sure of the skill. And he does not entirely trust his vassal monks any more than he trusts his lords.* It occurred to Ælfgifa that the Duke was probably the loneliest man she had ever encountered. No wonder his manners were a little rough. No wonder he leapt straight for suspicion. He had been thrust into a leader's role without any of Harold's natural advantages. The people of Normandy might respect William, fear him, but Harold's people loved their Jarl. She wondered just how many attempts on his life William had survived. This would need careful handling. *And you are a spy, Ælfgifa's conscience spiked at her, maybe you are not set to topple this Dukedom but you have been sent here to learn about the Duke.* She could buy trust with no other coin but trust.

"My sister's maid, a loyal ceorl since they were both children, was killed by bandits on the road to Wessex," she began.

"What the devil is that to me?" William demanded angrily.

"Truthfully, it is nothing to you. I should not trouble you with it if I knew who else to appeal to. My sister insisted that Suela accompany me rather than stay safe in convent walls. For her service and loyalty, she deserves to be remembered. I had no opportunity to tell Ealdgyth before I was sent here, Lord. Word may well have reached her already but I cannot rest easy until I have told the Queen how her maid died." Ælfgifa swallowed against a sudden, painful blockage in her throat.

"Yet you survived. How many men were in your escort, Lady?" William seemed to be measuring her response, trying to find a key to a puzzle.

"Not enough to ensure their survival or the rest of our party's, my Lord." Ælfgifa had no wish to speak of this. Her hands felt caked and sticky, as if covered with cooling, viscous liquid once more.

"Less touched by elves and more touched by God," William murmured. "How did you get away? The unvarnished truth please, Lady, if you wish me to consider your request."

"I was lucky or God was indeed with me," Ælfgifa said. "Suela killed one attacker before she died. Another was rolled on by his horse-" she saw William repress a shudder and nodded to herself. He would have seen enough of such things in battle. "They attacked me last, perhaps believing that I should give them the least amount of trouble."

"It would seem that error cost them, Lady. What did you do?" William's gaze was unblinking, intent. For the first time Ælfgifa caught a glimpse of the strategic mind that lay behind a comparatively unprepossessing exterior. You underestimated this man at your peril.

"One, I disabled, using trickery and a boot knife. I have no idea if he lived or died." She swallowed again. "The other... your Lordship will have seen the long knives—the seax—for which my people are named? They are not merely decorative. That man is dead. I was lucky, as I said." Ælfgifa was certain there was plenty of air to be had out here in the garden but she could not seem to suck any of it into her lungs.

"Lucky? An armed man against a woman? A small woman at that. That is more than luck. What purpose does God have for you to preserve your life so?" William believed her, against his will perhaps but she could see he believed her tale.

"I do not know, Lord. He has never seen fit to tell me."

William burst into sudden, wild laughter, making Ælfgifa first jump and then smile wryly. "Very well. Pen your message—in Frankish, mark you—and I will see it delivered to La Trineté."

Although she would have much rather visited the Abbey herself, she knew the Duke had just granted her a grand concession. She bowed her head and curtseyed again. "You are very kind, my Lord. You have my thanks."

"Go in now, Lady. It will be time to dine soon. I will not see you again for some time. I'll send someone to collect your letter if you have it ready by dawn. We march tomorrow." William turned away.

"My Lord?"

"Yes?" William replied with awful patience.

"Does it ever wash off? The blood, I mean?" Ælfgifa looked at him, trying not to appear vulnerable.

William opened his mouth but no reply was forthcoming.

"Ah," Ælfgifa said, as if the Duke had confirmed her own suspicions. "Farewell then, Lord. May God watch over you and grant you success." She turned and ran lightly from the garden, leaving William once again uncomfortably turning over thoughts she suspected he would rather never have examined, his head seemingly fit to burst.

***

With the right materials, it took Ælfgifa hardly any time at all to pen a short, descriptive missive to Ealdgyth. It took rather more time and a bone embroidery needle to prick a careful message to Brother Dubhne around the edge of the scrap of vellum, in holes and impressions so fine that to a casual observer they appeared no more than the crumbling of a poorly stretched piece of calf-skin. William's servant came and collected the unsealed letter. Duty done, Ælfgifa barred the door of her tiny, unheated chamber and lay down to an uneasy and fitful sleep.

($)HAPTER 37

$($)HESE were strange times. A noble Saxon hostage eschewing the company of her equals, content to grub in the dirt. At least William had, somehow, gained a skilled herbalist through it. If the fates of the men wounded at Mouliherne were any indication, the army was sorely lacking in skilled healers and surgeons. If the Elf-woman was as capable as she claimed – and he had no reason to doubt it— she may yet prove useful. And Helisande would look after her and prevent her from causing any trouble, at least.

In any event, William felt a twinge of guilt at doubting her motives. The letter she had written her sister was indeed entirely innocent in its content.

But if the whole Wessex family shared Ælfgifa's capabilities, then Edward was right to be wary of them. She had spoken particularly of Harold. Now he remembered what he had heard. Baldwin had been fulsome in his praise of the Saxon force and its commander. The heir to Edward's rival and evidently a fine commander, at sea or on land. Just the kind of man William could use. A stroke of bad fortune that Edward had exiled him—he was now in Difelin in Erin, so the spies said. Now he was no use to either of them, and might even become a challenge if things continued to go

446

badly for Edward. It was typical of his luck. Just as William entered into an agreement with Edward in the hope of gaining military support against Anjou, the King decided to get rid of his most capable generals and doubtless alienated a lot of decent fighting men, too. In hindsight, it seemed to William that King Edward had made his most kind offer more in the hope of securing military aid from Normandy in case the business with Wessex turned ugly. Military aid that could not be spared. Did Edward have no idea whatsoever what was happening in Normandy? That the Duchy was under severe threat itself, and not at some likely point in the future—right now. And his biggest problem was already a severe lack of men.

Just when William felt he was starting to get a grip on lordship, something else turned up to complicate matters. And that was without the bizarre and confounding Saxon woman he was now playing host to. It wouldn't be so bad, but he had come away from their conversations feeling that Ælfgifa would be able to comprehend his problems in a moment and dictate an obvious solution as if it were the answer to a child's riddle. If only she'd been born a man he might be worrying about her as a possible military adversary. God had a sense of irony. Or a sense of humor.

At least there was one bit of good news—an old enemy William had almost forgotten about, finally defeated. As they were preparing to leave for the Duchy's Southern Marches, a bedraggled, worn-looking war party trudged through the gates. Guy of Burgundy, starved out of his castle at Brionne, dragged to Falaise to negotiate. Beaumont, his beard now halfway down his chest and full of road dust, smiled grimly at William and presented his 'guest.'

William narrowed his eyes and looked at the man who had almost cost him his Duchy. Guy was thin, as well he might be after having been under siege for years. The Count affected to look defiant but to William's eyes he just looked tired.

"So, you finally starved the little turd out," he sighed to Beaumont. "Have him cleaned up and brought to my audience chamber. The lesser chamber."

"Aye, Lord," Beaumont grinned ruefully, explaining as a quiescent Guy was led away that the Count had surrendered in order to discuss terms, his castle still held by his men. In reality, he wasn't in much of a position to make demands. William expected him play for every concession he could get, but when his adversary was brought before him, William saw how beaten he was. Beaumont knew better than to relax his grip and allow any supplies through before the gates had been opened. Burgundy's men would not last long.

"Alright, what do you want?" he said to Guy as he took his place in the audience chamber.

"Lord?" Guy's brows creased. "I don't understand."

"I don't have all day," William huffed. "You want me dead and you want to be Duke yourself, obviously. You can't have that. But what do you *want*? You've been shut up in Brionne for years. You can go back there and starve for all I care."

Guy's eyebrows raised in surprise. William did not know what the Count had expected, but it was evidently not this. "To discuss... terms, Lord. Terms of surrender."

William rolled his eyes. "Here's what I'll allow. You can continue to live in Normandy if you wish. Keep a portion of your lands, but I'll require some in recompense." Hmm. Brionne was near Lanfranc's bishopric, wasn't it? He could at least do something for the cleric, after nearly having his holdings destroyed. "And some to the abbey at Bec."

Guy looked suspicious. "Very well, Lord."

"So a third to the Duchy, a third to Bec and you keep a third. And the castle to me." It was a good castle. Too good for the likes of Guy.

"Very well, Lord." Guy looked relieved. Perhaps it was better than he had hoped for, but maybe he was just glad it was over.

"That's settled then." William rose to leave. It looked as though the uprising that had nearly cost him his Duchy and his life was all but over. He could not feel any satisfaction. There was already another enemy to fight off. Was this what it was to be like? By the time one threat was defeated, two more had arisen? "There is one more thing, Burgundy," he added, as he reached the door.

Guy's expression changed to defensive once again. "Yes, Lord?"

"Rise up against me again, or give succor to my enemies, and I'll slice you into pieces in front of your own mother."

***

William wanted nothing more than to have a horse saddled and ride to confront Anjou. He knew though that he needed to gather his captains and advisers, decide a plan of action and make sure everyone knew what they were supposed to be doing. They had to wait for his uncle, William of Arques to arrive with his troops in any case, and according to the last messenger, he was still half a day away from Falaise. He took a breath. This was time that had been taken from him, but it had been given too. He should use it wisely, to prepare.

And the same went for the other resources at his disposal. "What's happening with our spies?" he asked Gallet when the inner council had gathered. "Have we got any in Martel's camp yet?"

"Yes, my Lord. A couple of grooms in Martel's stables."

"Grooms? No-one higher up than that?"

Gallet smiled. "Turns out stable hands make good spies. They see all the comings and goings. They're the first to hear when the lord's going out on campaign. And they can conceal messages in tack when riders go from place to place." He gave a snorting laugh. "Some more than others. One lad in Edward's stables thinks far too much of himself, but we get some useful tidbits."

William suppressed a grin. He doubted any of the nobles in his court would have thought of that. "All right. And have we rooted out everyone else's spies here?"

"Mostly, my Lord. That we know of. There are a few I've left in place so we can feed them on lies and nonsense."

"Good. I'd hoped as much. Anyone in Geoffrey's pay?"

"Yes, my Lord. A clerk in the treasury."

"Excellent. I want to try a bit of misdirection. Everyone listen closely." They all leaned in. "It's very important that we're disciplined about this. You all know Alençon and Domfront? All been there?" Nods and affirmations around the room. "All right, then you know that Domfront is very well defended, on a hill, with stone walls, and a keep built on an outcrop of rock not unlike Falaise castle here. Alençon, on the other hand, has only wooden ramparts, and it's on flat ground. The Sarthe is wide there, but runs slow, so we can get men across on boats easily enough should we want to attack both sides at once."

"So we're going for Alençon then?" Fitz asked.

"No. Domfront." A ripple of surprise went around the assembled Barons and knights. He gestured for calm. "Alençon is on the border, while Domfront is within Normandy, so I'm hoping it will be a bit harder for Geoffrey to supply. Most importantly though, Alençon is the obvious target. It's closer both to us and Henri, and will seem a much easier prospect. In case you were in any doubt, we're perilously short of men. With those still tied down at Brionne, for the moment, and the losses at Mouliherne, we simply don't have enough to encircle one well-defended town, let alone two. But if we can surprise Domfront unprepared and under-provisioned, it might fall quickly. If we go for Alençon first, that will give Domfront time to stock up for a long siege."

"Makes sense," Gallet nodded. "So you want me to tip off Geoffrey's spies that we're going for Alençon?"

"Yes, exactly," William replied. "In fact, everyone who doesn't need to know the plan will be informed we're marching on Alençon. And we will, until the last moment, when we'll swing to the West—by that time we'll be well within a day's march of Domfront."

"A sound plan, my Lord," Hubert de Ryes said. "But we'll need to move quickly. What about William of Arques? He's still half a day away, and his army will need rest and replenishment when they get here."

"I know. It can't be helped. I don't want to lose another day. I suggest we leave with what forces we have, as soon as we can. Fitz, I'd be grateful if you could see to my uncle's needs, fill him in on the plan and entreat him to follow after us as quickly as possible. If at all possible, I'd like it if the two armies could combine on the road, but I appreciate that they've already come a long way and it may be asking too much to have them march fast enough to overtake us. It won't be a disaster if he arrives a day late, but I'd rather avoid it if possible. I fear if we stay until his force is ready, we'll trip over each other and find more and more reasons to delay."

"I'll do my best, my Lord," Fitz said, looking as though the weight of the world was on his shoulders again.

"It's a good plan," Gallet said, "but what happens if they aren't fooled?" The others feigned to look as though they hadn't entertained the thought for a moment.

"We'll cross that bridge when we come to it. But Domfront's a little way from Geoffrey's territory, it will be hard for him to support. If we can't defeat them by surprise, we'll just have to keep harrying them, preventing them from resupplying, probing all the time for weakness, not giving them a moment's peace. I think we've learned a lot from Brionne about making life hard for the besieged without too much risk to our own people."

"Brionne took bloody ages."

"I know, but to be honest, we didn't have any idea what we were doing. Guy has taught us well."

"Now we've got him I'll teach him a thing or two with the edge of my sword."

"You bloody won't." William thumped the table. "He's still my man, after everything. If he puts a foot wrong again, then you can cut him into little bits as far as I care. But he'll be given a chance to correct his ways. I won't have my sworn lords fighting each other."

Everyone stared, and Gallet issued a sort of bark. "If you say so. My Lord."

Apparently no-one could believe he was prepared to be merciful. But did they not see? It had nothing to do with mercy. He had to play by the rules even if none of the others would. Even being a bastard. Especially being a bastard. "I say so. Don't worry, there'll be plenty of Angevins for you to hack to bits if you want to."

***

More marching. William was beginning to realize that war consisted far more of marching than of fighting. And waiting. Well, if his plan was good, there wouldn't be much in the way of waiting. Even as he thought it, he knew the chances of effectively surprising the defenders at Domfront were slim. They would have to somehow miss the presence of an approaching army. Still, if Geoffrey could be made to believe he was set on attacking Alençon, throw all his resources at defending the wooden-walled town, close his mind to other possibilities until it was too late... Put like that, it sounded so feeble. Nevertheless, it was possible to miss the presence of an army in the forests of Bas Normandy, especially if you were expecting it to be many leagues in another direction.

As he rode alongside his troops, hearing them talking about the plunder to be had at Alençon... At least they were convinced. He'd keep them slogging on towards the fake target until he was virtually convinced himself. And despite his instincts to rush, he forced them to keep a moderate pace to allow William of Arques to catch up, which happened on the third day. They were now such a large army, making such a noise and disturbance in the countryside, no-one could miss their advance. William wondered if Geoffrey would ride out to meet him and there would be open battle, his first since Val es Dunes, but there was no sign of any opposing force. Not even any skirmishers or raiders.

William allowed the detail of the plan to form in his mind, without discussing it with any of his captains. They had enough to worry about keeping their men together, fed and marching in the right direction. They would halt outside Argentan, a day from Alençon, set up camp as normal... Then leave an hour after dark and march at the best possible speed. If all went well, they'd reach Domfront before daybreak, well before they would be expected at Alençon. During a brief stop at midday, he gathered the others— Gallet, Montgomerie, Fitz, Henri de Ryes and Arques.

"By the end of today's march, we'll be eight leagues from Domfront. We'll camp at the crossroads outside Argentan. It would be the logical place to stop if we were intending to march on Alençon, only instead of following the road South, we'll take the North East road." He explained the night march. Naturally, no-one looked too happy about this. William nevertheless thought he'd got away without complaints when Arques seemed to change his mind.

"I've been marching twice as long as you, Normandy," he said. "My men are in little enough state to fight a battle as it is. And now you want them to march through the night too? My Lord."

454

"We'll take the reserve from your force. That will give a good number a rest."

"And have the best plunder go to your men?"

God's Left Bollock, William thought. *Where was the plunder at Mouliherne? And where were your men, Arques, when mine were dying in the mud for no purpose?* "When I'm King of England, every man who helps me here will have land and gold," he said, trying to keep the sneer out of his voice. He regretted it the moment he'd said it. The look on Arques' face told him he was right to.

"England, Lord? Do you jest?"

"No. As you know, my cousin is King there, and we have discussed the succession. But this is not the matter we are discussing now. As you know, time is of great importance. We need to strike when it's least expected if we're to have a chance of success."

"As you wish. My Lord."

They debated the order of marching, setting the 'battles,' groups of men under a commander with instructions that they would operate independently but in concert with those beside them. William found that arrangement easier to manage than a single mass with commanders trying to control a stretch of the line that could be fluid. They would be going straight into battle if everything went to plan, and there would be no time to arrange formations. Everyone would have to be in the right order, and know where they were going to be so they could attack as soon as they came out of the treeline beneath Domfront. Please God the gates would be open, the peasantry in the fields and the sentinels wiping the sleep from their eyes.

After they'd formulated the strategy, William moved back to the head of the column, letting himself be seen by the soldiers, exchanging a word or two with the knights and barons as he went. None of them yet knew that they'd be marching tonight as well, but in that way rumors had of spreading through an army like lice or the flux, he had little doubt that within an hour, everyone would know where they were going. It would be no bad thing now, anyway. It would at least avoid confusion later.

The army had sprawled out on either side of the road into the fields, filling folds in the ground but sagging away from a spinney on the left, wary of ambush even though it had been thoroughly scouted before the main force arrived. As he made his way back to the front, a shout drifted over the mutter of a hundred conversations, the clank of gear, the grunting of animals. He didn't pay it much attention, but another shout followed it. Where...? Over towards the trees. Men were jumping to their feet.

"What's going on?" he snarled at the nearest lieutenant. The man stammered something unintelligible and rushed off in the direction of the disturbance. In a few moments he was back.

"Spies, my Lord," he said. "Some of de Ryes' men surprised them."

"Did they get away?"

"I don't know, my Lord. I think so. I'll find out." He disappeared again and it was several minutes before he returned. "They escaped, my Lord. What happened is... confused. But it seems a couple of de Ryes' men went into the woods to get some firewood and discovered men watching us."

What? That shouldn't have happened. The pickets shouldn't have let anyone within a mile of them. *Damn! Bloody Flux!* "And is anyone pursuing them?"

"Yes, my Lord."

Well at least they were in pursuit. The lieutenant was still there. It seemed there was more. "What else?"

The man flushed. "It's unclear, my Lord. But the men who were surprised scattered. Some of them may have been... ours."

"Good God! We don't know?" Spies. In his own camp. Of course. Would he always be one step behind? William felt his heart thundering, and for an instant wanted nothing more than to draw his sword and swing it into the soldier's neck.

"It was said that there were four men in the wood. Only two fled across the fields. Henri de Ryes and his men have combed the trees, no-one could be hiding there. He thinks they may have been known, melted back into the army."

He took a breath, and ordered the man send word to his Barons to attend him, as quickly as possible.

"We are discovered," William hissed, when they had assembled. "Betrayed."

He explained. Horror and shock on their faces. Of course. *Idiots.* They didn't see just how this game was played, and how badly they were losing it. Except... Which of them were protesting too much? Montgomerie, who'd defied him over Talvas? Gallet, who never seemed to want anything? Who was selling him out this time?

"So there's no point in going to Domfront then?" Odo asked. "If they're warned, then we'll have no chance."

"No." William clenched his fists. "We march. Now."

"But my Lord," Fitz said, "If their defenses are prepared, it will be impossible to overcome them."

"There's still a chance. It may be that now Geoffrey's men know we have uncovered their surveillance, they'll expect us to call off the attack. Even if they do still think we're coming, we'll be at most an hour or two after they are warned. We may still be able to catch the town at least partly off guard. But we have to leave now."

To the men's credit, for the most part they dug deep into their reserves and marched for all they were worth. Most of them seemed to gain energy as they went, their enthusiasm building with the chance of battle. That was good. The confidence of the majority would win over those who were scared and tired. For the most part.

It did not surprise William in the least that it was Arques' men who started to straggle and string out the column. If he had been feeling charitable, William would have put that down to the additional days they had endured on the road. But Arques had been unenthusiastic about being called to support William, to say the least, even though he held his Barony of William. In theory, what was bad for William was bad for his uncle, who would lose his Barony if his liege Lord was deposed. He should motivate his men better, curse his diseased innards.

When they arrived at the edge of the woods opposite Domfront, the gates were closed, the walls manned. The fields were empty of peasants and animals. Even some fields of crops had been set on fire. The Norman army stood in the tree line as the first glimmers of daylight picked out the edges of the stone walls, exhausted, confounded, silent. William felt every man's disappointment more keenly than the burning in his calves, the blisters on his feet, but not more than the betrayal flaming in his soul.

CHAPTER 38

HELISANDE paused in chopping the scrubbed roots Ælfgifa had given her to prepare and grinned up through her honey-brown hair impishly. "Have I shocked you, m'lady?"

"No, not at all…" the words died on Ælfgifa's tongue and to her mortification she felt blood rising in her face. The two women were in the still room—William had been as good as his word on that score and over the last few weeks Ælfgifa had retreated there, and to the herb garden, as often as possible. She could not imagine Mabel de Bellême making more than a token protest when she absented herself from the ladies' solar day after day. They agreed on very little except this one item; that the more Ælfgifa was out of Mabel's sight, the better that day went for everyone. So Ælfgifa was grateful to William, it would have been unnatural not to be so. What his Grace, the Duke, had not mentioned was that Ælfgifa was to have the wife of one of his knights as a constant companion.

She would much rather have been alone with her thoughts and her churned feelings—still so raw since the attempt on her life, Harold's trapping her into life as a hostage, the exile from Edward's court and a hundred and one other hurts and slights, thought forgotten yet now piling misery upon pain until there was no path of logic to be found through the quagmire. Ælfgifa did not wish a companion. Certainly not one so relentlessly cheerful and mischievous. Or pretty. *There, Ælfgifa thought, I've named the true evil. I have a shallow nature just as everyone else does.*

Because Helisande was very pretty. That sort of prettiness that defied the kind of unearthly beauty Edith the Fair possessed, but somehow was more appealing perhaps because it was tangible. While she was still taller than Ælfgifa, Helisande was petite, slender and unconsciously graceful. Her eyes were large and luminously bright with intelligence and humor. Her complexion a very clear olive. Her mouth might have been made for kissing alone if it weren't for the flashing, sharp white teeth and sudden, wicked dimples. All of which might have been calculated to especially annoy Ælfgifa in her present depression except that there was no sourness in Helisande. No spoiled pout or sulkiness. She was a year or two older than Ælfgifa herself and had two children by a husband she clearly adored, and yet she seemed much younger. Ælfgifa realized that she herself had never engaged in the sort of innocent fun—and certainly not the less-than-innocent fun—Helisande encouraged her in. All Ælfgifa's games had been played with politics and strategy. It made her wonder if she had squandered her younger years. After all, just where had cleverness, cunning and learning got her? Exiled to Falaise, a political hostage.

It was impossible to resent Helisande, however. She spread such an aura of contentment and laughter where she went that within two minutes you forgot to be annoyed or grumpy. And the girl was impervious to sarcasm or snubs,

Ælfgifa reflected ruefully. She had certainly tried to put Helisande off, to freeze her with subtly barbed words and sly put-downs, when the girl had arrived the day after William's forces marched. After several attempts at getting rid of Helisande, Ælfgifa had reluctantly admitted defeat. The girl merely smiled unperturbed at Ælfgifa's witticisms, cruel or otherwise, saying she was neither clever not educated enough to understand the lady's meaning, before going straight back to cheerfully helping with whatever task Ælfgifa had set herself that day.

She pulled herself back to the present and arched an eyebrow at Helisande. "I am not shocked. I know my brothers have mistresses. I just... It seems so unlikely. You and the Duke."

"It was certainly a night to remember!"

"I really do not require details," Ælfgifa said hastily.

Helisande burst into peals of laughter. "Not for that reason, m'lady, although he's well enough as men go, I suppose. Better hung than some but no bull-"

"Helisande!" Ælfgifa knew they were alone but could not help a swift glance around to ensure no one was listening. "I do not think you should be talking of such things with me. With anyone! The Duke would not like it, I dare say. And what of your husband?"

Helisande's mischievous expression softened into one of wry amusement. "I don't talk so to any but you, m'lady. And you won't say anything. Besides I meant the assassination attempt. The first one."

"You were there?" Ælfgifa breathed.

"It's how I came to meet my husband." She paused. "It's never occurred to me how strange that is before now. Catching my future lord's eye whilst in the bed of another."

"Doubtless he liked what he saw," Ælfgifa said archly.

Helisande grinned. "It all fell out as it was meant to. The Duke escaped. Gallet became known as a most loyal supporter. I gained a husband."

Ælfgifa shook her head. "What I don't understand is this. Suppose you had borne the Duke a child? In my land the offspring of mistresses and lovers are often reared in the lord's household, sometimes as siblings to his legitimate issue. They may not inherit but they are not repudiated or scorned. In many cases the wife and the concubine are on good terms, even friends. But here? It is a shameful thing to be a bastard here, is it not?" Ælfgifa bit her lower lip, aware that she may be giving away more than she intended. The whispers about William's parentage could hardly escape her notice and she had sensed that the title of 'bastard' bothered him, however he tried to mask it. It reminded her sharply of the old Abbess so many years ago. *You wear your hurts too openly and too hard.* William was just such another as she had been. There was a desperate energy to his actions, as if he must forever be proving himself as worthy as one born the right side of the bed sheets.

Helisande shrugged. "It is as shameful as you allow it to be. Worse for a noble, I imagine. Less so amongst the small folk and the tradesmen. Of course the Church would have us believe it is a mortal sin but what isn't when it suits them? Do you think God is a jealous old man with nothing better to do than peer under a person's blankets at night? Seeing who lies with who and recording whether they be man and wife or not? Doesn't make sense, that."

Ælfgifa found herself chuckling at this blasphemous but astute observation. For an uneducated kennel master's daughter, Helisande was both bold and sharp-witted.

"I imagine it is of greater consequence if the girl in question is already married to another." Ælfgifa felt her mouth twist in a sour expression and Helisande grew sober and nodded.

"Alas few men wish to raise another's child so we have less license than men in our affections." Her smile was sudden, wicked and infectious. "Not that I have need – Gallet is quite enough, I assure you."

"And now I am sure you are trying to make me blush! It won't work," Ælfgifa said with mock severity.

"Did you never take a lover yourself, Lady?" Helisande murmured, eyes alight with curiosity.

For a moment Ælfgifa remembered the feel of Garyn's hands lingering on her waist as he lifted her down from her pony. And then her hands felt slick and sticky with his blood once more, and she heard his voice in her memory begging for confession and death. She swallowed hard against the bitter taste in her mouth and turned her face fully towards Helisande.

"I think God may have intended me for other pursuits than attracting lovers, don't you?" She smiled, hard and brilliant around the acid in her voice.

"Pfft!" Helisande said, shrugging dismissively. "God has nothing to do with it. Beauty of the face and body is entirely a matter of chance. I think you must frighten all your suitors away with that waspish tongue!"

Ælfgifa laughed half-heartedly. "Just such an answer as I would expect from a pretty girl."

But Helisande had teased out more of Ælfgifa's thoughts and feelings in a few short weeks than even her beloved family had ever done. She found her melancholy lifting. The cold wounds left, in the wake of all that had led to her imprisonment, healing. She had never had a friend who wanted no more of her than her company before, she realized. *And yet I must not grow too fond of Helisande nor let her become too close. I must not form attachments here, for surely I will not be here forever. What of the day when the information I send on to Harold and Ealdgyth means betraying those who have been kind to me here?* Ælfgifa shivered and offered up a half-formed prayer that such a choice would never have to be made.

CHAPTER 39

THE siege works had made good progress, despite the army being ready to collapse from exhaustion. No doubt suitable motivation was provided the men by the fact that they would be vulnerable to attack until the fortifications were complete. After a couple of days, four circular earthworks had arisen in the fields surrounding Domfront, the banks just high enough and ditches just deep enough to make them defensible. After a week, the walls were as high as a man and the first timbers in the wooden palisade had been erected. In another couple of days, the palisades were complete, and the majority of the army could rest and sleep without fearing raiding parties from Domfront. There had even been time for a hunt in the forest, with its well-maintained ways. The thrill of the chase was the only thing William had found to distract him from the terrible position he was in, militarily and politically.

Then the news had come—Geoffrey was marching on them. *Good, we've smoked the cur out*, William thought, and gathered his cavalry. They rode out and lined up on the edge of a low ridge before a broad flood plain, and waited. At least they'd be fighting downhill for a change... But they never saw the army of Geoffrey Martel. The scouts came in reporting that he had halted half an hour's march away. They waited, expecting Martel to wheel and flank them. William even sent out more scouts in case a second army was sneaking in to trap them between pincers. But no. Geoffrey waited, and waited, and in the last hour of daylight, began to pull back. The two armies had not laid eyes on each other. It was a battle of scouts. William returned to Domfront, half relieved, half furious, and the men set to work finishing the fortifications surrounding the town.

They had worked, but William knew what the men were saying. That they should have gone to Alençon. That they'd never break the walls here. That Martel was still close by, and if he chose to attack, then those walls would be the anvil against which The Hammer would smash The Bastard's bollocks. That only William's pride and stubbornness was keeping them here, making a bad situation worse.

Perhaps it was true. In part, anyway. There were other things that were being said. Mutters of *the Saxon woman!* or *the Saxon witch! No luck since she turned up...* Good God. Soon it would be *I saw a lamb born with two heads!* and *I saw a great sword in the sky pointed toward us!*

But he was certain they could defeat the town, as certain that the Saxon was merely an earthly woman cursed with a beast's face and a man's brain. And even if they couldn't break the walls or the townsfolk, he had to make the point. "I'm going to make it a living hell within those walls," he growled the next time one of his captains politely, respectfully suggested withdrawing. "Any border town could make a deal with my enemies and open its gates if we show weakness now. I intend to demonstrate what happens if they try it. Maybe they'll have Geoffrey speaking pretty words to

AN ARGUMENT OF BLOOD

them and promising them this and that, but they'll be...
mewed up inside their walls from now 'til Kingdom Come.
They'll be drowning in their own shit and carcasses by the
end!"

"They can just dump their shit in the river," Gallet
muttered. William turned his gaze onto the knight, and after
a moment's defiance, Gallet lowered his eyes.

No, it would take time, but the town must fall in the end,
or come to terms. William only hoped he was not bankrupt
before it happened. Keeping an army in the field was costing
somewhat more than taxes from the Duchy was bringing in,
or so his counsellors told him.

"Any news on Geoffrey?" he asked, changing the subject.
"Has he attacked anywhere else?"

"His army is still in the field," Henri de Ryes said. "Some
ten leagues South."

"Are they in a good position for us to attack?"

"They're well defended, and it would be easy for them to
fall back on Le Mans. My guess is that's what he would do."
De Ryes, Hubert's second son, looked pensive. Fitz had put
him in charge of provisioning, and it was a heavy
responsibility for an army in the field, away from familiar
territory. "Meanwhile we can't make full use of the land. If
our foraging parties get too close, they fall on us. I lost a
couple of men yesterday when a party was ambushed. We
were lucky most escaped, but our supplies are not abundant,
and it's becoming harder by the day to replenish them."

Was there anything that could give a glimmer of hope?
He glanced at Arques, but the baron looked quickly away.
Odo, on the other hand, seemed to regard the affair as a huge

468

game, and, in his own way, was just as useless as Arques. Fitz just seemed glummer than ever.

"When will we have siege engines?"

"We'll have some pirrières next week," Fitz sighed. "It will take longer to get the belfries ready, the enginers tell me. Not 'til the month is out. But the onager is well advanced, and we'll have that in two weeks, three if it rains a lot. It's lucky there's so much timber round here."

"Good. Gallet," William said, turning to the knight in what he hoped was a placatory manner. "Any intelligence at all? Anything we can use?"

"Not here." Gallet sighed and folded his arms. "It's a different story at Alençon."

"What do you mean?"

"It seems they were never even expecting us to go there. I had a few fellows out talking to the local foresters and they returned this morning. It's surprising how that love of Geoffrey seems to dry up in the presence of a little silver. The town never even prepared for an attack. They knew we were coming to Domfront the whole time."

God wither their cocks! William ground his teeth. He was being made to look a fool. Worse, he was being made a fool of. And then a realization like a bar of sun through clouds.

"Unprepared, you say?"

"Yes, my Lord. So far as my men could see, the town had made no moves to repel an attack. Arnulf's been boasting that you're scared of him, so they say."

Then there was a chance to make something of this, if they could act quickly. "All right. I'll take two thirds of the cavalry and one Battle's worth of light infantry, and we'll go and test their unpreparedness." Who to bring with him? He

469

wanted to keep Arques close, but with all the additional marching his men had done, it made no sense to drag them away now. And he was not ready for a confrontation with his uncle just yet... "All right. Gallet, de Ryes, Odo you're with me. Fitz and Arques stay here. Fitz has my full authority. Attack the town if a very favorable opportunity presents itself —otherwise restrict yourself to harrying their supply parties and stopping messengers. Don't give them a moment's respite. Not one. If Geoffrey marches on you, prepare to meet him and send word to me immediately. Fight if you must to maintain our position, but avoid it if you can wait until my return."

Fitz nodded, and Arques glowered but said nothing. Good enough.

"Those who are coming with me," William went on, "prepare your men. We go as soon as they can be ready. Tomorrow, at sunrise."

William attracted Gallet's attention as the captains dispersed to see to their tasks. "I want the others watched," he said.

"Your captains, Sire? Even your relatives?"

"Yes," William answered, ignoring the smirk in Gallet's voice. "I know it's possible that Geoffrey is following our moves and anticipating us, but he seems to know what we're going to do before we do it, and I am beginning to think someone here may be helping our enemy along."

"That business on the road?"

"Yes. It's possible Martel has people watching us and someone in the camp is getting information to them."

Gallet frowned. "I think you're right, my Lord, but I don't rightly know what we can do to stop it short of catching them in the act. They're bound to be a lot more careful now."

"That's why I want the others watched. Even if we can't catch them, they might not want to risk it."

The knight looked skeptical.

William tried again. "The fox may be cleverer than the hound, but the fox has to outwit the hound every time. The hound has only to catch the fox once."

"Well, of one thing we can be certain," Gallet said. "We aren't foxes."

"Then by God's hot piss, let us be hounds, and if one of them is betraying me, we'll rip them to shreds!"

Another march. Another slog to another battle, and that was if everything went right. At least with a few hundred horsemen and light infantry they could move faster and more freely than with the whole army. In two days they were before the town of Alençon, across the Sarthe as the morning mist began to clear from the water. And a second time they were confounded. The gates were shut and barred, the moat filled with water, the fields emptied.

"My Lord..." Gallet was as close to speechless as William had ever seen him. He looked a mixture of crestfallen and furious. "Forgive me. It looks like my reports were a pile of pigshit. I'm sorry."

"Perhaps." William surveyed the scene from left to right again. "They had warning, but not much. A day or two at most."

"My Lord?"

"We've been betrayed again."

471

The revelation clearly didn't make Gallet feel any better about it. And rightly so. Whoever had been passing information to Geoffrey had been doing it under Gallet's nose. And William's. They clearly still had a lot to learn about spycraft. At least no-one could reasonably blame this one on *the Saxon witch* who was back at Falaise. It probably wouldn't stop the more superstitious doing that anyway. After all, who knew how far the evil eye could see? And could he even trust Gallet?

"It won't be easy to stop them supplying the place," Henri de Ryes said. "The river goes right under the walls, and they can cover it from both sides."

What he said was true. The Sarthe passed perhaps threescore pieds under Alençon's Eastern wall. The walls were lowest there, with fewer raised castles, but they could not attack at that point, because there was a small fort on the opposite bank, that the town could keep supplied courtesy of a rope stretched across the water. They could even transfer men at night by boat in small numbers if they were smart about it. And if everything William had seen of Geoffrey Martel so far was accurate, the defenders of this place would be smart about it. He did not wonder that Arnulf had gone over to Geoffrey so easily. In fact, now he thought about it, Arnulf had probably deposed his father as part of a deal with Martel to give him lordship and protection. That maybe Geoffrey had duped his vassal, fitzGiroie, into provoking Talvas, and Arnulf encouraged his father to take bloody revenge...

The fury in William's ribcage was an ember, not flaring but giving out a steady, hard heat. It was the anger of a man proved right and who had not wanted to be. A man who knew himself outmatched.

"Well come on," he barked at de Ryes, Odo and Gallet. "Let's show our faces to my people."

They rode up to the river bridge, a little outside the range of a champion bowman standing on the ramparts. This was not a town likely to be surprised by an attack. Any houses or merchants' sheds outside the walls had been torn down – there was evidence of hurried demolition littered all around, but nothing that would help them get through or over the palisade. William could see skins being draped over the thatch of buildings near the palisade, to protect them against fire arrows and other projectiles. They stopped to watch a party of men clambering over the rooftops with the practiced ease of those used to spending half their lives up trees. And then one of them seemed to spot the group of horsemen outside their walls. He began shouting and jabbing. Then the men picked up the skin they had been about to affix and flapped it.

It took some moments before William could work out what they were saying, despite the still morning allowing the sound to carry.

"*Hides for the tanner!*" they shouted. "*Hides for the tanner!*"

Gallet cleared his throat awkwardly. "They recognized who we are then, my Lord."

This time the ember flared. It took hold, and heat burst through him. "It would appear they have," he replied, fighting to keep his voice low. "They didn't just know there was an attack coming. They knew I was leading it."

"What do they mean?" Odo asked.

473

William remained silent. After a few moments, he became aware of an intense pain in his jaws. It built, and only when he heard his back teeth squeak did he realize he'd been biting his anger down.

"They are referring to the descent of the Countess of Conteville," he hissed. The jeers carried on drifting across to them, with nothing in between to muffle the sound. Worse, the workmen's antics seemed to have attracted others. Sentries on the walls were shouting it too, and

"Mother? What? How? What have 'hides for the tanner' got to do with Mother? Her father was a steward, wasn't he?"

"And his father a furrier. But some... common folk like to simplify the story and say that the Countess was a tanner's daughter." *Reminding everyone that he had been born out of wedlock, to a woman of common descent. That's what I am. Bastard.*

"Oh, the wretches!" Odo yelped. "I'll see them all excommunicated! No, burned as heretics!"

"Don't you have to have a trial for that sort of thing?" de Ryes asked.

"Burn them all!" Odo screamed. "God will know his own!"

William leaned towards the bishop. "Calm yourself, brother!" Not that he was calm in any way himself. But it was wrong to show it outwardly. Rage was for battle, when it could animate a sword arm and inspire the legs to overcome exhaustion. And there would be a battle. By Saint Eustache's wrinkled arsehole there would be a battle. "I wonder could we get through the gate in one assault? Throw every man we have at it."

"We'd be under their arrows and spears and God knows what until we made a breach," de Ryes said grimly.

"And we don't know how many men are in the fort across the river," Gallet added. "They could sally and take us in the rear any time they like. Probably when half of us are across the river. Then the men in the town could sally, and that would be the end of that."

"We took Mouliherne by main force!" William retorted, already knowing the foolishness of it.

"Yes, my Lord," Gallet said softly. "And it cost us dear."

That was true. They might have had another two hundred men were it not for those killed and wounded back at that pointless tussle. But he had to fight someone!

And anyway, there was the fort. That would have to be neutralized before they could even consider an attack on the town... It didn't have much of a mound, and the gates did not look in good repair, but it was one more obstacle all the same.

But this was stupid. They'd failed. Lost any chance of surprise. They didn't have enough men for an all-out assault on a fortified town. A wooden wall, yes, but well defended it might as well be stone. They might as well return to Domfront. Damn them all, he would rip the town down with his bare hands! He could not let it be known for a single day that he'd taken such an insult without paying it back. If he lost ten men for every one they killed, if he was killed himself, it would be worth it just to be able to hurt the sons of mongrels. But the town... it was impossible.

The fort though... They could attack the fort! And then the good people of Alençon would have to watch their fellows being slaughtered, and do nothing about it. They could not sally themselves without being vulnerable crossing the

bridge. If only he had more footsoldiers and fewer horse. Well, they would just have to use the resources they had.

An hour later, a rough battering ram had been fashioned from a felled tree and the infantry were advancing with it, while a hail of arrows arced over the walls to keep the defenders' heads down. William sat his destrier with the cavalry, a bowshot from the gates, resisting the temptation to put the spur to his horse right then.

The thuds of the ram against the gate carried back to them, oddly out of step with the movement of the device. The enemy were now hurling rocks and spears at the soldiers below, but it looked as though the shields held above the ram were deflecting most of it. The gates were already beginning to sag a little. It wouldn't be long now.

"On my signal!" William called. Behind him, he heard a ripple of swords being loosed in scabbards, helms adjusted, hooves shuffling as the tension built.

The gates were flexing now, no longer solid barriers. A moment later a cry went up from the infantry as part of the left door collapsed. William could see a press of armed men clump to the breach. A few more bashes with the ram, while the fighting went on around them, and the gate crumpled.

He turned to Gallet. "Big enough for a horse?"

The knight pursed his lips. "A small one, perhaps."

"All right." He jabbed the spurs into his mount and remembered to yell "charge!" just as the beast took off.

His infantry were pulling back now, as planned. As his galloping horse covered the ground to the gates, William just had time to see the fort's defenders rush after what they thought were retreating men, and realize they faced a cavalry charge. The first man he encountered seemed to put up his

pike as an afterthought rather than as a determined defense against a mounted man. A push with his shield was sufficient to tap the weapon away, followed by a swinging blow with the sword, and the soldier was down. Then he was almost at the breach in the gate, which looked damned narrow, and managed to steer his rushing horse through it with no more than a bash on the left shoulder. Inside was a mass of men and pointed objects seemingly all jabbing at him. The first two men went down under his horse's hooves, the third received the edge of William's shield to the head, and the forth connected with the tip of his sword as he swung it wildly. The keen steel bit into the soldier's face, and almost yanked William out of the saddle as the horse rushed past. The rear palisade loomed up and William heaved on the reins, just managing to turn the steed's head before it collided with the wall, hoping that the rest of the cavalry would have time to stop or they'd end up in a pile of crushed horses and men.

By the time William had wrestled the horse around and raised his sword, the fighting was all but over. He looked in amazement. A dozen dead men lay on the ground, killed as the cavalry had burst into the fort. He spurred his horse back into the fray, swinging his sword, letting the momentum carry it through wide, slashing arcs and letting the final half a pied of wickedly sharp steel do the work. In moments, those men still standing had thrown down their weapons, fallen to their knees and were begging loudly for mercy. Gallet, after a moment looking stunned by the speed of it all, began directing the knights to round up the prisoners. Soon, they were massed in a knot at the center of the courtyard. William forced himself to relax his grip on his sword hilt. He had intended to kill every man here. He had not expected they would surrender en masse, but that no quarter would be asked and none given. And even then, it was one thing to cut down a man who throws down his weapon in the midst of a mêlée, but to slaughter a defenseless crowd? Even one that had been fighting him so recently?

No, it would not do. He sheathed his sword, dismounted, and moved to join Gallet and de Ryes.

Just then, a yell of "bastard!" issued from the crowd and a shape detached itself from the mass, hurtling towards him. William had just time to put his arm up, to take in a bearded fellow in a leather jerkin and leggings, an expression of fury. The impact never came – two of William's guard piled into the man and heaved him to the ground. The attacker was still yelling "bastard!" and "tyrant!" until one of the soldiers picked up his head by the hair and dropped it with a crunch on the ground.

The fury returned in a surge. These were his people. His! And they'd been poisoned against him by that traitor Arnulf, making common cause with his enemy. So the town bordered Maine, but it was held of the Dukes of Normandy by Royal decree. Did that mean nothing to these commoners?

"Let him up," William snapped. "To his knees, mind."

The guards hauled the bearded man up. William was about to ask him about his fealty, to swear his allegiance to his liege lord or forfeit his life. But the hatred burning in the eyes locked with his suggested he would only open himself to another torrent of abuse.

"He had this, my Lord." de Ryes offered up a long knife with an oddly curved blade, the cutting edge on the inside, and so keen it had almost thinned to nothing.

"What is it?"

"A pollarding knife, my Lord."

"Pollarding? What's that?"

"I understand the foresters round here cut the limbs off the trees with knives like this so they grow straight and thin."

"I see." William examined the knife, then looked at the man kneeling before him. If he couldn't punish Arnulf... Or perhaps he could, in a way. "Let me see, master forester. You hung out hides for the tanner earlier, which was most appropriate to your guest and liege lord. I wonder how I ought to treat wayward foresters in a manner that would be as fitting?"

The man's eyes had widened, and he tried to pull away, but the two men holding him gripped harder.

William waited until he was still again. "Pray, tell me more about 'pollarding'."

CHAPTER 40

HOWEVER skilled at observing and listening Helisande was—a fact attested by her endless supply of gossip—she was no match for Ælfgifa when it came to gathering information unobserved. All gossip was of roughly equal importance to Helisande, whereas Ælfgifa knew her ability to sort the trivial and mundane from the specks of true gold was the skill that made her so valuable to her brother, Harold. To Ealdgyth as well, now she was prepared to be honest with herself, and she was being honest, wasn't she? No more excuses made in her own mind for others using her to further their own ends, be they well-loved family member or otherwise. There was a freshening breeze, fiercer up here on the battlements of the western bailey, and it had rained in the night leaving the stone dark and cold. Ælfgifa pulled up the hood on her cloak and slipped past the sentries as they changed shift, finding herself an unobserved nook to sit in and look out at the drenched countryside. She supposed, based on how easily she had passed unseen, that she might find a sally-port and walk straight out of the castle if she truly had a mind to. In fact no such subterfuge would be necessary. It was a market day in the town, and supply wagons and drovers would be trundling their goods and beasts in and out the main gates later this morning. She might as easily rest a hand on an overloaded wagon and wander out with the crowd.

Once she might have done just that. Now Ælfgifa felt struck by a bone deep weariness of it all. It was no adventure, she was no longer a child and where exactly would she go? Her Frankish might be excellent but she was certain that she would be taken for a lady the moment she opened her mouth, lacking the soft blurring of consonants and rounded vowels of Helisande's accent which marked her out as country bred. Besides, no one who saw her face would forget it—nor would they be like to aid her. Ælfgifa felt a stab of longing to have been born plain and unremarkable, before thrusting such useless thoughts away.

There was also the question of honor. She scowled moodily out over the dripping forest. William had treated her well. Had in fact acquiesced to all her reasonable requests. She was not lonely for a companion. If the ladies of the court spurned her, as little did she care for them. She had a garden and a still room, and permission to visit the castle's dusty, neglected library—such as it was. Other than freedom, what more could she want for? The corners of her mouth curved in something akin to a smile. Wulfnoth seemed as happy here as he might be anywhere else. In fact Ælfgifa shrewdly suspected that he had more companions to play with here, where there was no Gytha to forbid him from exerting himself, than he did in Wintancaestre. He ran to Ælfgifa at the end of every day, grubby and scratched, often smelling of horses and dogs, full of tales of his small adventures. While she listened and laughed with her younger brother, she felt sad. If he stayed here very long he would never be fully accepted back amongst their own people. Just such a thing had happened to King Edward after all. Would Wulfnoth grow to be more Norman in his leanings than Saxon? Troubled by this thought, Ælfgifa did not register that she had been hearing the unmistakable approach of two sets of feet. Guards, most like, from the heavy tread and measured walk. Unperturbed, she stayed tucked in the nook. Surely they were not looking for her in any case.

Then snatches of their conversation came to her and she recalled just why she couldn't leave, even if she wished to. Harold had set her to find out about the Duke and his vassals. She was a spy.

"His Lordship was triumphant again, then?" Ælfgifa imagined this came from an older man, heavier set, perhaps of middle years from the timbre of his voice.

"Aye. 'Course he was!" A younger, less certain voice piped up defensively. "He can do anything, our Lord."

The older man guffawed. "Asce you ought to hold your tongue on the subject until you see his lordship butcher a deer!"

Ælfgifa listened in mystification. When on earth would William have butchered a deer? He'd made it quite clear that he thought all his folk had their place. Had he run short of a butcher just as he was down a scribe at present? She imagined the younger man scowling as she heard his sullen reply.

"Mother of God but won't you ever shut up about that festering deer hunt? T'was more than five years ago-"

"Of course you were barely out of a breech-clout-"

"And," Asce went on angrily, "the Duke pulled off a shot that no one else could manage. Not even you Berenger!"

Berenger was silent a moment. His tone was thoughtful as he replied. "Perhaps not, pup, but there wasn't much of a feast afterwards. His Grace shot the wrong deer. Damned if I know whether he's been shooting at the right deer ever since."

Ælfgifa, in her hiding place, felt a wave of gratitude towards Asce for asking the question she so desperately wanted to ask herself.

"What do you mean?" Asce sounded puzzled, fearful almost. "You're not saying his judgment is at fault are you? Berenger, *are you*? That's... that's treason..."

"No need to take on, boy. I just heard some things at mess that have made me uneasy. I never said his lordship didn't know what he was doing."

Ælfgifa could hear the frown in Asce's voice. "His lordship won at Alençon, that's what I heard. What else was there?"

There was a long pause while Berenger presumably decided how much to tell the younger guard. "They were warned Duke William's army was coming. Holed up tight, ready for siege. Then some bright spark gets the idea to make a joke of the hides they'd hung on the walls. You know the hides, boy? A town expecting siege will oft-times try to pad the walls some with ox and goat and horse hide. Pads of them hung over the battlements sometimes spreads the impact from catapults."

"I know this," Asce said impatiently. "What of it?"

"Don't know the truth of this, nor what followed. Someone in Alençon jeers over the wall that they'd hung out hides for the tanner. Put the Duke into a white rage, that did. Reckon a reminder of his less than noble origins is a sore point, not as there's any shame in an honest trade like. It was the punishment he meted out after they took the town that raises the chill on my flesh." Berenger paused again.

What did he do? What? Ælfgifa wanted to leap out of hiding and shake the rest of the story out of the man. Devil's bollocks, couldn't he tell an entire tale without these interminable pauses?

Clearly Asce felt the same way. "Berenger?"

"He had the perpetrators of the insult rounded up – by then I wager the townsfolk were only too willing to give them up. The Duke decreed that since they had a talent for entertainment, they could continue with it as their new trade. He made wounded mumpers of the lot of them." Berenger audibly swallowed.

Ælfgifa felt the flesh on her neck prickle. Her mouth had gone very dry. She had never liked to see maiming carried out as a punishment. It was rare anyway in England. Near as rare as a death penalty or declaring someone *nīthing*.

"He made them beggers?" Asce still did not understand.

"Reckon they'll be fit for work as anything else now, do you? He had the hands and feet of every one of them lopped off, the stumps sealed in boiling tar. Doubt they've much to laugh about in their new trade as jest-tellers." Berenger stopped abruptly.

"He... *all* their hands and feet? But then..." Asce sounded as if he might retch. Ælfgifa felt decidedly queasy herself.

"Aye. According to the story I heard," Berenger said grimly. "And the severed members cast over the town walls of Domfront to show the folk there what they'd be in for if they didn't open the gates."

"But that's not... honorable... and for an insult..." Asce rambled.

"Hush, boy. Now you steer close to treason. Remember, it's just a tale. Might be there's some truth in it, might be none of it happened the way I was told. Tales grow in the telling."

"But do you think it's so?" Asce demanded.

"The Duke I knew was certainly hardened enough to do such a thing. He's a cruel streak in him when his ire is up. Not a bad thing in a leader, long as it doesn't go out of bounds. Would his lordship carry out such a thing? I cannot say the truth of it. Unless he was in a rage, I would say no unless there was some great advantage to be gained."

"That's no answer, Berenger! The Duke is supposed to be great, knightly." Asce said furiously.

"Time you learned the difference then, pup. A great and good duke, should never be mistaken for a great and good man. A worthy leader does not mean that man is equally worthy." Berenger's voice was growing fainter as the pair walked on and Ælfgifa did not catch anything else they said.

She made no attempt to follow them, mind whirling from what she'd overheard. It was a horrific punishment to inflict on anyone, especially those able-bodied and used to work. And for such a slight matter as a jibe at one's circumstances of birth it seemed extreme in its cruelty. Yet fear was a powerful motivator if a duke or lord were trying to get his lands in order. Expedient cruelty could prevent further deaths, rebellions and punishments in the future. Ælfgifa pursed her lips. That was assuming what she had heard was true and not a battle-tale blown out of all proportions. There was always a root to a rumor but often it bore little resemblance to the final tale.

As much as she disliked the barbarism of such a punishment, she could see method behind it. *And if it is not true,* Ælfgifa thought, *William would be wise not to squash the rumors. To let his people wonder. He might have a few less sieges because of it.*

She glanced out at the rain-soaked forest again. The other ladies would be in the solar by now and she ought to make an appearance. Besides, Helisande would be looking for her. *Oh Harold,* Ælfgifa thought to her absent brother, *what will you make of my next letter? You sent me here to discover what manner of man the Duke is. Now I can tell you. He is either ruthless enough to enact a cruel punishment that even you would shy away from, or he is clever enough to let others believe it. He may not have any natural charisma or charm but his men follow him and have learned loyalty. Either way, he is a dangerous man. More dangerous, brother, than I believe you anticipated.*

The End

ABOUT THE AUTHORS

J.A JULES IRONSIDES

J. A. (Jules) Ironside grew up in a house full of books in rural Dorset. She loves speculative fiction of all stripes, especially fantasy and science fiction, although when it comes to the written word, she's not choosy and will read almost anything. It would be fair to say that she starts to go a bit peculiar if she doesn't get through at least three books a week.

She mostly writes fantasy and sci-fi. Often this leans toward the dark fantastic or dystopian forms of fiction. Occasionally there's some outright horror. Her passion for all things dark and dystopian stems from the fact that these narrative vehicles bring out the very best and absolute worst in people. She finds it endlessly fascinating to explore what it means to be human by—figuratively—putting her characters' backs to the wall. Often they'll even surprise her with the lengths they'll go to to achieve their goals.

As a keen martial artist, Jules has studied several disciplines but is most accomplished in Goju-ryu karate, which she has studied and taught for over twenty years. Her favorite things include books (obviously), slippers, cheese, and surreal conversations.

She lives in Gloucestershire, on the edge of the Cotswold way, with her boyfriend-creature and a small black and white cat, both of whom share a God complex. Her first book, paranormal mystery novel *I Belong to the Earth*, was published by Illusio & Baqer in May 2015.

For more information on Jules Ironside, please visit her website, **A Perfect Dystopia** .

ABOUT THE AUTHORS

MATTHEW WILLIS

Matthew Willis is stuck in the past, and likes to drag people back there for company. Fortunately, the past is a foreign country where very cheap short breaks are available. He occasionally breaks into fantasy and science fiction, stopping only to argue with people on Twitter about what actually constitutes science fiction. He lives in Southampton, roughly equidistant from the Titanic's former dock and the airfield where the Spitfire first flew, sharing a Blitz-damaged house with his university lecturer wife Rosalind and an imaginary zebra. For some reason, finding inspiration in history is rarely a problem.

Matt was born in the historic naval town of Harwich, Essex, in 1976 and grew up in a nearby village, never far from the sea. Matthew studied literature and history of science at the University of Kent, focusing on Joseph Conrad for his MA, and sailed for the university in national competitions where he didn't always finish last. He subsequently worked as a journalist for *Autosport* and *F1 Racing* magazines, and he has written for *Aeroplane*, *Flypast*, and *The Aviation Historian* in addition to maintaining the blog **Naval Air History**.

Matt's first novel, the historical nautical fantasy *Daedalus and the Deep*, was published in 2013. His first nonfiction book, on an obscure World War II aircraft, was published in 2007. In 2015, his short story *Energy* was shortlisted for the Bridport Prize.

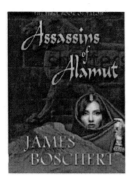

ASSASSINS OF ALAMUT
BY
JAMES BOSCHERT

An Epic Novel of Persia and Palestine in the Time of the Crusades

    The Assassins of Alamut is a riveting tale, painted on the vast canvas of life in Palestine and Persia during the 12th century.

    On one hand, it's a tale of the crusades—as told from the Islamic side—where Shi'a and Sunni are as intent on killing Ismaili Muslims as crusaders. In self-defense, the Ismailis develop an elite band of highly trained killers called Hashshashin whose missions are launched from their mountain fortress of Alamut.

    But it's also the story of a French boy, Talon, captured and forced into the alien world of the assassins. Forbidden love for a princess is intertwined with sinister plots and self-sacrifice, as the hero and his two companions discover treachery and then attempt to evade the ruthless assassins of Alamut who are sent to hunt them down.

    It's a sweeping saga that takes you over vast snow-covered mountains, through the frozen wastes of the winter plateau, and into the fabulous cites of Hamadan, Isfahan, and the Kingdom of Jerusalem.

    "A brilliant first novel, worthy of Bernard Cornwell at his best."—Tom Grundner

PENMORE PRESS
www.penmorepress.com

BODO
THE APOSTATE

DONALD MICHAEL PLATT

In a time of intolerance, following your conscience is a dangerous choice...

"In the meantime, a credible report caused all ecclesiastics of the Catholic Church to lament and weep."

-Prudentius of Troyes, Annales Bertiniani, anno 839

On Ascension Day May 22, 838, Bishop Bodo, chaplain, confessor, and favorite of both his kin, Emperor Louis the Pious, son of Charlemagne, and Empress Judith, caused the greatest scandal of the Carolingian Empire and the 9th century Roman Church.

Bodo, the novel, dramatizes the causes, motivations, and aftermath of Bodo's astonishing cause célèbre that took place during an age of superstitions, a confused Roman Church, heterodoxies, lingering paganism, broken oaths, rebellions, and dissolution of the Carolingian Empire.

PENMORE PRESS
www.penmorepress.com

Silk and The Sword
BY

Ron Singerton

Action Adventure, Crime, Mystery,
Roman History

Young Tacitus, torn from the girl he loves and accused of defiling his late mother's temple, is dragooned into the Roman army by his father Gaius, a bitter and unbending Centurion. With his father and seven legions, he joins General Marcus Crassus in an ill-fated attack on the sprawling Parthian Empire. After the Roman forces are decimated at the Battle of Carrhae, Tacitus, Gaius, and four hundred survivors venture eastward on the fabled Silk Road to find a river beyond a wall that will lead them back to Rome. Tacitus becomes the soldier he never wanted to be while battling bandits, trekking through frozen mountain passes, and dealing with a formidable foe on the other side of the world. But his greatest challenge is a personal quandary: should he return to Rome for his long-lost love or seek the hand of a princess in the mysterious land beside the Great Wall?

"A tour de force of Roman military survival across a long and arduous trek through the Parthian empire, the silk road, and into the celestial kingdom

PENMORE PRESS
www.penmorepress.com

Penmore Press

Challenging, Intriguing, Adventurous, Historical and Imaginative

www.penmorepress.com